Frank Coates was born in Melbourne and, after graduating as a professional engineer, worked for many years as a telecommunications specialist in Australia and overseas. In 1989 he was appointed as a UN technical specialist in Nairobi, Kenya, and travelled extensively throughout the eastern and southern parts of Africa over the next four years. During this time Frank developed a passion for the history and culture of East Africa, which inspired his first novel, *Tears of the Maasai*. He followed with *Beyond Mombasa* and *In Search of Africa*. *Roar of the Lion* is his fourth novel.

Also by Frank Coates

Tears of the Maasai

Beyond Mombasa

In Search of Africa

ROAR OF THE LION

FRANK COATES

HarperCollins*Publishers*

HarperCollins_Publishers_

First published in Australia in 2007
by HarperCollins_Publishers_ Australia Pty Limited
ABN 36 009 913 517
www.harpercollins.com.au

HarperCollins_Publishers_
25 Ryde Road, Pymble, Sydney, NSW 2073, Australia
31 View Road, Glenfield, Auckland 10, New Zealand
77–85 Fulham Palace Road, London, W6 8JB, United Kingdom
2 Bloor Street East, 20th floor, Toronto, Ontario M4W 1A8, Canada
10 East 53rd Street, New York NY 10022, USA

National Library of Australia Cataloguing-in-Publication data:

Coates, Frank.
    Roar of the lion.
    ISBN 13: 9 780 7322 8272 1.
    ISBN 10: 0 7322 8272 1.
    I. Title.
A823.4

Cover design by Natalie Winter
Cover image (background) courtesy of Getty Images, EO14146
Cover image (village) courtesy of Photolibrary, OSF1-00050019-001
Cover image (lion) courtesy of Shutterstock
Author photograph by Stephen Oxenbury
Maps by Laurie Whiddon, Map Illustrations
Typeset in Sabon 11/14 by Kirby Jones
Printed and bound in Australia by Griffin Press on 70gsm Bulky Book Ivory

5 4 3 2 1   07 08 09 10

To Max (Bruv).
And to Martin and Paul.
Brothers.

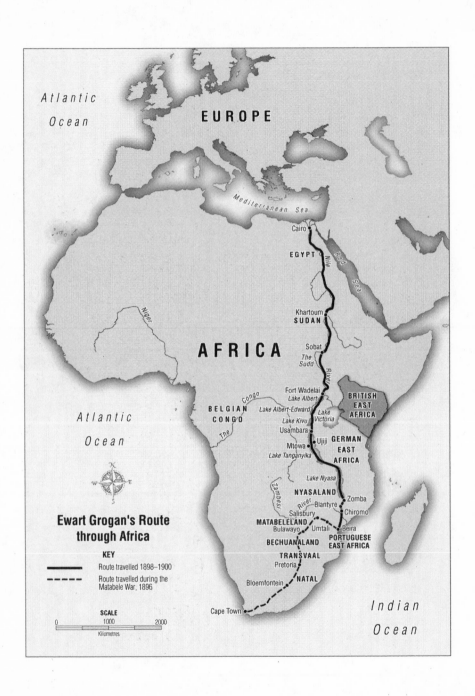

Atlantic
Ocean

EUROPE

Mediterranean Sea

Atlantic

Ocean

AFRICA

Niger

Congo

The

Cairo

EGYPT

Nile

Red Sea

Khartoum
SUDAN

Sobat
The
Sudd

River

Fort Wadelai
Lake Albert
Lake Albert-Edward
Lake Kivu
Usambara

Lake
Victoria

BRITISH
EAST
AFRICA

Mtowa
Lake Tanganyika

Ujiji

GERMAN
EAST
AFRICA

Lake Nyasa

Zambesi

NYASALAND

River

Salisbury

Blantyre
Zomba
Chiromo

MATABELELAND
Bulawayo

Umtali

Beira

BECHUANALAND

PORTUGUESE
EAST AFRICA

TRANSVAAL
Pretoria

NATAL

Bloemfontein

Cape Town

Indian

Ocean

N
W   E
S

**Ewart Grogan's Route
through Africa**

KEY

—————— Route travelled 1898–1900

– – – – – Route travelled during the
Matabele War, 1896

SCALE

0   1000   2000
Kilometres

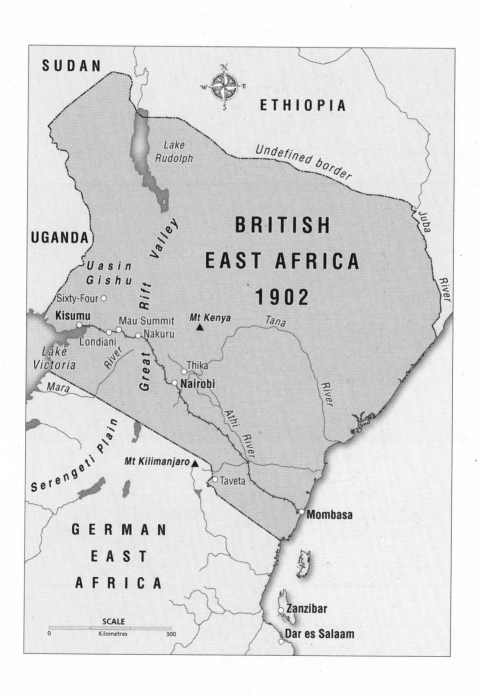

SUDAN

ETHIOPIA

Lake
Rudolph

Undefined border

Juba

UGANDA

BRITISH
EAST AFRICA
1902

River

Uasin
Gishu

Great Rift Valley

Sixty-Four

Mau Summit

Mt Kenya

Tana

Kisumu

Nakuru

Londiani

River

Lake
Victoria

Thika

Mara

Nairobi

Great Rift Valley

River

Serengeti plain

Athi River

Mt Kilimanjaro

Taveta

GERMAN

Mombasa

EAST

AFRICA

Zanzibar

SCALE

0   Kilometres   300

Dar es Salaam

PART 1

CHAPTER 1

1898

It was clear the German marching band were hopelessly, uproariously, unutterably, falling-down-and-beyond-redemption drunk. They had trouble keeping hold of their heavy brass instruments on the *Neptune*'s heaving deck, and any semblance of a formal playing formation had long been abandoned. But with true Teutonic grit, they kept their feet while belting out military arrangements, only occasionally missing a beat or note.

Ewart Grogan leaned on the ship's rail and turned from the band to gaze at the line of whitecaps breaking against the Pungwe River's sandbar. The beach, where the Indian Ocean surrendered its unbelievable blue to pale green shallows, was a mile away. Small fishing boats lined the shore, and beyond them sprawled the familiar outline of the ramshackle trading port of Beira.

It was two years since he had set sail from this same Portuguese East African port, at the age of twenty-two, swearing never to return. Being one of Cecil Rhodes' 'bloody troopers' had almost been the death of him here in Beira, for he had lain for perhaps days before a railway man discovered what he took to be a corpse in one of his empty railway wagons. But it wasn't wounds from the Matabele that had brought the young man to the brink of death; it was the bite of a mosquito.

Following his release from his contract with Rhodes' Chartered Company, Grogan had joined a small shooting expedition along the border of Mashonaland. It was meant to be a short diversion before he returned to England to decide what next to do with his life. The South African professional hunter in their party led Grogan and his three Dutch companions into bad country where the Englishman and one of the Dutchmen were struck down with a virulent fever. The Dutchman died, and the others took Grogan to the railway settlement at Fontesvilla where they helped him into a railway wagon bound for Beira.

He had little recollection of the journey, and no idea how long he had been in Beira before the railway man found him and took him to the hospital. The man later informed Grogan that had he not found his campaign medal while searching his pockets, he might have abandoned him there. Beira, he said, was over-burdened with drunken sailors who would often take refuge in one of his wagons after a night of heavy drinking.

The wind made a slight shift. Overhead, the light sail that the captain had set to hold the ship in its bobbing position beyond the bar flicked at its rigging until the helmsman trimmed his wheel. With the change in the wind came the unmistakeable, always exotic smell of Africa. Grogan filled his lungs with the moist pungent-sweet scent of over-ripe fruit, spices and vegetative decay. It brought with it an atmosphere of excitement and the promise of mysteries to be revealed.

Archie Battersby joined him at the rail. 'You know, Ewart,' he said, raising his voice above blaring trumpets and *oompah*-ing tubas, 'that entire band has been drunk since we left Cape Town. You'd think they'd give it a rest before we berth.'

Grogan nodded. 'I'd be glad if they gave the military marches a rest as well.'

'Aye, that too. But they're good drinkers, the Germans.' Archie patted his sides, making the sound of a flat palm on a padded beer keg. 'Lucky there was a Scot on board to give them a decent contest.'

At nearly forty, Archie was sixteen years Grogan's senior, and although his midriff bore the legacy of an unstinting enjoyment of fine food and alcohol, he was by no means unfit. However, in comparison to Ewart's rangy six feet and good shoulders developed during youthful summers climbing the Alps, Archie appeared a lot shorter.

In spite of the age difference, there was never any doubt it was Grogan's expedition that they were about to undertake. It had been Ewart's dream to hunt the deep recesses of the African wilderness since he was a child, although it wasn't until recent events had provided the final impetus that he decided to make the journey. Archie had been an acquaintance, if not a close friend, for years and was keen to join him. Ewart knew him to be an affable character and was pleased to have him as a companion. That Archie's aunt, another of Ewart's acquaintances, was happy to dole out some of her considerable wealth to finance the trip was very much in Archie's favour.

The band paused and, to a man, downed instruments and reached for their steins.

In the startling silence that followed, the first officer bawled a string of guttural commands.

'Seems the captain has finally decided the tide is in flood,' Grogan said, as deck hands scurried aloft to drop the sails.

'A tricky manoeuvre from what I've heard,' Archie added.

Grogan's eyes went to the deck cargo where all their belongings were tied down. The only piece that was not under the heavy green canvas was his instruments chest. He'd had it removed from the other cargo, ready to be unloaded under his supervision. He daren't place the handsome rosewood chest in the hands of ignorant stevedores. It was a thing of beauty and a prized possession. Its contents were equally precious, as the chest held his artificial horizon, sextant and chronometer.

The stiff on-shore breeze soon had the *Neptune* going at a good clip. It heeled over, cutting a brave line through the swell, and charged towards the sandbar.

'What do you know of the draught of the *Neptune*, Ewart?' Archie asked.

'Nothing,' Grogan answered, peering intently, as was Archie, at the on-rushing line of breakers. 'But surely the captain —'

The band launched into an ear-smashing rendition of the German national anthem. There was a slight tremor beneath their feet — as if something heavy had shifted below decks. A moment later there was another jolt, and then their careening vessel ran aground on the sandbar.

The German marching band fell like ninepins. Brass instruments skittered along the deck, as did most of the passengers.

Grogan clung to the railing and watched in horror as the band's beer keg broke from its roped enclosure and tore down the deck in an erratic, wobbling path towards the cargo.

Above the dreadful grinding of the ship's keel on the sandbar, and the cries and moans of the passengers, Grogan heard the unmistakeable and heart-rending sound of splintering rosewood.

Archie took hold of the lobster's carapace and broke open its abdomen with what, given their mood, Grogan imagined would have been a satisfying crunch.

'I am truly tired of Beira,' Archie said, unceremoniously dumping part of the carcass on Grogan's plate. 'I'm particularly tired of the heat and this sweat I seem to be continually swimming in.' He took a mouthful of his beer and made a face. 'I'm also tired of drinking this piss the South Africans call beer.'

The interminable delays Grogan and Archie had endured while awaiting the arrival of their supplies had confined them to Beira for longer than patience could bear, and there were times when Archie's complaints wore thin. But Grogan, mindful of the long journey ahead when he would have only Archie Battersby to share a contemplative pipe or a sip of whisky with, simply smiled and tore free a piece of lobster meat with his fork. 'At least you have to admit the lobsters are good. And cheap.'

They were eating on the balcony of their hotel, overlooking the Indian Ocean and the scatter of squalid waterfront stalls whose only assets were a pot of boiling water and a tank of dancing lobsters. If Grogan needed cause to complain, it would be the incompetence of shipping agents who didn't seem to have a clue why his instruments had not been returned from repair in Durban.

'I've been thinking about a few things,' he went on. 'Why don't we do a spot of hunting while we're waiting? I'm sure there's plenty of game further inland. We could hire a few porters and take a trip up the Pungwe and take a look.'

'Hunting?' Archie grinned and took another long swig of the insipid beer. 'Now you're talking. After all, isn't that what we came here for?'

Grogan shrugged. He'd found that Archie frequently devalued their mission to the level of a hunting jaunt, which was actually the least of it, but he let the comment pass. His own main purpose in taking a trip up the Pungwe was to test his health and stamina against the type of climate and terrain they would experience during their trek. He was worried that the ill-health that had laid him low while soldiering with Rhodes would return to stymie his greater plans. A hunting trip would also serve to deflect any suspicions from the French, of whom there were many around Beira, about the real purpose of their trek. It would not do to alert the French Intelligence to their greater objective, which was to penetrate far deeper into the interior than he wanted the French to know until absolutely necessary.

'Anyway,' Grogan said, 'it will give us a chance to try our skills with our new weapons. I particularly need to check the sightings on the 4-bore.'

'Bloody good idea, Ewart. The sooner the better as far as I'm concerned.' Archie tore off another piece of lobster, and stuffed it into his mouth. He nodded to the book in Grogan's lap. 'What's that for?' he asked, his voice muffled by lobster meat.

'I've decided to keep a journal of our trek. Nothing for publication, mind you — rather more like a diary than a journal.' Grogan gave the book a pat. 'I've already made a start.'

14 March 1898. Beira
Beira is a galvanised-iron expanse of ugliness surrounded by sun-baked sand, awash with strong drink, and populated by Portuguese ruffians. Of the last, Archie and I have already found three, who interrupted our dinner and insisted upon pointing out the inferiority of the British race and the superiority of their own. We were able to demonstrate in a few short minutes how the British won the empire. Our meal was not further troubled thereafter.

Beira is undoubtedly bigger, uglier and more morally corrupt than I remember it following the end of my tour of duty with Rhodes. I shouldn't doubt it is also more dangerous, with the jetsam from a dozen countries haunting the bars near the harbour; while, sadly, the charming old Portuguese mansions are in decay.

We chafe to begin our journey, but are forced to await the return of my instruments which are getting a thorough going-over in Durban after the damage caused to them by the Neptune's clumsy arrival into Beira.

I had forgotten that Africa has a time standard all its own. It runs at about a quarter of the speed that one requires to get anything done in a reasonable time. This seems even worse here in Beira where there is altogether too much good living to be had. I am having a devil of a job rounding up porters for our trek across Africa. It seems that life is too easy in Portuguese East Africa. There is no incentive for the natives to pick up a 60lb load and carry it far from their homes and into places beyond their wildest imaginings.

The Portuguese seem to have lost their sense of adventure, and have passed that sad state of affairs on to their indolent natives.

CHAPTER 2

Momposhe Ole Matipe puffed out his chest and tugged his red *shuka* higher onto his skinny frame. It sat in place until he exhaled, when it slipped down again to cling precariously to his pointy shoulder. His mother had given him the new garment when she shaved his head in preparation for his circumcision. Soon he would join the *il barnot* — the shaved ones — in many days of celebration of their elevation within the tribe. The garment was bigger than he needed, but he didn't complain. His lanky body was slowly filling out, and a man's hair was sprouting from his man's body parts, for he was beginning the journey that in a few years would see him become a warrior — one of the feared Maasai *moran*. He was conscious of his new status as he walked slowly and erect behind his father's herd, his bald scalp shining like a polished black stone. He patrolled the herd's flank, keeping an eye on his father's signals and keenly watching for any obstinate cow that might flinch from entering the Boer's stock dip at the last moment.

Dipping the herd was new to Momposhe. In fact, his father's herd was the only one the Boer farmer allowed to use the dip. He imagined it was because his father had offered a kindness to the Boer at some time. He was like that, his father, helping people with his skills in medicines and soothsaying. Perhaps he had helped the Boer with a troublesome cattle blight, and in return for such a favour the Boer let his father's cattle use the therapeutic waters.

The Boer and his children — a girl and four strong boys — had completed their dipping and were moving their cattle into a holding yard at the side of the house.

The Boers on this farm were among several families who had come from the south over recent years. Where they came from, nobody in Momposhe's tribe knew. That they had trekked for many months was apparent from their dour appearance, and their heavy ox carts had taken a full wet season to cross into the Purko Maasai's Uasin Gishu grazing land. Boers permitted no obstacle to stand in their way, fording the smaller streams, and floating possessions and stock on large ungainly rafts they built to tackle the rivers in flood.

The Maasai had watched the Boers come, and they had watched them build their strange high-roofed houses on the Laikipia and Uasin Gishu plateaus. They watched the men curl long lashes of the *kiboko*-hide whip along the backs of bullocks, and the children run behind, crushing soil clods under large bare feet, or chasing baboons from the maize with sticks. Soon it became clear the Boers had no intention of moving on.

The young Maasai men were incensed and talked of war, but the elders, Momposhe's father included, cautioned the *moran* against intemperate actions. They reminded the hot-headed young warriors that since the days of the white man's smallpox they were few in number — too few to risk a war with the whites who had proved they could quickly assemble a strong force, and whose weapons could slash through a line of charging, whooping *moran* like a savanna fire could lay waste the dry-season grass.

Momposhe understood their rage. This was Maasailand, and the Maasai herds had been free to roam the Laikipia Plateau as the seasons decreed for longer than anyone remembered. But Momposhe paid heed to his father who counselled patience. He said it was possible that the white man brought benefits as well their diseases. There was no doubt the wily Kikuyu had profited from their presence, providing food supplies to the growing number of travellers and settlers in exchange for *mericani* cloth, iron wire, axes and many other strange offerings. The Maasai only had their cattle, and a Maasai man would not trade them for his life.

Momposhe ran to a recalcitrant cow and waved his herding stick at her. She shook her head, flicked her tail, and rejoined the herd crowding at the race that led down into the dip.

Although everyone — even Momposhe — knew of ticks and the diseases they carried, none of the Maasai was aware of the curative powers of the dip. Even if they were, he doubted whether any would risk their precious cattle to such a bizarre practice. But his father, Marefu Ole Matipe, was a man familiar with medicines, and knew many things about cattle. He was not afraid to try something new if it was beneficial to his herd.

Momposhe's mother was at the rear of the herd, coaxing the cattle forward with gentle words of encouragement. Many years before, Marefu had taken her as his bounty following a raid on the tribe's hapless Kikuyu neighbours. Now she was free to visit her family, but always returned, smiling, to his father. Although a Kikuyu and not born knowing about cattle, she could speak their language and understood their moods like no other woman. His father had given her high praise by saying she was almost as good as a Maasai. It was the reason his mother was allowed to help in the herding.

Normally Marefu would be assisted in the herding by his children, but Momposhe was his mother's only child. When Momposhe asked why, she told him that something had weakened inside her after the difficult time she had giving birth to him.

Momposhe would sometimes recall this when out on the savanna tending his father's goats. He wondered if he were at fault somehow, and if his mother blamed him for the *weakness*. It made him feel bad because recently, and belatedly, his father had taken a second and then third wife.

Marefu made regular visits to his new wives, and their young children, who stayed in their home village. He would be away for days at a time, and Momposhe's mother would fret until he came back. For many days after returning, his father could do nothing for himself before Momposhe's mother had it done for him, exactly as required. Keeping his wives in distant *enkangs* was just another of his father's many strange habits, some of which, like the dipping, he had picked up from the Boer family.

Momposhe knew his father was very wise and, like an empty pool, he soaked up the drops of wisdom that fell like rain from his father's lips, in preparation for the day he would assume a position of importance within the tribe, taking his place as a leader on the council of elders like his father. But before that would be his time as a *morani*, one of the protectors of the tribe. Once he was circumcised, his training would begin in earnest.

Momposhe raised his herding stick and pointed it at the wooded hills above them at a launch angle. He made practice thrusts, and imagined the day when his spear would fly through the air into an enemy's heart.

The Nandi warriors who assembled above the Boers' farmhouse were unaware that Marefu Ole Matipe, a member of the Purko Maasai, was also on the farm they were about to attack. Not that it would have made any difference. They had lost patience with the white men who crossed their land, grazed their cattle on it and broke the soil for their crops. Others had come from the east stringing copper wire on wooden poles from one horizon to another without a word of regret or justification. The Nandi had tolerated enough. It was time to fight, and to take the spoils of war.

Concealed by a thick stand of trees, the warriors tested the edges of their spears and stabbing swords. Beaded necklaces adorned their throats, and beaded strings held their hair and glossy black feathered headdresses in place. Black skin gleamed with a sheen of sweat earned on their long, loping trot to the homestead.

Below them spread the Boers' farm, fat with sheep and cattle, and, like a ripe berry, ready for the picking.

Their leader clicked his tongue. All eyes turned to him. He showed them the bright edge of his sword, and in a crouched huddle they followed him down the hill to the farmhouse.

*   *   *

Momposhe's father was speaking to his cattle, calling them by name. His voice, soft and deep, came as a song of praise. 'You, Crooked Horn, come through, my beauty. Ah, there you are, Wild Eye, move along. Well done. Come on, come on Patched Quilt. Good girl.'

When his father's song abruptly stopped, Momposhe glanced over to him. Marefu was staring beyond the farmhouse into the hills. Suddenly he dashed towards the gated fence, snatching up his spear as he ran.

Momposhe stood rooted to the spot, shocked into inaction by his father's strange behaviour. Then he saw the Nandi.

They came rushing down the hill like a lethal storm — silent, except for the swish-swish of naked legs through the grass, muffled footfalls and the stifled gasps of exertion. Deadly. War shields flashed in the sun. Spears bristled, dark and sharp.

His father's roar cut through the silence and brought the Boer farmer's head up from his line of cattle.

The white family were instantly transformed by the crisis into a military machine. They quickly gathered at the farmhouse door where the wife, stout and usually unhurried, handed out ancient firearms with swift efficiency to the Boer and her older sons. The younger boys and the girl armed themselves with farm implements — a shovel, pitchfork and stake — and positioned themselves at the door.

Suddenly realisation struck. Momposhe gave flight to his long legs and dashed through the mud and cowshit, flashing ineffectually at the air with his herding stick, towards where his father stood. Marefu parried the thrusts of a Nandi spear with his own, and danced around fence posts to evade others.

The Boer and his boys charged into the fray. There was the crack of a rifle; the boom of a shotgun. The raiders ran among the cattle, hollering and whooping and waving their arms. The terrified beasts scattered in panic. A Nandi warrior made a dash at the house, and the girl jabbed him in the groin with her stake. He fell with a look of amazement and pain. One of the Boer boys was skewered by a Nandi stabbing sword. The Boer and his eldest son thrust the noses of empty guns at their attackers.

Marefu wrested his spear from one of the Nandi as Momposhe arrived, using it like a dagger instead. Momposhe slashing, whipping, flaying. Crying in rage.

In the background the women's screams.

A Nandi loomed behind his father, wielding a club. Marefu fell, like the tallest tree in the forest surrendering to an axeman's blows.

A blinding flash of pain. Darkness crept across Momposhe's eyes like the sun setting, and he fell too, so slowly, into the mud.

CHAPTER 3

Archie lowered himself wearily into his folding camp chair. The Pungwe River, fifty yards away down a sandy bank, caught the sloping rays of afternoon sun as it made its sedate journey to its meeting with the ocean, a hundred miles away at Beira. It had been a hard and frustrating day of hunting: he and Ewart had tramped endlessly through waist-high grasses in pursuit of a few skittish gazelles that remained forever out of range. Earlier they had sighted a small herd of buffalo, but it came to naught as they disappeared into the morass on the river's edge. Not a shot had been fired all day.

'Bloody mosquitoes,' he said to himself, slapping at his knee. 'Sun's hardly out of sight and the little buggers are all over a man.' He turned in his chair, craning his neck towards the camp. 'Rodriguez! Where's my bloody whisky?'

A muffled reply came from the stores tent.

'Humph,' Archie responded, and sat quietly, contemplating the changing colours of the water.

Grogan came up from the river. 'Mind if I join you?' he said. 'Or would you rather continue to mumble and curse alone?'

'Be my guest.' Archie swept his hand towards a chair. 'Misery craves company. Or is it mirth?'

'Misery sounds right,' Grogan said, lowering himself onto the canvas seat.

'You can't talk. If you'd seen your face when that barrel smashed into your precious chest ...'

Grogan nodded sadly. 'I liked that chest. Got it in a little Asian port called Singapore.'

'On your convalescence jaunt,' Archie added. He was one of many friends who had convinced Grogan to take his round-the-world voyage, so the sea air could revive him. He had looked like hell when he'd returned from the Matabele war suffering from malaria, and the abscess on the liver he developed as a consequence made matters worse.

'It was more than the chest,' Grogan said. 'Those instruments are vital for our work in central Africa, and beyond.'

Archie grimly noted Grogan's continuing reference to their original plan, which was to walk all the way to Cairo. Realistically, Archie didn't expect otherwise at this stage of their journey. Although the walking during their hunting expedition had been tough in parts, it was nowhere near as tough as it would no doubt become when they finally began their journey proper. He anticipated some discussion then of the folly of their ultimate plan and, if necessary, how to change it, when they became fed up with the rigours of interminable trekking. It was the possibility of changing their plans that Archie believed was behind their agreement to keep the true extent of their journey secret to all but close friends and family.

Archie had to admit that Grogan had never left any doubt that his objective was to make the journey from Beira to Cairo. He would then be able to claim to be the first man to have walked from Cape Town to Cairo because he had already completed the first section with Rhodes. To Archie, it had been an interesting concept, but one that he felt to be quite unachievable, and was therefore inclined not to take it seriously. However, he kept these thoughts to himself.

Archie's personal objective for the expedition was to hunt. He had been a keen hunter from an early age, when his aunt would take him up to her Scottish estates to hunt deer and pheasant. Although he knew that Grogan was keen to bag a few trophies of his own, Archie had the strong impression that his young friend had a different and much stronger motivation to continue on to Cairo. And it was not merely to serve Queen and country. He gained an inkling of what it might be when they were discussing who among their family and friends knew the details of their proposed trek. In a rare moment of candour, Grogan let it slip that he had included the father of a certain young lady in California in his confidence. Archie had been unable to elicit more, and knowing what he now did about Ewart's determination, he was pretty sure that's how it would remain unless Grogan decided to enlighten him.

There was only one point that undermined Archie's conviction that Grogan would soon realise the challenge was beyond them and come to his senses. It was that steely determination in the young man's eyes. If he had something to prove to this person in California in marching across Africa, then he would do it. Archie, and all those who knew Ewart Scott Grogan, were acutely aware that when this intense young fellow set his mind to something, there was nothing, short of death itself, that would stop him.

Grogan and Archie persevered for a week on the Pungwe despite only a few fleeting glimpses of game. The animal life seemed to have been decimated throughout the whole area. They suspected it was due to intensive hunting.

A guide they had recruited locally led them to Mtambara's *kraal*. Mtambara had been an important chief in his day, but was now reduced under Portuguese influence to little more than a figurehead. He was a diminutive old man, decked out in a dirty patch of cloth and a bandolier of leather and white beads. Grogan took his hand in greeting. It was thin and his grip was weak.

Mtambara seemed addicted to snuff. Throughout their meeting, while Grogan and Archie sat on the offered chairs, the chief squatted on his haunches, resting his bony arms on bony knees. Every few moments a long thin arm would drop down to a snuffbox at his feet and dip into it like a heron poking in the dirt for grasshoppers. Lifting his pinched fingers to a nostril, he would then halt his conversation to sniff vigorously.

Mtambara's older son, the heir apparent, was an even more insignificant creature, seeming constantly to be in a drug-induced stupor. But the chief's second son, Jim, was quite a live wire and looked smart in a khaki shirt and trousers. He told them that the hunting was better on the Sabi River, on the other side of Umtali — the town on the border of Portuguese East Africa and South Africa.

'We are after lion,' Archie said, immediately interested.

'Yes, sir, there are lion. Many lion. And I can be happy to be your guide. I can show you where they are.'

Grogan felt sure that if they had expressed an interest in polar bears, Jim's answer would have been the same, but they agreed to let him try his hand. Alone, they seemed condemned to wander in a fruitless search for game.

Jim proved to be an endless source of information about the country through which they trekked. Educated in South Africa at a missionary school, he had a good grasp of English and used it with the typical clipped accent of South African Englishmen. After a walk of two days from the *kraal*, the view from a high veldt revealed a rich green carpet of grass spreading towards the border, slashed occasionally by the silver water of the Udzi River. They made camp on the last rise before descending to the river valley. Grogan sat and stared at the unbroken stretch of purple hills that ran into a misty and distant northern horizon. He was far from where he wanted to be. The shifting image to the north concealed the land that was his true destination.

'That way Nyasaland, sir,' Jim said at his side.

'I know, Jim. It's where we will soon be heading.'

'Ah, very good, sir. You will like it, I think. It is very beautiful. More beautiful even than here.'

In the days that followed, they found no signs of lion. They spotted a number of antelope and managed to bag a few.

For Grogan their hunting interlude only succeeded in increasing his frustration. The futile, halting pursuit of game didn't even give him the chance to test his stamina in a forced march as he had planned, but he knew he had to curb his impatience. Without his instruments he could not complete the important survey work he had set himself.

Two days later, Archie came down with a mysterious illness and was unable to walk.

'Maybe we should go back to Beira,' Grogan offered.

'And sit stuffing ourselves with lobster for weeks while we wait for our supplies?' Archie shook his head. 'I'd rather take my chances up here. I'm sure I'll be all right in a day or so.'

'Then why don't you rest here with the bulk of the supplies? I'll go on ahead to the Sabi and make a reconnaissance to see if it's worth our trouble, and come back to meet you in Umtali.'

Archie agreed, and Grogan had his chance to pit himself against the African bush.

He marched his men twenty miles along the Udzi. The following morning he set off again, this time across country to Umtali — a forced march of sixty miles in nineteen hours. It was the test of strength he wanted.

He celebrated that night with a brandy and soda in Umtali, and fell asleep feeling elated that, although tired, there were no lingering side effects from the punishing trial of his stamina and general health.

23 April. Umtali
Previous twenty-four hours in a haze of fever.
I cannot describe the desolation of spirit this brings me.
Sick at heart.
It would appear that the fever and I are to be constant companions.

When Grogan pressed through the swinging doors of Umtali's newest hotel some nights later, he winced at the cacophony emanating from a motley assortment of musicians belting out an unremarkable jig on the temporary platform erected to facilitate the Grand Hotel's grand opening.

It appeared as if the hotel was making every effort to live up to its name. A number of mirrors were set into the walls at various angles, reflecting the light from a dozen dazzling spirit lamps hanging from wall fixtures. Coloured paper ribbons festooned the walls and ceiling, and were gathered into bunches at each end of the stage where two scantily clad women were performing high kicks to the accompaniment of cymbal crashes. Other women, similarly dressed and heavily mascaraed, moved among the crowd holding aloft silver salvers crowded with all manner of drinks. A juggler was sending a number of coloured balls and what appeared to be a chamber pot into the air, and a clown was doing card tricks in a corner.

The revellers themselves were no less extraordinary. There was a red-turbanned Arab in a black tuxedo, a Chinaman in traditional silk garb with slippers that turned up at the toes, and a dubious-looking bearded fellow in a taffeta dress. Others appeared to have come straight off the land in their bib-and-brace overalls and battered hats. Laughter filled the air, as thick as the tobacco smoke.

The colour and movement made Grogan's head spin for a moment, and he gripped the bar to steady himself and await its passing. He had not quite recovered from his fever; the only reason he was there at all was to overcome the numbing boredom of the days spent awaiting Archie's arrival. He promised himself he would stay for just a few minutes.

'Hello, blue-eyes, are you sure you should have another drink?' The woman by his side at the bar was dressed in a flowing green gown with a feathered hat, and held a sequined mask up to her eyes on a long gilt stick. 'I was going to offer you one, but then I noticed you were already drunk.' Her olive skin glowed in the lamplight and a heady perfume wafted towards him as she languidly waved her fan under her chin.

'I'm sorry to disagree, madam, but I'm not at all drunk. Haven't had a drink for days, in fact.'

'Of course you haven't, dear boy, that's why you almost fell against the bar.'

'I didn't fall. I ... I'm ... it's just a little touch of the fever.'

She dropped her mask to reveal a cluster of smile lines at the corner of her brown eyes. 'In that case, you'd better have a whisky. You can buy me one too.'

Grogan awoke to see Jim's grinning face looking down at him.

'Jolly fine party, sir!'

'Wh-what?'

'I said I think your party last night was jolly fine, sir. Do you think so?'

Grogan looked around the bedroom. It was his room, but how he had reached it the night before, he had no idea. A buzz of pain hovered at his temples. He blinked his eyes to clear his vision, which was slightly fuzzy.

As his eyes continued to roam the room he caught sight of his reflection in the dressing-table mirror. He was fully dressed above the waist, and absolutely naked below.

He sat up with a start and looked at Jim as if he alone held an explanation, but Jim's black face was a picture of innocence, with a grin from ear to ear.

CHAPTER 4

The grasses, spreading as far as the eye could run before tiring, waved across the breadth of the valley like a soft old blanket held to the wind. A hill, speckled with smooth round stones, climbed gently from the grassy surrounds to a tumble of boulders, which some said had fallen from the sky when *Enkai* released his leather thong to let all the Maasai cattle come down from heaven.

Momposhe stood on the rise below the boulders, his small herd of goats scattered below him, sucking on a grass stem. His skills were still insufficient to truly understand the subtleties of sweet grass, but he knew enough to know the stock enjoyed the fodder of their new valley.

It had been their valley since Momposhe's section of the Purko Maasai moved there to avoid the tribal wars that had swept Maasailand. Most of the *moran* had gone to fight the Ildamat section, because the Ildamat Maasai had attacked their friends, the Keekonyokie. This caused the Purko warriors to dance, to demand respect from the Ildamat, and to sing songs of war. The Purko came together in numbers that blackened the savanna, and then they jogged away in a thundercloud of dust. Only the women, old men and boys remained behind to tend the herds.

Somewhere across the wide savanna Momposhe imagined mighty battles being fought, for the other sections had joined the war and he knew the *moran* of his *enkang* would win great honour by causing the grassy plains to run with the blood of many enemies. Momposhe did not know why there was war between the brother sections. All he knew was that hostilities had existed between them for as long as he could remember, before they finally erupted into bloodshed.

He desperately wanted to go with his *moran*, but he was yet to be circumcised. He looked at his miserable little bean pod, knowing it would not grow to be like the *moran*'s sausage-gourd until it was cut. It was smooth and soft, like a fat caterpillar. Without his father, there was no one to ask the elders to call the circumciser, and without circumcision he could not prepare for warriorhood.

The boy picked up a stone and threw it angrily at a secretary bird that was taking advantage of the insects and rodents disturbed by the goats' foraging.

A grass season had passed since they arrived in their valley. He well remembered the long rains that came before their move. They were the rains that fell on him as he and his father were taken from the Boers' farm where they had been dipping their cattle before the Boers — all seven of them — were slaughtered by the Nandi. It was a terrible day, that rainy day, when he and his father put his mother's body, also a victim of the Nandi, in the ground. When they went back to the smouldering ruins of the farm there were white men there in uniforms. They were very angry, and took Momposhe and his father to a cage, where they stayed for three days without food and only the rain that leaked through a hole in the roof for water. On the fourth day the men tied his father behind a mule and took him away. When Momposhe tried to follow they chased him off.

Now another rain season was approaching and again Momposhe would beg his father's brother to arrange the circumcision, but he knew the answer would again be no. His uncle said it was a father's duty to arrange a circumcision. Momposhe knew it was also a father's duty to pay the circumciser's fee, and it was more likely the heifer than the tradition that troubled his uncle.

The sun had begun its slide to the distant range that the Maasai called Mau, and Momposhe decided it was time to head back to the *enkang* and closet the stock safe from the predators of the night. As he approached the collection of huts encircled by its protective *boma* of thorn bush, he saw a man climbing the hill. By his blue cloak, shaved head and walking staff, by his long pierced ears heavy with wooden plugs, Momposhe knew the man was an elder, but not one familiar to him. Perhaps he was a visitor.

Fifty paces away, and Momposhe's chest heaved and jumped as if it had become a cage for a small monkey. He dropped his herding stick and immediately retrieved it without taking his gaze from the man, still not daring to believe his eyes. It was Marefu Ole Matipe — his father — striding towards him.

But his father's face was troubled and he walked like a man pursued by a demon. Or perhaps it was Momposhe who had committed some heinous crime that his father had heard about and he'd dashed back from his white man's prison in order to punish him. Momposhe didn't care about the reason. His father was here, and even if he had come only to deliver his beating, Momposhe would be happy.

Now his father drew near. Now his sad black eyes met Momposhe's, and stared at him as if at someone they didn't recognise. Momposhe froze under the hunted, haunted gaze. Then the hard lines at the corners of his father's mouth softened and he reached for Momposhe. And drew his shaved head to the warm flesh of his flat belly and held him there.

It was said by those in the *enkang* who knew such things that a Maasai could not endure the white man's jail; could not abide the removal of the sun, the confines of a cage, the loss of dignity. Momposhe therefore thought his father would die, and had steeled himself never to see him again. He shed no tears. It was not becoming to one who aspired to warriorhood.

But here he was, holding him, feeling his father's heart pumping blood through his body. Strong and alive.

A tear fell from Momposhe's eye. It hit the ground with an eruption of dust. But he was happy.

* * *

The six elders sat in council around the fire. Momposhe, told to remain at his uncle's hut, peered from the darkness, finding spaces between those watching the gathering to study the half-circle of old faces. The flickering firelight added more wrinkles, and their eyes were in deep shadow, strangely unfamiliar and disturbingly expressionless.

His father, Marefu, stood stiffly before the old ones, his back to Momposhe, but the boy could hear every indignant word his father said. He began by reminding the elders that they had abandoned him, an age-set brother, to the whites, and asked whether they would have done so if he had been confronted by a lion rather than by the men in uniform.

'No,' he said, answering his own question. 'You would rather die with me than abandon me. The years are not too many for me to remember the day of my first lion kill. Do you remember, Leponyo?' He turned to look at the old man at the right of the semi-circle. 'It was in the time of the red moon, was it not? A big drought following the season when the hyenas took sixteen sheep. Yes, I can see it in your face. You are with me there again. The savanna grass crushed flat around us. You beside me. We enraged the lion with our chanting and dancing. Do you know that? Yes. You and I. Shoulder to shoulder. Shield to shield.'

Momposhe edged closer; close enough to see his father's eyes move on to the next man.

'*Ai*, Sekento,' he said. 'We ran all day, you and I, to make a raid on that Kikuyu village beneath Kinangop. You took a beautiful red bull, and I took a beautiful young woman — the one that would become my wife. You knew her too, Sekento. She was a sister. Do you know I buried her that day at the Boers' farm? Yes, I buried her in the ground as the whites have demanded we do, instead of letting the night predators take her as is our custom. But in so doing, I was found by the soldiers. I was not worried. I had done nothing wrong, but they took me to their court and to their jail. It wasn't for many moons that I understood they thought I was in a Maasai raiding party that finished the Boers. Those whites are so stupid, ah? How could they not recognise the Nandi spear in the Boer's back?' He smiled derisively before resuming his fierce expression. 'But you knew it was a Nandi spear, did you not, Sekento? Of course you did. And you, Leponyo, and you, my brother Ilampala. All of you knew the Nandi did the killing.' He moved his eyes from one to another, holding them with his gaze until each was forced to look away.

'All of you,' Marefu repeated with disgust. 'But none would come to speak for me with the whites.' His voice was like a razor-sharp *simi* slicing the meat from their bodies. 'May a beast of prey devour you!' he said, to gasps from the gathering. It was the worst curse a Maasai could put on another, but no one dared reproach him.

'I expect no better from you when the whites come for me again. They will, for I have killed an *askari* in making my escape. How could it be otherwise? I could not stand another day in that dark, cold place. How can any man endure such barbaric treatment, no matter the crime?'

Marefu found Momposhe at the edge of the firelight, and the boy saw that his father was sad, immeasurably sad, and not angry as he had been.

'I am leaving,' Marefu said. 'You have shamed and disgusted me. You will not see me again, for I am no longer a Maasai. I disown you. I shun you. You no longer exist.'

Momposhe followed his father all through the night. Even when the lion stalked them, they kept walking. When the eastern sky warmed with violet and pink, they still did not pause but walked on into the fullness of dawn, when Marefu finally stopped.

The boy remained standing as his father squatted in the shade of a baobab. They had exchanged not a word all night. Now Marefu nodded at the shaded space in front of him. Momposhe sat.

'I know what is in your heart, Momposhe,' his father said. 'We will discuss what must be discussed now, and when we have finished it will be done, for I will not speak of the Maasai from this day on.' He looked at Momposhe. 'Do you understand, my son?'

'I do.'

'Then tell me, what is in your heart?'

Momposhe could not find the words. He looked up into the tortured limbs of the baobab. They clawed at the awakening sky, as if reaching for its streaks of gold. How could he explain how his forlorn hopes of becoming a member of the *moran* had been instantly revived by his father's return, but then dashed again following his father's irretrievable damnation of the entire tribe? One side of him wanted to scream his anger at the injustice of it all; of being robbed of his right to become a true man. Another part of him understood his father. He knew how much he had been wounded by his age-mates' treatment of him. Age-mates were closer than brothers. Their bond was at the core of the Maasai's survival, the heart of the tribe's formidable military strength, for an age-mate would never desert another on the field of battle. Side by side, in a tight phalanx of shields and spears, they were invincible, for no one could break that invisible bond. But now Momposhe's chance to enjoy such a relationship was at great risk. It was too difficult for his mind to encompass all the conflicting emotions.

'You have followed me, but you are not sure if you should have.' As usual, his father had gathered a scattering of thoughts and pressed them into a few simple words.

'Yes, Father. I am sorry.'

'Don't be sorry. It is I who am sorry. I have damned all my brothers, and now stand to lose my son.'

'I don't want to lose you, my father.' The baobab frowned down at him, warning him not to disgrace himself with tears. Momposhe screwed his fingers into a knot and bit his index finger. 'What should I do?'

'You are an *olaiyoni*, a big boy. Soon you will be offered the chance to join the *moran*. These things you will forgo if you come with me. It is for you to choose. Do not fear that I will be angry with you, because I know it is in every Maasai boy's heart to join his brothers. I will miss you, but I will love you no less if you leave.'

The baobab made no offer to help. It stood above him, its leafless arms spread in a gesture of detached disinterest, when a moment before it had been ready to condemn.

'What can I be if not a Maasai?' he asked.

'I can see that the whites will soon become the strongest tribe. They have many fearsome weapons and their numbers grow, whereas the Maasai wars will reduce us to nothing, and we will only be able to observe the division of our lands.'

'Do you mean I should join the whites?'

'I don't know their customs. You must first study them, then decide for yourself.'

A shaft of sunlight broke from behind the baobab's thick branch and fell into Momposhe's eyes. 'I want to go with you, my father.'

Momposhe and Marefu walked for days without food, and with only the calabash of water, which was never enough.

The land was dry, game was scarce and fleet of foot, and water to fill the gourd was difficult to find. When they did fill it, it was with the gritty, malodorous brew of near-empty waterholes. Their path was very long, and so far as Momposhe could tell, it was a path leading to nowhere.

On the fifth day, Momposhe fell down, and was unable to stand for some time. Soon after, his father followed a pair of wheel ruts to a farmhouse. Marefu hesitated at the gatepost before planting his spear in the ground.

The pair of them moved towards the farmhouse, and stood there in the sun until Momposhe's legs began to buckle again. Finally the door opened and a hand gun poked out, held by an old white woman who did little more than peer at them through the crack of the door opening. She spoke bravely, but the breathy falter at the end of her words told of her fear.

Marefu replied — as respectfully as Momposhe had ever heard his father speak — in the melodious tones of the Maa tongue. It made no impression on the woman, who now needed two hands to hold her gun. She remained so for some time, then the door closed.

Momposhe looked up at his father, who kept his eyes on the door, resolute in his stand. Again they waited, and again Momposhe's knees grew weak.

The woman re-emerged, with her revolver in her apron pocket and a cloth bundle in her hands. She approached warily, and Marefu pushed Momposhe forward to accept the cloth parcel. As he took it, the woman smiled at him. Momposhe almost fainted as the smell of fresh bread filled his nose and made his mouth run with water.

He and his father retreated to the gatepost, and Momposhe's belly swelled with the hot bread that the white woman had made into little round cakes.

They were not so lucky in the days that followed. They were in the high plains where the nights were cold, and they were chased away from many farmhouse doors with no offer of food. Momposhe suspected the farmers feared the Maasai, for everywhere there were the signs of war. During their march they had found a battlefield strewn with the bodies of fallen *moran*, their flesh torn and partially devoured by scavengers.

On the third day after finding the white woman with bread cakes, they came upon a white man labouring with a heifer that was stuck in mud beside a waterhole. The farmer's face was very red. Momposhe could see that the heifer was not unwell and should have been able to extract herself from the mire, but she refused to, as heifers often chose to do for reasons only cattle knew.

Marefu and Momposhe approached and observed the man's pushing, pulling and shoving at the heifer for some time. Eventually, the white man put his hands on his hips and muttered something to the two Maasai. An awkward silence followed as neither Marefu nor Momposhe could understand him, but it was obvious the man needed help. Marefu handed his spear and walking staff to Momposhe and went to where the heifer lay in the mud, making the occasional mournful mewing call. He leaned over and put his mouth to her ear, making similar loving talk that Momposhe had seen men of his *enkang* do when cattle were ill.

He stroked and patted her and the heifer became calm. Then he gave her a slap on her tail, and the heifer gave a few energetic kicks and lurched to her feet.

The white man stared at the retreating heifer for a moment, then burst into laughter, slapping his thigh and slapping Marefu on the back.

Momposhe ate well that night, and the space the white man gave them in the hut he used for his calves was warm and comfortable.

CHAPTER 5

After leaving Umtali, they stalked the Sabi River for days, but Jim's promise of lion proved to be the overly optimistic boast that Grogan had always suspected. He and Archie decided to retreat to reconsider their next moves. Jim bade them a cheerful farewell and headed back to his father's village as if it had all been a merry frolic. Grogan thought that for Jim, at least, it probably had been.

Sitting in the dining room of their Umtali hotel, the bones of a very tough chicken now picked clean, Grogan said, 'I've been giving this some thought, Archie, and I now realise what we've been doing wrong. Instead of wasting our time with natives or amateurs, we should find ourselves a professional guide. Someone who can be guaranteed to find our lion. I imagine there'd be someone in Beira for the job.'

'Good idea. We've been galloping all over the shop without luck except for the antelope you found before I arrived.'

'Not much of them either, I'm afraid. A couple of gazelle. That touch of the fever laid me low. Not well enough to go chasing after them.'

'You were a sight when I finally got here. Whatever happened to you? It didn't look like the fever to me.'

A vivid memory of loud laughter and bare thighs flashed into Grogan's mind. 'Something in the food, I suspect,' he mumbled.

In spite of his resolve, the recollections would not leave him: the hotel bar in a riot of colourful banners, loud music and dancehall girls especially invited from gold-mining towns all over South Africa. Drinks passing between him and several strangers. Whisky. Too much.

For days following, as he waited for Archie, he had been very conscious of his penis. He monitored every one of its sensations as if it were a predator inside his trousers. Whenever he had the chance, he made an excuse to be alone to give it a thorough examination. In time he realised all the itching and other strange sensations had been a creation of his imagination, or perhaps of his guilt.

'Then you think we should take another look at it?' Archie asked.

'*What!*'

'Getting a professional guide.'

'Oh, yes ... I think we should. As soon as we get back to Beira.'

26 May. Urema River
Our prospect of sport improved immeasurably when we came across Mr Dan Mahony, Portuguese East Africa's foremost guide and an acquaintance of mine from the Matabele war. He agreed to lead us north of the Urema River to where he said there was plenty of game.

The country we walked through was extremely fertile, the white millet growing to a height of twelve feet and carrying enormous heads of grain. The people, who are evidently flourishing, build neat grass huts and keep them clean.

Archie bagged a good lion within hours of making camp on our second day. Archie! Was my medal for shooting at Cambridge for naught? I am in a state of agitated impatience and firmly resolve to redress this disparity.

Grogan set out at first light with Mahony as guide and Mahony's best man as his gun-bearer.

They came onto fresh scat at a waterhole an hour out of camp, and followed it with only the buzz of flies and the twitter of early birds in their ears. They lost the trail a number of times and had to backtrack to recover it.

As the sun climbed into the immensity of the African sky, the spoor — paw prints as large as dinner plates — disappeared into long grass. Mahony looked at Grogan, shaking his head.

Grogan stared into the grass. The lion's path was obvious, laying aside a swathe as it thrust its huge head through. Even with that parting, Grogan could see no more than a few yards. The lion obviously knew it was being followed, and had chosen ground to its advantage should it decide to attack.

'Dan,' he said, 'let me go in alone.'

'Don't be stupid, Ewart,' Mahony responded. 'There'll be another lion, another day.'

'Maybe. But this is my first. How many hunters bag the first lion they see, Dan?'

'Hardly any.'

'Exactly.'

Grogan took the rifle from the gun-bearer, whose lip had turned white where he'd bitten it, and pressed on into the long grass.

'Ewart!' Mahony hissed behind him. 'I can't allow this!'

Turning back with a grin, Grogan said, 'I absolve you from all responsibility, Dan.'

Mahony shook a fist at him as he turned and melted into the grass. 'You always were a bloody pigheaded tear-arse, Grogan,' he muttered.

The head-high grass absorbed all other sounds apart from the crush of dry stalks that grew to fill Grogan's awareness. The lion relentlessly stuck to its path, rarely diverging offline by more than a foot and giving Grogan a clear view of the way ahead. It also gave him confidence that the lion was still in front of him.

The heat became stifling. Sweat trickled down his face, dropping onto his already saturated shirt. He stopped. Utter silence instantly surrounded him. The broken line of grass ran on ahead as it always had, but he suddenly realised that the lion could have doubled back and be waiting on either side, coiling its massive muscles beneath it in readiness for the pounce.

The real danger of the stalk in long grass now dawned on him. He strained to see through the towering growth on either side. His ears rang in the silence. Then a deep, faint, breathy sigh came in spasms from somewhere out there. After a moment more, he convinced himself that the sound was ahead of him, and possibly moving away.

He pressed on, stopping every few minutes to calm his breathing and to listen. On one occasion, the sway of seed heads at the end of the path told of the lion's proximity. This reassured him, as he felt confident that his eye and quick reflexes could drop the lion in a frontal attack. Sometimes the sighing sound was not there, leaving only an unnerving silence. On these occasions Grogan found it almost impossible to force himself forward. His rifle became slippery in his grasp.

After ten minutes of this cat-and-mouse game, the land began a gentle rise, imperceptibly at first, but soon he could see the boulders on a *kopje* about a hundred yards away. Unbelievably, there was his lion — a large male with a magnificent reddish mane — giving Grogan an instant to find its chest in his sights and let loose the lead-nosed .303.

The lion dropped with a last defiant snarl, and lay still.

4 June. Pungwe River
We have witnessed the plenitude of Africa. Mahony led us to an Eden near the Pungwe River. It is a dream fulfilled. Upon breaking from the wooded hillside, we beheld a landscape covered by an enormous herd of animals. Where the plain was at its widest — in the direction of the Urema and the NW extremities of Gorongoza's Plain — it was black with game. There must have been in the order of 40,000 wildebeest within our sight. They parted as we approached and swallowed our tracks as we passed. A variety of other antelopes, zebra and the larger ungulates were also visible in considerable numbers.

Archie and I chased three eland for eight miles without success. We camped where we were, and Archie, again the lucky one, spotted buffalo emerging from a donga in the early evening and shot four with his double .303.

Archie has yet to understand buffalo and treats them with careless disregard. They have earned my respect from the many stories I have heard of their fearless courage and cunning nature. They kill far more in Africa than his lordship, the lion.

Archie and I dropped a buffalo from a large herd this morning. As we approached the 'dead' beast, it suddenly struggled to its feet and charged us from thirty yards. I fired both barrels of the 4-bore into its chest, which had not the slightest effect. Without the time to reload, I shamelessly took to my heels. Archie, quite recklessly, stood his ground, as if defending the barricades of a fort. He fired a single shot and brought the beast down three yards from his feet. He promptly went weak in the knees and called for a brandy. I hazard a guess that it will be the last time he treats the buffalo in such a cavalier manner.

All in all, Archie has had a miserable time these last few days. This morning, shortly after we struck camp, his portliness, which I constantly remind him will prove a burden in the months ahead, proved his undoing. We were crossing a bridge of matted vegetation when he disappeared through it into the river below. No doubt the ever-present crocodiles were delighted at the arrival of the unexpected bounty, but we pulled him out before any harm was done.

Archie decided to spend the day in pursuit of his and Grogan's heavy luggage, which had still not arrived. His first task was to find the Portuguese shipping agent — difficult in itself — and give him a piece of his mind. He said he would start by checking the bars along the waterfront. Grogan wondered how far Archie would get before an ale in each bar became the end of it. Nevertheless, he wished him good luck, and said he would continue his recruitment campaign for porters.

Grogan had seen a Watonga village on one of their hunting trips along the Pungwe, and searched for a boat to take him up river to find it again. He had met other Watonga on the Zambezi when he was scouting for Rhodes. They reminded him of the exuberant Zulu in stature and humour, and of the Matabele, who were not afraid to eye a white man across a battlefield and could fight with honour. He knew the Watonga to be a proud people, with respect for a leader. He would need to find men with these qualities in abundance if they were to survive the ordeals in the trackless centre of the continent. He had been unsuccessful to date, so decided to change his tactics with the Watonga.

Two hours later, Grogan marched into the Watonga village dressed in his pressed drill tunic and a full regalia of ribbons. Upon inspection, his own decorations seemed insufficient, so he'd added others. On his cap he had sewn two brass buttons from an old military greatcoat and a pair of holey silver dollars he'd bought in a market in southern California. His sleeves were decorated with pieces of red, white and blue cotton, and from his shoulders and chest dangled sections of gold fringe cut from the hotel's gaudy dining room curtains.

He stood in the middle of the village and slapped his leg with his swagger stick, which was, in actual fact, the cleaning rod from his old Snider rifle.

'My friends,' he said, projecting his voice so all could hear, even though, by necessity, he was using an interpreter — a man from the village who had been adopted by a mission school as a child. 'I am here today to offer you a great adventure. This adventure is a journey of many, many moons to faraway lands. If you are one of the chosen ones to accompany me on this adventure, you will see the deep water of Lake Tanganyika — a splendid sight to behold. Then we will go north again to yet another lake, even mightier than Tanganyika, and cross mountains with rivers of fire, and beyond them more mountains, so high that the water is as stones.'

In the pauses for translation, he watched the expressions on the Watonga's faces. They had fallen into a deep silence.

'Out of the fourth lake flows a mighty river,' he continued, 'which, after following it for many moons, will take us to the home of the white man, whose number is more than the grains of sand on the shores of the great ocean at the mouth of the Pungwe, and whose *kraal* is larger than the hills.' Still the Watonga remained spellbound and Grogan began to feel confident of success. 'There, at the famous city of the white man, there is a great salt lake — the water without end — where your northward journey will cease. But even then your adventure continues, for

I will send you home on a boat even larger than this village, and upon returning you will be welcomed as heroes by your people. Your brothers will never tire of hearing your stories, and your children, and your children's children, will sing songs praising your memory.'

There was a long silence as the crowd digested all this.

A voice came from the front rows. The interpreter said, 'They want to know how you know all this if you haven't already seen it.'

'Tell them that white men know very much, and what we don't know we learn from books.' He pulled a book from his pack and held it up for all to see as the interpreter related the answer.

Another voice came from the gathering, bringing a great deal of laughter.

'What did he say?' Grogan asked, as the crowd drifted away.

The interpreter tried unsuccessfully to suppress his smile. 'He said that the Watonga are known for their storytelling and lies, but this white man has defeated them in their own sport.'

Grogan watched his recruitment drive disintegrate before his eyes. However, one man held his ground, while a few others lingered on the edge of the village clearing.

'You there,' Grogan said, waving to the man. 'Come forward. Are you interested in joining my adventure?'

The man was tall and well-muscled and his intelligent eyes held Grogan's for some moments before he said in faltering English, 'I will come with you.'

'Excellent! And who are you?'

'I am Makanjira.'

The interpreter explained that Makanjira was a minor chief — a young man awaiting his chance at leadership behind a line of more senior men. Grogan believed himself to be a good judge of character, and thought Makanjira to be a natural leader who would make a good head porter or gun-bearer.

Of the others loitering nearby, he signed up four, including a small boy whom he appointed as camp factotum.

On the boat journey back to Beira, he congratulated himself on his decision to keep a diary as it was unlikely he would be able to recall all the unexpected complexities of the expedition without it.

CHAPTER 6

Bruce Dalton was a no-nonsense person in just about everything he did. He had to be to make a living in the harsh climate of the hills outside Londiani.

When he came to the highlands after his wife's death it was to farm his allotted plot of land. Farming had been in his family's blood for generations, whether growing potatoes in Ireland, or more recently in his father's case, running rubber plantations in India. He had picked up the finer points in his mother's milk, even making a decent fist of bananas when he was down on the coast.

He began to farm grain and vegetable crops, while around him his neighbours were making good money out of cattle. Somehow he gathered the impression they had found the path to easy money — low risk and high profit — so he ploughed nearly all of his limited capital into beef cattle.

Standing in the home allotment now, where he had gathered the worst of his herd, he understood he knew absolutely nothing about cattle. They were sick. Many had already died, and he was staring financial annihilation in the face.

Marefu and the boy were standing with him, perhaps waiting for him to give the orders on how to end this evolving disaster. Dalton had even called his Kikuyu maid to act as translator should he have any instructions to give to his Maasai labourers, but all he could do was shove his big hands deep into his pockets and feel sorry for himself.

The boy, Momposhe, edged towards him. Dalton could see him out of the corner of his eye. He was a good stamp of a lad, intelligent despite his lack of English, and a willing worker with his father.

'What is it, boy?' he said without taking his gaze from his ailing cattle.

The boy stammered some words to Bernase, the Kikuyu maid. She listened, then turned to Dalton. '*Bwana*, the boy says my father would know what you are doing.'

'What am I doing? What does it look like I'm doing? I'm staring at my bloody dying cattle is what I'm doing.'

The line of translation ended at Marefu, which prompted a long conversation between him and his son. Dalton idly wondered how his cynicism would cross the language barrier.

'My father asks what you do for your cattle,' came the response.

Dalton sighed and shook his head. 'I have no idea.' His answer was more an expression of his despair than a reply to the boy's question.

Again his words went from the boy to the man.

Through Bernase the boy said, 'My father knows this disease, *bwana*. We call it *olodoa* — the sickness — and it is very bad for cattle. They suffer, then they die.'

Dalton turned to the boy, of a mind to chastise him for his impudence, or maybe to give him a clip under the ear to go on with. He didn't need his nose rubbed in the obvious. Then he recalled it was the boy's father who pressed the issue. He glanced at the older Maasai, hoping to find an expression there that he could take issue with. Marefu met Dalton's gaze with eyes full of concern. There was no callous indifference to his plight as he might have expected, but an empathy that transcended all their verbal limitations. Dalton realised he had, until that point, dismissed Marefu as one incapable of understanding the finer points. The language barrier was formidable, creating a huge distortion of his understanding of the other man. He guessed Marefu was around his own age, but unlike Dalton, he was tall, slender and lightly muscled — a beanpole with a spring in his heels. Decorative strands of beads lay against his chest almost covering two raking scars that must have been there for many years. They ran from his shoulder to his navel.

'Can you cure this sickness?' he asked Marefu.

The answer came back promptly. 'Yes.'

A further conversation ran between Marefu and the boy, who said, 'My father says he cannot cure all, but those that have not gone too far, he can try.'

Dalton nodded. 'Then tell him to try.'

Marefu handed his walking stick to his son and went to the nearest animal. It had discharges running from its nose and sunken eyes. He bent to smell its breath which came laboured from its mouth. There were small eruptions on its gums. He patted the cow, and put an arm over its back, and another under its belly to feel the strength of the shivering fit that racked its body.

Marefu directed his words to Momposhe but kept his eyes on Dalton.

The boy said, 'This cow is very bad. If we save her, we can save many.'

Dalton nodded. 'Tell him, *thank you*. And let's get on with it. We can only do what we can. But tell him this: I want to work beside him. I want to learn.'

Momposhe tried to concentrate, but couldn't. While he should have been studying his father's work on Mr Dalton's sick cow, he was distracted by the *enkiti,* who he could see from the corner of his eye. She was staring at him again.

He knew she was not permitted to be out in the savanna, because her father or the Kikuyu maid had often come looking for her on occasions such as this and called her back to the farmhouse. It had happened many times before, and Momposhe wished Dalton, who had gone to Londiani that morning, would come back, because she was a nuisance. A small girl — an *enkiti* — should not be allowed to distract an *olaiyoni* — a grown boy — from serious work.

Behind his righteous indignation was concealed a flaw in his conscience, because hadn't he, Momposhe, been guilty of staring at the *enkiti* when he first arrived at the Daltons' farm with his father? But that was understandable, because the girl — whose name was Darling — was most peculiar. Small, with long honey-coloured hair and eyes like the sky at dusk before the short rains begin — a mix of greens and a touch of grey.

Marefu slapped the cow on its tail and it plodded back to the herd.

Darling was on her knees, making finger-marks in the dust. She stood when she caught Momposhe's derisive expression, and dusted her hands, before turning and, with her head high and with deliberate steps, marching back to her house.

When Marefu and Momposhe arrived at Bruce Dalton's Londiani farm, his cows were suffering from rinderpest — what he was soon to learn was referred to as an infectious febrile disease. Nobody in the district had a clue about it. Some said it came into British East Africa through infected Indian beasts. Dalton had no idea, but he did know that he and his neighbours faced ruin. So when Marefu said he could cure his herd, Dalton had little to lose by giving him a try.

He thought the old Maasai must have some hocus-pocus tricks, because over the following weeks, he saved most of Dalton's herd whereas his neighbours lost nearly every animal to the disease.

Overwhelmed with gratitude, Dalton asked what the Maasai would accept as payment. Momposhe said that his father would be thankful to remain tending the cattle. This was more good news, for Dalton had realised there was more to raising beef cattle than he had thought. In a rush of relief he insisted on making some further contribution.

The boy translated for his father, who reflected on it for some time. Finally, he said he had no need of anything more than a roof over his head and food enough for his belly, but said that if the *bwana* would see to the education of his son, it would more than pay for his simple assistance with the cattle.

Dalton readily agreed. In fact, he was surprised and delighted at the opportunity. He had always had a deep respect for what he termed 'the learning'. His own formal education had been limited, but throughout his life he had grabbed knowledge as a miser might grab at pennies.

It was with some satisfaction then that in the following weeks Dalton watched Momposhe and his daughter head up the track to the Londiani schoolhouse.

He was very pleased with himself. His cattle had survived the rinderpest, he had survived financial ruin, and he had gained the services of an expert cattle man. His only cost for the entire thing was to send the boy to school. Even that was a bonus, as Momposhe would learn English and be able to be his translator.

Bruce Dalton was at last able to smile with satisfaction, knowing that things were turning out well at last.

CHAPTER 7

20 July 1898. Chinde and the Zambezi River
After four long months our agent finally found our heavy supplies. For some inexplicable reason they had been sent to Durban, were mislaid, found again, and hastily dispatched not to Beira, as we'd hoped, but to the Zambezi port of Chinde.

In those four months I have subdued the wildlife, made studies of all manner of agricultural techniques for future reference (although I have some difficulty explaining why I thought such a study needed to be done), sent a collection of butterflies to the Natural History Museum at Oxford (some of which, according to my reference material, may be hitherto unknown to science), and made extensive ethnological notes on the Wakonde tribe, who work metal and carve wood to make weird and wonderful musical instruments.

In other words, I have done all but make a start to my journey. But now, thankfully, all that is behind us. We sailed to Chinde and we are now on the Zambezi; a river with no banks as far as I can tell, for we have been steaming upstream for a full day without sighting land.

It is a dreary, hot, monotonous journey. Our only excitement occurs when we run aground on one of the numerous sandbanks, which we do regularly. The crew on board pole for their lives, and dozens more are in the water, pushing and pulling at the boat while trying to avoid becoming a meal for one of the enormous Zambezi crocodiles.

28 July 1898. Chiromo
On the 24th we disembarked at the junction with the Shiré River and were transferred onto the Peters for the rest of the journey to Chiromo.

Food was almost non-existent, so Archie and I did a spot of fishing from the rail of this floating tea kettle, generously described as a steamer. Having landed a couple of fine specimens, our problem became how to make a meal of them. There was no bread, butter, milk or Worcestershire sauce, without which life, or at least native cooking, is intolerable. Luckily, we were able to buy fowls, eggs and tomatoes at riverside villages along the way.

Chiromo is laid out at the junction of the Shiré and Ruo rivers. Most people who spend any time here are laid out too, in another sense. On the north-west side, the town is hemmed in by the vast Elephant Marsh, now a closed game preserve owing to the inconsiderable slaughter of the beasts in time past. When the wind is from the marsh, mosquitoes in their millions are blown onto the town's hapless occupants.

Just prior to our arrival, a lion appeared in the town in broad daylight and carried off a native.

Grogan led Archie up the path to Chiromo's grandest house. It was a square building suspended on stilts with verandas on all sides. The space beneath the verandas was concealed from view by flowering vines clinging to a white-painted lattice. Pots of the most beautiful orchids dangled from the veranda's supporting beams on long copper chains.

When they reached the top of the steps, they found a gardener pouring water into a large pot plant beside the front door. He was a most dishevelled creature wearing tattered khaki shorts and an undershirt that might once have been white. He paused in his work to give the two men a curious look.

'We're here to see the vice-consul if you please,' Grogan said in a businesslike manner. 'I have letters of introduction from Lord Battersby.'

The gardener carefully lowered his watering pot and stared first at Grogan and then at Archie.

'Well . . .?' Grogan prompted impatiently.

The man simply blinked his eyes, which were a watery blue, made more startling by their contrast against his weather-beaten, sun-tanned skin.

'Did you not hear —'

'I'm MacDonald,' the man said, clearing his throat. 'The vice-consul.'

Grogan glanced at Archie, whose mouth hung open momentarily.

'I'm sorry,' the vice-consul said, wiping his hands on his shorts. 'Not used to visitors. Except on second Tuesdays when the veterinary officer comes around. MacDonald, James.' He extended his hand.

Grogan shook it. 'Ewart Grogan,' he said, and then presented Archie, who he introduced as Lord Battersby's youngest son.

'Archie,' MacDonald said, pumping his hand. 'Glad to meet you.'

He invited them into the parlour, which was heavily shaded and remarkably cooler than the blistering heat outdoors.

'Proper tropical design,' he said in response to Grogan's remark. 'I had a house just like this when I was a customs officer in Port Darwin back in the eighties.' He then went on to describe the architectural features in some detail.

Over iced drinks and an exchange of news, both local and from overseas, MacDonald invited them to stay for dinner. 'Indeed, why not bring your personal effects and stay here? I live alone, and there's plenty of room, as you can see.'

At dinner — which was fish stunned by one of MacDonald's .303 cartridges fired into the Shiré at close range — conversation was halted by the coughing call of a lion. A moment later, it was answered from another direction. MacDonald shook his head. 'That's our lullaby almost every night, I'm sorry to say.'

Grogan retold the story they had heard about the native being taken during broad daylight.

'Absolutely true, Mr Grogan. Absolutely true. Sadly, it's not unusual. Only yesterday I found leopard spoor in the street in the morning, and in the Ruo the crocodiles have an easy life near the natives' bathing places.'

'There seems to be an extraordinary proliferation of wildlife around Chiromo, Mr MacDonald,' Archie said. 'I don't understand why.'

'Chiromo — it means the joining of the rivers. Wasn't the Garden of Eden situated in just such a place?'

'I suppose you're right, but as far as I know, the Almighty spared Adam and Eve from the predation your townspeople seem to suffer. These man-eaters are running amuck wherever they please.'

'Ah, you're so correct, Mr Battersby,' MacDonald sighed. 'But what can I do? There are so many. Do you know, almost the entire white population turned out to slay that lion the other day, but it got away completely untouched. Shots were fired at him from all manner of weapons, from five to five hundred yards. But still he wandered around, the least excited individual in the town. I'm afraid there's not a hunter within a week's march of Chiromo who's prepared to help.'

Ewart and Archie exchanged glances.

Archie was first to speak. 'Mr MacDonald, perhaps you will allow us to be of some assistance in that regard?'

Ewart reached down from the tree and took the two rifles from Archie. 'Got them,' he said in a lowered voice. 'Now, see if you can climb up here beside me.'

There were muffled curses from the darkness below.

'There's a hole a few feet up the trunk. Use it for a step,' Grogan said.

After several minutes, during which he heard Archie fall at least twice, his companion scrambled onto the branch beside him, wheezing with exhaustion.

'P'raps it wasn't a good idea to open that other bottle,' Archie said, burping loudly.

'I told you that after the third,' Grogan replied.

MacDonald had again served them a wonderful meal that evening, complete with fine wine. Around 11 pm, after Archie had demolished the wine and started on the brandy, they left to begin their watch for the lion that had terrorised Chiromo.

Their *machan* was set in a tree outside the town near the lion's last sighting. Below them a nervous old goat bleated into the darkness, which was broken only by the light of a three-quarter moon floating lazily in and out of wispy clouds.

'It's not cricket, you know,' Archie said. 'Shouldn't use a bait like this.'

'Normally I'd agree,' Grogan whispered. 'But this isn't for sport. This is to eliminate a man-eater. And if you sit like that you'll fall off. Why don't you straddle the limb like me?'

'I can't. Hurts my balls.'

'Then don't sit on them! For God's sake, Archie ... that *blunderbuss* you're carrying would knock a man off a horse.' He referred to the 4-bore Archie had in his lap. Grogan had his trusty .303.

'Hmm.' Archie burped again. 'Years ago I helped get rid of a man-eating tiger in Kashmir. Like this. With a bait. Not good. But this is the lord of the jungle. Deserves better.'

'We can debate the niceties in the morning. Now be quiet; if he's near, you'll frighten him off.'

'Right you are.' After a moment's silence, Archie said in a rasping voice, meant to be a whisper, 'Lucky for his kind he's not the only lord of the jungle. There's always more to carry on the line.' He held his tongue for a while, then after further thought added, 'A bit like the British system of hereditary peers, isn't it? You have a string of 'em in case the eldest is 'liminated.'

Grogan ignored him.

A lion roared somewhere in the distance — a long call followed by a series of shorter sobbing coughs. The lion was proclaiming its domain.

They both listened without saying a word. The call came again.

'He's a long way off,' Grogan said. 'When there's silence we'll know he's serious.'

An hour passed, punctuated by the whining of numerous mosquitoes.

Archie began to snore. Grogan gently shook him awake.

'Is he here?' Archie asked with a start.

'*Shh*!' Grogan hissed. 'Not yet. Be patient.'

The lion had been silent for the entire hour. A number of times Grogan thought he'd heard telltale sounds, but nothing eventuated. The goat wasn't just a lure; it would alert them when the lion was approaching.

Some time later he heard a low grunt come from the darkness beyond the tethered goat. He held his breath, trying to catch another sound to better pinpoint the lion's location, but it remained quiet. His ears rang in the total silence. Inexplicably, the goat was silent too. Perhaps the grunt had been a bush pig.

Archie shifted in his sleep and his 4-bore slid from his lap. Grogan made a grab for it, but missed. Almost at the same instant, Archie fell backwards off the limb and hit the ground beneath the tree with a thud and a muffled 'Oomph'.

'Archie?'

A low moan came from below.

Grogan found a place in the tree to hold his rifle, and edged his way along the bough.

A strange sound came from the darkness below — a twang like a released bowstring. It was the goat's tether drawn taut.

Then the goat began to bawl in panic.

Grogan was at the bottom of the tree before realising he had left his rifle in the branches.

'Archie, are you all right?'

'My arm. Bloody hell!'

'Come on, get up.' Grogan strained his eyes into the surrounding bush, which was a collection of indistinct shapes dappled by the moonlight.

A moaning grunt came from the shadows, followed by the faint snap of a dry twig.

Archie heard it too.

Grogan could faintly hear the sound of the lion's exhalation — a sigh of anticipation.

The goat continued to tug at the halter, periodically making a pitiful bleat of fear.

Grogan's straining eyes misted with tears. He was afraid to blink them away in case he missed the charge from the darkness. He squatted and searched the ground around him for Archie's 4-bore.

Shadows moved — under the influence of the moon or the lion, he wasn't sure.

He felt the cold steel of the rifle barrel under his fingertips.

The lion charged — a silent, powerful surge of raw power.

As he quickly drew the rifle into his shoulder, a number of images flashed through Grogan's mind: the almost perfect camouflage of the lion's black mane and tawny coat against the mottled greys of the bush in moonlight; the utter silence — even the charging lion seemed to bound soundlessly out of the night; and, finally, the iridescent green of its shining eyes.

A deafening explosion erupted from Archie's 4-bore.

CHAPTER 8

James Coleman stood with his back against the enormous open fire, rocking on his heels, and — as was his habit — laying down the law to the three young men in his clipped East Coast accent. Occasionally he would take a puff of his cigar, or use it to jab at them for emphasis.

'I tell you,' Coleman said, 'the Philippines is just the first of them. We'll free Cuba, and when we do, McKinley can just sit back and wait for Spain to sue for peace.'

Coleman would not agree he was 'laying down the law'. He would insist he was merely passing on the benefit of his three-score years to his two sons-in-law and the young man who hoped to win the hand of Gertrude, the youngest of his three stepdaughters. It was his habit to hold such court in his study immediately before dinner, over an early-picked semillon, while the women gathered in the drawing room. He had become accustomed to being heeded — no matter the audience — after he had made his money; not in gold, as many had tried but failed to do in California, but in agriculture and timber.

The Napa Valley was wooded in those early days, and his forest concession provided the seed capital he needed for the vineyards. Supplying wine to the burgeoning population of San Francisco was the beginning of an empire that now billowed out from his mansion in the valley.

When he met, and later married, Elizabeth Watt in London,

she was a widow with three young daughters. Coleman had been in England to arrange distribution of his wine and citrus fruit, and although she was twenty years his junior, he had swept Elizabeth off her feet.

'The sinking of the *Maine* in Havana merely gave us the excuse to invade,' he said. 'The president had no choice after that.'

There was a light tap on the study door and Gertrude entered, swishing the long hem of her skirt to one side. 'Papa, we are all famished! What *are* you talking about for so long?' Her lustrous long brown hair was piled on the top of her head and held there with a large gilded pin.

'Ah! My dear Gertrude,' Coleman said, his wide smile parting his thick white whiskers. 'We are almost done.' He waved his hand to indicate she should join him. 'Come in, my darling.'

'Only for a minute, because Mother sent me to fetch you.'

'Good evening, Gertrude,' the young man, Morris, said, grinning at her.

'Oh, hello, Morris,' she answered with what Coleman recognised as a poor attempt at enthusiasm.

'You look stunning in that dress. Is it new?'

Gertrude looked down at the long boldly striped navy and white dress, which was nipped at her narrow waist, and nodded. 'Yes. I was in San Francisco last week. At the Golden Rule Emporium. But I'm not sure I like it now.'

'Morris is right, my darling,' her stepfather said. 'You look very fetching. Now, gentlemen, would you please go ahead into the dining room while I have a brief word with Gertrude.'

The three men obediently filed out the door.

'You don't need to say it, Papa,' she said without prompting.

'At least you could be a little more enthusiastic when he comes over.'

'Morris is nice, and quite a gentleman, but you know I'm not interested.'

'He's a fine young man. Good family up there in Calistoga.'

'I have already met a fine young man, thank you very much.'

Coleman shook his head. 'Sweetheart, I don't think we'll see him again. For all his bold talk, I don't expect he'll show his face after making such an outrageous statement.'

'You don't think he'll do it, do you? Well, I know him better than you, and I know he will.'

Coleman took her hand into his and patted it. 'I just don't want you wasting your time, or burning any bridges.' He smiled at her. 'For my sake, will you at least be pleasant?'

'I shall be cordial and polite. More than that, I can't promise.'

He shook his head with a begrudging smile. 'Why is it I can intimidate everyone but you — the youngest person in this house?'

'Because I know you're a big marshmallow.' She fluffed up his white whiskers and pecked him on the cheek. 'Now come — dinner's ready.'

Gertrude climbed the stairs, smiling. The night had been pleasant, and Morris had been his usual charming self. She was flattered by his attention, and under normal circumstances would have given him more encouragement, but the young man with the bold talk and outrageous statements, as her stepfather put it, was the one she wanted.

She opened her bedroom door. The room was bright, with every light ablaze. Her maid had a fascination with the new electric gimmickry. Gertrude switched all of them off except for her large bedside lamp and the one above her writing desk.

She sat at the mirror and unpinned her hair. It fell in a tumble around her shoulders. Picking up her ivory-handled brush, she idly began to run it through her long auburn tresses. Normally Molly would be there, fussing over her and readying her for bed, but this evening she wanted to be alone. The letter had arrived earlier that day, and although she had read it immediately, she wanted to do so again at greater leisure so that not a word was missed. She put down her brush and slipped the letter out of its slightly soiled envelope.

19 August 1898
My Darling Gertrude,
    I received your very welcome letter upon reaching Blantyre. It was all the more appreciated, or should I say

cherished, coming as it has from halfway around the world to find me. But find me it did. I am both delighted and amazed.

My heart soared upon reading your words of love. I can only assure you from the bottom of my heart that I feel the same. Sometimes, when the evening is calm and the work of the camp is done, I sit in quiet contemplation of your beautiful features, your gentle hand in mine, the music of your laughter. I recall the many joyful moments we shared — treasured the more since our time together was so short. I wish that my trek was done so that I could be back in your arms and feel the thrill of your embrace.

You shouldn't worry yourself about my health for it has been quite good, apart from a little bit of fever, which of course is all part of being in Africa.

I can vividly recall a night at the campfire during the Matabele war when Rhodes was in a contemplative mood. He said that Africa needed men of vision and courage to stir it from its sleep; men who could grasp his concept of a British axis running through the continent from south to north. Pointing directly at me, he said, "You younger men must devote your lives to this great task." Little did he know that it sparked a flame in my mind that even now is about to leap into life. My preliminary survey for the railway line through the region of the great lakes in Central Africa will be my humble contribution to Rhodes' grand vision.

Presently, I am in Nyasaland — about 60 miles SSW of Blantyre under the terraced cone of Mount Chiperoni, which stands amidst a circle of lesser peaks. Great woodlands of the wild loquat, mahobahoba, cover the lower slopes, and crystal-like streams, which cascade through bamboo valleys, tumble down through ferns and orchids to scar the face of the mountain.

Standing on a ridge one sees the endless forest-clad plain running east to Portuguese East Africa and the Indian Ocean. The surrounding mahobahoba forest is resplendent, with many flowering trees on the rises with gold, red, russet and browns (so common in our northern autumn) appearing in great display. In the areas where, for some inexplicable reason, an open plain appears among the trees, a carpet of purple flowers attempts to overwhelm the green. Here and there on the Blantyre side are the well-ordered coffee plantations lending an air of discipline to the rampant natural beauty. For a fleeting moment I thought I might be back in West Sussex, such was the gentleness of the cool air and the greenery and pleasant colour of the coffee flowers.

It pains my heart to witness such beauty without the one I love at my side. Perhaps one day ...

What I am saying is that Chiperoni is exceedingly beautiful, with cool days, and evenings and nights quite cold. The streams are icy. There are no mosquitoes or flies — quite a relief compared to the swamps of the Pungwe, and the bedevilled flats of Chiromo where the wind blows clouds of mosquitoes from Elephant Marsh.

In the forests, elephants are attracted to the small sugary fruit of the mahobahoba tree, becoming, I believe, intoxicated by the fermentation. Unfortunately, I have been unable to bag an elephant due to the dense forest into which they can quite literally disappear.

I am travelling alone at this time because poor old Archie suffered a broken shoulder in a nasty fall from a tree. He is convalescing in Chiromo and we cannot proceed until he is mended. It greatly frustrates me. I imagine time slipping away like the sands in the glass. Do you realise, my darling, that I recently turned twenty-five? My life seems to have stalled in this wilderness beyond the Empire. There is so much to do, so much to achieve. I cannot afford to waste time.

Archie's injury even prevents him from hunting with me, which, as you may well imagine, peeves him greatly. However, he cannot complain too much about missing his hunting. Checking my notes I find that between us we have bagged six lion or lioness, two hippo, seventeen wildebeest, ten impala, fifteen zebra, three eland, five

Lichtenstein hartebeest, three tsessibe, four waterbuck, eleven reedbuck, one oribi and six buffalo.

Upon reflection, I realise the account of our trophies might distress you, my darling. If so, I am sorry, but I have yearned for this opportunity to hunt since I was a child. In fact, I have four childhood dreams that I hope to realise while tramping north. They are to bag an elephant, a lion and a rhino, and to set eyes upon Lake Tanganyika. Strange, you may think, but my childhood was one dogged by ill-health. Our family physician warned that due to my delicate heart I would be forever bound to life in the English countryside. Oh, if he could see me now. But my four dreams kept me fighting to overcome my afflictions, the aftermath of a near-deadly attack of measles.

With the same determination I will complete this journey, and prove to your stepfather I am a man of my word.

My promise and our dreams are our secret. Archie knows nothing about them, or the promise I made to your stepfather. Archie thinks our expedition is all about bagging a few trophies, and surveying Rhodes' railway line.

I will spend my days suffering unbearably from impatience until I hear from you again, but will remain encouraged by the loving words of your last letter.

Until I hear from you again (God knows when or where that might be),

I am, your adoring slave,
ESG

CHAPTER 9

4 December 1898. Zomba
It is nearly nine months since we arrived in Africa, and we,
that is, Archie and the complement of porters I engaged to
supplement my five worthy Watonga, today steamed up
the Shiré towards Lake Nyasa.

We have on board all our luggage, save for our full-plate
camera, our spare chronometer and aneroid barometer, my
set of dress silks and spare cotton shirts, which have
apparently been lost in the many circuitous miles our
belongings have enjoyed. Such are the pleasures of African
travel.

Big game hunting is always exciting, but I must confess
to a waning interest as days turned to weeks, and weeks
turned to months, while we waited in Chiromo, first for
Archie's shoulder to heal and then for another wretched
bout of my fever to abate.

While waiting, I carried out an extensive survey of the
forms of agricultural activities in these parts. I have notes
prepared under separate cover in relation to sugar, coffee
and brick-making industries hereabouts, and will make
them available to the appropriate authority upon returning
home.

Everywhere one looks there is opportunity in all manner
of endeavours, but without the magical catch-cry of

'Gold!' Africa remains utterly ignored. Nyasaland has boundless potential. It reminds me of New Zealand, where the hardy British settlers have made a most wonderful fist of the opportunities by dint of strong will, fortitude and hard work.

Eventually we resumed our northward journey, but our progress was crab-like, that is to say, slow and sometimes sideways, due at least in part to my fever, which lingers despite my coddling.

I have conceded to Archie's nagging and agreed to stay put in Zomba where the cooler air will aid my convalescence. Meanwhile, Archie will go to the northernmost point of Nyasa to begin the process of recruiting the larger body of porters we will need for our crossing of the Tanganyika plateau.

Before he leaves, Archie and I will visit the Governor to pay our respects.

Zomba's Government House was a large, picturesque timber and stone building with a delightful tropical garden. It had a tennis court and croquet lawn — such as lawns are in the tropics — and a large patio, where the Governor, Sir Landers Caldwell, led Archie and Grogan for afternoon tea. They took a seat at one of the many garden settings under the trees surrounding the tennis court.

'Tea will be along presently,' the Governor said. 'In the meantime, I'd like to know more about your expedition, Mr Grogan. You say you are travelling all the way to Cairo? Extraordinary.'

Grogan smiled. 'Not particularly, Sir Landers. It's simply a matter of application. A matter of applying oneself to a task that is like many others, with a beginning, a middle and an end.'

'Granted, but an extraordinary task nevertheless. I do believe that no one has ever done it before.'

'Quite right, Governor. We shall be the first.'

'If we succeed,' Archie added.

'Pardon my asking,' the Governor said. 'But why? I mean, why are you doing it?'

'Why do men attempt any difficult undertaking?' Grogan replied. 'It is part of mankind's make-up to seek challenges so as to measure the extent of his capabilities. But if you are asking me what are the specific objectives, I would say it was to carry out a preliminary survey to determine the feasibility of a railway running south to north through the continent.'

The Governor blinked. 'Really?' Grogan couldn't tell if he was stunned by the idea, totally disinterested, or simply didn't want to concede that he'd heard of Rhodes' bold plan. The railway was not government policy, and many argued it would be provocative, challenging French and Belgian interests in the region.

'And to collect some good specimens along the way,' Archie added.

'Ah, a spot of sport,' the Governor said, nodding enthusiastically. 'I understand that kind of objective, Mr Battersby.'

'Between us we have bagged six lion or lioness, two hippo, more than a dozen each of wildebeest, impala and zebra — I can't remember exact numbers. Oh, and three eland. Plus a few bucks — waterbucks, reedbucks, those sort of things.'

'Splendid!'

'And six buffalo,' Archie finished, satisfied he had covered the majority of them.

'Are you proposing to do any hunting while you're here? Because I know a few —'

'Not really,' Grogan interrupted. 'We are only taking a short rest in Zomba before pressing on.'

'Ah! Then you must both join us tomorrow. We have a little bit of social tennis on Saturdays. It helps for us to get together from time to time. You know — relieves the boredom.'

'Actually, it's only I who will remain here for a few days. A touch of malaria. So I really should rest. Archie is going on to Karonga's *kraal*, to find some porters for our onward journey. We've been having the devil of a time finding enough ever since leaving Beira.'

'Very wise. It's close to season's end and the natives will want to be home for the harvest. Karonga is as good as any to find

58

them.' The Governor glanced over Grogan's shoulder. 'Oh, look! It's Emily. What a surprise,' he said.

A young woman was crossing the tennis court towards them. She wore a crisp white uniform and walked with a confident, athletic stride.

'I'm sorry to interrupt, Landers, but Sophia said I should.'

'Certainly. Come, come, meet Mr Grogan and Mr Battersby.'

Her hand was soft and warm. Grogan had almost forgotten the touch of a woman's hand.

'Gentlemen, this is Miss Emily Hitchen, our nurse at the District Clinic.'

They exchanged greetings.

'I was just inviting these gentlemen to our little tennis tournament, but without luck, I'm afraid.'

'Really?' she said, making a small frown. 'Such a shame. We don't have many visitors. It's a pity you have to leave so soon.'

'Only I am leaving, Miss Hitchen,' Archie said. 'Ewart is here for a few more days.'

'Then you must join us, Mr Grogan. Do you play?'

'Occasionally,' he said. 'But I'm a bit rusty. May I come as a spectator?'

'Of course you can, can't he, Landers?'

'By all means, old boy. More the merrier.'

'Then it's settled,' she said, her smile revealing small, white, perfectly formed teeth. 'Tomorrow it is.'

Grogan accompanied Archie for the first mile of his journey to Lake Nyasa. It was early morning and the crisp air was refreshing. He felt the exercise would do his health good.

The Governor had arranged a few porters for the trip to the lake — a matter of a day or so. This meant Grogan could keep Makanjira and his lieutenant, Zowanji, in camp to guard their equipment and supplies, allowing Grogan to take a room at Mrs McPhee's small guesthouse — the only one in Zomba.

Archie's caravan consisted of fourteen men and the cook's assistant. This was sufficient while they were in the relatively inhabited regions, but after leaving Lake Tanganyika they would need a much larger caravan to carry many more supplies as well as the gifts needed for safe passage through hostile lands.

After the first mile Grogan felt strong enough to continue for another. It would also give him time to cover a few more details with Archie.

'Regardless of the number of porters you recruit, Archie, you'll wait for me in Karonga, won't you?'

'I will, Ewart. Don't worry.'

'It's just because I don't want us to become too far apart.'

'I know.'

'I won't be far behind, you understand. And these porters ... try to find some Watonga if you can. They seem to be a good bunch. I'll be along in a day or so. As soon as I regain a little strength.'

'Yes.'

'Why are you smiling?'

'I'm wondering how your malaria will stand up to a day's feverish tennis.'

'Tennis? Don't be absurd — I'm only going for the tea party.'

'Not if Nurse Hitchen has anything to say about it. She seems very persuasive. I'll bet you're on the court within an hour of arriving. Maybe even thirty minutes.'

'Nonsense.'

Grogan lay shivering under a blanket in his sweltering room at Mrs McPhee's guesthouse, ruefully recalling the tennis match that, three days ago, had led to his relapse.

Doubles, Miss Hitchen? Why not?

They were only beaten in the third set, but it was madness. Even as he accepted Emily's persuasive invitation he knew he would regret it. She was not to know of the twinge of pain he'd felt in his lower back that morning. Nor would she have been aware of the effect that her clinging cotton tennis dress had on him as it wrapped around her thighs during her singles game against Mrs Carmichael.

During the tea party that followed, in which he thought he might have slipped back to civilised England without knowing, he put the pain from his mind and simply enjoyed the sparkling conversation and the tinkle of Emily Hitchen's laughter.

There were periods in the days following when he'd felt the worst had passed, then the fever would rush back at him and his head would throb like a four-pound hammer was thumping inside it. That morning, his pain had been replaced by a chill. Now he was hot. He threw off his nightshirt and kicked the sheet and blankets from him.

There was a knock on the door followed by a muffled voice. 'Mr Grogan, it's I, Mrs McPhee.'

Grogan quietly groaned. 'I'm not able to come to the door, Mrs McPhee,' he said as politely as he could while retrieving his sheet from the floor.

'May I open, Mr Grogan?'

He suppressed a curse. 'Please do,' he said, pulling the sheet to his chin.

'Mr Grogan?'

'Emily! I mean, Miss Hitchen.' She was standing in the doorway of his room — a palliative angel in her starched white uniform — while Mrs McPhee, the full-bosomed proprietor, smiled benignly behind her.

'I hope you don't mind. I heard you were ill.'

'Oh, it's nothing really. Just a little fever.' Sweat trickled into his eye. He quickly brushed it aside.

'*Och!*' said Mrs McPhee. 'Look at him! The poor man's in dire need of help. I'll leave you be, Emily. Call me if you need anything.' She pulled the door closed as she departed.

'I've brought you some medicine,' she said, approaching the bed. 'Do you have quinine?'

'No. I mean yes. A little.'

She put her medicine box on the bedside table and, opening it, pulled out a bottle of quinine powder.

'Do you have a tumbler? Ah, here's one.'

She quarter-filled the glass with water from his flask and placed it on the table next to her medicine box. Next she took a measuring spoon and tapped the white powder into it, taking care not to spill it.

Grogan watched her frown of concentration.

She stirred the quinine into the water and sat on the side of the bed. 'Now, here,' she said, holding it in front of him. 'Take this.'

He sat up, conscious of the sheet slipping from his chest.

Emily placed a hand behind his head as he tilted it back to swallow the quinine and water.

'Yuck!' he said, giving an involuntary shudder.

'More water,' she said, taking the glass from him, and handing it back when she had filled it.

Grogan swallowed it all, spilling some on his chest. He coughed when it caught in his throat. Emily patted him on the back and, when the spasm passed, took a small towel and gently wiped his chest. He became acutely aware of her touch. Her hand on the back of his neck, the titillating caress of the towel on his neck and upper body.

'My, you have got a fever, haven't you?' she said, noticing the bead of sweat drop from his jaw to the side of his neck before running down his chest.

'Hot and cold,' he said in a hoarse voice.

Emily poured a little water onto the towel and wiped his brow, the back of his neck, and ran it down his bare chest to his midriff.

His erection could not be controlled.

'There, there,' said Nurse Hitchen. 'Don't be embarrassed. I know a man has his needs.'

She took the hem of the sheet in her delicate fingertips and gently pulled it down.

CHAPTER 10

My dearest, darling Ewart,
I am sitting at my little writing desk beside my bedroom window, which looks out over the vines. The berries are setting, and the sun is shining, but I see none of that. Instead, I see you reflected in the glass, standing behind me, stroking my hair, which you did so enjoy doing.

I see your strong blue eyes, no, not blue, what are they? Sometimes they are blue and sometimes they are an iridescent green. Am I being fanciful? Perhaps.

My fancy is born from the loneliness I suffer. The long days pining for a word from you drag on. I have no way of knowing if you receive my weekly utterances as I fear our letters cross on their interminable journeys.

Although I have received several of them, sometimes arriving three and four at a time, I wonder how your letters can possibly find their way to California. I imagine stoic mailmen crossing great distances from the outposts of Empire. I see them skirting mountains, pressing through dense jungles, fording raging rivers and tracking over sandy deserts (are there deserts in Africa?), finally arriving at a seaside port only to begin another enormous journey, this time across the oceans to me.

I worry that my letters, returning in another mailbag, get lost in one of those rivers or jungles. I fear that all my words of love will die out there, lost forever. What if the bag carries more than one letter of mine? I could die thinking of it.

We (that is Mother, Father and I) went to England at the beginning of May (I sent a short letter from there. Did you receive it?). England was cold and wet. Father wanted to find new buyers for our expanding supply of oranges. Mother and I spent some time shopping. I couldn't resist taking her to see bridal fashions. She is sworn to secrecy, of course. Papa thinks I have forgotten you, and I would hate to deprive him of the surprise when you triumphantly return!

This time we made our homeward journey by way of Chicago and the Great Northern Railroad. Chicago is a very progressive city with buildings even taller than those of New York and London.

Upon arriving, Father announced our homecoming with the usual grand party. He never misses the opportunity to pass on stories of his business successes in England to all his neighbours. He also never misses the chance to, yet again, introduce his unmarried stepdaughter to society. I shouldn't be so unkind as he means well, but I don't need these continuous "coming out" announcements. I sometimes feel I've become an old spinster and my family (that is to say my stepfather at least) is worried that I will soon be of an unmarriageable age (I'm not even sure if that is a word). I must humour him, because I have found that if I mention your name he becomes silent and brooding.

Oh, how can I fill these pages with trite stories when what I really want is to fly to your arms, and to smother your delicious mouth with kisses?

It is better that I end this tear-stained letter lest I be tempted to take my imagination into places quite unseemly for an unmarried lady.

Be safe, my darling, and remember how much I love you.
Yours forever,
Gertrude

The fine white sands of Lake Tanganyika's beach tugged at Grogan's boots as he struggled towards the water. He had been on the move for six weeks, celebrating Christmas Day at Karonga's *kraal* with a cup of tea and the company of Dr Castellote — the physician for the telegraph company — who had nursed him through a malarial coma.

The doctor was also travelling north, and had only come to Grogan's assistance when Makanjira paddled out to his ship to beg for assistance. Castellote told Grogan that the malaria was inflaming his liver, and could bring on another attack of liver abscesses which would quite likely kill him. He counselled returning to the coast as soon as he was fit enough, and taking the first ship for home. Grogan thanked him for his advice and said he would think about it.

Archie had not been waiting at Karonga's *kraal* on the northern tip of Lake Nyasa as they had agreed. He'd left word to say he had gone on to Lake Tanganyika, and that he would meet Grogan there instead. Grogan had been infuriated. Archie surely knew he hadn't enough porters to get him to Lake Tanganyika. It was while recruiting more porters that Grogan had fallen ill.

Now, depleted by exhaustion, Grogan put all that behind him and allowed no thought to enter his mind other than the immediate task, which was to complete the journey across the wide expanse of shimmering, scorching sand to the waters of the lake. Behind came his porters, eager to reach the refreshing waters, but silently keeping a respectful distance like a congregation following the Eucharist. They were not permitted to assist him when he stumbled — that had been made clear when Grogan's fever-weakened knees buckled in the soft sand at the start of the one-hundred-yard journey. Each step was an accomplishment; every ten paces a monument to perseverance.

Thirty yards from the water and the heat-haze cleared enough to reveal tall, curling breakers rising under the influence of some force deep within the immeasurable blue depths to pummel the shore and send a froth of wavelets scurrying up the sand to greet him.

He fell, and his hands sank into the wet sand. He could hear the hiss of wavelets kissing each individual grain before disappearing into the lake's inexhaustible depths. His mouth watered at the sight and scent of it.

Finally, he was there. He fell to his knees in the breakers and filled his mouth with handfuls of sweet fresh water. He flung it about him and felt the almost irresistible urge to allow himself to sink into its calming, cool depths and sleep.

Revived, he waded through the breakers, rejoicing at the buffeting they gave him, and gazed out over the turbulent shore towards the blue beyond. The flicker of a hippo's ears appeared in the lull between rising waves, and further out, no land, hill or mountain intruded between where he stood and the distant watery horizon.

The African Lakes Corporation's steamer *Good News* groaned as the swell on Lake Tanganyika rubbed it against Kituta's wharf timbers. Grogan rested against a pylon and tamped tobacco into his pipe. Makanjira was supervising the loading of their remaining cargo items. They would soon be heading north in pursuit of Archie. Again he had left word that he was forced to move on. Grogan's fever was gone, leaving him thirty pounds lighter, but he still steamed with anger at Archie's wilful behaviour.

He rummaged in his top pocket with his free hand and found a match. Puffing his pipe into life, he tried to put his anger behind him and gazed out over the blue expanse of Lake Tanganyika.

Gertrude came unbidden to his mind, as she often did in his contemplative moments, but this time her memory brought with it a twinge of conscience. He was a young man who relished challenge and seldom failed to conquer it, but twice his willpower had been challenged, and twice he'd failed the test. He had always been highly charged with a strong attraction to members of the fair sex, but until the incident in Umtali had not had the opportunity to satisfy it. He tried to put the unpleasant thoughts from his mind. The affairs in Umtali and Zomba need not be repeated, but they had nothing to do with Gertrude, nor affected his love for her in any way.

The steam whistle of the *Good News* sounded, summoning Grogan to the next round in his adventure.

4 April 1899. Lake Tanganyika
At last. We departed Kituta aboard the *Good News* which is filled almost to overflowing. However, cockroaches outnumber passengers hundreds to one. They inhabit every corner of the ship, and some are the size of mice. My mosquito net sags under their weight. I wondered if it would survive the night, but need not have worried. Makanjira, who has appointed himself as my personal guardian while I remain in my weakened state, dealt with the problem. This morning I found the space surrounding my hammock strewn with cockroach corpses.

The uncomfortable morning became an almost unbearable afternoon as the temperature climbed to 100°F shortly after noon, and continued to rise.

A furious storm came out of the north and lashed our boat, throwing us around in seas the character of which I have not seen since the storm-strewn Atlantic. I understand such storms are not uncommon and often have dire consequences. They are formed by the tropical heat in the deep gullies among the surrounding mountains, and dash down quite unpredictably. I fully expected the little rust-bucket would turn turtle on us, and then heaven help us all.

The men moaned and prayed that Allah would save them, but I could see from their countenances that they were less than confident He would.

Almost all aboard suffered terrible seasickness as the storm continued into the late afternoon. Upon the onset of evening, the wind dropped and the seas almost immediately calmed.

6 April 1899. Lake Tanganyika
The captain has agreed to put into M'towa where I am hopeful of at last finding Archie after I had a chance meeting with two Belgian priests of the Pères Blancs order. They told me they had seen an Englishman of Archie's appearance a month ago, heading north.

I should have been more polite to the priests, but I had some trouble holding my tongue. The problem is that after *witnessing many noble attempts by various religious bodies to bring their so-called enlightenment to this continent, I have decided that their involvement in the life of ordinary Africans is impertinent. I happened to share these views with the White Fathers before they told me about Archie.*

Still, I hold by my words. What right have they to impose their sanctimonious clap-trap on the lives of these simple folk? In many instances they are likely to upset the often admirable state of society in Africa. Given the appalling misery at home, is there not enough work for all of them back in Europe? I can see naught but trouble and misery if these self-seeking souls continue to dismantle traditional customs and rituals, many of which are the foundations of an ordered society that has existed for centuries, nay millennia. I shall have none of it.

CHAPTER 11

Momposhe viewed the *enkiti* with quiet unease. He, the *enkiti* and her ugly yellow dog were on their way to school in Londiani, but the girl was dragging her feet again. She seemed to delight in provoking him. He didn't understand why, and had been unable to find a solution to their daily confrontation, short of actual violence.

If anyone should be dragging their feet it was Momposhe, whose job it was to escort the *enkiti* along the dusty track that ran out of the farm, up the rise towards the escarpment and into Londiani.

After many months of confusion, he now knew enough English to realise the *enkiti*'s name was Jessie, not Darling as he had thought. She was the daughter of Mr Dalton, the farmer who Marefu helped with his cattle. Momposhe and his father still lived in Dalton's barn because they hadn't yet been asked to leave. It seemed an arrangement that suited everyone. Marefu tended the cattle, Momposhe did odd jobs, and Dalton fed and housed them.

One of Momposhe's odd jobs was to take Jessie to school. It was a tolerable task until the time when his father and Mr Dalton decided he should have an education. The teacher agreed to let him join their classes, and Momposhe's drudgery began in earnest.

After his first day at school, Momposhe protested to his father. He had been forced to join a class that included girls, some of whom were even younger than Jessie. Marefu shrugged and refused to budge. He made it known that if Momposhe was to join the white tribe he had to learn their ways, just as he would have had to learn Maasai ways if they were still with the tribe.

Momposhe suspected his father had other things in mind. For a long time, communication between Marefu and Bruce Dalton had been very difficult. A simple instruction from Bruce to Marefu, a single sentence perhaps, required two intermediaries. Dalton would ask Bernase to translate from English to Kikuyu — her mother tongue. Momposhe, who had picked up some basic Kikuyu from his mother, would make a rough translation from Kikuyu to Maa for Marefu, who had been too proud, or too lazy, to learn Kikuyu from his wife. The result was seldom better than a series of disjointed words — the meaning lost along the way. Subtleties were impossible.

Questions were the most difficult, requiring a round trip through the translation go-betweens, providing at least four opportunities for error. Answers often bore no conceivable connection with the question. Dalton might ask, 'Have you seen the red heifer with the white patch on the hindquarters that looks like a star?' The returned answer might be: 'On that night there was no moon at all. Rain was in the air.'

Momposhe thought that learning Maasai ways had always been more interesting than school. School was a strange place, with mysterious rules and unfamiliar customs, and the stuffy, sometimes hot classroom was initially no fun. But as each month passed, Momposhe became less like a Maasai and more like a Londiani schoolboy.

The task of fitting into their new life was no easier for his father, who was also learning the white people's customs and the equally strange rules of farming. Not that he had become attached to the Dalton household. He said little to anyone, including Momposhe. Something had happened when the white men threw Marefu into jail that time and even the relative safety of the Dalton farm could not undo it. Or maybe it was the burning hatred that he held for the Nandi, who not only killed his wife, stole his cattle and caused him to be thrown into a stinking hole, but also forced him to flee his home in case he was again put in a cage.

Jessie was again dawdling, and now bent over a flowering shrub at the side of the track. She picked a flower, sniffed at it, and made a show of fixing it into her hair. 'Don't you think this is pretty, Momposhe?' she asked.

He ignored the question. They would be late again, and the teacher would beat him, not her. He walked back towards the girl. Her ugly dog with the spotted pink and black tongue glared at him. Momposhe glared back. He would not be intimidated by a girl's dog. He stood beside her, waiting until his presence intruded upon her attention.

The yellow dog growled a warning.

The *enkiti* peered at him with those strange greenish eyes. They held a wordless question, as if she had no idea why Momposhe was looking exasperated.

He extended his hand to her.

She studied it for a long time, and then took it.

She walked happily all the way to school with her soft white hand clasped in his.

'Where have you been, Momposhe?' Jessie asked, a little petulantly. 'I've been looking everywhere for you.' She plopped herself down on a log under the tree by the home lot.

The Maasai boy looked down at her, a superior smile on his face. 'I have been helping my father. We were doing man's work,' he said haughtily.

'Doing what, exactly?'

'Nothing that an *enkiti* needs to know.'

'Were you castrating the sheep?'

Momposhe, a little crestfallen by her guess, changed the subject. 'What is it you want of me?'

'You promised to teach me something Maasai.'

'I am busy. Can't you see that?'

'If you don't, I won't help you with your studies. And you'll make Mrs Mitchell really cross with you.'

Momposhe sighed and slumped to the log at her side. 'So if I must, I will.' He liked the sound of the phrase. It was something he could imagine Bruce Dalton, or his teacher, saying. 'What is it you want to know?'

'I don't know, silly. If I knew it I wouldn't need to ask.'

It was another thing she did to tease him — playing games with English words. He could also play word games. '*Oiyote*,' he said.

'What?' she replied.

It was the word the Maasai used to introduce a riddle, and he asked her one exactly as he had learned it from his mother.

'Momposhe, don't be mean — you know I can't speak your language.'

'Oh, really? Then maybe you need to go to Maasai school until you are clever like me.'

'Ple-e-e-ase,' she begged him.

He relented and repeated it in English: 'I have two skins, one beneath me, and one over me. What are they?'

Jessie immediately entered into the spirit of the game. 'Hmm ... An umbrella,' she said. 'No ... I give up. What is it?'

'The bare ground and the sky.'

He rattled off another string of Maa, before translating for her. 'What am I? I am long, but I cannot reach a goat's udder.'

'A tree! No! A snake. Oh, I don't know, what is it?'

'The road to Londiani.'

They laughed. Jessie clapped her hands. 'Oh, I wish I knew some riddles too.'

'Didn't your mother teach you?'

'No,' she shook her head, and smiled at him. 'I never knew my mother. She died when I was a baby.'

'Oh,' he said, regretting her sadness. 'I too have lost my mother. But not so young as you. It must be very bad.'

'It's not so bad. Papa says if you don't know what it's like, you can't miss it. I think that's right. Only I miss having no brothers and sisters. I'm the only one in Londiani without at least two or three.'

Momposhe was feeling guilty for turning the game from fun into sadness. 'Then I will be your brother,' he said, 'and when you want me, you can call me.'

Jessie sniffed. 'But how can I call you if you are far away? You're always out with your father and the cattle.'

'You do like this,' he said, cupping his hands and forming a gap between his thumbs. He blew across the opening to make a breathy musical note. 'Then you whisper your message into your hands, and I will hear it.'

Jessie, delighted, cupped her hands and made a warbling whistle.

'What do you call it?' she asked him.

'I don't know. It does not have a name.'

'It must have a name. Everything has a name.'

'No. Not everything.'

'Of course it does. How do you talk about it if it doesn't have a name?'

He was becoming agitated again. 'Very well. It is called when-you-put-your-hands-together-and-whisper-to-your-thumbs.'

'Silly,' she said. 'I will call it "Jessie's telegraph". Like the one along the new railway line. No, I'll call it "Jessie and Momposhe's bush telegraph".'

Momposhe smiled. 'I think put-your-hands-together-and-whisper-to-your-thumbs is easier.'

'*Through* the looking glass, Momposhe. T-h-r-o-u-g-h ... through.'

'Through,' he said through gritted teeth.

'That's better,' the young girl said. 'Now, let's begin.'

Momposhe thought that she turned the page with a superior gesture, as if she had written the story herself. He very much disliked schoolwork with Jessie. She was far too authoritarian. They always studied in the kitchen, which closed around him when Jessie became bossy. To make matters worse, Bernase loitered in the background, ready to make fun of him if he made mistakes.

'It is a stupid word,' he said defiantly. The *enkiti* must be taught that a girl was not a man. She had no right to attempt intimidation. That was a man's prerogative.

'Pooh to you,' she said.

Bernase put a hand to her mouth, and with the other held her large belly to contain her laughter.

73

'What is pooh?'

'Cow shit.'

'*Ai*, and now you speak so bad to me.'

'Badly,' she corrected.

'What?'

Bernase was at the edge of his vision. He knew she was barely able to hold back her laughter.

'You should say badly, not bad.'

'No. It is bad. You speak bad.'

'Momposhe, really.' Jessie closed the book with a sigh and frowned at him. 'Mrs Mitchell said I am to help you with your studies. To catch up with the rest of us. Now come.' She opened the book again. 'We were up to page ten.' She put her finger on the first line.

Momposhe read: '*Curiouser and curiouser!*' cried Alice.' He paused. 'What is it meaning, this word, "curiouser"?'

'It's not a real word.'

'Then why must I learn it?'

'Because.'

He waited for her to continue before realising 'because' was all the explanation he would get. It was just another way to tease him. His anger grew, but he could contain it. Such trivial tests were no match for his new self-control. He stood, glowered at Bernase, put the book on the table and walked from the kitchen with as much aplomb as he could muster. 'I have learned sufficient for today.'

Outside, the heat felt good on his skin.

'*Sufficiently*,' came Jessie's voice from inside the house.

Momposhe stormed off.

At the corner of the barn he paused, looking down at his bare feet. They were pale with the powdery dust from the beaten earth. He suddenly had an overwhelming desire to have shoes. To own shoes — strong, solid leather shoes that would keep out the dust. A white man was defined by his shoes. If Momposhe was to become a member of the white tribe, he must have shoes.

The Purko Maasai were far away, in both distance and ties. There in Londiani Momposhe was in the white man's land.

74

He recalled his father's warning that if he wished to join the white tribe he had to learn their customs and their ways. To have shoes meant to have money, and to have money meant to know enough about the white man's world to find ways to possess it.

He bent down and rubbed his hand across his feet, removing most of the dust, then turned back to the house, determined to get to the bottom of the word 'curiouser'.

CHAPTER 12

Before Grogan slipped into the dugout canoe that would take him to shore at M'towa, he gave some last-minute instructions to Makanjira. His headman would take all the equipment and supplies to Ujiji, set up camp and await his arrival with Archie.

Later, while climbing the sharply rising hill to the village of M'towa, it occurred to Grogan that he had put everything vital to sustaining his life out there in the wilderness into the hands of an African tribesman he had never met until a year ago. He rationalised that Makanjira and his lieutenant, Zowanji, could have robbed him several times during his many periods of illness, but hadn't. It felt strange to have formed such a strong bond with a man so culturally, educationally and, in fact, in all ways dissimilar to himself.

His niggling annoyance with Archie intruded. He had continued to push northwards despite Grogan's instructions and knowing of the danger of splitting the caravan in two. Grogan tried many explanations, but could find no cause for it. Archie was not the type to grab control of the caravan and therefore take the kudos for the expedition to himself, so why did he continue to defy Grogan's orders? He was at a loss to know how to approach him. It had been three months since they were last together, and while he admitted to feeling a great deal of relief that he would not be left to travel alone through the wilderness ahead, starved of civilised conversation, he was certain they could not succeed if his position as leader was not accepted.

He decided to reserve his judgement, and await Archie's explanation before giving vent to his frustration.

When he found Archie in his tent on the hill overlooking the lake, he was shocked. Battersby was no longer the robust man he had been in England, nor even when they were last together. His skin was grey and his sunken, jaundiced eyes peered out from dark hollows. His slightly portly body was now of skeletal proportions, and his fingers — which constantly fiddled — were spindly and shaking.

'Archie!'

'Ewart, good to see you.' He smiled wanly and struggled to his feet.

'Archie ... I had no idea ...'

Archie sank to his seat again, defeated by the effort. 'Sorry, still a bit weak.'

'What happened to you?' Archie's condition so shocked him, he had forgotten his anger.

'Malaria.' Archie tried to smile, but his voice broke as tears welled in his eyes. 'Ewart, I damn near died!'

Grogan put a hand on his friend's shoulder and sat beside him. 'Well, man ... how are you now?'

Archie nodded, as much to bolster himself as to reassure Grogan. 'I'm going to be all right, I think.'

Archie told him of his two months of fever and the pain that racked every muscle in his body. Struggling ever northward in an attempt to find a healthier climate to battle his fever, he finally came to M'towa and Dr Castellote — the telegraph company doctor — who nursed him through the worst of it.

'He died,' he said in answer to Ewart's question. 'Dr Castellote. He died last week after saving my life. They buried him up there.' Eyes wide, he indicated the hill above the camp. 'Imagine, Ewart, being buried here in Africa. In the bush, so far from home. So far from your family and everything you know. It would be terrible.'

For the briefest of moments Grogan knew Archie's fear as if it were his own; saw the horror that such an isolated ending etched in his gregarious friend's imagination. Archie's fear was not of death, but of a *lonely* death. Dying alone meant your life had been reduced to nothing. If there was no one there to witness its passing, it was as if it had never happened. To Archie, this was the worst possible end.

Grogan sat with him, patting his shoulder consolingly, and they talked. The conversation wandered through the leafy avenues of Green Park, along Park Lane, and eventually to Regent's Park, Queen Mary's Gardens and the zoo. Archie allowed the conversation to venture into Grogan's Sussex, but only because he knew it. He was happy to go anywhere but Africa, where vast spaces, strangers, and strange circumstances pervaded. Grogan spent two hours visiting familiar places with his friend, knowing that he needed the comfort that only home could give him. But Archie's realisation that they might not make it to Cairo alive had sent a tremor of fear through him that Grogan thought it might take him many long days to overcome.

21 April 1899. Ujiji
Ujiji has always intrigued me. It is the single most historic spot in all of Central Africa. It was, however, as childhood dreams invariably are, a trifle disappointing in reality. A few white buildings scattered here and there, a mango tree, a palm, and the shore of Lake Tanganyika. Nothing much.

How many times had I sat huddled over that book beneath a flickering candle, devouring the words used to describe that one scintillating historical moment when here in Ujiji Stanley met Livingstone?

How many times did I imagine myself to be the avenging warrior charging up the shoreline of Lake Tanganyika into Ujiji, the heart of the great slave-trading canker, to rescue hundreds of hapless slaves?

Indeed, how easily does the name Lake Tanganyika roll off the tongue, when not a year ago it was merely part of my boyhood dream.

Archie and I hired donkeys to treat ourselves to a ride into the town. We passed rows of grinning skulls — a reminder of the last days of the Arabs' slave trade. We secured lodgings in a substantial old mission house owned by a couple of non-resident Greek traders. Shortly thereafter, an invitation to lunch arrived from the Governor, a German by the name of Hauptmann Bethe. We accepted with some reluctance. The Germans have been moving aggressively towards British Uganda so we hardly expected a fraternal greeting. However, Governor Bethe and his three officers gave us a royal welcome. Bethe has a large round face, a handlebar moustache and sticking-out ears, but his manners and hospitality were impeccable.

Before lunch had even appeared on the table, the Governor had surrounded us with a bewildering array of alcoholic beverages. Surprisingly, we were invited to commence with a port. Then followed vermouth, champagne, claret and beer. Lunch was finally served around four, and we started on port again. I was able to restrain myself and took my beverages in moderation, but Archie, ever the opportunist, was in for everything.

The conversation turned to the matter of our journey north. I was reluctant to provide any details, and more than once had to divert Archie from squawking everything. Instead, I tried to elicit some information from Bethe, asking what route he would recommend. The Governor said it would most definitely be via Tabora, as the north road was virtually unused and very dangerous. He said they were always chasing raiders from the Congo, which was the reason most of the lakeside towns on the Congo side were virtual fortresses. All the Congolese officials gathered there for safety, because in the outlying regions there was anarchy. Armed bands of natives and army deserters roamed the area, destroying everything in sight. He said that desperate men, unable to tolerate Leopold's harsh rule, would slit our throats for a handful of maize meal. Archie pressed the Governor for details, and sat transfixed during the telling. I could see it would not take much to persuade Archie to head towards Tabora, and keep travelling east until he hit the Indian Ocean.

When lunch was over towards the end of the afternoon, the Germans again pressed us to take more drinks. I said I wondered if it was wise to mix so much alcohol, especially given that it was 110 degrees outside.

Bethe replied that it was wise to do so for health reasons.

Intrigued by his answer, I asked him how so.

The Governor leaned forward in his seat, the more to emphasise the point, and said it was a known fact that no teetotaller had ever left Ujiji alive.

Tembi, the small Watonga boy who Grogan had appointed cook's assistant while in Ujiji, brought in two cups of steaming tea.

The section of the mission house made available to them consisted of three large rooms, the largest of which they used as a sitting room. It was spacious, with shuttered windows and high ceilings. They had a separate entrance sheltered by an open-sided thatched awning, which gave protection from the fierce western sun but allowed what breeze existed to make its way inside. The furniture was simple but well-made. A solid wooden table with six tall straight-backed chairs commandeered the rear wall. A number of cushioned chairs with side tables filled the remainder of the space. Garish Greek seascapes festooned the walls — the only stimulus in an otherwise bland colour scheme.

Tembi placed the tea on the low tables beside Grogan's and Archie's chairs, and silently departed.

Archie took a sip and groaned.

Grogan cast a glance at him and smiled. 'Bear up, Archie. Remember, no teetotaller has ever left Ujiji alive.'

'I'm not sure one could define this condition as *alive*,' Archie said, holding his forehead as he sipped his tea. 'The Governor has some curious ideas about entertaining. It must have been dinner time before we had lunch.'

'Some curious ideas about the region he governs too. I can't believe what he said about King Leopold. I hold no brief for the Belgians, but Leopold is a well-known philanthropist in the

Congo. Bethe's talk of torture and slavery is surely just a German's view of a disagreeable neighbour. Did you find any suggestion of it while you were in M'towa?'

'Too ill, I'm afraid. Most of the time I didn't know where I was, nor the day.'

'His opinion on the danger of the northern path came from a totally different perspective, in my view.'

'Do you mean you don't believe him?'

'Not at all. The Governor is simply testing us with a few little games to try to discourage us.'

'So you mean we're not going to Tabora as he suggested?'

'Of course not. That little piece of advice about taking a small army — something he knows we're in no position to do — came not from an over-active imagination but rather from a more calculating side. He doesn't want us to go north, so he can divert us from the volcano area, where our survey work will begin.'

'But why would he do that?'

'Because the Germans are interested in running a railway from Dar es Salaam, on the coast, to Lake Victoria and then Uganda.'

'Well, what are we to do about the lawlessness he spoke about up north?' Archie asked.

'We'll take it as it comes, dear fellow. As we have all the other distractions we have had to face.'

Archie said no more, but Grogan caught a hint of the expression he'd seen when his friend had spoken of his terror of dying alone in the Africa wilderness.

2 May 1899. Ujiji
At dawn our caravan, now one hundred and fifty strong, departed Ujiji.

It appears strange to our eyes how these men, driven by necessity to the task of beasts of burden, can leave the safety of their homes and trek into a wilderness knowing naught of the perils that await them, and do so in such a festive and exuberant mood. A high-pitched voice rises in song, and a chorus of bass voices answers. Feet stamp in the dirt, a kudu horn pierces the morning air, and the haunted sound of a conch replies. The sixty-pound chop-boxes of food, folding chairs, stretcher-beds, tents, and bags of alum and salt for curing hides are lifted to the men's heads and the long line begins its tentative shuffle forwards. Each of the pagazi, or porters, carries a flat tin water bottle with a stitched felt cover, and their daily ration of posho in a three-pound sack strapped around their waist.

It was a slow start towards Usambara at the top of Lake Tanganyika, which I understand is typical of the first day of a large caravan. It was not until four in the afternoon that the last of our men departed the outskirts of Ujiji. We made camp shortly thereafter. Our methods will improve over the coming days, and I am confident that a more respectable daily rate of twelve miles can be achieved.

The Germans provided us an armed escort to deter any early desertions, which can occur shortly after a porter receives a portion of his pay in advance and before the caravan has moved too far into hostile territory.

Our supplies are not excessive considering we will be travelling into a no-man's-land, but consist of the following: food; ten milking cows and twenty-five goats; tents, beds, collapsible baths, tables and chairs; medicine, including a large quantity of quinine, permanganate of potash (which I firmly believe can cure almost any affliction known to man if administered promptly and in sufficient strength) and Elliman's Embrocation (a proven aid to muscular pains); my library, including veterinary, flora and fauna references as well as the classics; tobacco; two spare Union Jacks (one of which will be presented to Her Majesty at the end of the walk); ammunition; surveying equipment; and gifts for the chieftains through whose territory we must pass.

Makanjira is concerned. Most of our new contingent of porters are Manyema; a tribe renowned for their strength and stamina, but also for being ill-tempered, ill-disciplined thieves. He also says the Manyema have not given up their cannibalistic tendencies.

Soon after leaving Ujiji, the caravan followed a path along a high treeless ridge. Seven thousand feet below, Lake Tanganyika was lost in a heavy mist that clung to the mountains until early afternoon. In the late afternoon, Grogan called a halt to pitch camp before darkness and the chill air of evening caught them exposed on the mountain. That night the porters complained bitterly about the cold.

Archie and Grogan suffered too. The chill brought a return of their fevers. In addition, Archie had swollen septic hands caused by mosquito bites suffered on their first night out. They added to his litany of complaints, which he voiced loudly and often.

Archie's hands worried Grogan — not the infection, for it would soon be cured by the permanganate of potash he had liberally applied; rather it was the fact that Archie had ignored a fundamental precaution. Even the porters used mosquito netting while on the steamy, low-lying lakeshore. Archie's lapse was a symptom of a man who had become dangerously reckless. And while he alone was responsible for his condition, he swore and complained during his misery.

When he wasn't complaining he was reminding Grogan of the joys of civilisation and how he missed them. Grogan tried to ignore him, but could not help recalling that he had chosen Archie as his travelling companion not for his skills in navigation, his map-making ability, nor his knowledge of Africa and its ways, but because he was affable and stoical. Now it seemed these traits would be in short supply on the trek.

Archie had changed.

CHAPTER 13

22 May. Usambara
Weakness of limb and lethargy of heart have curtailed my
diary entries these last several days. My fever returned, but
more disconcerting was the liver abscess, which has flared
again. Before dropping into a sleep I was unable to
control, I heard Archie tell the German administrator here,
Lieutenant von Gravert, that my temperature was 106.9°F.

Fortunately the Germans in this thriving settlement have
organised affairs with Teutonic thoroughness. We enjoy
the facilities supplied by Lieutenant von Gravert, and my
health is slowly improving.

Archie is stricken with the responsibilities of camp. In
my waking moments I see him as a mother hen, dashing
around, forever on the lookout for disasters. In periods of
lucidity I enquire about our preparations to proceed.
Archie prevaricates.

At Usambara, the sand formed over millennia by the pounding
waves of Lake Tanganyika blew in ceaseless drifts up the shore
where it rose into dunes some fifty feet high. Behind one such
dune, Archie organised the setting and the running of the camp,
while Grogan ranted and raved, lost in a hallucinatory world.
Archie thought the fever might actually be a blessing in disguise
for Grogan. Before lapsing into a coma, he had such terrible

pain in his abdomen that he yelped each time he was moved. His liver abscess was again inflamed.

While Grogan tossed in his fitful sleep, Archie spent some time with Lieutenant von Gravert, who made it abundantly clear that he didn't believe a man in less than perfect physical health could survive the trek to Lake Kivu — the next of the great lakes in their journey. So far as the lieutenant was concerned, the mountainous country to the north of Kivu was the end of the known universe. The volcanic barricade, with its jagged floor of petrified lava and swirling, sulphurous air, represented the gates of hell — a no-man's-land. Archie didn't mention that not only was Grogan proposing to march beyond that barrier into Uganda, he intended to go onward to the Nile and Cairo — nearly a thousand miles away.

Archie had always thought the journey to be merely a romantic fantasy for Ewart, and that good sense would prevail when the situation became serious, as it now was. He decided to enlist von Gravert's assistance to explain the situation to Grogan. When Ewart had been lucid for a couple of days, and his abdominal pains appeared to have abated, Archie invited Lieutenant von Gravert into the camp. He made sure his friend was comfortable on his camp stretcher, tucking a pillow made from a canvas bag stuffed with clothes behind his back.

The lieutenant went into excruciating detail about the difficulty of carrying enough supplies over what was essentially uninhabited land, the lack of water and any semblance of formed tracks, and the wild savages said to periodically rampage through the region. In summary, he said, 'I understand from Mr Battersby that your hunting expedition has been quite successful. You have your trophies, your adventure stories to relate when in the company of your family and friends. So my advice to you, Mr Grogan, is to stay where you are until you regain your strength, and then return to the coast for your sea journey home. While you are still able.'

Grogan listened patiently to von Gravert's clipped and efficient English. When the lieutenant finished he thanked him, and then turning to his friend, who had remained silent throughout the monologue, he asked, 'What do *you* think, Archie?'

Archie sighed and shook his head. He'd been expecting this. 'Ewart, I said I would join you on your expedition, and I will not break my word. But we have achieved most of what we set out to do. It worries me that your health has become an issue. Lieutenant von Gravert believes it may mean your life.' He shrugged. 'Maybe I just don't understand. What is it that drives you? Why is it so important for you to go on against all the odds?'

Grogan, with a wince of pain, pulled himself to a sitting position. 'Can you see through the tent flap, Archie? Out there to the north? It's the Rusisi Valley — the very gateway to Central Africa. I've gazed up that valley every waking moment I've had these last few days. At the Rusisi's source is Lake Kivu — a lake never before seen by an Englishman. Burton, Speke, Grant — none of them. Even Livingstone and Stanley never set eyes on Kivu. But we will, Archie, you and I.' He allowed himself to relax against his pillow. 'Some things are worth risking one's life. Finding an unknown lake in Africa is well worth the consideration.'

The Rusisi River begins as a mad fifty-mile dash down its valley, collecting several equally eager tributaries along the way until its violent journey ends twenty miles short of Lake Tanganyika, in a mosquito-ridden labyrinthine swamp. With their feet firmly planted in the mud of the swamp, and leeches and other parasites invading their clothing, Grogan and Battersby could see before them all two thousand feet of their climb to the mountains that enfolded the next of the great lakes — Kivu.

A climb of two thousand feet over fifty miles was not an arduous task for a caravan such as theirs, but the two white men were waging an almost constant battle against malarial fever. Archie was managing far better than Grogan, who had not recovered from his earlier bout. On the third day, Grogan was so exhausted from dragging his aching body over the broken ground alongside the Rusisi that Archie ordered the men to build a stretcher, or *machila*, for his friend.

'I'll not be caught dead in a confounded machila,' Grogan said in a breathless voice when Archie had it brought up for him.

'Dead is what you will be, dear boy, if you don't use it. But if your pride won't allow it, perhaps your head will. We're doing less than five miles a day at the moment. At this rate we'll not be in Uganda until Christmas.'

Grogan grumbled about being rid of the stretcher the moment his temperature dropped, but over the following days his condition worsened.

As Grogan hovered between life and death Archie agonised over his choices. He could return to the swampy and unhealthy lowlands, or press on into the unknown land of Lake Kivu.

Lieutenant von Gravert's blunt opinion, which he shared with Archie just before they departed Usambara, was that if the journey to Lake Kivu didn't kill him, Grogan would probably revive in the higher, cooler air.

Grogan opened his eyes. He blinked, and rubbed at them. There was nothing but an oppressive, suffocating blackness. He had been blinded in some violent altercation that he couldn't recall. His only other sensation was a headache, which pounded like a drum in his ears.

What seemed at first to be total darkness was soon revealed to be a moonless sky, but one hung with low blood-red clouds. He was floating some distance above hell, its asphyxiating air rotten with decay. He imagined he was being carried to Valhalla and ultimate peace. Floating past him were the devil's hovering gatekeepers, carrying lanterns that dripped molten silver to an unyielding black earth. A moment later they were fishermen gliding across the lake, spears poised above the phosphorescence of their bow waves and the dull red glow of volcanoes on the horizon behind.

Makanjira's strong hand held Grogan in his litter until his raving moderated.

The pounding in his ears stopped suddenly and an eerie, keening call came in its place. It was the voice of a fallen angel crying for its lost paradise. He tried to turn from the demons that held him immobile, to fight back at the monsters that threatened to suffocate him with their hellish breath, but he couldn't move.

Some distance away he heard Makanjira speak, and Archie reply. They were talking about him, but he couldn't understand a word they said. He was filled with enormous sadness. Not only was he, Grogan, lost in this alien world, but the people who had trusted him to lead them from it were also trapped.

12 June. Lake Kivu
After days wafting in a malarial wilderness, I awoke this morning with only a slight temperature. The wind had blown the volcanic plume from the lake and I could not but wonder at the beauty of Lake Kivu and the eddying mists above fading hills, redolent of mystery. My fantastic dreams seem a fitting entry into this unknown land.

The broken shaly ground of the lake shore makes walking somewhat akin to marching through porridge. At times we were forced into the cold waters to skirt around impassable bluffs. At other times we took to the mountains, where swift flowing streams presented a problem of a different kind for our cows (which I brought for the purposes of fresh milk) and goats, which had to be manhandled across the waters. More than once a goat was swept away, but our Manyema can swim like tadpoles and made a contest to see who could first reach the animal to rescue it.

Soon we will be in the kingdom of the mighty Watusi. I will not be carried there, and have retired my machila and dozen boys.

A commotion arose at the front of the caravan. Grogan, who had been guarding the livestock at the rear with a couple of *askaris*, hurried through the bush to find Archie in earnest discussion with Zowanji.

'It's the Watusi,' Archie said in answer to Grogan's question. 'There's a large party headed our way.' As he spoke, drums began to beat out a brisk repetitive rhythm.

'Any sign of weapons?' Grogan asked Zowanji.

'There are many warriors. Many spears,' he said.

The Watusi had a reputation for their aggressive demands for *hongo* from caravans. It was said that what they couldn't obtain as gifts, they took by force.

Grogan checked his rifle and ammunition clips. 'All right. Zowanji, you stay here. I'll need you for translation. Archie, you'd better go to the rear with half the *askaris* in case our friends try to steal our cows. Make the *askaris* understand they are not to shoot unless I give the order.'

The porters had set down their loads and were nervously chattering to one another.

'And Archie,' Grogan added as he turned to go, 'everybody is to stay calm. Find Makanjira and tell him to spread the word. Stay calm. No panic. And tell the porters not to look so bloody nervous.'

Archie nodded and headed towards the rear of the caravan.

Grogan slung his rifle over his shoulder and stood facing the track and the wall of dense undergrowth that surrounded it. The drums continued to grow in volume as they approached. In a strange way, he felt they were reassuring. At least he knew where they were and there would be no sneak attack. Then he wondered if that was the Watusi's intention.

He didn't have long to ponder it. Two lines of tall spear-carrying warriors came marching towards him, and then stood back, pressing themselves into the bush at the side of the track. Next followed dancers with coloured rattles and bells. They gyrated and flung themselves from side to side. Finally, an impressively decorated man, over six foot in height, emerged with a body of attendants. They carried feathered fans, an elaborately carved chair, and a flowered gourd of *pombe* — the potent native beer. A separate attendant carried the vice-regal sucking straw.

The chief came forward with a graceful and nonchalant stride, and stood, head erect, his eyes on Grogan, as Zowanji interpreted his introduction. He was Chief Ngenzi, the highest vassal to the king of Ruanda. Grogan nodded, and introduced himself as Grogan, master of Venters in the county of West Sussex, and fellow of the Royal Geographical Society. His claimed membership of the Society was presumptuous, but on the spur of the moment was the best he could do to inflate his credentials.

The chief nodded and waved several young women forward. They offered bananas, fresh vegetables and bags of millet. Grogan's men brought forth five bolts of *mericani* cotton, two rolls of copper wire and an assortment of beads.

When the polite exchange of *hongo* was concluded, with much bowing and smiling, the chief made it known that he would escort them back to his village. It soon became clear that this was no mere suggestion, for he would listen to no amount of excuses from Grogan that he had no time for socialising. It was also clear that Chief Ngenzi was accustomed to having his own way.

Grogan called the caravan to order and followed, unsure if they were Ngenzi's guests or his captives.

CHAPTER 14

25 June. Ishangi
Chief Ngenzi led us into his village and welcomed us in a
most hospitable manner. He also presented us with further
gifts — four goats, each led by a young woman of the tribe.
There followed a confused exchange between our
interpreter, Zowanji, and the chief. Zowanji informed us
that the young ladies were also intended as part of the gift
— this said with no small amount of glee on his part.
Archie and I tactfully pointed out to the chief that this was
not the white man's custom, and that we would happily
accept the goats but not the women. The chief nodded his
understanding, but I fear that something was lost in the
translation, because for the remainder of the formalities he
regarded us with a very curious eye, wondering perhaps
about the white man's preference for goats.

All was forgiven apparently, for the chief organised a
farewell celebration in our honour (I finally convinced him
of our pressing need to move on). A great feast was set
before us, with gourds full of the bitter pombe beer that is
so much enjoyed in these parts.

The young warriors were first to rise to the sound of the
drums, stamping their feet into the dust of the fireside and
brandishing spears in a mock show of their warlike
ferocity. Their skin, of which there was a considerable

expanse on show, was coated in sweat or some form of oil, making their taut muscular bodies shine like polished ebony in the firelight. It was clear that they had taken their share of the pombe for they were wide-eyed and frothing at the mouth in their excitement.

The reedy sound of flutes joined the drums, and a number of the tribe's young women joined the warriors in the dance. The women were very scantily dressed indeed, with the merest suggestion of feathers covering their nether regions. The trepidation I harboured at the outset of the festivities was confirmed as the performance progressed. Soon I felt I was bearing witness to the devil's carnival.

Archie and I excused ourselves as soon as we could without offending our host, although I suspect he will scarcely remember our departure as he also had taken a great deal of the pombe. When we arrived back at camp, Makanjira and Zowanji were awaiting me. They spoke to me in confidence, warning against allowing the Watusi to follow us when we departed the following day. They said it was well-known that the Watusi are thieves and that nothing would be safe in their presence.

Grogan stirred to the muted sounds of men awakening from sleep. He'd had a fitful night, troubled by the tantalising vision of naked young women dancing for his enjoyment. He could almost feel the firm dark flesh of their thighs; savour the tangy taste of their full breasts. Above him, the velvet night sky was softening into a pastel dawn. It took some time for his sleep-befuddled head to take it in, but Grogan suddenly realised his tent was gone.

Makanjira stood nearby, solemnly observing Grogan's growing comprehension. 'It is gone, *Uyaba.*' His head porter used the name *Uyaba* whenever matters were grave. Grogan hadn't had a chance to query its meaning.

'I can bloody well see that, Makanjira! Question is, where has it gone?'

'The Watusi, *Uyaba.*'

'That's it! Come with me.'

Grogan stormed over to Archie's tent to find his friend stumbling through the flap, eyes bleary with sleep. 'Ewart! What's up?'

'What's up is that our friend Chief Ngenzi has stolen my bloody tent!'

Archie looked to where Grogan's tent had stood and asked, 'What else is gone?'

A half hour later they had confirmed they were missing two sixty-pound tin boxes and two canvas kitbags. Included in the lost items were the sextant, thermometers, the artificial horizon, a bag of one hundred sovereigns, many of Grogan's clothing items, including all of his trousers, notebooks, and many photographs of the early part of their walk.

Grogan said he was going to Ngenzi's camp to retrieve them.

'You're what?' Archie asked, incredulous.

'We can't let them get away with this, Archie. We'll be fighting a rear-guard action for the next hundred miles if we do. I'll take a couple of men and see what I can do.'

'A *couple* of men!'

'We need to show them we're not afraid, but also that we don't want a war. A couple of men and a bit of British pomp should do it.'

While Grogan made ready, Archie unlocked the armoury and issued ten of the men with Snider rifles. He hastily organised a drill to demonstrate how they would defend the camp at close quarters with fixed bayonets.

When Grogan returned he had strapped on his revolver and an old French dress cutlass, and armed Makanjira and Zowanji with Sniders. 'What do you think?' he asked Archie, rattling the cutlass in its scabbard.

'Ewart, I think you're stark, raving mad.'

Chief Ngenzi's village sat beside a small stream in a clearing below low hills. It was a peaceful scene, with women gathered at the stream washing clothes, and children running through the shallows, splashing and laughing as children do. From his hiding place on one of the hills, Grogan peered down on the village through his small telescope. About fifty armed warriors ambled about in the general vicinity of the two entrances leading to an inner circle of huts. The largest of which, in the centre, he presumed was Ngenzi's.

He consulted with Makanjira and Zowanji. They confirmed that the small number of warriors almost certainly meant that Ngenzi was not expecting a retaliation for his raid. The warriors were merely precautionary.

Grogan gave the men his instructions, which were not to shoot unless he fired the first shot, then led them down the hill in file.

They were almost on the inner circle before the warriors were alerted to their presence. As Grogan had hoped, they were uncertain what to do. One of the more courageous made a dash at him, but Grogan withdrew his cutlass and flashed it above his head, making threatening advances as he did so. The warrior halted and withdrew to rejoin his comrades, who watched in confusion as Grogan marched towards Ngenzi's hut.

Ten minutes later, when he re-emerged with Chief Ngenzi at the end of his sword, the entire village had assembled. Ngenzi's full army were behind them, extending across the stream and into the surrounding hills on all sides. Grogan glanced at his two Watonga headmen. Neither could drag their eyes from the enormous gathering that encircled them.

Archie patrolled the perimeter of the camp, checking on the positions of his ten armed men and ensuring that all the porters remained within the circle of packing boxes he had established as a bulwark. The livestock had been hidden under guard some distance away.

He cracked his knuckles and checked his timepiece. Ewart had been gone for more than five hours. He estimated that the walk to Ngenzi's village would take two for the round trip. He began to suspect the worst. At any moment, he expected the full might of Ngenzi's thousands of fearsome warriors to descend on them. Archie realised that his young friend was inclined to be impetuous, but on this occasion it had become critical — the safety of the entire caravan was at stake.

He wondered if he should have objected more strongly, but then admitted that it probably would not have helped. When

Ewart Grogan was intent on doing something, God alone could prevent him. Archie doubted if even God could break that iron will.

Returning to his position, where the barricade faced the direction of the Watusi village, he sat and stared into the green wall of foliage. Just as his buttocks began to grow numb on the hard wood of a packing case, he heard the sound of snapping fronds and muffled voices.

He stood, and called *psst* to the nearest of his guards. The warning flittered around the camp. He had no time to do more, because the voices were coming closer, the sounds seeming amplified by the total silence that had fallen over the camp.

'Hello, Archie,' he called.

'Ewart, you're back.'

'Demonstrably,' Grogan said, grinning.

'And you're all right.'

'You sound surprised, my friend.'

'No! Well, yes, I suppose I am.'

Ewart unbuckled his cutlass and turned to Makanjira. 'Take a few of the boys down the hill to bring up the cattle,' he said.

'Cattle? You've brought cattle?'

'Yes, they're my hostages. For the return of our goods.'

'Good God! What exactly happened down there? Did he have any warriors waiting for you?'

'I'll say. A formidable force you might call it. I estimate five thousand of them.'

'No!'

'Strung all around the surrounding hills. Full battle regalia.'

'But how did ... why didn't they —'

'I judged the cattle a fair exchange for safe passage out of their valley with their chief. Anyway, at the end of the day, the cattle are probably better hostages than Ngenzi.'

'But ... where is Ngenzi?'

'Tied up in one of the little valleys.'

'You ...?'

'I snatched him from his bed. Lazy bugger apparently doesn't arise until ten. I then had the initiative. I demanded the return of our equipment and belongings, and said that I understood it was only a few wrongdoers in their midst who were at fault and must be held responsible, but that I would confiscate their cattle and hold them until the items were returned.'

'And how did they take that?'

'Not very well. One or two made a bit of a show, but I waved the cutlass around my head and they gave it up.'

'They gave ... What then?'

'I snatched around two hundred of their cattle.' He smiled as if he had been on a child's treasure hunt. Then, looking around the camp site, he said, 'You've made some rearrangements. I'd love a cup of tea.'

Archie was still open-mouthed.

Grogan shrugged. 'So much for the so-called terrifying Watusi warriors, eh? Two rifles, one revolver, an old cutlass and plain old British pluck stood five thousand of them at bay.'

30 June. Bugoie

I keep our caravan in close formation during the day and maintain a doubled guard at night, although we left Ngenzi's valley some days ago. I regrettably had to concede defeat in the game to retrieve the last of our possessions. A thorough search of the countryside unearthed a few items, but our important scientific equipment was not found. I am now unable to complete the railway survey with the precision I had planned. I shall make triangulation sightings as best I can and keep more thorough notes.

Although seething with frustration, I sent the Watusi's cattle back to their village. The thieving Ngenzi had been chastened by his ordeal, but essentially got off scot-free.

The loss of my clothing, particularly my trousers, is another matter entirely. At present it is not a problem, although within a matter of weeks it may be.

Bugoie is a land like no other we have seen on this journey. In the northwest I spied the mighty volcanoes that I wish to study, and this evening I climbed an isolated hill to better see what lies ahead.

To the south lies Lake Kivu, a mirage, changing with every subtle shift of the light. At one moment it is a deep sparkling blue, with islands ringed by necklaces of white sand. At other times, when thunder is in the air, it is a mysterious place with dark promontories and shadowed headlands. A wide plain, here and there broken by forest, runs from below me to the west to meet the volcano Kwijwi and a wall of high mountains. Mount Götzen, its plume of choking sulphurous smoke climbing skyward, sits to our north. With its equally forbidding neighbours, it would appear to present an impenetrable barrier to our onward journey.

From this point forward I believe ours will be the first European footprints to mark this strange land.

The scene has great beauty, but perhaps I have been foolishly swayed by idle stories that come to me from the small villages we pass. For all its beauty, the land ahead appears to hold a somewhat sinister air.

CHAPTER 15

Dalton cursed and leaned all his weight on the arm of the spanner, but the rusted bolt on the plough blade refused to budge. He stood and took an oil-stained cloth from his pocket. Wiping his hands, he said, 'We'll have to go back and get a chisel for this one.'

It was Dalton's way of dealing with intractable problems. He felt that by articulating them they became more manageable. It didn't matter that Marefu, standing behind him, couldn't understand him. It was the words, not their understanding, that eased the situation.

'C'mon, Marefu, we'll have to —'

His Maasai herdsman was nowhere to be found. There didn't even appear to be anywhere he could have hidden — the field was only partially ploughed, but what remained of the grass could surely not conceal a man. 'Strange ... he was there a moment ago,' he said to himself.

A movement against the skyline caught his eye. A group of horsemen were coming over the rise from the direction of Londiani. He watched them approach. Within a few minutes he could detect the uniforms of five *askaris* — four natives and a white sergeant.

'Mornin',' the sergeant said, touching his hat.

'Mornin', Sergeant,' Dalton replied. 'What can I do for you?'

'Nice day,' the sergeant said, sitting back on his saddle and pushing his hat to the top of his forehead.

Dalton was never completely at ease around the constabulary. It wasn't that he was a habitual offender, but, like everyone else, there'd been times when circumstances required a more pragmatic view of the law. 'I suppose it is if you've time to admire it.'

The sergeant's expression hardened. Dalton hadn't meant it to come out quite so harshly, but at the same time he had no inclination to waste his day yacking to policemen about petty crimes.

'Yes, well, we're doin' a run through the Londiani area lookin' fer a murderer.' It was obviously intended to impress upon Dalton that he was also a busy man, involved in important law enforcement business. He waited for Dalton to make a response, but he didn't.

'Yes, a murderer,' he went on. 'Maasai chap. From over by Sixty-Four.'

Dalton nodded.

'Murdered and mutilated a Boer family, he did. Wife and kiddies — the lot.'

'When was this?' Dalton asked.

'Few months back.'

'It's taken you a while to get here then,' Dalton commented.

'Harrumph, not my bloody idea of it. The Assistant Commissioner got a bee up his arse, didn't he? Probably from the DC himself.' He straightened his hat. 'Anyway, I'm interviewing all the natives in the area. Do you have any working for you or not?'

Dalton looked around his unploughed field. 'If I did, I wouldn't be ploughing this lot on my own, would I?'

The sergeant bristled. 'No need to be uppity about it, mister. Just doin' me job.'

'As am I.' Dalton said, adding a smile.

'I'll bid you good day then,' the sergeant said stiffly, and signalled his men to follow.

Dalton watched them gallop out of sight, then picked up his spanner, weighed it heavily in his hands, and headed back to the house.

*   *   *

The old building that Dalton used for a barn was dimly lit. One lantern hung over the stalls he used to pen young calves against the tooth and claw of the night. It was empty at the moment. The other light sat at his feet beside his chair, casting strange shadows around the walls and onto the two black faces opposite him.

Marefu was on a low stool, his boy on the straw-covered dirt beside him, but in a position that allowed him to see both Marefu and Dalton while he translated for them.

Dalton had waited all day for Marefu to return from wherever he had fled when the *askaris* came. It had given him ample time to consider the possible folly he'd made in not telling the police that he knew their man. Not only knew him, but was in fact employing him, and had done so since soon after he had committed the murder.

He still couldn't quite fathom why he hadn't reported him. He'd never had a liking for the police. It probably went back to his Irish ancestry. The sergeant, in particular, with his high-handed, superior attitude and piggy eyes, reminded him of the dockside police who'd belted young seamen like him for perhaps being a little under the weather and taking a rest before getting back to the ship. Or it might have been his confidence in his ability to read a man and know what was in his heart even if no words were exchanged, rather than rely on the prattlings of a wigged beak.

Still, he realised he might have brought a murderer into his household, and there was little Jessie to think of, and Bernase. His rifle, resting across his knees, was his insurance, just in case he had misjudged his man.

He watched Marefu's face as Momposhe told his father what the *askaris* had asked Dalton. Marefu seemed unperturbed, replying to his son in calm tones.

'My father says, yes, they were searching for him.'

'And why were they after him?'

The boy didn't need to confer. 'Because he escaped from the white man's jail in Sixty-Four.'

'Nothing else? Why was he in prison?'

Momposhe exchanged words again. 'He doesn't know, sir.'

Dalton gave Marefu his sternest look. 'Something happened on that Boer's bloody farm, and if I don't get the gist of it, I'll toss you and your father out in a whisker.'

The boy looked at his father, but changed his mind. 'I can tell you what happened on the Boer's farm, sir. I was there. There is no need to trouble my father.'

Dalton hesitated at this, then conceded. 'Very well, let's hear it.'

The boy's voice was barely audible. The hoot of a barn owl and the shuffle of cattle in the home lot were the only sounds to punctuate the telling of a story that Dalton could scarcely believe. If it hadn't been for Momposhe's expression — a mixture of remembered horror and immense sadness — he would have called it the imaginings of a troubled mind.

After the boy had finished, he sat there ashen-faced and trembling. Dalton stood and briefly rested a hand on the boy's shoulder, before leaving him and his father in the darkened barn. As he walked back into the night, across the dried grass stubble to the house, he wondered how long it would take the boy to again lock away the memories of that day of utter horror which Dalton had forced him to remember.

Dalton was sitting under a lantern working on a damaged harness. Jessie came into the room unnoticed, and sat on the chair opposite, waiting for her father to become aware of her.

After five minutes' wait, she said, 'Papa?'

'Hmm?' he answered, squinting for the end of the wire he had pushed into an old stitching hole.

'Why don't I have a brother or sister?'

'Jessie, you know your mother died just after you were born.'

'Well, why don't I have any older brothers or sisters?'

Dalton put down his pliers and looked over his eyeglasses at his daughter. 'Darling, what's this all about?'

'I was just wondering ...'

'Wondering what?'

'I was wondering what my mother was like.'

'Oh.' Dalton removed his glasses. 'Haven't I already told you this?'

'Yes, but I was still wondering.'

'Hmm, well now, let me think. Your mother. Her name was Marie, and she was born in Portugal, near the town of Lisbon.'

'Where's Portugal?'

'A long way away. Near England. And her parents went to Portuguese East Africa when she was little, but things didn't work out, so —'

'Why didn't things work out, Papa? Did they have the rinderpest there?'

'No, I don't think so. I don't know why things didn't work out, they just didn't, so they moved on to India.' He paused, expecting another interruption, but it didn't come. He recalled explaining where India was the last time the conversation had come up. 'And when she grew up, she took a position as governess in a Portuguese–Goan home.'

'A governess is a kind of teacher,' Jessie said.

'That's right.'

'And what did my mother look like?'

This was Jessie's favourite question, and the one Dalton was never loathe to answer. 'Ah, she had skin like silk, and a colour much like yours — a touch of the sun. Her hair was like yours too, but a shade darker.'

'Was she was pretty?'

'Very pretty. Just like you, my darling. Fairly tall for a Portuguese, I reckon. And slender too.' He paused, a picture in his mind like it was yesterday.

'And how did you meet her, Papa?'

'We met while I was on home leave from the ships. She was escorting her charges around the market and I happened to be there too. She certainly caught my eye. We were married by the time I went back to sea.' His smile made Jessie smile too.

'And then you came to East Africa.'

'And then we came to East Africa.' His smile faded. 'We thought there was no future for us in India. My father said the days of European managers in the rubber there were numbered. So we left Goa and came to East Africa to give the rubber a try.'

He remained silent, and his eyes went back to the harness on his knee.

Jessie came to his side and kissed him on the cheek. 'Good night, Papa,' she said.

'Good night, darling.'

Dalton picked up the harness and pliers and began to search for the wire end again, but he put them back on his knee, thinking about Jessie and her continuing interest in memories of her mother.

He wondered how things might have been different had Marie been alive. Would she approve of his raising of their child? How might Jessie be different if she had a mother to turn to for all the issues girls must face, and that Dalton had no clue about?

He had no doubt her question about brothers and sisters came from her loneliness. It was a problem he could do little about, but he'd hoped that the lopsided friendship between her and Momposhe might go some way to easing it. His only concern was that her association with the Maasai boy might turn his pretty daughter into more of a tomboy than she already was.

He looked down at the harness. There was just too much work on a farm to afford him the time to raise a daughter properly. It wasn't the first time he had considered finding another wife, but, as before, he knew he would take the idea no further.

Jessie's need to be reminded of a mother she couldn't possibly remember was a mixed blessing for him. He wanted her to know about her mother, and repeating the same old stories probably helped to strengthen them in her young mind. But each time he did so, it took him back to a time and a happiness he knew he could never repeat. In reminding Jessie about Marie, he reminded himself how much he missed her.

CHAPTER 16

12 July 1899. Gwamu
It is clear that this region is the boiler room of Africa; it is from here that the huge engines that drive the entire eastern part of the continent receive their power. Not only is the land mass constantly changing shape and dimensions with the upheaval of lava from deep within the planet's belly, somewhere among these lofty heights surely lies the elusive source of the Nile.

I have named the mountain to our west Mt Battersby. A curl of smoke is visible through the day and an angry glow reddens the clouds at night. The similarities to Archie, third in line to the Earl of Garnsworth, were irresistible.

A local chief who came to trade for salt warned me that the mountain range, named Mfumbiro, 'the place of fire', is waterless and certain death awaits those who attempt to cross the chain. The old fellow had a flair for the dramatic for he added that demons live in the volcanoes and are known to emerge periodically to eat people.

Zowanji glanced nervously at the peaks as he translated the old man's fantastic story. I warned him to keep the story to himself. There are enough excuses for the porters to down their loads and refuse to move without adding the ravings of an old man.

Grogan needed to explore the region around the volcanoes because it was this area that posed the greatest threat to the viability of the railway. But the old chief's warnings about water and the difficult terrain advised caution.

Grogan and Archie discussed their tactics, and agreed that the main body of the caravan, under Archie and Makanjira, would take the long route to the south of the volcano, while Grogan would take a party of seventeen, including three guides borrowed from the old chief, to explore the region to the north of the peak.

The two men had prepared their respective caravans and were ready to leave.

'It looks like you'll have a hell of a walk, Ewart,' Archie said, eyeing the smoking volcano.

Grogan's eyes followed Archie's. The mountain was a monstrous mass of black basalt. At a distance there appeared to be patches of vegetation clinging to islands of soil undefeated by the eddying lava flows. 'It does, but we're travelling light, so we should be able to manage it.'

'How long do you think it will take you to get around it?'

'Oh, I expect no more than a week.'

'Let's hope we can find each other on the other side.'

'There's always someone to ask. You can't go anywhere without a small entourage of locals poking their noses into whatever you're doing.'

'Hmm, come to think of it, I haven't seen a soul these last few days,' Archie said. 'Most unusual.'

'Well, one way or another I'll find you. Keep to the lake, and I'll follow the shore until we meet.'

'Aye. Well . . . we're ready. I'll get my lot moving.'

'Right you are, Archie.'

They shook hands, Archie holding the grip a little longer than Grogan who then gave a call to Makanjira to rally his small team.

'Ewart,' Archie said, as Grogan walked away.

He turned back to him, but when Archie remained silent, he asked, 'What is it, Archie?'

'Um, nothing. Except . . . you will be careful out there, won't you, old chap?'

Grogan smiled. 'I will. You too.'

Grogan stormed into the old chief's village with Zowanji puffing at his side. They had made a forced march to confront him about the three guides who had disappeared the night before.

'Tell him,' he demanded of Zowanji when they found the old man.

The chief listened before he and Zowanji had a brief exchange.

Zowanji turned to Grogan. 'He says they are not here. He says that not one of the three have returned to the village.'

Grogan glared at the chief — a gesture that usually prompted a reconsideration of the facts. 'Tell him I want them found. Tell him I want them punished for their cowardly behaviour,' he said through tight lips.

Zowanji did as he was told. The old man remained impassive, making his reply in a firm but measured tone. Grogan watched his eyes carefully.

'He says he cannot punish them for they are not here, *Uyaba.*' Zowanji had a tremor in his voice.

Grogan looked at him, but Zowanji could not meet his eyes. He realised he had been in a rage for the entire day that it had taken to return to the village. Zowanji obviously felt too close to the firestorm for comfort.

Failure was a bitter pill. They had barely begun the trek around the volcano when the first three guides disappeared in the scrub before they reached the lava flow. The next three showed little enthusiasm for the task, repeating their chief's warning about the lack of water and the sharp lava that would shred the porters' feet.

Grogan issued orders for the men to make sturdy sandals, and to carry plenty of water, but the two forward guides disappeared before long, and the third attempted to bolt but Grogan recaptured him. In an attempt to frustrate any further escape attempts, he tied the guide to himself with a short length of rope for the remainder of the day. But the next morning he too was gone. Grogan found it quite strange. He'd had some experience with desertion among porters and guides, but seldom found them prepared to leave sight of camp after dark without an armed escort.

In spite of his anger and frustration, Grogan found it difficult to disbelieve the chief who seemed to be sincere. The deserters might have remained hidden in the bush until they were sure it was safe to return.

'Very well,' he said with resignation. 'Ask the chief where he thinks they are if not here?'

He could see from Zowanji's expression that he was not going to appreciate the answer.

'He said he has already told you that answer, *Uyaba.*'

Grogan nodded and smiled cynically. 'Demons. He says they have been taken by demons?'

Zowanji, abashed, nodded.

21 July 1899. Lava slopes, Mt Battersby
This afternoon, a group of natives came across the lava slopes towards us. We were at first delighted to finally find someone to trade with, but they were a miserable lot, starving and dishevelled. With great difficulty we unravelled their story. They had been living a desperate life on the edge of the forest, afraid to return to their food gardens because of the Baleka, who, according to them, are a tribe of cannibals who have entered the region from the Congo and now loot, pillage and murder everyone in their path.

I discounted the story of cannibalism as one merely intended to soften my heart towards their pleas for free food, which I gave them to the extent that I could afford, for they were clearly very much in need of sustenance.

The old chief's prediction about water proved to be correct. Grogan had no food left and the caravan had been on water restrictions for two days in the baking sun of the lava slopes. The going was made even more difficult because of the jagged surface and the ridges and chasms in the lava.

In one chasm they could hear water burbling far below, but it was too deep to climb down without great risk. To follow the chasm either up the lava slope towards the water's source or down to the jungle floor, where it might become accessible, was a gamble of water against time. Grogan decided to take a risk and press on.

The caravan stopped for a rest around the heat of noon. Three porters failed to arrive. After an hour waiting, Grogan fired a few shots to help them find their way. The volcano rumbled a reply.

Grogan had considered the three men trustworthy, for they had shown no previous inclination towards desertion. The warnings he had received about the mountain began to prey on his mind. He regretted not arming Zowanji. Should an attack come from the Baleka, cannibals or not, he would only have his .303 and revolver to repel them.

The missing porters had been carrying two precious water calabashes. Grogan had given up any hope of finding natives to trade with for food and water on the lava slopes. With the exception of a few terrified pygmies, who fled on their approach, they had seen no one. He decided to return to the base of the mountain.

They edged downwards to the rim of the forest, where they entered an eerie swirling mist. Grogan guessed it was caused by the moist jungle air meeting the hot dry air of the lava slopes. The going was even more difficult, with masses of vines, and piles of broken and torn vegetation caused by the mountain's recent eruption. The scene was of another world — one of violence and destruction. The porters became decidedly nervous and muttered among themselves.

Fearing more desertions, Grogan took to the slopes again, now under the cover of light cloud. They were rewarded by a light, but steady flow of rain, which they scooped from the lava into their calabashes.

On the following morning they were at last in sight of the edge of the lava field. The complaining Manyema porters, who had tried every ruse to have Grogan return before he showed them his .303 and reminded them of their contract, hobbled on with more purpose in their step. Pockets of vegetation became more common and soon they were back on more familiar wind-worn grassy slopes. The only reminders of the recent eruptions were islands of jagged igneous rock flung there by the explosive force of the magma.

Under the brooding brow of the volcano, they passed one deserted village after another. The effects became quite unnerving, even for Grogan, who briefly considered the option of turning back. But the waterless expanse of lava did not appeal, and if the Baleka and their grisly habits were real, Archie and the body of the caravan would soon be entering into their domain from the southern side of the volcano. They had to be warned. Grogan checked his .303 and ordered the men onwards.

At midday, he called a halt to allow the porters to rest. They slumped down where they stood, for there was little vegetation to use as a shelter against the sun and wind; nothing to break the monotony of the rolling grasslands on the lower reaches of the mountain. Grogan unslung his water canister and moved ahead to take advantage of a slight rise. The wind shivered the clumps of fibrous highlands grasses and soughed among the volcanic rocks that stood like grotesque guardians of the slopes.

A hundred yards away was a thatched-roof village, empty, he imagined, like the several they had already passed that day. Then he heard what sounded like a baby's cry. He cupped his ear against the whispering wind. After a few moments it came again — a faint cry almost lost in the rolling ocean of hunkering grasses. Casting a glance back to the men, he decided to let them rest and tend to their bloodied feet while he went to investigate.

The empty village, silent, still, reminded him of a corpse. The external signs of what had once been a living entity were there: the huts; a threshing rack. The low platform where the women would sit to sew and mend. Halved coconut shells — the playthings of children. A row of water pots. But it was what was missing that spoke of recent, violent disruption. There was no chorus of voices — men and women, old and young — engaged in the ebb and flow of village life. No aroma of meat roasting on an open fire. Nothing to be seen of the children, or the sound of their shrill voices.

He stood beside the empty goat pen. There was fresh dung in the enclosure, but the stock were gone. A millet crop, partly harvested, stood on a neighbouring hill.

The baby's weak cry came again. Grogan moved cautiously into the circle of huts. The wind parted a layer of thatch from a hut, and as silently let it fall back into place. Most of the woven door covers had been torn from the huts, but the one where he thought the sound had come from was closed tight. He reached for it, pausing a moment to ready himself for what he might find, then flung it open.

A young goat bleated as it ran past him. It stopped at the last hut to take water from an overturned, broken pot before trotting off.

The corded muscles of Grogan's shoulders relaxed. He took his hat off and wiped his kerchief across his forehead, then ran it around the brim of his hat. He took a deep breath. A hint of the volcano's sulphurous vapours came on the wind.

Ahead, above the flank of the mountain, the sky was vivid blue, broken only by the long white tails of scurrying cirrus clouds and a circling squadron of small, black shapes.

He didn't need his binoculars to know they were vultures.

CHAPTER 17

Gertrude's mare kicked the earth as she walked it along the end of the vine rows, giving rise to the fecund aroma of rich Californian soil. She loved harvest time when the vines, heavy with fruit, drooped to the ground, and the itinerant pickers, like blackbirds, fluttered from vine to vine, singing as they plucked and dropped the berries into panniers on their backs.

The pickers gathered like a swarm of bees around nectar at exactly the time when she and her stepfather agreed the grapes were ready for harvest, almost as if they too were aware of the nuances of grape maturation. Previously, Gertrude had dismissed the possibility that these wandering, uneducated workers could have opinions on the immediate prospects of rain, the indefinable concepts of humidity, temperature and soil acidity, but of late she had begun to have second thoughts.

Just as she was gaining an understanding of the African blacks through Ewart's letters about his travels, which discussed their knowledge of medicine and the intricate art work they produced, so Gertrude began to consider the pickers as individuals rather than as a collective. She wondered if some had inherited skills from their ancestors — people that the world had hitherto considered ignorant and incapable of the higher notions of science and art.

Ewart's letters told her of tribes in a place called Nyasa who could weave intricate baskets from native fibrous plants, and others who could beat metal into wondrous forms representing animals and birds and even people. Others made the most amazing musical instruments, and their king searched his realm for voices to add to the royal choir. He fed and housed the singers in a comfort unknown outside the royal household. It was true that he also blinded some of his favourite choir members to ensure they remained in his service, but he demonstrated at least one civilised aspect in what many would say was total savagery.

What of the women? Ewart had spoken of their lives: their obeisance to their men; their stoic, even manly labours. They carried children on their backs while tending the crops, and could reduce a fallen tree to a pile of firewood in a day. But throughout what many might call a wretched life, Ewart believed these women were content, even happy. He didn't say how he knew, and Gertrude was intrigued by it. Were they happy in their ignorance? Or were they fully informed members of a society that had developed roles that ideally suited every section of their community — men and women, old and young?

Ewart's enquiring mind had explored these roles in some detail while observing the women's daily lives. It was the women who built the huts, and walked miles with their lithe, cat-like tread to another village to trade a bag of millet for a bunch of bananas. In some tribes, he told her, the women moved about in near nudity, and thought nothing of blatantly watching him bathe. He said they seemed amused merely by his presence. They had musical laughter.

Would he feel such equanimity if the women were white, Gertrude wondered. Did he harbour any other feelings for these women? Were they only interesting because of their contrast, or were they intrinsically enticing?

She realised she had drawn her horse to a halt and had been staring at the muscled, sweaty shoulders of one of the Negro pickers as he worked the row nearest her. The man was young and handsome in his own way, and was now self-consciously glancing back at her as he continued working.

Gertrude tried to imagine how closely linked this young man was to the rich cultural mixture Ewart had described. She pictured him in Africa, forming works of art from metal, singing love songs to his young woman, making love under a warm yellow moon ...

She suddenly felt hot and flustered, and as the man looked back at her again, she kicked her horse into a canter.

Grogan's caravan approached the western side of Mt Battersby, where the slopes became gentler and the grassland gave way to occasional pockets containing scrub and stunted acacia trees. The vultures he had seen from a distance were feeding on carrion that was scattered around yet another empty village. There were scores of them, squabbling amongst themselves over the meatiest pickings. The ripple of desultory conversation that had occupied the porters during this easier section of the march stumbled into silence.

One of the huge black birds attempted to take flight with something large in its talons. It struggled to gain height, but was forced to release its load as it wheeled towards the caravan. The object bumped to the ground, and rolled to Grogan's feet. It was a human head. Glazed eyes stared up at him as if in horror.

Grogan fired off a round from his .303 and the flock took flight, abandoning their grisly feast. Their departure revealed body parts strewn across a wide area, like meat scraps thrown from a butcher's block.

Only the Manyema appeared impervious to the horror of the scene, supporting the Watonga's insistence on their latent cannibalism. But all of them scanned the surrounding hills in fear, as they realised that the rocky crags were now the possible abode of murderers. The caravan's remaining local guide was on his knees, face covered, whimpering like a frightened child. The Watonga huddled together, as if in the company of their own people they might be spared the gruesome sight. Even Makanjira and Zowanji appeared on the point of bolting, terrified; as indeed was Grogan, who dared not show it.

From the hill above the village came a shout. A cluster of black figures appeared in outline against the clear sky. More gathered as they watched, and with a mighty howl the whole mob of around a hundred came storming down the hill towards them.

Grogan was stunned. He had never witnessed such overtly aggressive behaviour, and for a moment wondered if it were some strange local welcoming ritual. He looked around his men for an indication that this was indeed the case, but found nothing but stunned disbelief and fear. The defining response was from their local guide, who had lost control of his bladder.

Grogan bellowed to the guide, demanding to know what was going on. His whimpering reply came: 'They are the Baleka, master, and they have come to devour us.'

Grogan grabbed his rifle from Zowanji and dashed to a stunted shrub where he took careful aim. At a range of two hundred yards, he dropped the Baleka at the head of the charge. The leading group barely paused, and came on as before, their wild animal ululations now sweeping the mountainside.

At a hundred and fifty yards, Grogan dropped three, and a moment later, at around a hundred yards, downed four more. The leading contingent were effectively eliminated, and the following group, who had seen the effects of the soft-jacketed bullets, lost their enthusiasm and disappeared into a field of millet.

There was a long period of silence. Grogan cast an eye over his men. They stood petrified, staring into the millet, barely daring to breathe in case their movements prompted another charge from the Baleka.

A howl cut the air. It came from a rock in the field, where two of the Baleka raised their spears in defiance, the sky at their backs. They began to whoop and yelp to encourage their fellow tribesmen to renew their blood lust.

Grogan adjusted his sights for eight hundred yards and fired off two quick rounds. The Baleka ringleaders dropped from view.

'Come on!' Grogan shouted to his men, and they dashed to the village where he felt they would have a better chance should another attack eventuate.

They gathered in a close circle and looked around in horrified disbelief. Scattered among the huts were the remains of the hapless villagers. Coils of human entrails were strung to dry on a rack; a body, skinned to the bone lay at the entrance to one of the huts, surrounded by vultures and vermin.

Elsewhere there was a tattered forearm with strings of half-raw meat hanging from it. He saw a head with the brain exposed, partly eaten.

Grogan was shocked and revolted, but a morbid fascination made him continue to search the surroundings. He found another head, this time with one gnawed cheek, the other burned to a charcoal shell. It lay on the ground beside a stool, as if the diner had put it to one side while he went to refresh his drink. The scalp had been peeled like an orange. Offal and excrement were everywhere. The stench was indescribable.

Grogan felt the rise of bile, and emptied the contents of his stomach in a rush of vomit. Still gagging, he led the caravan from the village at a brisk pace, forgetting the immediate threat of the Baleka in his haste to be gone.

Darkness had fallen by the time Grogan's caravan came to a halt for the night. They had kept up a double pace all day, and had no energy left to pitch camp or to cook. Grogan felt it wiser anyway to make do with the dried meat than to risk exposing their position to the Baleka by their cooking fires.

The absence of a tent was another matter. Lying under only a covering of stars left him feeling insecure and unable to sleep. He marvelled at the amazing psychological effect of a flimsy piece of canvas, but no amount of rationalisation could convince him of its absurdity. As he lay there, tossing and turning, his thoughts went to Archie and the main body of the caravan. Grogan knew he had been lucky to catch the Baleka offguard, and that his caravan's small numbers had enabled them to swiftly make their escape before the Baleka could regroup. Under different circumstances they would be all dead and probably gracing the cannibals' table. He couldn't put aside the vision of Archie leading the heavily laden caravan through one of Lake Kivu's many deep valleys and being set upon by the Baleka savages.

Grogan's group were now on the south-western flank of the volcano. Lake Kivu, and Archie's party, could not be far away. Maybe the Baleka had already been to Lake Kivu on their sweep to the north, looking for fresh blood? He finally gave up all attempts at sleep and went out to check the sentries instead.

Alone in the dark, he felt much more secure. He had always trusted his ears and senses against any other man. He had honed his skills in Matabeleland, and they had proven a life-saver on more than one occasion.

His worries about Archie would not leave him. For the first time on the trek, Grogan felt the painful stab of conscience. Archie, and all the men on this expedition, had put their lives in his hands. It was a frightening responsibility, and for what? For a whim, a fantasy, that he, Grogan, had concocted for his own selfish purposes. What was his noble quest to win the woman he loved against the one hundred and fifty men who were now at risk of their lives?

A chill came over him. He dropped his face into his hands and prayed he could reach them before the Baleka did.

For most of the next day Grogan's caravan moved quickly through the grassland at the foot of the mountain without incident. He was feeling confident that they had given the Baleka the slip, but later in the day, as they were pushing through a dry swampy area with grass above their heads, their guide came rushing in, jabbering at Zowanji. Finally, he made it known that a Baleka raiding party was forming on their flank.

Fortunately for Grogan, he had his weapons at the ready, as he'd realised the swamp was an ideal place for an ambush. When he reached a modest clearing that gave about a thirty-yard circle to stop the enemy's rush, he handed his revolver to Zowanji and made ready for the onslaught.

Within minutes the Baleka attacked. Grogan shot the leader and his nearest companions, but lost two men before they were driven off.

They continued a running skirmish for the remainder of the day, finally losing them at sundown.

Dinner was a sombre affair with every rustle in the grass and night bird's call quickening the heart.

In the following two days, Grogan drove the porters at a withering pace. The usual middle-of-the-day rest period was ignored. They marched into evening and dropped, shattered, too tired to eat the miserable rations they had been reduced to. Before first light he had them on their feet, loaded, and off into the glimmering dawn. Pity any porter who collapsed and refused to get up, pleading exhaustion. Grogan would wave the *kiboko* over him, threatening his hide if he didn't get moving.

On the second night he realised they were all in danger of a breakdown. He had allowed no time to look for villages to trade with, in case they found the Baleka instead, and their food was insufficient to maintain the energy needed for the forced march. If they didn't find the lake the next day, Grogan knew he could not make the men continue. They were at the stage where he felt they might rather die than maintain that killing pace.

The waters of Lake Kivu had never looked better to Grogan as he stood on a ridge with Mt Battersby at his back. Finding a column of smoke rising from its shore, with the almost certain prospect that it was Archie's camp, made the vista even better. He and his caravan had slept less than ten hours in the previous three days.

The Union Jack was flying proudly from a bamboo staff when they arrived in camp. All was in order, as he'd hoped. Two tents — Archie's and his own — were pitched in the centre beside the valuable stores tent. Loads stood in orderly stacks, and the smaller porters' tents ringed the whole camp.

Archie came out of his tent as soon as the camp attendants saw the arriving party and set up a barrage of hoots and shouts of welcome. He gave Grogan a bear-hug, and tears of joy filled his eyes when he held his friend at arm's length to see how he had fared. 'My God, Ewart!' he said. 'You look ghastly!'

'Thank you, Archie. I was going to say that you looked a little pale, but now I won't bother.' But his wan smile conveyed his relief that the nightmare was over.

Grogan dismissed his men, who immediately staggered off to find a place to rest, and he and Archie retired to canvas chairs outside their tents. A strong cup of coffee initially made Grogan's head swim, but revived him sufficiently to hear Archie's news.

He had suffered a bout of fever soon after beginning his search for Grogan along the flanks of the mountain. This had caused him to make a retreat to the lake, and he was now almost fully recovered. He said he was about to set off again on the following morning. Grogan told him his fever had probably saved his life, and recounted the story of his meeting with the Baleka.

'We've had no sign of them here,' Archie said, 'thank God. But we've had the usual rumours, which I ignored. Do you think we should strengthen our guard?'

'A good idea, although I suspect they've retreated to easier pickings.' Grogan was pulling at his boot, but hadn't the strength to get it off. Makanjira, standing nearby, came to his aid.

He continued his story while Makanjira struggled to remove the boot. 'The Baleka not only prey upon the tribes, they vindictively destroy food gardens and slaughter cattle. The few survivors are in a state of near-starvation. Ah, that's better,' he said when the boot finally came off.

'Bloody hell, Ewart. Your feet are disgusting!'

Grogan tentatively wriggled his toes. His foot was putrid and wrinkled from days of immersion in a wet woollen stocking and leather. The stench was overpowering.

He prodded at it. 'Ouch!' he said. 'There's something in my toe. It's been giving me hell over the last few days, but with the Baleka around, I didn't dare take my boots off.'

The cause of Grogan's discomfort was found to be a jigger flea — a parasite about the size of a pin-head that burrow under the skin to lay its eggs. His small toe was a mass of putrefying flesh.

Archie rolled his eyes. 'How revolting,' he said.

Makanjira stood looking down at the toe, shaking his head sympathetically.

'Do you know how to handle these things, Makanjira?' Grogan asked.

'I do, *Uyaba*.'

Grogan nodded before again examining his toe. 'And I suppose permanganate of potash won't do the trick on its own?'

'No, *Uyaba*.'

Grogan sighed. 'Archie? Do we have any medicinal brandy left?'

In the evening, after Grogan had consumed a half-bottle of brandy, Makanjira skilfully extracted an enormous jigger flea from under his small toe, complete with a sac of eggs the size of a pea. Only the bone and the top part of the toe remained intact, but Grogan had by that time fainted and did not need to see it.

CHAPTER 18

11 August. Katwe
Our tramp through the Rutchuru Valley returned us to
steaming jungle and mosquito-infested papyrus swamps.
Immediately my fever returned and I was again reduced to
the status of invalid, riding my machila. Lions followed us
for days, circling our tents each night and disturbing our
sleep with a most unholy ruckus.

Archie informed me that not twenty-four hours ago my
temperature was 108.4°F. I'm not sure that this is
medically possible, but I did not dispute it.

These ongoing bouts unnerve me. I wonder how long I
can continue the battle against the fever. What if my
strength eventually fails when I am deep in the bush, far
away from medical assistance? I know it preys on Archie's
mind too. He has been at my side night and day during
these difficult times. I sense he is ever more feeling the
strain, and would be quit of this expedition in a trice
should I indicate my willingness. After I return to this
world after being temporarily lost in delirium, I often find
the camp run-down and Archie in tattered shirt and torn
trousers. I am forced to remind him that, until our
circumstances are sufficiently dire that we cannot keep up
appearances, we must at all times consider the effect our
actions and appearances have on the natives, and do our

utmost to maintain the standards expected of British gentlemen. He may be an unsightly nurse, however I cannot fault his dedication to bringing me through the fever.

Three days ago we crossed by canoe the channel connecting lakes Albert Edward and Ruisamba, and came onto British soil once again in the administration town of Katwe. Our brief sojourn here provided us with our first opportunity to sleep under a roof since leaving Ujiji some four months ago. Unfortunately we shared the room with thousands of mosquitoes and armies of rats. My sleep was interrupted on several occasions by the irritating whine of a mosquito in my ear, or the need to eject one or more large rodents from my bed.

This morning we began our eighty-mile march to Fort Portal, nicknamed Fort Gerry. It was Sir Gerald Porter who declared Uganda a British protectorate a few years ago, in 1894, but not before the brilliant Lord Lugard argued strongly for it and finally convinced the pussy-footing Liberals that if they didn't do so, the Germans would take it. So before leaving Katwe, our first camp in British Uganda, Archie and I toasted Lugard — that giant among mere men — on the shores of Lake Albert Edward and the border between Belgian and British spheres.

To the east of our trail lie the Ruwenzori Mountains, first sighted in 1888 by Jephson and Parke on the Stanley mission to rescue Emin Pasha from the Dervishes of the Sudan. In the second century, Ptolemy named them the Mountains of the Moon, though how he knew of them, much less saw them, I, like many others I suspect, am at a loss to explain. He claimed they were the source of the Nile. By all accounts he was not far from the truth.

I have had nothing from Gertrude these last several months, and I pray there will be something at Fort Gerry.

Fort Portal was little more than a collection of huts and lean-tos surrounding a small stockade. But it was a British post, and Grogan moved the caravan along at a clipping pace, impatient to reach the fort and hoping that he would find a bundle of mail awaiting him.

The administrator, Bagge, a florid man who had spent the last fourteen months on the post, cordially welcomed the two men. He arranged some accommodation for them and was keen to continue the conversation, but Grogan interrupted as politely as he could and asked if there was any mail for them.

'Yes! Of course!' the administrator said. 'Silly of me. You'll be keen to catch up on the news of the world I suppose, eh? Come, let me get you your mail and newspapers, and we can continue our chat at supper, what?'

There was a separate bundle of mail for each of them, and a stack of newspapers. Grogan abruptly took his leave. He rushed back to their hut like a Scrooge with a bag of pennies, found a quiet place shaded from the sun, and untied his bundled letters. Scanning quickly through them he found about a dozen from Gertrude, and many others from friends and family. He spent some time sorting them, savouring the delicious moments before beginning to read.

Gertrude's letters illustrated all the many facets of her personality. From one to the next she jumped from playful to serious; cerebral to silly; enigmatic to candid. She dissected her life to date and, as he had done for her, revealed her secret dreams. She wanted a grand house with many children — did he prefer sons or daughters? A rambling garden where they could rollick with their children without a by-your-leave to anyone. She thought that California was pleasant, but would he prefer England? Or anywhere else?

He learned about her family, and each individual's little idiosyncrasies. He learned, for instance, that her older sister's husband wore a toupee and dyed the sides of his hair to match it. The result was a disastrous montage of different colours and textures which the family pretended not to notice.

She sent him a very long letter from the snowy mountains of Colorado where her whole family had gone for the Thanksgiving weekend. She had sprained an ankle in her first hour on the slopes, and spent the remainder of the holiday with it propped up on a pillow.

He quickly scanned them all, knowing he would return to them again and again over the coming weeks until the next British outpost. In the last of her letters she wrote:

My Darling Ewart,

What bliss! A parcel of letters from you arrived today. A flood of wondrous words from your hand. I could not wait, but flew to my room to devour them and pen an immediate reply. I say immediate, but I forget the endless delay it takes our words to travel the world from one end to the other.

And all your adventures! I hardly dare to breathe as I read them. Dear Ewart, I cannot think what I would do if you were hurt. Please promise me you will be careful.

I am sorry to hear of your continuing ill-health. You say it is nothing, but I say again, you must be careful.

Since last writing, Papa has joined Mother and me in London and set about 'introducing me to society'. I tried to humour him for he is such a dear. Mother, of course, knows of our plans although I had sworn her to secrecy. It all became such a bore that I told him I was not interested in being put on show like one of his navel oranges! But he would not be dissuaded, so I told him about us.

I shan't tell you his exact words, good manners forbid, but suffice to say he was animated about the subject. I staunchly defended you, pointing out all the wonderful achievements you have already accomplished. He will soon learn better and admire you, as I know all my family will.

After a few days he quietened. He still huffs and he puffs, but I believe he is now reconciled to my plans to wait here in London until you arrive.

London is a wonderful city, but not so wonderful as it will be when you are here, and can show me all the interesting places you know so well.

I told Mother that you suggested we make arrangements to meet your family when we were here, so she bullied Papa into arranging it. It was quite a simple matter really and we entertained all of your siblings save young Hilda who was at boarding school, and Dorothy who is abroad with your Aunt

Abigail. I suspect we shall meet them anon. We had a very pleasant afternoon. Cook excelled herself with a collection of tarts and savouries.

Please don't think me impertinent for here offering my impressions of them, because I found them all to be perfectly delightful and pleasant.

Your nearest sibling in age, Philip, is not at all like you, is he? I can't imagine him in the tropical sun with that fine Celtic complexion. He quite impressed my stepfather with his knowledge of the accountancy profession.

Next in line is Norman. Or is it Margaret? Anyway, Norman I found to be quite a serious young man. Oh, I know you will dispute it, but I think he quite resembles you in appearance. Margaret, on the other hand, is quite exceptional, although I see in her bold red hair the connection with some others in your family. You have just the merest suggestion of red in your lovely fair hair. I suppose I should call it golden, it sounds more dramatic.

Archibald was persuaded to play us a short composition on the piano. I think he is of that age (did he tell me he is nineteen?) where he is just getting over the mortification of late adolescence that we all suffered. Ah, but having said that, I see no sign of such suffering in your youngest brother, Quentin. He was home from naval college and, from what I deduced from the asides, not in such good graces as the family would hope. It didn't seem to bother him though. He was quite the live wire, clearly unaware of the stigma of being seventeen. He is the little brother I always wanted.

So, now you know that I have convinced my stepfather to let me stay in London, and that I have met your siblings, and, to some extent, managed to avoid disgracing myself in their company, there is only one thing left for me to do: to throw my arms around you, tell you how much I love you, and welcome you home like the conquering hero that you are.

Stay safe, my love,

Gertrude

PS. I almost forgot. In your letter from the town with a strange name — was it Zomba? — you say you played tennis.

Tennis, indeed! I cannot for the life of me imagine you playing tennis in Africa. I don't recall you telling me that you even played. There is so much for us to learn about each other, isn't that so? The people you met sound very agreeable folk. Tea parties and tennis. What other surprises do you have in store for me?

I cherish every thought of you.

I relive every moment, brief though they have been, from the time we met until that day when you left to continue on your way.

I cannot bear this interminable waiting.

Come swiftly, safely home, my love.

I love you.

Gertie

Grogan closed his eyes, and willed a vision of Gertrude to mind, but it was Nurse Emily Hitchen, with her soft hands and starched white uniform, who intervened. He was stricken with remorse, and rubbed his eyes hard, trying to eradicate her memory and its attendant guilt.

But Emily would not leave him. The subtle aroma of talcum powder and antiseptic lotion came to mind, the dim light through the window on that hot Zomba afternoon, a cool sponge on his burning flesh.

He leapt to his feet, and stormed out of the compound in a sweat.

CHAPTER 19

Archie had been pacing the perimeter of the Fort Portal stockade for an hour. He couldn't delay the issue any longer. When he saw Grogan approaching their two-room shack, it was with feelings of relief and dread.

He hurried up to him. 'Ewart. A moment of your time, if I may?' he asked, wincing as he said it. He sounded like a butler intruding upon his master's busy schedule.

Grogan, surprised, and a little amused by his formality, nodded. 'Of course, Archie.'

Archie insisted he enter before him, and then took a seat after Grogan did, choosing the comfortable woven chair under the window. He sat back, clasped his hands behind his head, then removed them, sat forward and studied them minutely — as if the answers were written there in a small print.

'I've been stalling for the last three days,' he began. 'Ever since I got the telegraph from England, you know, with our mail. Well, anyway, I must return to England.' He glanced up to Grogan, met his eyes — those intensely blue, resolute, unblinking eyes — and then dropped his to resume studying his hands. 'Immediately.'

He waited for a response, and receiving none looked again at Grogan, who had opened his mouth but was yet to find his power of speech.

'I know, this is a terrible setback for you. For us. But the telegraph has been relayed from one British post to another, trying to find me. And there it was — is. *Urgent family business*, it said. And then it detailed all the nonsense that's been happening over there. *Requires your immediate attention at home.*' He paused and took a deep breath before sitting back in his chair.

'Um ... well,' Grogan began. 'Whew, Archie. What can I say?'

'I know, Ewart. Beastly hard luck.'

'It's ... quite a surprise to —'

'I know, I know, I should have —'

'We've come so far, and —'

'— hate to do this to you —'

Archie realised he was babbling. 'Look, Ewart,' he said, raising his hands to call a halt to it. 'I've been over every angle of it. Can't be helped, I'm afraid. But a horrible, truly horrible situation to put you in.'

Grogan was silent for a few moments, taking it all in. 'Yes,' he answered slowly. 'It is.'

'Of course, no one needs know we might have taken it all the way to Cairo,' Archie went on. 'I mean, it was a bit of a lark really, wasn't it? A hunting trip. And it's not as though we haven't plenty to show for it. Trophies all over the shop. Proves the success of it, eh?' He was hoping Grogan would see the positive side, as he had himself after deliberating on it for hours.

Grogan ran his hands through his hair, which had grown long like a lion's mane over the months of travel. 'This is very difficult for me, Archie.'

'I understand, old chap. Look, we'll have a bit of a spell here in Fort Portal, do a spot of hunting. A day or two can't hurt. And then we'll make our way to the coast. I understand there's good hunting around the Great Rift Valley.'

Grogan seemed surprised by his plans for them. 'I think you misunderstand me, Archie. I'm not going back with you.'

'What?'

'I'm not going with you. You can go. You must go. But I must go on.'

'Go on? Ewart, are you mad? You can't go on alone. Why it's ... it's suicide!'

Grogan's familiar smile returned. 'I don't intend it to be.' He seemed lost in thought for a moment, and then he shrugged. 'But I must go on. Whatever the cost.'

30 August. Fort Portal
My Manyema porters have been misbehaving again. With too much idle time on their hands, they have taken to the strong local pombe with disastrous results. Last night they raided the fort's milk supply, and in the course of that crime attacked a number of the Sudanese guards, leaving them beaten and bloodied.

Bagge ordered them flogged. This was apparently the last straw for the Manyema, who demanded to be released from their contracts so they could return home to Ujiji. I had hoped they would remain with us to journey's end in Cairo, but felt that to force them to stay would likely provoke more trouble than it was worth, so, reluctantly, I paid them off, farewelling each one personally before they departed south. The Manyema are a bunch of scoundrels, quick to temper, but also ready to laugh when the issue passes. I believe they thoroughly enjoyed their romp through Africa with me.

Archie Battersby came to me with the news that he must return home to England at once. He was greatly distressed to have to tell me this, and admitted that he had tried to form an alternative solution rather than desert me in the middle of Africa.

I was stunned. Archie has been my constant companion for eighteen months, and at times the only person within more than a hundred miles who could carry on a conversation with me. He did not elaborate on the family situation, and of course I could not pry into his private affairs, but I wondered about his news. I wondered what could remain urgent over the weeks that it took the telegraph message to find him, and further remain so for the additional period it will take him to return to the coast and then to sail to England. It is a journey of more than eight hundred miles to reach Mombasa and the ship for home. What event could remain urgent for so long?

Upon reflection, I realised that a number of situations could possibly fulfil that criteria, and I tried to put the matter of the content of the message from my mind, but some perverse demon forced unworthy thoughts to intrude.

I can't help but wonder if the almost constant drain on Archie's health has finally taken a toll on him, mentally and physically. Like me, Archie has almost continuously suffered from fever these last six months, along with infestations of the hideous jigger fleas and a host of similarly disgusting parasites. There is also the constant craving for the simple comforts of life. For food. There have been few occasions when we have enjoyed a nourishing meal. At one time we were reduced to eating, or at least attempting to eat, an elephant's trunk. Ten hours of boiling could not make it chewable.

How unreasonable is it to wish for a comfortable bed, a night's sleep without being invaded by blood-sucking mosquitoes, or a morning not requiring a search of your boots in case a scorpion or large spider decided to make a home of one of them during the night?

I can hardly blame him if he did decide that his stamina is not up to the remainder of the walk. He was never as fit as I, and is, after all, sixteen years older. When we started out, he was a good two stone overweight, although that problem was soon solved.

I may have answered hastily in saying I would press on. The idea of continuing to Cairo, a journey of over two thousand miles, without the company of another like-minded spirit, has made my heart sink, and I admit to spending the remainder of the day considering the prudence of attempting it alone.

This evening I took a walk to the wooded hill on the outskirts of the fort, and sat alone with the night sounds and the stars to contemplate my situation. I decided it is true that to continue alone is fraught with danger. Who can I trust to guard my stores when necessity forces me out of camp? Who will be at my back if the caravan is attacked? Can I trust my Watonga to guard the camp while I sleep?

I have satisfied my childhood dream of bagging a lion, a rhino and an elephant. I have seen Lake Tanganyika, and surveyed the unknown parts of Central Africa so that Her Majesty's domain might be extended to her continuing glory. But the most important ambition — to prove myself worthy of the hand of the woman I love — has not been achieved. Could I go to her father and say I intended to walk from the Cape to Cairo but managed only part of the way? Would he look kindly upon that result and congratulate me for my good effort? No. It would simply prove to him that I am a man more able to talk than to act.

I will continue. Alone if I must.

In the days before he would lead his reduced caravan from Fort Portal into the notorious, untamed reaches of the upper Nile, Grogan wrestled with the ghosts of doubt. He could not recall any time in his life when he had entertained, for even a moment, any doubts about his ability to accomplish something he had set his mind to achieving. No intellectual challenge had ever defeated him in the long run. Nor had the technical and physical demands of scaling the Matterhorn as a nineteen-year-old. He had not lacked the courage to face a thousand Matabele howling across the veldt towards his isolated post with the intention of bloody murder. Nor had he succumbed to the profound horror, the brutal emotional assault on the soul, of the sight of a feast of human flesh.

He returned to his letters, leafing through them in search of an elusive something to nourish his embattled spirits, but put them aside again. He knew there was nothing but his own will that would see him through the coming ordeal.

'Are you sure you won't need more tobacco?' Archie said, pointing to the chop-box that contained most of Grogan's luxury items, like Worcestershire sauce and candles.

'No, I have plenty for the next few weeks,' Grogan said, patting Archie on the shoulder. 'Don't worry about that. Just be sure to get my supplies to Wadelai on time.'

'I will. As soon as I get to Kampala, I'll send them on.' Archie still looked downhearted. Grogan was reconciled to his situation, but Archie remained distraught about his decision to leave.

Grogan's caravan was lined up on the point of departing Fort Portal. Archie was having the usual last-minute problems with his larger contingent, and would be delayed a further day or so.

'What about that India rubber bath?' Archie asked as an afterthought.

'Don't you remember? A hyena got that way back in Mukinyaga.'

'Did it? Oh, yes, I remember now. You were furious.' A grin forced its way through Archie's gloom to brighten his face. 'Stormed off into the *bundu* in hot pursuit, you did.' Now he laughed, hard, as Grogan recalled he'd done at the time. 'I can still see you, steam coming from your ears. Getting tangled up in your cartridge belt and rifle's shoulder strap.'

Grogan couldn't help but smile, as much in recollection of the incident as in relief to see that Archie's mood had finally lifted.

Archie rubbed his eyes, letting the remaining chortles drift away with the memory. 'We had some laughs amongst all the shitty bits, didn't we?' he said.

'We did, Archie. Enough of them to make up for all the mosquitoes, cannibals and wild animals.'

'Well ...' Archie cocked his head and raised an eyebrow. 'Almost,' he added with a smile.

He extended a hand to Grogan, 'God speed, old chap,' then drew him into a brief, firm embrace. 'God speed, and good luck.'

'You too,' Grogan said. 'I'll see you in London in a few months.'

'Aye. You will.'

Grogan nodded to Makanjira, who shouted an order to move out. As the caravan marched off, Grogan gave a final wave to Archie, who saluted him and bawled an order of his own to his men to get on with their work.

But on the hill overlooking the fort, as the head porter's voice lifted in the high-pitched call of their first marching song and his men answered in throaty response, Grogan turned back to see Archie's distant figure raise a hand of farewell one last time.

CHAPTER 20

Bruce Dalton tied his tired old mare to the schoolyard gatepost and hitched up his trousers. At the top of the three steps to the veranda that surrounded the single-roomed building, he glanced down at his shoes. They were dusty, and it took an act of will to resist cleaning them on the back of his trouser legs.

He was at the school following a request from Jessie's teacher. Following her summons, was more the point, for Alice Mitchell was a woman of formidable resolve, and had been Londiani's one and only school teacher for longer than anyone could remember. Dalton had no idea what she wanted to talk about, but suspected it would be to do with Jessie's recent lack of interest in her books — even the storybooks she'd loved to read aloud to him in the evenings — and her growing interest in the farm and hunting.

Alice had an angular face, heavily lined, with deep crevices that added parentheses to her thin, tight lips. It was a face, Dalton believed, that could stop a clock had she had the inclination. But for all her aloof austerity, nobody doubted that she was a dedicated, even gifted teacher. It was just that Dalton, like many poorly educated men, felt incompetent in the presence of knowledgeable people. That Alice Mitchell was a knowledgeable woman made matters worse.

She sat at the front of the empty classroom, scribbling a note on the topmost of a stack of dog-eared papers. When she saw him approach, she carefully placed her pencil on her desk and pushed up the sleeves of her thin cardigan to reveal scrawny, freckled forearms.

'Ah, Mr Dalton,' she said, making the expression that passed for a smile. 'Please.' She indicated a chair.

'Hello, Mrs Mitchell,' he said, trying not to sound gruff as he often did as a result of his nervousness.

'Thank you for coming.'

'Not at all. Is there a problem?'

'You might say that,' she said, the smile, such as it was, quickly fading. 'I'm afraid that Our Jessie is falling behind again.'

It was always Our Jessie, as it was Our Freddie or Our Edith. Alice took her job to heart.

'Oh?' Dalton asked, disingenuously.

'Yes. She is decidedly lacking in diligence.'

He paused to carefully choose his words for his response.

'Diligence, Mr Dalton. Attentiveness. Industry, if you will.'

Dalton reddened.

'As a consequence, her work suffers. She is falling behind the others in her age-group.'

'I see.' He began to fidget with his fingers. 'Well —'

'I have placed her on yet another remedial program. The purpose of asking you here today was to inform you of this, and ask that you take steps to ensure she attends to the special assignments I have set her.'

Dalton nodded.

'If you are unable to help — I mean, if you haven't the time — you might see if Momposhe can assist.'

'Momposhe?'

'Yes. He is doing extremely well. If Jessie had just an ounce of Momposhe's motivation there'd be no problem.'

Dalton struggled to comprehend it. He stared at her.

'Motivation, Mr Dalton. It means —'

'I know what *motivation* means, Mrs Mitchell,' Dalton retorted, then regretted his outburst. 'I'm sorry. This, ah, comes as a surprise.'

'I often find that parents are ill-informed of their children's progress in school, and therefore ill-equipped to rectify the situation. Hence the necessity for meetings such as this.'

But it wasn't learning about Jessie's poor performance that surprised Dalton; it was the news that a formerly illiterate Maasai, with no schooling whatsoever, had become a model student.

The teacher sat waiting for his response.

'Yes! Of course. I'm sure they appreciate your interest,' he said. 'As I do,' he quickly added.

On his way home, in the slanting shadows of dusk, Dalton dissected his impressions of Momposhe and realised he had made the same mistake with him as he had with his father.

As the Maasai were unable to speak English, he had assumed they were unintelligent, but in the case of Marefu this was clearly incorrect. The older Maasai had extensive veterinarian knowledge and a vast pharmacopoeia at his command. The fact that he had learned his skills from unconventional sources did not detract from the intellect needed to apply it.

He realised that he may now also need to consider Momposhe in a similar light.

Momposhe walked guardedly into the farmhouse room that served as the Daltons' kitchen and sitting room. It wasn't that he was afraid of Bruce Dalton; merely unsure of how to behave in his house. There were conventions about when to sit, and when to stand. He was also unsure of how to address Dalton. The farmer had told him to call him Bruce, but Momposhe had learned the proper form of address for adults at school and felt uncomfortable using his first name.

Bernase, the kitchen maid, showed him in.

'Hello, Momposhe,' Dalton said.

'Good evening, Mr Bruce,' he said.

'Sit. Sit,' Dalton waved a hand to a chair. 'Tea, my boy?'

'No, thank you, Mr Bruce.'

'Then you won't mind if I take mine, will you?'

It was Dalton's form of humour. Momposhe smiled and shook his head.

'Well, will you at least sit while I do?' He indicated the chair again.

Momposhe sat.

'I've been speaking to your father,' he continued.

Momposhe's heart sank. His father had said nothing about this. This meeting might not be good.

'We both agree you should go on after term ends.'

Momposhe wrinkled his brow in confusion.

'To another school, of course.' Dalton took a sip of his tea. 'Nakuru, for a starter.' Momposhe's continuing astonishment and silence prompted him on. 'Then we'll see, but by all accounts you're quite a student. Mrs Mitchell tells me you have the ... the motivation to go on with it. Doing very well, according to her. English — obviously. But also good with the numbers, and history and ... Well, top of the class in just about everything.'

Momposhe nodded, the realisation that Dalton was defining his future now finally dawning.

'What do you say about that?' Dalton sat back, pleased with himself. He made a hat of his entwined fingers and, placing it on his head, leaned back in his chair and crossed one leg over the other.

Momposhe suddenly felt very warm. Uncomfortably warm. The black iron stove seemed to be radiating immense heat. With difficulty, he kept his emotions under control. Dalton had just described a dream that he had scarcely dared contemplate before that moment. He had been approaching the end of the school year with dismay, knowing that the wonderful world Mrs Mitchell had only begun to reveal to him in the last year or so would be snatched away. It filled him with despair. A light had been illuminated in a corner of his mind, and he feared the dark that would take its place if he couldn't continue to learn.

But although Dalton's news would be a dream fulfilled, the thought of leaving the farm filled him with anguish. It was another step away — a massive one this time — from his Maasai culture. There had been a number of smaller steps taken since the first leap, when he decided to follow his father away from his *enkang* and the only life he had known up until that point. Each day since he had learned a little more about the ways of the whites, and lost a little more of his memories of his old home. Did he ever actually take milk in a gourd, pour the fresh warm blood of an ox into it, twirl a stick in it to remove the gory filaments, and drink it with relish? He could scarcely recall such a thing happening, but knowing it had occurred almost every day in that far-off time and place amazed him. Was he sure he wanted to abandon forever his childhood desire to become a warrior, a *morani*?

A flicker of concern crossed Dalton's face at Momposhe's lack of response. 'What is it boy? Don't you have something to say for yourself?'

Momposhe scrambled to untangle his thoughts. 'What can I learn at Nakuru, Mr Bruce?'

Dalton sat forward and scratched his head. 'At Nakuru? Well ...' He took a sip of his tea. 'I imagine there'd be, ah ... more advanced studies. Yes, that's it — studies along the lines of Mrs Mitchell's class, but more ... um, advanced.'

'Will I learn about England and Scotland and other parts of the world?'

'Surely. That's geography. It's sure to be taught there.'

'And the ways that Englishmen make their laws and keep their people together?'

'Laws and government and such ... Now, that I'm not so sure about. Let's not get ahead of ourselves, Momposhe. That's sounding more like college than Nakuru General.'

'Is college where people learn about all the important matters?' It occurred to him that there must be a higher centre of learning, as there was where elders of the Maasai congregated to discuss important matters.

'That's true, but before you go running off to college in Mombasa or wherever, you haven't answered my question about Nakuru. Do you want to go on after this year or not?'

Momposhe's face split with his broad smile. 'Oh, Mr Bruce. More than anything.'

Jessie's head had been fuzzy with sleep, but when she heard her father's voice through her bedroom door, and realised he was speaking to Momposhe, she crept out of bed and sat by the door to listen.

So Momposhe would leave their farm to spend school days in Nakuru. Until that moment, she hadn't appreciated how much she loved having the Maasai boy around. With regret, she realised she had been mean, selfish and nasty to him. He, on the other hand, had been stoic in the extreme, forever disregarding her tantrums and bad behaviour.

She crawled back into bed and curled into a ball. She willed herself not to cry. She would be no worse off than she had been before Momposhe and his father arrived on their doorstep two years ago. She would still have Wonder, her big faithful dog, and there were school days when she could mix with the other children at Londiani. And she expected Momposhe would return most weekends, so why was she so upset about losing him?

Jessie was only vaguely aware that Momposhe's relationship with her had changed significantly over the last two years. He had entered her life and taken on the role of younger sibling — someone to be instructed in almost every aspect of farm life and how to behave at school. But over recent months he had become Jessie's hovering guardian angel, the big brother who rejoiced in her successes, and became merely saddened, rather than enraged, when she behaved badly towards him. Jessie's unawareness of this reversal in status was another endorsement of Momposhe's personality. He moved easily between the roles of big brother and tutor, friend and autocrat, without Jessie knowing it.

She fell asleep and dreamed of a classroom — not hers in Londiani, but an important classroom with rows and rows of big books and a huge globe spinning on its axis on the raised platform beside the teacher. When she looked more carefully, she realised the teacher was her dog, Wonder. He slobbered at her with his usual huge grin and pointed at the globe, which had come to rest to reveal the smiling face of Momposhe.

Dalton watched Jessie gallop across the home allotment on her mare, her honey-coloured hair streaming in the wind, and her big yellow dog at her heels. He shook his head in amazement. It was three weeks since Momposhe had started at his new school — a period during which his daughter had moped around the farm, barely able to rouse herself for meals. Now, however, she had bounced back to her exhuberant self, apparently without a backward thought for her lost companion.

She slid from the mare and ran to the gate, slipping the latch and ruffling her dog's ears, before a leaping remount and a slap to the pony's rump sent her careening over the swaying grasses again.

Dalton gave half a shout for her to close the gate, but realised it was a waste of breath. He had chastised his daughter for not shutting the home gate numerous times without it ever having achieved a lasting result. When it came to rules, Jessie had a simple philosophy: she would obey them only if she could see a reason for them. In this case, she probably reasoned there was seldom any stock in the home lot, and as the gate could equally well be open as closed, she decided to suit herself about it.

He walked across the enclosure, closed the gate and slid the latch back into place. Jessie was now a diminishing figure on the grassy rise. In a moment more she would be gone. She had her .22 slung over her shoulder, so she was probably off on one of her hunting expeditions. He smiled. There wouldn't be a duiker or dik dik safe for miles around.

Again he pondered his decision to allow Jessie to hunt. If she had been a boy, there would have been no issue, but a girl . . . He wondered what Marie would think about her eight-year-old daughter gallivanting all over the hills. He could almost hear her sweet voice reassuring him.

You're a loving father, Bruce.

I do my best, but I worry about her hunting.

I know you do, my darling.

She's always been a wilful girl, Marie.

I know.

Quite wilful, in fact. If I forbade her she would probably defy me.

She might. Perhaps she should be in the kitchen with Bernase, learning how to cook simple meals.

But Dalton knew his daughter had no interest in cooking, or almost anything girls of her age did. He felt that if she'd had a sister Jessie might have been persuaded to indulge in more feminine pursuits.

Again he felt the stab of pain recalling his folly in bringing his dear delicate wife to such a pestilential place as the coast of British East Africa. If they had stayed in Goa, Jessie would have had many siblings, and Marie would still have been with him. From experience he knew such thoughts spiralled into a depression, and, with an effort, he again turned his mind to his daughter.

Jessie was like a half-tamed monkey, behaving properly — as he had taught her — until her mood changed, then, for no known reason, she would do the most outlandish things.

Oh, Marie, I am so unsure of everything I do with her. Do I force her to study harder? Do I put her in dresses, although she hates them? Do I insist that she learn to cook and sew? At times I am overwhelmed, my dear. I worry at times.

Of course you do, my darling. But you can only do what you can do. You don't have to be a perfect father. You only have to be a good father. And you are. In the end, finding happiness is Jessie's responsibility. We can only pray that she succeeds.

CHAPTER 21

In the fortnight following Archie's departure, Grogan had a particularly bad time of it. He suspected that suffering alone contributed to his discomfort, and the fact that Archie would be making most of his eight-hundred mile journey in the relative luxury of ferry and train only made it worse.

Grogan was travelling with a reduced caravan consisting of twenty of his original Watonga, including Makanjira and Zowanji, two armed Waruanda, a dozen Manyema who had been languishing in the Fort Portal jail when the others departed, and the cook boy from Ujiji. He planned to recruit more in Wadelai when the new supplies Archie would send from Kampala arrived.

They were crossing the Semliki Marshes where the grass was over ten feet high, making a matted wall that was as tough as whipcord, with small spines that detached themselves and set up an intense irritation in the skin. It was home to great herds of elephant, which they could hear trumpeting nearby, but which remained invisible for the many days they spent in the claustrophobic confines of the marsh grass. The elephants' submerged, two-foot deep footholes trapped them often, demanding an enormous amount of precious energy to pull free. Concealed too were crocodiles and irate hippos. Grogan was forced to shoot several of both at close quarters.

Far more annoying were the clouds of mosquitoes, which harassed them day and night. Grogan's face swelled with their bites. He took to pacing about while eating his meals, trying to avoid swallowing them. At night he piled heavy items around the skirt of his mosquito net and eliminated those trapped inside before retiring. But before he could fall asleep he would hear the whirlwind of wings and, upon lighting a candle, would find hundreds under the netting with him. If there were a thousand more it would not matter, for there was no place on his skin that was not occupied by one of the most vicious — the small, black variety that seemed able to find their way through the fine netting.

Supplies ran low as the difficult terrain consumed the days. Grogan found to his horror that he had used his last candle, and his nights were made even more uncomfortable without the solace of a book. The swamp water had reduced his feet to grey mulch, and his boots were on the point of disintegration, requiring running repairs at the beginning of each day, when he would bind them together with twine.

After seven days they emerged from the swamp to find the land bleached by drought. The Wanyoro people's maize and millet crops had failed, leaving them on the point of starvation. Grogan shot three hippo to provide them with meat.

The Wanyoro came from all around to collect a share of the meat and to learn how the white man could provide such an abundance of food. Makanjira achieved the status of minor celebrity by holding up the .303 and explaining how it worked. Pressed for a demonstration, Grogan brought down a couple of gazelle at around four hundred yards. Immediately, an eerie silence fell over his audience. A brave member of the Wanyoro came forward and pointed to a number of dots on a hill some three miles distant. He informed Grogan that they were wildebeest, and could he please shoot one to demonstrate the killing range of the rifle.

Grogan said it was impossible, and the crowd filtered away, dejected. He later learned that Makanjira had boasted that the weapon was able to bring down elephant at a range of five miles.

Gertrude wandered around the corner of the garden wall and stopped to admire the kilted knights guarding each gatepost. Their stone sword hands were raised preparatory to striking down interlopers who dared to storm the entry to Venters, the Grogan family's estate in West Sussex. But one knight's arm was missing.

'I broke that off,' a voice behind her said.

'Oh!' Gertrude turned, startled, to find Quentin there.

'Sorry, I thought you saw me.'

'No. What are you doing?'

'Waiting for rabbits.' He had a rifle resting nonchalantly over an arm.

'I see. And when will that be?'

'Any moment now. They come creeping onto the lawn around late afternoon or dusk.'

Gertrude nodded. She liked Ewart's youngest brother. He reminded her of Ewart in many ways. Unlike all the other siblings, he had a sense of humour, and could be quite irreverent, where the others were very well-behaved in her presence. She felt that he would develop Ewart's magnetic charm in a few years, and, as Gertrude knew she would have to be with Ewart, the woman who won Quentin's heart would need to be constantly alert to the attention of other females.

'What do you mean, you broke it off? Broke what off?' she asked.

'Sir Leroy's sword arm.' He jutted his chin at the knight with a missing limb.

'And how did that happen, Quentin, if I may ask?'

'A 10-bore. Two hundred yards.'

'Quite impressive. I would have used my Rigby .375.'

'Do you hunt?'

'A little.' She looked up at the battered statue. 'Leroy is something of an odd name for an English knight, isn't it?'

'He wouldn't be English. The Grogans are from Irish stock. Not that anyone can remember that far back in history.'

'Well, it doesn't sound Irish either. If it's anything, it's American.'

'His name's not Leroy. At least I don't think it is. I just made it up. The other one's Dwayne.'

'Definitely American.'

'I must have named them when I was doing American history. I'm going there one of these days, you know.'

'Oh? When?'

'When I go to sea. After graduating from the naval academy.'

'Then you must come to visit me in California. If I'm still there.'

'Are you really going to marry Ewart?'

She smiled. 'Who said that?'

'Ewart did. Not to me, to Philip. He tells Philip everything.'

He studied her closely, making Gertrude feel uncomfortable for the first time.

'Why would you marry him?'

'Well, if I were to marry him, it would be because I loved him. And he loved me.' She raised her eyebrow. 'Is that so hard to believe?'

He thought a moment before answering. 'A little. It's just that he's such a prig.'

'Ewart? A prig? Quentin, don't be ridiculous. Anyway, how can you say that about your brother?'

'He's a bore. A bossy bore. Ever since Mother died he's been unbearable.'

'Being the oldest, I expect he feels a responsibility to be your guardian. By the way, who looks after the estate and things while he's away?'

'Half-brother William.'

'You have an older half-brother? I didn't know.'

'William is over fifty. He's more like an uncle. We have thirteen half-siblings in all.'

'Goodness! That means your father had twenty-one children?'

'That's right.' He was grinning at her amazement. 'Father must have been a randy old bugger, eh?'

Gertrude's mouth opened in surprise. There was mischief in Quentin's eyes. She tried to maintain an expression of umbrage, but couldn't hold back, and burst out laughing with him.

Fort Wadelai appeared from the steaming river flats like a phoenix rising from its ashes. Grogan, accustomed as he was to numerous false alarms, where a town would appear and as quickly be gone in the shimmer of a heat mirage, contained his excitement until the caravan had almost reached the outskirts of the settlement.

When he was convinced the town was real, he became acutely aware of his shoddy appearance. Chief Ngenzi and his thieving Watusi had reduced his wardrobe to a pittance. His trouser-legs were torn. He had only one puttee remaining of the pair that had survived the theft; the other was lost in an elephant foothole in the Semliki swamp. With the exception of his double terai, which he felt was essential to protect him from the worst effects of the sun, he was a bedraggled mess.

He tried to arrange his tattered shirt into a semblance of propriety, but it was no use. The shirt-tails remained trapped by his trousers, but the sleeves flapped like grubby boat pennants. His trousers had been flayed by a hundred fallen branches and a thousand thorny bushes and vines. His skin was also in shreds due to a period travelling in a canoe on Lake Albert when he'd tried to preserve his failing wardrobe by removing all but his trousers. His resultant sunburn and subsequent peeling had caused open-mouthed astonishment among his porters.

15 October 1899. Fort Wadelai
What joy it was to see a white man again! Upon reflection I am sure I startled Lieutenant Cape, RA, with my enthusiastic greeting, but it has been so long since I have had the opportunity to converse with another European, let alone an Englishman, that I was quite overcome.

My joy was quickly overshadowed by the news that the supplies sent by Archie had not arrived. There was a note from him confirming the shipment and details of the expected departure date of the consignment.

Lieutenant Cape said that he had not received supplies for months due to the severe drought which affected the entire countryside, and was himself short of food. He posited the view that my supplies might have been stolen. I cannot entertain such a disaster and have decided to bide my time here.

Instead of a bounty of letters, I received but a few. Thankfully, there were three from Gertrude, making me wonder again at the process by which they arrive.

Cape and I decided to go hunting for the pot in the Shuli country. There was plenty of game about, and we bagged a few good sides of meat on the first day, salting them down and sending them back to the fort with the boys. We also had some sport, killing four rhino and a good elephant with tusks of 71 lbs and 61 lbs.

The wait for Archie's consignment aggravates me. I am torn between my desperate need for supplies and my equally strong desire to be gone from here so as to complete my journey as quickly as possible. I must be patient, for to proceed without proper supplies would be deadly.

These last few days have been quite testing. The fever comes and goes. It rages through me like a grass fire on the savanna for hours, causing me to lose all sense of time and place. Then I have lucid periods, but with no energy, where I sit for what seems like hours, staring out over the Albert Nile as it surges inexorably northward.

Gondokoro is the next (and last) chance to receive mail, but by then I may be able to take a steamer, perhaps all the way to Cairo.

A steamer from Gondokoro will ensure that the end is in sight.

After waiting four weeks for his supplies, Grogan decided to press onward, travelling lighter and therefore faster. His protracted, and ultimately pointless, delay had developed in him an irrational, and sometimes desperate urge to be home.

He dismissed his remaining Manyema porters, giving them explicit instructions to return home by way of Kampala rather than risk annihilation using the more direct route.

His company of eight, comprising his five loyal Watonga, the cook boy from Ujiji and two Waruanda *askaris*, pushed off onto the Albert Nile in five canoes. They made good time in the swift current, although they were initially blocked on several occasions by huge floating islands of papyrus grass, which forced them to clamber out and drag their canoes across their surface before resuming their journey on the river.

Hippos were a continuing problem, threatening to upturn their craft. One particularly persistent and belligerent bull chased them for over half a mile before a shot from Grogan's revolver caused him to abandon his game.

Apart from being vigilant for errant hippos, Grogan began to relax and feel reassured that his mighty trek had entered a serene stage, befitting of its conclusion on the Albert Nile, which ran steady and wide on its dignified journey north. It would take him and his caravan eighty miles to Dufilé. Beyond Dufilé was the Bahr-el-Jebel, or White Nile, which would then join its sister, the Blue Nile, for its final two thousand miles to the Mediterranean. He could almost taste the strong bitter coffee of Cairo.

Grogan dared to dream of Gertrude, London, and a chilly Christmas at home.

CHAPTER 22

At another time, Grogan might have been tempted to take a detour of a mere fifty or sixty miles from his northward path to witness the Victoria Nile come bursting from the narrow ravine that confined it and tumble nearly one hundred and fifty feet to the level of Lake Albert. But between him and the Murchison Falls was a mountain range, and in any case, he was in no mood for sightseeing. He was becoming increasingly sure that at Gondokoro a steamer would be available to take him to Cairo. His rush northward was becoming an obsession.

Grogan felt very pleased with himself as the five canoes moved downstream at a steady pace of about five knots. While two porters steered his canoe through flotillas of tiny cabbage-like floating plants, Grogan allowed himself a respite from the continuous demands of the caravan. He lay back against his canvas pack and indulged in a rare nap, lulled by the lapping waters and the canoe's gentle rocking.

'*Uyaba*.' The annoying voice came from far away.

'*Uyaba*,' it persisted. Makanjira had drawn his canoe up, and was paddling alongside. '*Uyaba*, do you hear that sound?'

Grogan was irritated about being interrupted for such a trivial point. All he could hear was the lapping of the waters and the keening call of a fish eagle hovering above the river in its search for prey. 'I can hear nothing, Makanjira. Now let me sleep.' He pulled his hat over his eyes, and tried to regain the blissful tranquillity he had lost, but at the edge of his hearing Makanjira was yabbering to someone. He ignored it, then came the call again, this time in a different voice. '*Uyaba!*'

He opened an eye. 'What is it, Zowanji?' It was only his lethargy that threw a blanket over his anger, restraining the outburst he might otherwise have made. *Could a man not take a moment's rest without being harassed by stupid minions?*

'*Uyaba*, look.'

Grogan sighed and sat up. The surrounding terrain had changed. The gently rolling hills running away from the banks had grown steeper and more rugged. And they were closer. The river had narrowed, and gained in speed — he estimated it was running at about eight or ten knots. He looked at Zowanji, who was holding an insistent finger towards a fine cloud hovering over the river. Now Grogan could hear it — a faint but deep moaning coming from the cloud of spray ahead. A cataract!

'Go! Go!' Grogan yelled. 'Makanjira! Paddle to the bank! Zowanji, get those men moving!'

Grogan picked up a spare paddle and pulled hard at the river. His canoe — towing a cargo load behind — was in the lead for only a moment, then the three lighter canoes passed him, heading for the bank.

The waterfall was no longer a murmured rumble, it was thundering. He could see the vast eddies leaping above the level of the river before plunging into the abyss.

Two hundred yards to the waterfall's edge. Fifty yards to the bank. The canoe was a matchstick on the bucking waters.

Grogan strained every muscle to the paddle. 'Harder! *Go!*' he screamed at the three porters in his canoe.

The others were already on the bank — a hundred yards away.

'Cut that canoe free!' he yelled back to the porter at the rear. In a moment their many precious supplies swept past them towards the cataract.

The men on the bank were running, scrambling over the rocks, trying to keep up with Grogan's canoe which was being swept downstream at an increasingly rapid rate. Zowanji had a rope. He threw it to Grogan's canoe. It fell short. The men on the bank were shouting, yelling encouragement, but the roar of the waterfall reduced their cries to wordless mouthing.

Zowanji cast his rope again. Grogan lost his paddle in reaching for it, but caught its very end and gathered it in with both hands. He braced it against the bow of the canoe.

When the drag of the water took up the line's slack, the rope was nearly wrenched from Grogan's hands, but he hung on. The canoe swept in an arc against the taut length towards the bank, where Zowanji and Makanjira clung with all their strength.

Grogan and the three men scrambled over rocks to the shore. Twenty feet away, the tumbling waters roared and snarled their annoyance.

Gondokoro stood on a rise above the river bank. Grogan could see the fort, with its white battlements and Union Jack hanging limply from a flagpole above the gate. He attempted to quicken his pace, but the pain in his liver shortened his step. He tried to ease it by pressing a hand over the spot, but it didn't help. Eventually he reached the fort and found the commanding officer in his hot little office — a tall, lean, middle-aged captain, keen to exchange news of the outside world with Grogan.

'Really, Captain Dugmore, you are surely better informed than I on the state of world affairs,' Grogan pointed out. 'My latest news is from Wadelai. Three weeks old even there.'

'Three weeks! They get their news from Uganda, I suppose. We have to rely on the bloody steamer from Bohr. So far, we're out of luck.'

'The steamer? Where's the steamer?'

'That's what we'd like to know. Haven't seen the old tub for weeks. Months, actually.'

'What happened to it?'

'Who knows? Probably stuck in the Sudd.' By the look on Grogan's face, the captain realised the new arrival knew nothing about the Sudd. 'It's a swamp, Mr Grogan. But the biggest swamp you could ever imagine. Hundreds, no thousands, of square miles. I don't suppose anyone knows the true extent of it. The Nile surrounds it, or flows through it. More often than not, it appears to disappear into it. A floating papyrus wall so thick that an elephant can dance on its surface; so strong that it can trap big river steamers.'

Grogan sank to the chair he had previously declined. The captain took his seat behind his desk. 'Is there something wrong, Mr Grogan?'

Grogan stared at him. *Is there something wrong?* How could he ask such an imbecilic question? The captain's florid face was innocence personified. Although he could be no more than forty, his skin showed the damage that time in an unrelenting sun could do. His lips were cracked and his forehead was flaky. There were pieces missing from his ears. He was sunburned from a recent prolonged exposure, perhaps on an excursion to the outer edges of his known world. Dugmore was a man accustomed to irregular mail deliveries, but Grogan, having become so obsessed about reaching his destination, felt that every piece of news from home was a lifeline to draw him through the remaining watery wastes.

'The mail,' he croaked. 'There's no mail here?'

Captain Dugmore shook his head. 'Not for months.'

'And there's no other boat to take us down river?'

'Afraid not. Not until the *Kenia* gets back. Could be weeks.'

Grogan stood, bringing a sharp return of his pain. He shoved a hand under his belt and pressed on his liver to ease it. He needed air — the claustrophobic atmosphere of Dugmore's small space was suddenly suffocating.

Outdoors it was scarcely any better. He took a deep breath, filling his lungs with the scent of the river — the compacted mud, the rotting vegetation, the sickly sweet odour of drying fish on the racks beside the bank. Grogan was a man who searched for, and often found, a bright side in every piece of bad news, but there was nothing to give him a haven of hope in the face of such crushing disappointment.

The river moved inexorably northward to Cairo, but downstream was a monstrous papyrus maze, waiting to trap him like a fly in a web.

29 November. Redjaf

Difficult times demand difficult decisions. Last evening, Captain Dugmore introduced me to Captain Henri, the Belgian commandant just downriver from Gondokoro.

Henri and I shared a convivial evening made particularly noteworthy by an amazing array of wine and spirits. During the course of the evening the Belgian captain offered me a passage north to Bohr, where his steamer will join the search for the British launch missing from Gondokoro these last four months, and the Belgian paddle steamer that accompanied it. He also promised to assist me in a search for an onward connection, for if the river is passable, from Bohr I will be able to continue down the White Nile — or the Bahr-el-Jebel as it is called hereabouts — to the Nile, and Cairo.

Such generosity made it a very difficult decision. How could I accept assistance from the very country that only a few years ago almost succeeded in wrenching parts of the Sudan from British grasp? On the other hand, to refuse meant waiting months in this hellhole, or attempting to walk out of it. Pride waged war with necessity.

For better or worse, I have decided that we will leave Redjaf in a few days. Perforce, by means of a Belgian boat.

My liver abscess has worsened. I cannot walk without experiencing excruciating pain. My haste towards the Mediterranean is becoming more than impatience to be home — it may be a matter of life or death.

Grogan and his eight men sat aboard the Belgian steamer as it paddled downstream through an endless ocean of papyrus. He had seen papyrus in Kew Gardens on a visit one chilly day in autumn. It was a handsome specimen with stately, bold stalks supporting a burst of lacy green mop-top fronds. In the pale light that struggled through the glasshouse roof, the papyrus appeared delicate, barely able to hold its upright stance. But in its countless millions on the banks of the White Nile and in the many huge floating islands that blocked their passage, the papyrus formed an oppressive living mass that threatened to surround and consume the boat and all its occupants. On the rare occasions that they steamed into a clearing — an opening within the surrounding sea of greenery — the papyrus was still there, standing on the horizon like a vigilant enemy forming its ranks preparatory to an attack.

But in spite of the oppressive heat, the blood-sucking mosquitoes and the papyrus, Grogan was able to take a complete rest from the ordeal of the march. His liver condition eased over the weeks on board, and apart from a remnant touch of the fever, he was as well as he had been for months.

Makanjira was seldom from his side during his bouts of illness. He hovered around him like a guardian angel with a water flask, or tobacco for his pipe. As his health improved, Grogan found his head porter's attentions increasingly irritating, but the man couldn't be dissuaded from his fussing.

'You take little, little only, *Uyaba*,' he said when Grogan choked on a mouthful of water.

'Yes, Makanjira, I understand.'

'And *Uyaba*,' he said, peering at him earnestly. 'You must take care. Take much resting.'

'Yes, Makanjira. Don't be such an old hen.'

He nodded, frowning. 'What is hen, *Uyaba*?' he asked after a moment's reflection.

'A silly bird.'

He nodded again, considering this information.

'And what is *Uyaba*?' Grogan asked, realising he had accepted the title for the better part of two years without ever getting around to asking.

Makanjira nodded as he did when he understood the question, but couldn't formulate an answer. '*Uyaba* is *uyaba*,' he offered. When he realised this would not suffice, he went on, '*Uyaba*, you are a lion. The leader of this pride.' He indicated the caravan. 'And we follow.'

23 December. Bohr
We have finally reached Bohr — a paradise of malaria, misery and mosquitoes — through Kero — a howling waste in a wilderness of swamps. Again, I am decimated

by bad news. The Sudd is blocked. All three passages have been cut off due to the failure of the annual rains that flush the islands of papyrus and weed downstream.

Dishearted by the news, I am nevertheless resolved to challenge the Nile on foot.

CHAPTER 23

The butler led Archie down a wide carpeted hall into an elegant drawing room. A welcoming fire flickered in the grate under a mantelpiece that supported a large gilt mirror. Lacy curtains cast a veil over the view across St James's Square, but allowed pale winter light to enliven the rich colours of the room.

The young woman who stood as he entered, and approached with hand extended, had an elegance to match the décor and a smile to exceed its brightness.

'Mr Battersby? So good of you to come.'

'Miss Watt. Delighted.'

'Please, call me Gertrude. We've been in California so long we've forgotten all that formality. Or at least I have. Please, won't you take a seat?'

Archie thanked her, and lowered himself into the shapely Georgian chair opposite her.

Gertrude Watt was not the raging beauty he had expected to find as the fiancée of Ewart Grogan. She was charming, yes, had a delightful smile and good features, but would more likely be described as 'handsome', although that seemed too horsy for such a stylish woman. She was not by any means the starchy spinster that her age of twenty-four might suggest. Nor was she the typical simpering 'Papa's little pet' that many young women of well-to-do families feigned these days.

As they made polite conversation preparatory to moving on to discuss Ewart's situation, he realised what it was about this woman that interested Grogan. Gertrude was a bright young creature, not afraid to express a view on most matters, but she made her point in a captivating, disarming manner without persisting to the point beyond politeness. He could imagine Ewart — not one to hold back on any issue — finding a worthy match in Miss Watt, whatever the topic of discussion. Without allowing himself to dwell on it too much, he fancied she would be a match for him in bed too, such was the vigour of her personality.

'And when did you arrive back here in London, Mr Battersby?'

'Only a fortnight past. I'm still setting up house again, out near Regents Park.'

Gertrude nodded and fell silent.

Archie said, 'I presume you have asked me here to elicit some news of Ewart, Miss Watt.'

She needed no further encouragement. 'How was he when last you saw him, Mr Battersby?' she said, leaning forward on her sofa.

'He was well, quite well.'

'I understand, that is, he has written to say, that he suffers from fevers. As I believe you did too.'

'Yes, we have both been taken down with it at times. It's quite normal, I'm afraid.'

'He has said little of the other condition he had before leaving England. A problem with his liver.'

Archie was unsure how much to reveal, as Grogan himself was not one to make much of his grievances. 'Oh, I imagine he has a touch of it now and then. But he's otherwise quite well. Very fit, in fact.'

'Oh, you have no idea how relieved that makes me feel, Mr Battersby.'

'You shouldn't worry, ma'am. He will be fine, and home before you know it.'

'That is my other anxiety. I have heard nothing these last few months. Not since September. When will I see him? It has never been so long between letters. Sometimes I get eight or twelve at once, and then nothing for weeks. But now it's been three months.'

'Now, now, no need to fret yourself. It's Africa, remember. I was more often amazed that anything reached us at all, let alone that it took so long to do so.'

Gertrude dabbed at her nose with a lace handkerchief. 'I'm sorry, Mr Battersby, it's just that I've been sitting in London these last four months expecting Ewart to arrive any day, and it goes on and on.'

'I can imagine how you feel, dear lady. But it would have been better had you stayed at home in America to await the news. The telegraph lines from Cairo will rattle with the news of it when he arrives there. They know nothing of this whole adventure, nobody does, and it will create a sensation when they learn of it. Your young man will be the toast of London, of the world, when he reaches Cairo, you'll see.'

Gertrude nodded. 'Thank you for your kind words of encouragement, Mr Battersby. But I would rather have my Ewart home now, an unknown, than suffer another day not knowing where he is and how he is feeling.'

In Bohr, Grogan's liver complaint eased, and he went for a walk to explore the old Dervish fort and its bleak surroundings. He took Zowanji with him, hoping to find someone to trade with.

The fort had been abandoned only a year before, but already the the cottonbush had overgrown the battlements, and the white ants had commenced their work, removing the grins from the scattered skulls of past hostilities.

They came upon a group of Dinka, thought by the likes of the explorer Sir Samuel Baker to be the most formidable warriors on the Upper Nile. Their name meant 'men of men' in their language. Their numbers had been greatly reduced by the Dervishes, who stole their cattle and therefore their wealth. Grogan had been warned that, because of it, they had a great mistrust and antagonism towards all outsiders.

The tallest among them were head and shoulders above him — some close to seven feet tall — with lightly muscled bodies, angular shoulders and gangling arms. They were completely naked except for several strings of glass beads around their neck and one or two at the wrist, and a ring of ivory above one or both elbows. A marabou feather in the hair was a touch of fashion favoured by a few. Their bodies were caked in ash, which Grogan imagined was to guard against mosquitoes, but made them appear like grey, long-limbed phantoms. The impression was reinforced by their manner of walking, where they appeared to pause, leg hovering, before putting each foot down.

Zowanji had no success engaging them in conversation. Through sign language he tried to make it known that they should come back to Grogan's camp to barter, but to no avail.

As Grogan and his interpreter walked away, the men of men watched them go with sullen, arrogant eyes.

25 December 1899. Bohr
Christmas. How could I have imagined I would be home by now? I still have at least a further fifteen hundred miles to go.
I celebrated the day with fish coaxed from the Nile with a stick of dynamite.

While Grogan was recruiting porters and trading for supplies, the supply ship *Kenia* arrived in Bohr after nearly four months trying to cut its way through the Sudd towards Khartoum. It was under the command of the American, Captain Anvil Mulders — a man said to know all there was to know about the Nile after navigating it for fourteen years.

Grogan found the captain on the bridge of the *Kenia*. He was short and heavy-set — solid rather than fat — with a heavy greying beard from which poked a foul-smelling cigar. He told Grogan that, in his opinion, the Nile downstream was at its lowest ebb in over one hundred and fifty years because of the severe drought in its upper reaches. He said it would be impossible to land anywhere more than ten miles north of Bohr because of the build-up of the papyrus. He also said it got worse further north, and that if Grogan continued downstream until he met the Sudd it would mean cutting his way through something like fifty miles of weeds to reach true land.

'In other words, Captain,' Grogan said, 'continuing to Cairo by river is completely impossible.'

''Xactly,' Mulders said around his cigar.

It was Grogan's worst nightmare. 'What do you know about the track by land?' he asked.

The captain removed his cigar. 'Are you tellin' me you're plannin' to walk to Cairo, young fella?'

'I am, sir.'

'Then you're a bloody fool, sir!' he said, and thrust his cigar back in his mouth.

Grogan, undaunted, continued, 'Maybe, but you have just now told me there is no other option, so I must. You'd oblige me by telling me what you know of it up ahead.'

The captain chewed thoughtfully on his cigar for a moment, then sighed and said, 'If your heart's set on it, then I guess I must. I don't know anything about the track, as you call it — nobody does. But I can tell you what I know about the general lay of the land, if that helps.'

Over the next hour Mulders described what he knew of the river and its surroundings. He spoke of the various people along its course, who you could trust and who you couldn't. He gave advice on the trade goods that were much in demand by some and thought totally useless by others. In conclusion, he described what Grogan must look for to know when he was beyond the Sudd and able to rejoin the river.

'All the streams running into the Nile are brackish up to that point, and run west. They're called *khors*. Past the Sudd the *khors* are all fresh water, and flow north. When you get to that point you're forty miles from a town called Sobat, where you can begin looking for your river transport.'

'And how far is it to that point, Captain?'

'Well, I can tell you by river it's about three hundred miles.' He squinted through a cloud of tobacco smoke at Grogan. 'So that'll give you an idea, but on the river all I have to worry about is the blacks, the papyrus and the crocodiles. You got all that and then some. I can say that in your case, young fella, it's gonna be one helluva three hundred goddamn miles.'

Grogan thanked him and stood to leave.

Captain Mulders removed his cigar, and spat on the deck to one side. He extended a hand and peered up at Grogan through the squinted eyes of a man forever searching the river for trouble. 'Good luck, Mr Grogan,' he said, shaking his head in reluctant admiration. 'You're one crazy bastard.'

Invigorated by his new-found knowledge, Grogan began recruiting for porters in earnest, but he found only a few who were interested, and of that sorry bunch there were even fewer who were even vaguely suitable. After waiting until the last moment, in the hope of attracting more suitable applicants, he made his choices and told Makanjira to ready the caravan for immediate departure the following morning.

In the cool light of dawn, as he made his inspections up and down the line, he wondered what he had been thinking when he hired his new porters. His recruits included a scruff of a boy, hardly a yard tall, an old Egyptian Dervish prisoner with a gammy leg who was on reprieve provided he departed the town, and a man who he had been warned was a criminal lunatic and should be kept in chains after dark as he was inclined to howl at the moon and prowl about in a most disconcerting fashion.

His caravan therefore consisted of eighteen, including the two Watonga headmen. One of the Waruanda had died of the fever, leaving him one Waruanda *askari*, the other four Watonga, two boys, the criminal lunatic, the lame Dervish and the youth from Kero. Captain Henri had used his influence to provide five Congolese *askaris* to assist with the passage through hostile Dinka territory.

With the reduced number of porters Grogan was forced to further economise on what he considered to be his few simple comforts, leaving behind his beloved stretcher bed and a comfortable canvas chair.

6 January 1900. Southern Dinkaland
I have suffered the lethargy of fever these last few days, and now, forcing myself from it, I find that the century, indeed the millennium, has passed me by.

The river here is a vast expanse of grass, here and there darting inland to form long, twisting lagoons. They are a devil to walk around.

Between the lagoons, the land supports a surprisingly large number of Dinka, but they are no more amenable to trade than the tribes around Bohr due to the dry conditions and the previously mentioned decimation of their herds.

These Dinka seem more primitive than those I first met. They greet me with boisterous enthusiasm, prancing about like herons on their long lanky legs and spitting on me as is the customary salutation. They carry long-bladed spears, a shorter pointed fish spear, and a heavy club made from a purplish wood.

To win the Dinka's good graces I promised to provide them a supply of meat by shooting elephant, of which there are many hereabouts. The old boy I bagged had tusks that must have weighed over 80 lbs. It almost made me weep to leave the ivory behind, but I have no porters to carry it. The Dinka learned the reason for my lament and promised to carry the tusks to a station where they will arrange for them to be sent to me. I thought this a great joke, but, not to spoil their fun, wrote down an address in London. How gullible the Dinka must think we whites are. Nevertheless, I kept the smile from my lips.

The constant attention of our towering companions is making my men nervous. It is impossible to be rid of them as we cover no more than ten miles a day in the heavy going of the swamps. The Dinka, meanwhile, amble along on a parallel course, obviously with more time on their hands than we.

At night it is worse. A tall ghostly figure occasionally moves through the shadows beyond the edge of firelight and is gone before it can be identified. The silence is interrupted by soft footfalls, or perhaps it is merely the splash of a fish, but the disturbances truly tighten the nerves.

Makanjira and I share guard duties. On my watch I surround myself in a cloud of local tobacco, which has a particularly pungent smoke, praying for morning, but the blood-sucking insects cannot be denied. By morning I feel their poison has put me into a drugged daze.

CHAPTER 24

Grogan stumbled from his tent, angrily scratching his newest batch of mosquito bites. He rubbed at his puffy eyes and found Makanjira standing at a deferential distance. The headman knew better than to intrude upon Grogan until he had exorcised his frustration at losing another night's sleep to the parasitic insects.

'Well?' Grogan asked moodily.

'The Waruanda *askari* is dead, *Uyaba*,' Makanjira replied without ceremony.

Grogan was not surprised. The poor man had been battling fever for weeks. 'Where is he?' he asked.

Makanjira pointed to the edge of the camp, and led the way to where the *askari*'s body lay. He had wandered away from his tent, probably in a feverish daze, and fallen among the long grass. His skin was a mass of bites.

'Poor bugger's been sucked dry,' Grogan muttered to himself. 'Very well then, see if you can find some dry ground to put him in, Makanjira. Then make ready the — What is it, Zowanji? For God's sake, you're like a bee in a bloody bottle.'

Makanjira's lieutenant was shaking his hands in anxiety while waiting for Grogan to allow him to speak.

'*Uyaba*, that porter — the one you brought from Bohr who makes noise at the moon — he is gone.'

'Gone?' Grogan looked around him. As far as the eye could see was nothing but grass stirring in the faint breeze that accompanied the sunrise. 'Where in the hell could he go?'

'I do not know, *Uyaba*, but he has taken your clothes.'

The air filled with Grogan's rage, until he regained his composure and ordered Zowanji to take another man and go after the deranged porter. If necessary he was to drag him back in harness.

Two hours later, Grogan's mood had not improved. He decided they had waited long enough and started out with Makanjira to find the criminal lunatic, or at least the search party. They found both about a mile from camp. The lunatic had decided to go home, taking Grogan's clothes as *hongo* for the Dinka.

Grogan spent the best part of the day recovering his clothes, a blanket and a spare mosquito net from the nearby Dinka. He managed to retrieve all but one of the pairs of trousers Captain Henri had kindly given him. The big Dinka in possession of them steadfastly refused to give them up. Grogan decided they were not worth an incident and begrudgingly left them to him.

The errant porter giggled throughout these protracted negotiations. By the end of them, Grogan was in a foul mood and eyed the man with unconcealed disgust. He was very tempted to boot him out of camp and back to Bohr, as he wished, but knew that if he did, he would have to abandon more equipment or supplies. With visions of impassable swamps, grassy wastelands and possible famine facing him, he could ill afford that luxury.

10 January. Southern Dinkaland
I awoke at dawn to the incessant sound of buzzing. My hands were numb from bites, and I could feel the swelling mounds of irritation around my eyes, ears, neck and face. I was possessed by a moment's madness.

I must have been ranting incoherently, because Makanjira and Zowanji came running with their rifles. They watched in amazement as I grabbed the night lantern from my tent and emptied the paraffin into the papyrus before putting a light to it. The twenty-feet-high grass was green at the base but dry above. It caught quickly. A terrific sheet of flame, capped by a vast cloud of smoke that caught the red lights from the fire and the golden touch of the dawn, afforded a picture of indescribable grandeur. It thundered away like a rolling sea of molten iron, licking up the country as it sped eastwards, devouring the grass and its hidden hordes of flying, biting insects.

I knew the fire would not rid me of the pests, but it was a delightful moment of revenge, giving me the satisfaction of knowing that I had annihilated billions of the little beasts.

We have left the waterlogged land of the Nile behind, where pythons were as common as daisies in a field, and are now entering a flat land of baked clay, thorn and palm scrub.

The Dinka, of which we now have a new batch, have become increasingly annoying, prying into our belongings and pilfering small items. I have tried to bribe them off by offering gifts of Diamond Jubilee medals, but they now demand more — my equipment and supplies. It grows hourly more tense.

One Dinka giant demanded my trousers. I don't understand the sudden attraction of that particular item of apparel. When I refused, he stamped and waved his arms like a spoilt child. When this had no effect, he rushed at me with club raised. This was too much. I took him by the scruff of the neck, and gripping him firmly in the vicinity of where he wished my pants to be, ran him out of camp. This I followed up with a drop-kick delivered by my iron-toed boot. It had the desired effect — the warrior retreated amid howls of amusement from his fellows.

Grogan was suffering constant bouts of malaria, which left him lost in a delirium for days on end.

He decided to lead his caravan away from the swampy surroundings of the Sudd, with its constant drone of mosquitoes, and into the baked earth to the east of the Nile.

The land was flat, limitless and covered with coarse grass more than five feet high. Here and there were dotted clumps of borassus palms and large anthills like pale imitations of the tall Dinka. The numerous narrow *khors* ran to the west, indicating that he was still short of the Sobat, where the Sudd came to an end and large steamers plied the navigable Nile all the way to Cairo.

Where, earlier, the water in the swampy wastelands of the Sudd had been his concern, it was the scarcity of it that worried him in the grasslands just fifteen or so miles away from the river. The *khors* were a brackish concoction of mud and foul-smelling liquid, but there was little else available.

Throughout the day a few Dinka, who kept their distance but were never out of sight, followed them. Makanjira thought there were many different individuals who alternated their watch over them. Grogan scoffed at him for having an overly active imagination, but when they paused for a rest around midday he climbed an anthill to reconnoitre the path ahead and estimated there were about five hundred Dinka concealed in the grass surrounding them.

He kept the presence of the Dinka to himself. His men were already nervous enough. The tall, naked visitors moved from the concealment of the grass like shadows, and as silently disappeared. Grogan found it unnerving to see the occasional Dinka perched on one leg like a black stork on an anthill, knowing there were countless more somewhere in the grass.

He climbed another anthill when they stopped in the late afternoon to pitch camp. Now he estimated there were about a thousand Dinka in the area. Long black lines snaked through the grass like a swarm of *siafu* ants, converging on them from all directions.

Immediately the tents were set, about five hundred warriors surrounded the camp, demanding trade items. Since they had nothing to offer in exchange, Grogan refused. The warriors became belligerent, strutting through the camp and shoving the men out of their way, lifting anything they found lying about. Zowanji lost his temper when one warrior took his plate and spoon.

Grogan knew the Dinka would not tolerate any retaliation from the Watonga, so he strode up to the warrior, who stood fully eight inches above him, and hit him with a firm right cross, setting him flat on his buttocks.

In one voice the assembled Dinka let out a loud *h-o-o-o*, and a naked young blood sprang into an aggressive war dance, brandishing his spear — not at Grogan, but at one of the *askaris* who was nervously doing his duty, standing on guard with his rifle at the ready.

Grogan intervened and broke the Dinka's spear, then gave two or three warning cracks of his heavy hippo-hide whip as the warrior retreated. This halted the first intruder, but others advanced with menace. Drawing his revolver, Grogan let off a volley over their heads and advanced, firing shots and cracking his whip.

The tension was too much for one of the Watonga porters who dashed past Grogan shouting, 'We are all done! We are all done!'

It was the spark that finally ignited the Dinka. One warrior hurled his spear, piercing one of the Congolese *askaris* in the chest. He fell dead at Grogan's side.

Other warriors launched into the attack, laying about them with clubs and dropping *askaris* and porters all around. Grogan fired his double-barrelled rifle, taking first the chief, then one of his lieutenants, in quick succession. He dodged a spear and, drawing his revolver, dropped two more warriors before wounding another with his last cartridge.

The fighting closed around Grogan, who made a stand with Makanjira, Zowanji and one of the *askaris* who had not bolted at the first charge. In close combat, the warriors' clubs came raining down on the four men. Grogan took the brunt of one blow on his forearm, and fended off another with his empty rifle. The warrior rounded for another blow and Grogan shoved the rifle barrel into his midriff, pushing him off balance while he quickly slipped a bullet into the chamber, cocked and fired it.

The dumdum cartridge blew a massive hole in the warrior, spraying his comrades with blood, gore and intestinal parts. Such destructive power was unknown to the Dinka, who took to their heels *en masse*, howling with dismay and anger.

Grogan climbed a termite's nest and found the war party had retreated to about three hundred yards. Three or four of the leaders were watching from an elevated vantage point, apparently in conference before mounting another attack. Grogan loaded the .303 with another two dumdums, took careful aim in the fading light and squeezed off a shot. One of the leaders was knocked back with such force he took another down with him.

The Dinka retreated again, this time to about seven hundred yards. Grogan could hardly see them, but sent another volley in their direction. Whether he struck anyone or not he couldn't tell, but the entire party dispersed into the grasses.

As darkness closed in, the warriors were invisible, but their ominous calls of *h-o-o-o, h-o-o-o* continued into the night.

16 January 1900. Dinkaland
The Dinka continue to follow, but they have done little more than watch us from afar. I continue to take pot shots when I get a chance. After I downed a man on an anthill at six hundred yards, they now watch from a distance of a mile or more.

Two of the three men who had taken terrible blows to the head during our battle came out of their swoon quite mad. One died last night. I patched the others as best I could. One had a gash two inches long and open to the bone of his temple, and the other had two gaping holes on the top of his skull.

We have again moved closer to the river, but the Sudd goes on, never-ending, and the khors continue to run determinably west, and are brackish. Occasionally we stumble upon a small island of dry land, but it is as flat as the marsh and affords no vantage point from which to plot a better path forward or to relieve the tedium of endless green.

Against my strict orders, one of my Congolese askaris lagged behind, and disappeared. We searched and called for him for hours, but we could not find him. I fear we will never see him again.

I opened my last box of cartridges to find them lying in a rusty sediment. I salvaged a handful of those I thought would not be dangerous to fire. The shortage of ammunition is immaterial so far as hunting is concerned, for there is no game to shoot. Even the countless waterbirds keep their distance, or are so small that my .303 would annihilate them, leaving nothing but feathers to eat. My concern is that another raid by the Dinka would finish us.

The swamps are wearing us down. It was foolish of me to return to the river. It was better in the open where at least we could drink the air without the fetid taste of mouldering vegetation constantly in our mouths. Tomorrow we head for the dry ground again.

My health worsens. I have experienced bouts of vomiting, and suffered mightily from diarrhoea, due, I believe, to the foul water that is our only choice. My fever wafts over me almost daily, and the liver abscess that I had thought passed returns without warning and lays me low in hours of agony.

I seem to have lost the ability to recuperate. Perhaps it is the melancholia, which comes unbidden and at strange times. I wonder who knows of my situation. Who cares? Sometimes I feel we are trapped in a green maze. Isolated and lost. At the mercy of thousands of heathen warriors. Other than Gertrude, one or two close friends and immediate family, no one knows of this ambitious undertaking. And if they did, what could they do? What can anyone do to rescue us?

Now, as I ponder the lonely road north, through more of this abominable climate and intolerable terrain, I can no longer torture myself with the option of abandoning the whole affair. There is no way back. If we don't make it beyond the Sudd, we shall all die.

CHAPTER 25

'Zowanji comes!' Makanjira cried. The remainder of their party came out of resting places and gathered around the borassus palm where Grogan had slumped in the shade.

Grogan had sent Zowanji to try to find a Nuer village. There were a number of Nuer in the area — people of similar stature as the Dinka but without their bellicose manner. He hoped they could trade for food. They'd had no luck for days, principally because word of Grogan's rifle had spread across the grass plains like a dry season fire, rushing from village to village in advance of their arrival.

Grogan tried to rise, but his legs would not respond. He fell against the borassus palm, and then used it to stand upright. His near-collapse alarmed him, and it showed in his surprised expression. He quickly composed himself, but not before Makanjira noticed it and rushed to his side.

Grogan shoved him away. 'Get off! Leave me alone. Damn fool, Makanjira. I'm all right. Can't a man miss a step without a general panic breaking out?'

Makanjira held Grogan's elbow for a moment more before stepping back, abashed.

'Zowanji! What have you found for us?' Grogan called, but he knew the answer before the man replied.

Zowanji dropped his head. 'Nothing, *Uyaba*. The people ran away.'

'Ran away? Even from you, alone and unarmed?'

'I am sorry, *Uyaba*. I found the Nuer village, as you asked, and I went slowly slowly to them, but they cried out and ran away. Soon the village was empty. I could find no food to bring.'

'Very well,' Grogan said. 'We'll try again later. Makanjira, load up. We go.'

Makanjira gave the order, although it was hardly necessary to repeat it, as their small caravan had shrunk even further with another death — this time the youth from Kero, who had been bitten by a cobra.

Grogan moved out, leading the column. Before he'd gone half a mile, his head began to swim. He took a mouthful of the vile brackish mud that was in his water flask and tried to put the dizziness from his mind. He had battled nausea and diarrhoea since arriving in the area of the Sudd, and he still suffered from fever and the pain from his liver abscess. But he refused to concede to his body's demands that he rest. He knew he was racing against the odds. Hunger would be the most patient killer. The Dinka would be more decisive. Once they realised he had no ammunition, they would close in for their revenge without delay.

He continued on, his head swimming. When they arrived at a wall of grass, about twelve foot high, he stopped, unable to decide which way to go. It was a simple choice between pressing on through the marshland and tackling the swamp along the river, or going east to circumnavigate the marsh grasses. And it was a decision he had made many times before. But the longer he stood staring at the grass wall, the more anxious he became. He felt as if a sword hung over his head and his fate turned on his choice. He stood looking first at the grass, a green wall that might run a hundred miles to the east, and then he turned to the west, where the Nile played its cruel games with crocodiles, sink holes and suffocating swamplands.

He was conscious of the men's attention on him, waiting, as he looked from east to west, unable to move. He sensed Makanjira exchange nervous glances with Zowanji. The cook boy put down his load and sat on it, resting his chin on his fist.

All of this Grogan understood, knew he had to make a move one way or the other, but was incapable of doing so.

He dragged his eyes from the hypnotic effects of the puzzle and his gaze fell on Makanjira. 'Damn you, Makanjira!' he bellowed. 'I knew I shouldn't have listened to you. We should have stayed on the river. I told you that! Now look at this! Why did you —'

The thought that he was losing his mind came vividly into focus. It had been *his* decision to leave the river, as it was for all important matters. It was he, Grogan, who was responsible for their plight — no one else. He struggled to defeat the feelings of shock and confusion. He could see that Makanjira wished it to be true — that it was indeed he had who insisted on leaving the river — but it wasn't so.

Grogan indicated by hand that they would take the path through the marsh grass. He cleared his throat. 'Load up, Makanjira,' he said in a soft voice. 'We go.'

After several hours of beating a path through miles of towering marsh grass, Grogan and his men again emerged into a featureless plain that ran before them as far as the eye could see.

The first of the shallow, slow-moving *khors* they came upon was salty, and like all they had crossed to that time was flowing to the west. Grogan began to wonder if the mighty Nile would allow anything to escape it; even the insignificant trickle of brackish water that the *khors* provided was drawn inexorably to the river. He understood that the Nile's junction with the Sobat River marked the end of the Sudd, and it was to the Sorbat that the *khors* would run when they neared it, but he couldn't compel his mind to grasp that simple geographical explanation. In his imagination, the Nile was sucking everything from the surrounding land — the water, the wildlife, and perhaps even Grogan and his men.

Zowanji spotted a marabou stork at some distance and alerted Grogan to the possible meal. Grogan would not chance one of his remaining bullets at such a range. He shushed the men and crept forward, taking cover as best he could in the grass, which at that point was less than waist-high. The bird was searching for lean pickings among the grass tufts, probably for frogs, snakes and insects. It looked as thin as a stick, but it was their best chance for food in a week.

Grogan moved unsteadily through the grass. The heat seemed exceptionally strong that morning. A line of sweat ran down his cheek and slid under his jaw. An incessant fly worried his ear. The marabou seemed unaware of his approach, high-stepping through the grass and bobbing at its prey.

Grogan hated marabous. He couldn't recall a settlement anywhere in Africa whose refuse pit was not home to at least a dozen of these tall, hunch-shouldered, ugly, bald-headed, mottled creatures. They reminded him of parsimonious undertakers, too cheap to afford a decent suit. They fed on stinking carrion and offal, yet here he was salivating at the prospect of adding one to his cooking pot. His stomach rumbled loudly in anticipation.

He knelt to rest. The strain of carrying his heavy rifle in a crouched stance was testing his stamina. He took a few quiet breaths, looking back to where he had left the men, but they were hidden from sight. The grassland hummed with heat, but was silent except for the sighing breeze in the grass stems. He wiped his hand across his dripping brow and pressed on.

The marabou was now at a range of a hundred yards. To go further was to risk being discovered, sending the bird into flight. He tried to bolster his confidence by recalling he had a dozen Cambridge shooting prizes in his trophy cabinet for distances over a hundred yards.

He took up a comfortable position on one knee and raised the .303 to his shoulder. A sharp spasm stabbed at his gut and his stomach churned. He rested his arm on a knee until it passed, then resumed the firing position. The rifle seemed extraordinarily heavy. He had difficulty holding it steady and swayed so that the marabou became lost behind the rear sight. He muttered a curse at his incompetence and settled back to the task. He held steady. Steady.

The concussion split the silence and reverberated across the plain. The explosion momentarily stunned Grogan. It was a mere .303 — an infant in his formerly extensive armoury — and yet the recoil had almost knocked him down.

He climbed shakily to his feet and anxiously searched the grass. On the horizon, a low white cloud of impossibly distant water birds rose above the green wall of papyrus, and the marabou, an unlikely aerialist at the best of times, was in pursuit of them — a fast-disappearing blot in the limitless blue sky.

20 January. Nuerland
This morning Makanjira woke me with the pleasing news that my homesick lunatic had disappeared in the night. This meant another lightening of our loads. There was little choice; my tent — lock, stock and barrel — had to go. I know there will be nights when I will regret this. To make matters worse, I found my remaining two tins of tobacco to be mouldy.

Mosquitoes continue to hover about me in clouds. I can scarce breathe without ingesting them. I also have a stiff arm, thanks to the Dinka who tried to brain me.

One of the Congolese askaris has an infected foot, making it difficult for him to walk without enduring near unbearable pain.

The khors are brackish. Running west.

Grogan could not sleep even though he was totally exhausted. Each time he vomited, he felt his feverish head would burst. He was trapped in a vicious circle where he craved water but the swamp was his only choice. The brackish soup hardly had time to settle before it was violently ejected, leaving him dry-retching until his abdomen ached.

Others in the caravan suffered almost as severely, but their greatest enemy was hunger. They were all very weak. Grogan measured progress by the hours of suffering, rather than by mileage. Their days started when they crawled out of their grass caves, and ended when the late afternoon sun mercifully allowed them to stop, to stalk the grass for anything edible, and to seek sleep. Only unconsciousness provided escape.

For an hour or so, Grogan had been listening to two lions calling to one another somewhere out in the plain. They finally came together about a mile from the camp, and joined forces to regale the night with their rasping, moaning message that the grassland was their domain. He listened to their coughing grunts approaching until they were silent, then he struggled to his feet and walked to the edge of the camp where the moonlight softened everything with its cold silvery light.

Rustles in the grass and the occasional crush of a paw on a dry stem told of their proximity. Grogan let the gun hang loosely in his curled fingers.

His ears pieced together the fragments of sound to make a pattern out there in the grass. One lion had stopped some distance out. Only one set of large padded feet troubled the undergrowth as it continued to creep forward. A pause — perhaps to raise its nose to test the air. A change of tread, maybe to avoid a brittle patch of foliage. Then the lion was standing at the edge of the flattened grass. For many long minutes it was not there, and then its cold golden eyes were on him as if it had been there, staring at him, all night.

Grogan could sense the power of the animal. Raw, pure power. It was the ruler of the night; no other could claim its crown. No beast. No mere man.

They stood, the lion and Grogan, neither moving, neither making a sound. Grogan felt removed from the setting, as if he were not a participant but a spectator in this scene where a deadly animal was facing off its prey in the moments before it leapt and tore him apart. He wondered how it would end.

The lion yawned and the moonlight flashed from a long white canine. It turned its head, as if searching for its mate concealed somewhere in the grass, and licked its enormous jaws. In another moment it was gone.

Grogan glanced down at the double 10-bore in his hands. It seemed puny. He released the catch and opened the barrel. Peering down the gleaming empty chambers, he could see the grass at his feet.

Another day began. Grogan arose while the wash of yellow and pink still hung low in the east, and stirred his men into action. Every hour travelled before the sun was high was a chance to reduce the cravings of thirst.

They had covered but a handful of miles before they were strung out across the flat grass plain like a line of tattered washing.

As the heat of morning climbed, he had to threaten the three Watonga with a touch of his *kiboko* if they didn't get up and move on. They mumbled and wept, but made an effort. Fifteen minutes later, they were lagging again. The Congolese *askari* was even further behind, painfully nursing his poisoned foot every step of the way with the help of a makeshift crutch. Zowanji, the best of them, was at his side. Grogan called a halt under a stand of palms.

Makanjira passed Grogan a water flask. He took a sip, but his thirst got the better of him and he allowed himself the luxury of a mouthful, which he choked upon, wiping his mouth to remove the bitter aftertaste. He handed the flask back to Makanjira with a grimace. The others began to straggle in, dropping into the welcome shade of the palms.

Grogan was soon restless to continue. His mind, consumed by cravings for food and fresh water, still ignored his body's need for rest. Before he realised he had made the conscious decision to rise, he had struggled to his feet, using the serrated pole of the palm as his aid.

The men were scattered around like broken toys. None had the energy to move. They needed more rest. Even Zowanji, strong and usually energetic, lay like a rag doll set down against a tree trunk. The three Watonga sat together under their own palm. The Ujiji cook boy was a few paces away, already almost asleep. The others were listless and silent. Only Makanjira met his eyes, ready to stand and call the order on Grogan's word.

Grogan made a feeble hand gesture to say they could rest a while longer, but himself felt compelled to inspect the way ahead. Leaving the men where they were, he struggled through the tangled grass that clawed at his legs, now stripped bare of the bottom half of his trousers. After a few moments he reached another of the *khors* that had blocked every mile of their passage. It was just twenty paces wide, but experience suggested the muddy bottom would pull at their tired legs and try to drag them down.

There was something about this *khor* that appeared a little different. He moved further into the shallows while trying to unravel his thoughts. He could see his boots. That was different. The bottom had not become turgid with mud. It was sandy.

He brought a cupped hand to his lips. The water tasted sweet. He tested it again. It was fresh. And it was flowing north!

CHAPTER 26

Grogan's initial elation at finding the fresh-water *khor* quickly faded as he realised they had at least a five-day walk to the settlement along the river. Looking around his men, he saw no sign of the energy that had brought them stumbling into the *khor* to drink their fill. They had all improved miraculously with the fresh water and a brief rest, but the hunger remained, and the fifty-mile march that awaited them to Sobat was daunting.

With one craving satisfied, the other seemed to fill the space of the two. Grogan wondered at their chances of catching a fish or snagging a water bird. They sat on the banks of the Sobat River, contemplating the task ahead.

Grogan's eyes meandered upstream, above the scattered palm tops along the river. In the glare from the sandy bank it was difficult to see clearly, but he glimpsed what he thought to be a moving palm trunk. Not moving as if blown by a non-existent breeze, but moving towards them. He blinked hard, not trusting his eyes, or his mind, for the first few moments.

Then it became clearer. He stood and moved towards the vision, passing Makanjira and Zowanji, who were bathing their feet in the shallows.

'Look,' he whispered, still not daring to put a name to his vision. He stood and let his rifle fall to the sand.

Makanjira looked up at him and then stood too. 'A boat,' he said, as if not trusting himself either.

The moving palm tree emerged to reveal a small ketch coming down the Sobat under sail.

Captain William Dunn had the group in his glass. *A group of natives*, he thought. *Settlement scavengers, by the look of them.* He ordered the corporal to have a soldier lower a boat, and to row them to the bank to investigate the group.

One of the men on the bank was heading towards the place he had chosen to set ashore. He was unarmed, but Dunn decided to take no risks. The area was notorious for attacks by ruffians such as these, ejected from their clans for some tribal crime or other. It was not unknown for such groups to spring an ambush on British patrols for the prize of their weapons and tunic buttons.

The sailor held the rowboat steady while he and the corporal stepped onto the sandy bank. The native kept coming, seemingly unafraid.

'Wait here with the boat, Corporal,' the captain said. 'And keep a ready eye on this fellow while I try to find out his little game. Don't play about with him or any of his mates. If his mob makes a move towards us, shoot them.'

'Yes, sir,' the corporal said with a snappy salute.

Dunn walked smartly along the bank a few yards, determined to show he was not intimidated by this fellow's forthright manner, coming as he did, stumbling through the water without a backward glance. He levered a cartridge into the chamber just in case and waited for him to come up.

When he was quite close, the native raised his hands and, to Gunn's utter astonishment, said in quite remarkable English, 'Thank God, old man. You're a sight for sore eyes.'

'Wh-what are you doing here?' Dunn stammered.

'We're on our way to Cairo, old chap. Can't tell you how pleased I am to see you.' The effort seemed to have left him breathless, as he held his midriff while sucking air. 'I thought I was going to have to walk the whole bloody way.'

'Quite,' Dunn said, still not fully recovered from his surprise at finding a white man so far from civilisation, and on foot. His skin was almost black, but an Englishman — of that there was no doubt.

Dunn suddenly remembered his manners. 'I'm so sorry. I'm Captain William Dunn, officer in charge of the Sobat fort.' He extended a hand.

'Grogan. Ewart Grogan.'

'How do you do?' the captain asked.

'Oh, not too bad, thanks,' Grogan replied. 'How are you? Had any sport hereabouts?'

'Just fair, but there's nothing much here. I say, would you care for a drink?'

'Actually, that would be splendid.'

'Do come aboard then. And bring your boys. I'll get cook to hurry on lunch. Had any shooting? Seen any elephant?'

Grogan said there hadn't been much these last few weeks.

'Pity,' Dunn said.

Grogan stared at his reflection in the mirror on the cabin wall. He hardly recognised himself. Even after a good scrubbing he was still almost black from the sun. He was quite dismayed. He felt he had done everything possible to protect himself from the equatorial rays, which were well known to induce feebleness into otherwise healthy individuals. He had even managed to retain his spine pad throughout all his ordeals.

After his wash, the ship's kitchen put on a wonderful lunch for them. The men were accommodated on deck, while Dunn and Grogan kept to the relatively cooler air of the ship's scullery. It was quite a light lunch, which was fortunate. Grogan had difficulty resisting the urge to bolt down his food and probably make himself ill, so he kept to Dunn's lead. Unfortunately, the captain was a very slow eater and it took the best part of an hour and a half for them to make their leisurely progress through the clear soup, beef and vegetables — tinned, but seeming to melt in Grogan's mouth — and, finally, scones and tea.

During the course of the meal they discussed the war and various world affairs. Eventually Dunn got around to asking the question that must have been on his mind since he found Grogan on the banks of the Sobat.

'You know, old chap, when I first saw you on the banks of the river I thought you were a renegade native, or worse, a confounded Frenchman.'

Grogan smiled.

'So where the devil did you come from?' Dunn filled Grogan's glass.

'I've been on an expedition for quite a while now. I started at the Cape of Good Hope.'

The captain burst into laughter, nearly choking on his wine, but his mirth subsided in the face of Grogan's continued silence.

'I take it you're joking, old man.' Dunn forced a smile, but was clearly offended. 'Otherwise you must take me for a fool.'

'Not at all,' Grogan replied. 'I left Beira in March 1898. If my reckoning is true, that's a month shy of two years. But I earlier walked from Cape Town to Beira, so in all I say I started from the Cape.'

Dunn took a large tumbler of water and swallowed it almost entirely. 'I'm sorry, sir,' he said, realising the man was serious, 'I've misjudged you. What did you say your name was?'

'It's Grogan. Ewart Scott Grogan.'

21 February 1900. Cairo

I am alone in this room with its lofty ceiling and its frieze of filigreed masonry atop starkly white stuccoed walls. The room is unadorned but for two items of furniture: a bed with posts that taper from the floor, beginning as thick as a man's thigh, to the top where finely carved pinnacles support a mosquito net with diaphanous tails fluttering in the breeze from the river below; and this simple desk, where I now sit to quietly contemplate what has transpired. Soon the seductive offerings of civilisation — the food, the drink, the exquisite sound of a female voice — will cause me to forget, and so I must study my diaries and commit measured comment to paper.

I must write now while the passion borne of immediate recall still heats my blood; to commit to paper all the emotions, all the visions and perceptions, before they wither.

But can I forget the desolation of desolations, the infernal, howling waste of weed-choked river, mosquitoes, flies, fever, and insects of every variety imaginable, and some unimaginable, that would bite, sting or suck the life out of a man? The blood-curdling howl of the cannibal. The thorns and sharp stones. The petrified lava flows that lacerate the feet. A land both waterless and waterlogged. I have passed through it, and now have no fear of hell.

I should commence with my reason for making this mad expedition. I could say it was simply to satisfy my childhood dreams of hunting lion, rhino and elephant, and the desire to gaze on a lake in Africa that few white men have ever seen, or will ever see. Or I could say that my journey was driven by the desire to honour Her Majesty's imperial wishes — for the glory of Empire. But will such simple reimbursements balance all that wretched torment? To confess the truth, that it was an obsession — a motivation of the heart — that drove me to conquer Africa would be equally unbelievable by some. But what mortal man could endure such privations without a higher motivation? It was the pursuit of one woman's love — a woman whose promise, more than any other driving desire, inspired my quest. Oh, how I wish these next weeks would fly so that I might once again sweep her into my arms and kiss those gentle lips.

Home. How long has it been? But I know the answer exactly. It is two years less two weeks. There was not a day that I did not count the hours — even in the depths of the fever when I would drift in and out of that hell of fire and pain.

Now I sit with full belly and full pipe, scarcely believing I have made this miraculous transition from near starvation and endless discomfort. How many civilised men realise what immeasurable pleasure there is to be had from fresh bread, cool beer, clean linen, a crisp copy of The Times? And what of friendly conversation, laughter, and a healthy debate about Irish Home Rule? I am like a condemned man given a reprieve, and see the world as I have never seen it before.

I can scarcely believe that after all these many solitary months, when my only companionship was illiterate natives, I can still enjoy isolation. The days have been full since arriving here, so it was with some relief that I accepted the Commissioner's offer of this room, allowing me time to rest before I attend yet another celebratory dinner before we finally sail for home.

Looking at my battered journals, I wonder how I should begin. From Cape to Cairo: an improbable dream to the few who knew my plans at the outset. The less polite would say — if not to me, then to any other who would listen — it was a fool's mission; a death march. But I have always known that the will of a determined Englishman could defeat any mere adversity, or the sum of such adversities, placed in his path.

Perhaps I should write chronologically, the better for my readers to grasp the time it took to complete the task. I could start in Cape Town with Rhodes' call to arms to put down the impudent Matabele insurgents; the journey north as one of his scouts, fighting through impi ambushes; the arrival at Bulawayo, fever-racked and near death. But no, the real journey begins on the iridescent Indian Ocean, up the Shiré River to Chiromo. Steaming up beautiful Lake Nyasa, where small black children play among the ruins of Arab slave dhows, little knowing what atrocities were committed in the name of commerce on those sinister ships. The dark heart. The uncharted wilderness where my men disappeared as if by magic. The landscapes of smoking volcanoes, of jagged, petrified lava, of literally impenetrable jungle, of sinister forces of men and miseries endured. And towards the end, where we descended into hell — an unimaginable horror. The lakes, the rivers. The swamps. The unpredictable hippo, able to break a man in two with the power of its massive jaws. The shadowy crocodile. The interminable mosquitoes — all so vividly etched in my mind.

Or instead, I could write about the sport, the people, the potentates, the terrain. And the adventures, comic and tragic.

There is time to begin it, if not to finish, for the ship leaves Cairo tomorrow for home — to where my heart is. To my darling Gertrude.

PART 2

CHAPTER 27

1906

The locomotive clanked and jerked down the long Nairobi platform, engulfing the vendors, touts and merchants in a cloud of billowing steam until, with a shriek of metal and a long sigh, it came to a stuttering halt. An air of expectation fell over the train, silent in that instant, except for the ticking of cooling steel. Then a passenger compartment door opened, followed by another, and the entire mass on the crowded platform advanced in a boisterous surge.

A tall man in a linen suit swung open a first-class carriage door, and paused a moment to regard the bustle of activity with satisfaction. It reminded him of San Francisco years ago, when he'd arrived there at the end of a long sea journey during which he met his wife. The air even smelt like California: dry, hot and hinting of oriental spice, rotting vegetation and wood smoke.

Now that passengers were alighting onto the platform, the activity became frenetic. New arrivals, alone or appearing a little uncertain, were easily spotted and a small coterie of eager would-be helpers quickly gathered around, entreating them to choose them above all others. It was their guesthouse, their horse and cart, or their offering of the very best plots in the town, the White Highlands and all points in between. For the man in first class it had been a long journey, beginning with a sea voyage from Cape Town and broken only by a brief sojourn in Mombasa, which was neither refreshing nor enjoyable because of the intolerable heat and humidity. He filled his lungs, appreciating how Nairobi's high altitude managed to thin and cool the air while the strength of the sun left him in no doubt that the town was in the tropics.

He stepped down from the carriage, brushed back the slightly tawny fair hair that fell across his forehead and captured it under his wide-brimmed hat, giving it a pat to settle it. The throng did not immediately inundate him, although a few vendors pressed closer, regarding him with acute interest. Perhaps it was his expression, which, regardless of the faintly affable smile that played on his lips, left them in no doubt that he was a man who would not be cajoled into a hasty purchase. No, it was the eyes. Those nearest him were enthralled by their brightness; there was an indefinable element to their colour. In one light they were the ice blue of the morning sky before the sun could warm it, but in another instant they were tinged with a yellow-green flare that added fire. They were the eyes of a lion — eyes that had the power to immobilise a man, absorb him and, only with luck, to mercifully release him.

He was searching for someone, this man with the eyes, but he was not at all concerned when the person could not be found. Instead, he reached a hand into the carriage to assist a lady to the platform.

She alighted, brushing at the persistent red dust of the Taru that still clung to her dark blue ankle-length dress. Her white hat with a matching blue netting sat at a jaunty angle. She seemed a little mundane to be part of the fire-eyed man's world; not pretty in the way that young girls can be pretty, with pert noses and smiling eyes and full lips, but not plain either. She was what people in English drawing rooms might politely describe as 'fine-looking'. Then she smiled with delight at the carnival on the station platform, and she was transformed. Her eyes sparkled, her cheeks rounded, softening the rather sharp line of her chin and nose, and her complexion warmed to a most flattering pink. Even the wisps of auburn hair that escaped her hat now seemed to elegantly frame her face.

Her appearance on the platform was a signal for the vendors to finally abandon caution and converge upon the couple.

'Mr Grogan?' A voice came forcefully over the heads of the crowd. 'Mr Grogan ... is that you?' A man in a black bowler hat and fawn jacket fought against the throng converging towards the platform gate.

'Over here!' Grogan replied, waving.

The man in the bowler shouldered his way towards the couple and offered his hand. 'Charles Ringer,' he said with a broad smile.

'Ewart Grogan,' the man in first class replied, giving the hand an energetic shake. 'So good of you to come yourself, Major.'

'Not at all. Delighted to meet you, sir.'

'May I present my wife, Gertrude? Darling, this is Major Ringer of the Norfolk Hotel.'

'Charmed, ma'am,' the major said, inclining his head and adding a ceremonial click of his heels.

Gertrude offered her hand, which he took between fingers and thumb.

'Pleased to meet you, Major. I understand your hotel is — what did it say? — the most prestigious accommodation north of Dar es Salaam?'

'I'm flattered that you have been reading our promotional literature, ma'am, and I can assure you it is absolutely true. As you will soon see, ours is the only stone hotel in town. Thirty-eight rooms and two suites for married couples — one of which is reserved for yourselves. The roof is completely of tile construction. Hot and cold running water. A French chef. I'm sure your stay with us will be pleasant.'

'I'm sure it will, Major.' Gertrude smiled.

'No need to oversell it, Major,' Grogan said, patting him on the shoulder. 'We've already paid our deposit.'

'Indeed you have. Then let me take you there without further ado.' Ringer pointed to a gate at the side of the platform. 'We'll take this exit. As you can see, it's a bit of a dog fight over there.' The main exit was jammed with passengers, their luggage and the press of locals. The major waved to the porters to gather the

Grogans' luggage, then 'Follow me, please,' he said, leading the way.

The crowd that had escaped the platform now filled the quadrangle at the rear of the station building. Here was assembled a motley array of wheeled vehicles: rickshaws, dog-carts, mule buggies, carriages, wagons with bullock spans, landaus, gigs. And there were men mounted on horses and donkeys.

'Morning, Ali,' Ringer said to a man in breeches and knee-high gaiters. The man touched his hat with the heel of a long riding whip.

'Ali Khan,' Ringer said in explanation to Grogan. 'Owns most of the transport around here. Got his start by driving a herd of horses all the way from the Benadir Coast. If you need anything, from a trap to a twelve-span ox wagon, Ali's your man. His stables are in Market Street.' The major pointed towards a scattering of sheds and low timber buildings.

The reception crowd spread out from the station like a multi-coloured fan. At the centre, nearest the platform, were the white businessmen, mainly in dark suits and hats. Forming an inner circle were the Asian artisans and traders — the tailors, food vendors and general merchants. This group favoured flowing white *kanzus*, and colourful *kikois*. There was the occasional turban-clad Sikh in a pin-striped business shirt and waistcoat over a pair of voluminous white cotton breeches. The outer circle was composed predominantly of blacks. Rickshaw boys, servants awaiting their masters' orders, and curious tribesmen, in town for no other purpose than to witness the twice-weekly arrival of the train and the strange assortment of *wazungu* who came with it to their land.

'We didn't actually get into specifics in our correspondence, Mr Grogan,' Ringer said. 'What is it, exactly, that you are looking for in British East Africa?'

'All in good time, Major. I'm sure my wife will appreciate a touch of shade and perhaps a cup of tea before we get into all that.'

'Of course. Inconsiderate of me. It's just ... curiosity, I suppose. Your reputation precedes you. Ah ... here we are.' He stopped at the side of a buggy where a small black boy stood in attendance beside the mule.

Ringer waited for his guests to be seated before saying that the boy would take them to the hotel and that he would follow in another cart with their baggage. The boy leapt onto a high-perched seat and, without a backward glance, gave the mule a flick with the reins. The buggy jerked forward and Gertrude gave a giggle as they were thrown back into the seat. They rolled out of the congested quadrangle onto a rutted dirt track grandly signposted Government Road. It was generously wide, with buildings of many shapes and sizes lining its length.

The first substantial building they passed was a freshly painted timber construction with the sign 'Joseph and Sons — General Merchants' fixed above the corrugated iron veranda. It had a pair of large glass display windows on either side of a glass-panelled double door. 'Tailoring for both Ladies and Gents' said a sign painted on one window. 'Boots, Groceries and Soft Goods' said another on the opposite side. The proprietor, either Joseph or his son, leaned in the doorway, arms folded, eyeing the passing traffic.

Through a gap in the line of buildings Grogan caught a glimpse of lurid purple and orange stands sprawling on the far side of a low-lying stand of papyrus — a market of some sorts.

A cluster of small, decrepit *dukas* — the ubiquitous Indian trade stores — followed a row of more substantial stores on Government Road. In the front of one was a pair of mewing lion cubs, tethered to a post. Following the *dukas* was an impressive double-storey stone building bearing the signage: 'Elwood Dobie — Watchmaker & Jeweller'. Written by hand on a wall panel at street level was: 'Special — Lion Claw Hat Pins', and below it: 'Elephant Hair Bracelets'.

The tantalising aroma of roasting coffee wafted to them from a shop declaring: 'T A (Tommy) Woods — Coffee'. Mr Woods stood at his shop door, and nodded to the Grogans as the mule buggy passed.

Corrugated iron was the predominant building material, particularly for the older, smaller buildings, while weatherboards, and the occasional brick or stone establishment comprised the remainder. It was not surprising, therefore, to find that 'The Machine Metal Works — S Medicks', occupied the biggest premises on Government Road. 'Ridging, curved corrugated iron, baths, tanks, guttering and pipes', a sign said, adding in another: 'Two Curving Machines — not a hair's breadth deviation from the line of curve'.

There were other, lesser, roads leading from Government Road to smaller tracks, but these were sparsely lined with storerooms, and residences built of rough-hewn timber, many with simple thatched roofs.

About a quarter of a mile from the station, the buildings of Government Road thinned and weed-covered vacant plots began to appear. All carried details of the vendor's agent. Among the many Asian names, Ewart made a note of the name R O Preston on one of them.

The road became more of a track, which made a long curve towards a red-roofed building at its apparent end. 'The Norfolk' was proudly displayed on the gable above a wide veranda. Around the veranda ran a white balustrade with criss-crossed timber struts beneath the handrail. A white picket fence completed the image of a well-groomed establishment. Behind the Norfolk rose lightly wooded hills, and further into the distance was a dense forest.

The boy drew the buggy to a halt at the foot of the stairs, and a doorman wearing a spotless white *kanzu* and red fez trotted down to help Grogan and Gertrude from the buggy.

'Morning, *sahib, memsahib*.' His smile illuminated his black face. 'Welcome to the Norfolk,' he said, bowing, his arm sweeping towards the steps to the veranda. 'Please.' He put out a hand to assist Gertrude.

Just then Ringer arrived. He stepped from the cart, leaving the doorman to arrange the disposal of the luggage, and led the couple into the cool, dark interior.

The dining room was not large, but elegantly decorated and furnished. A long narrow mahogany table lined with straight-backed chairs ran the length of the room. Ringer caught Grogan's eyes resting on a large hole smashed through one wall under a painting of a fox hunt.

'Oh, ah, yes ... we have a little maintenance to do following the Turf Club meeting last week.'

Grogan raised his eyebrows a touch.

The major continued, smiling a little uncomfortably. 'We managed to get the filth out of the carpet — horses can be such messy animals — but I'm afraid the other William IV chair is done for.' He nodded to a single elaborate chair beside a mahogany coffee table.

'What happened?' Gertrude asked innocently. Grogan had been trying to frame the same question more diplomatically.

'Oh, didn't I mention it was a meeting of the Turf Club?'

'Yes, you did, but ...'

'Turf Club, Colonists Club. It doesn't seem to matter.' Ringer examined a mark on the dining table, licked his finger and dabbed at it, then whipped out a white handkerchief and polished the spot. 'They sometimes get a little playful after the evening's business is done, or sometimes a dispute becomes a little heated and ... well.' He realised he had been mindlessly airing problems best kept from the guests. 'Not that it will be a worry for you,' he said, trying to sound reassuring. 'It's all in hand now. So ...' he hurried on, 'let's go onto the terrace and we can have some drinks and discuss your schedule.'

Grogan glanced at Gertrude before saying, 'Drinks would be wonderful, but I wonder if we could trouble you to have them sent to our suite? Mrs Grogan would like to freshen up before we do anything else.'

'Most certainly, Mr Grogan. I'll have Mwindi prepare them for you. What would you like, Mrs Grogan?'

'I'd like an iced tea, if you don't mind.'

'Certainly. And Mr Grogan?'

'Make that two iced teas, and two gin and tonics.'

'Hmm, eau de Taru Desert ... my favourite perfume.'

'Ewart, stop,' she giggled, playfully pushing him away from where he was nuzzling her neck. 'The steward will be here in a moment with our drinks.'

'How do you expect me to wait a moment longer? It's been four days!'

'It's been two and you know it. Naughty boy.' She straightened her skirt which he had pulled out of shape. 'Now just be patient, I want a nice relaxing bath.'

'Two days? Are you sure?' He removed his hat from the bed and hung it on the stand by the door.

'Yes, only two, although I swear I thought I was going to die in that heat.'

They had been a week on the ship from Cape Town. In Mombasa, Ewart could barely wait until she had gained her land-legs before he was caressing her and tickling her nipples. She could never resist him for long, even when suffering the after-effects of seasickness.

'That won't be a problem here in Nairobi, my darling. Hot days, stimulating cool nights.' He parted the curtains and opened the window to the garden. 'Can't you just taste the freshness of the air?'

'I will when I get this dust off me. He did say they had hot water, didn't he?'

'Yes. Will I run the bath for you?'

'Yes, please.' She lifted one of the ports onto the bed.

'Gertie ... you should let me do that for you.'

'You forget, Ewart, I was expected to do my share on the farm.'

'Well, you're not in California now. And I'm sure your stepfather wouldn't have had you lumping oranges, if that's the term.'

'You lump hay bales, but never mind, it's done. I only want a fresh set of clothes.'

He was beside her at the bed. 'I like you best in no clothes.' His hand went around her waist and inched to her breast.

There was a discreet knock on the door.

Ewart took the tray from the steward and thanked him. 'Your tea, my darling,' he said, handing her the gin and tonic.

'To us and our new life in Africa,' she said, holding her glass aloft.

'To us and our future fortune,' he said, clinking her glass with his own.

*　*　*

The sign boldly said: 'The Exchange (Nairobi)'. *Rather grand*, thought Grogan, as he approached the desk where a man of about forty, with a pencil-thin moustache and a rather severe parting in his hair, sat on a high stool, papers strewn in front of him.

He regarded Grogan in silence as he approached. One eye was narrowed into a squint as if he was peering into sunlight. At best, his expression could be described as analytical. He waited for Grogan to speak.

'Mr Preston?' Grogan enquired.

'Mr Grogan.' The handshake was firm and friendly, belying Grogan's impression of hostility.

'How do you know me?' Grogan asked with a guarded smile.

'You arrived on yesterday's train.'

Grogan remained silent.

Preston smiled. 'It's not a conspiracy, Mr Grogan. Nor have I been spying on you. I heard you came first class. You see, I still have some friends on the railway. And from the look of that fine suit, well, I thought this is surely our new well-to-do man in town. If you'll pardon my audacity.'

'Nice deduction, Mr Preston,' Grogan said, finding the man's confrontational humour a little odd for one in the real estate business. 'So, on that score, there's no need for me to tell you why I'm here?'

'Not quite,' Preston said. 'But I'll warrant it's about land.'

'You disappoint me. Your hoarding would suggest that — an estate and house agent, it says. "A man with nearly ten years experience in British East Africa". To retain your reputation as a mind-reader I'm afraid you'll have to do better.'

'Well, you might have also entered to buy a rifle or ammunition,' Preston said, pointing to the glass display cabinet where a number of firearms were exhibited. 'Or a cricket bat or tennis racquet.' He indicated more shelves on the opposite side of the room. 'A strong young fellow like yourself could certainly be a sportsman.'

'Point taken. And you were correct in the first place. I am interested in property, so ... shall we get down to business?'

'Certainly.' Preston pointed to a couple of chairs beside the firearms display and joined him there.

Grogan took out a slim pack of cigars and offered Preston one. As he lit it, he said, 'Before we go into details, Mr Preston, perhaps you wouldn't mind telling me about your experience as an agent.'

'I only got started late last year. Been doing a bit of this, a bit of that, beforehand.'

'Then how do you claim to be — what does your sign say? — "the best agent in Nairobi"?'

'Any fool can sell real estate, Mr Grogan. It's knowing the land, the condition of the terrain, the weather, the mood of the local tribes, that will decide if an up-country property really suits you. And in Nairobi, it's knowing who owns what and whether he can be trusted.'

Grogan gave it some thought. He liked Preston's direct manner of speaking. 'If that's the case, where did you get all this knowledge?'

'If you're like everyone else, you will be looking for land somewhere along the railway. The so-called White Highlands, perhaps. The Administration is keen to sell. They need settlers — thousands of them — to make the railway pay. I know every inch of that country. I've tramped over everything within fifty miles of it. There're few who know BEA like me — of that you can be sure.'

'And how is it that you know it so well?'

'I built the railway line — me and seven thousand coolies. There's not a rail, tie or key laid that I didn't supervise. Every last mile of it, from Mombasa to Kisumu.'

Grogan nodded, impressed. 'And how much of this land is yours to broker?'

'Not much. You're looking at a railway engineer, Mr Grogan, not a landowner, although I have a few plots here in Nairobi, some with houses I built myself.' He paused to take a puff, and studied his cigar. 'But I'll help you find the type of land you're seeking, be it for farming, forestry or speculation, and arrange an introduction to the vendor — for a small consideration if you are satisfied. If you aren't, there's no charge. I hope you'll agree that's fair.'

'Hmm, yes, fair enough, Mr Preston. Very fair. Shall we proceed on that basis?'

'As you wish.' Preston went to his desk and retrieved a dog-eared notebook from a pile of papers. 'Now ... what is it you're after?'

'I want a town plot here in Nairobi. A good site for commercial premises. I don't want it anywhere near that bazaar with a stink you can smell for a mile.'

Preston jotted down a note and nodded. 'You've a good eye for business, Mr Grogan. This town is going to grow. And fast.'

'I'll need about ten or twenty acres.'

Preston's eyes widened before returning to his pad. 'Ten or twenty acres,' he said to himself as he wrote.

'I'm also interested in a few hundred acres of farmland. Close enough to Nairobi to keep an eye on.'

'There's been a couple trying farming out Fort Hall way. Rubber, cotton, rice. Charlie Bonser was doing all right for a while, but a couple of years ago he got washed out. The rains came and took the crop straight out of the soil.'

'I'm thinking of trying my hand at coffee.'

'Coffee ... There're a few acres of coffee out Kabete way. Seems to do all right.'

'Kabete, you say? How far is that?'

'About two hours' ride.'

'See what you can find.'

Grogan leaned back in the chair and let a stream of cigar smoke escape as he reconsidered his tactics. He had planned to use someone like Preston to find his smaller interests in and around Nairobi, but for the larger holdings he felt he would need to talk directly with the Administration. After an unprofessional, almost bumbling beginning, Preston had impressed him. He was the antithesis of the government bureaucrats that Grogan would be forced to deal with at some stage during the negotiations for his forest concession. He had such a natural antipathy towards the typical sanctimonious pen-pushers in government that he decided to progress as far as he could without them.

'Mr Preston,' he said.

Preston lifted his head from his notes.

'You would have seen plenty of forests in your travels, would you not?'

'Forests? As a railhead engineer, I saw more trees than I cared to.'

'Are you familiar then with cedar forests?'

'I am, sir. My men cleared thousands above the Great Rift Valley.'

'I see.' Grogan stubbed out his cigar. 'Then do you think you can direct me to those forests?'

'Aye. Is it forest land you're after now?'

'Yes. Something like a hundred thousand acres would do.'

CHAPTER 28

The dog's enormous tongue lolled from the side of his drooling mouth in what he might have thought was a beguilingly ironic smile. His barrel chest heaved from the exertion of the chase and, as the girl shook her head in feigned disapproval, he had the decency to avert his eyes for a moment to make a disgusting slobbering swallow before the mottled pink and black tongue reappeared, dropping globs of froth to the baked earth where they made large rust-red spots.

'Honestly, Wonder,' Jessie said with resignation in her voice. 'I don't know why you bother.' Jessie Dalton was a willowy fifteen-year-old, with long fair hair, and olive skin that reminded her father, Bruce, of his deceased wife. 'You'll never catch warthogs in this type of country.' She waved a hand, encompassing the knee-high grass undulating to a distant hill beyond which the massive shape of the Aberdare Ranges rose like a blue-green dream. 'And that's good luck for you — that old man warthog is just too big for you.'

The girl favoured patched overalls and checked shirts, as did her father, and it was fortunate she did — there was no money for girl's clothes, apart from the one printed cotton dress she wore to occasional social outings in town with her father, or to church, which was seldom. But that suited her. She had no use for skirts that only got tangled when taking her seat on her bay pony.

Jessie dropped to her knees and gave the dog a hug. 'You mustn't try to fight everything that comes near our farm. Do you understand that, Wonder?' she said with her cheek against his neck, feeling the powerful beat of his heart in her ear. 'Don't you remember the hyena? Nearly killed you, you silly boy.'

She put a finger on the dark grey scar that showed through the bald patch on his side. Wonder's flank rippled at her touch.

'You're getting too old to go after everything that moves.'

He gave her an impulsive wet lick to show there were no hard feelings.

Jessie had never known a time when Wonder was not around. With no other child within a half-hour's ride of the farm, her earliest memories were of Wonder — her playmate, her guardian, her confidant. Her brother. She loved him with the fervour of a child alone in an adult world for the first seven years of her life. Only after Momposhe came to Londiani did she find another human being to call a friend.

Only a person who had known the dog for a lifetime could love such an ugly creature. He was big, decidedly shabby, with a ghastly orange coat, and had incorrigible bad manners, like passing wind when in the presence of visitors he disapproved of, and dropping mauled, lifeless snakes on the veranda when the mood took him.

Wonder was an indeterminate age, and Jessie just three years old, when he arrived at the farm shortly after the Daltons did. Bruce Dalton had tried to send the dog on his way back then in 1894, not because he didn't need the company — he was a widower — but because he didn't trust an animal with such a fierce countenance around his little daughter. But the dog simply refused to leave the farm — or, more particularly, the little girl. He would conceal himself whenever Bruce or Bernase were close at hand, but always remained within sight of Jessie. There were many occasions when, to their horror, they would find him sitting alert and on guard beside the child, his disgusting pink and black tongue dripping drool onto the child's pillow. In time Dalton was obliged to accept the dog's insistent presence as a matter of fact. He would not admit it to

Jessie, but she knew that eventually, and begrudgingly, he began to admire the animal's unrelenting individuality.

Jessie stood and checked the sun. A breeze came up with a hint of the chill that could quickly fall over the highlands as soon as the sun set. She was at the furthest part of her father's land, near the rising *kopje*. It was said the stones had some significance for the Maasai, who used to graze this land years before her father was granted a lease. The old-timers of the district said the local Maasai would visit the *kopje* at various times and practise their magical ceremonies.

It reminded her of Momposhe, and she remembered she hadn't sent him a message in days. Leaning her rifle against a rock, she cupped her hands, and forming an aperture between her thumbs, blew across them to make a musical note. She repeated this several times, then whispered her message to the wind: 'Momposhe, come home. Come home.'

The bush telegraph, she called it, and it was her and Momposhe's secret — a secret method of communicating over great distances that he had taught her years before. Now he disavowed any belief in it, saying it was the game of children, but Jessie still swore by it.

'Well, let's see if it works this time, Wonder,' she said.

The dog cocked his ears and stood to attention as she slung her rifle across her back.

Jessie laughed at him. 'Come on boy. It's getting late,' she said, bending to ruffle Wonder's tattered ears. 'Let's get back before Bernase thinks I'm lost again.' She put her foot into the stirrup iron and swung easily up into the saddle.

Jessie had done the hunting for the pot for as long as she could shoulder a rifle. Initially she'd accompanied her father, but as the work of the failing farm demanded more of his time, he was forced to allow his daughter to carry on alone. But her hunting forays had returned slim pickings during the last week. The short rains had arrived, allowing the game herds to disperse into the new native grass pastures far from the farm waterholes that had kept them in close attendance during the long dry spell. The warthog had been her one real chance for meat, but Wonder's impetuous belligerence had forced her to drop her aim, losing the shot. The ugly old boar was probably too tough anyway, she thought resignedly. And it would have been too heavy to hoist into the saddle. She glanced back at the dog and smiled. Wonder loped behind, his grotesque tongue lolling from the corner of his mouth, the almost deadly encounter with the warthog boar now forgotten.

As she came within sight of the farmhouse she saw a familiar figure standing in the yard waiting for her.

'It worked! The bush telegraph worked! C'mon Wonder,' she yelped, and kicked the bay into action. 'It's Momposhe!' The pony leapt forward and Jessie's long fair hair streamed behind her as they galloped over the short grass.

She reined the bay in and swung down from its back. Momposhe's second-hand navy blue suit was tighter across the shoulders and shorter in the leg than she remembered it being when he went off to the Mission College in Mombasa. Western clothes never really suited him as much as the elegant, red knee-length *shuka* of the Maasai that he wore draped so rakishly from a shoulder. With his arms crossed, leaning against the fencepost, he seemed somehow more confident, more grown-up. But it was still Momposhe.

She strode across the yard to him, grinning. She hesitated a moment, looking up at the young black man who remained leaning against the fencepost, then, despite his teasing indifference, she flung her arms around his neck and gave him a hug.

Laughing, he eventually prised himself from her embrace. 'Look at you,' he said, running his eyes from her scuffed farm boots to her frayed overalls and finally arriving at her floppy-brimmed felt hat. 'Still an *enkiti*.'

She pouted and threw a half-hearted slap at his arm. 'I'm *not* a little girl. I'm fifteen already!'

'Well, well, and a real lady also, I see.' He was smiling, but was a little more reserved than she remembered him. It seemed that each time he went away he came back a little different.

She grabbed his hand and led him to the log under the pepper tree that was used for a seat. 'Sit,' she commanded playfully, dragging him down on the log beside her, and studied him until he turned his face away, uncomfortable with her intense scrutiny.

'Now, Momposhe, you'll tell me everything,' she said. 'What have you been doing? Have you got a girlfriend? How's school? What are you going to do now?'

'Well, for one thing, I'm not Momposhe any more.'

'You're not?'

'No, I've decided to change my name.'

'Why?'

'Because it's not fitting. If I'm going to become a lawyer, I can't be Momposhe. No. I must be known as Marcus.'

'Marcus?'

'Yes. Marcus is a lawyer's name.'

'It sounds very British.'

'British is good,' he added with conviction.

'So you'll be Marcus Ole Matipe?'

It seemed he hadn't considered the whole name, and after a pause to think about it he said, 'Yes, Marcus Ole Matipe.'

'Hmm . . . It sounds rather nice, but what about your father? What will old Marefu say?'

He was silent for a moment. 'My father will understand.'

Wonder swaggered up, panting, and flopped in the dust at Jessie's feet. He let his muzzle drop to his paws and released a loud nostril sigh, sending a puff of dust into the air.

'The ugly one is still at your side,' Marcus said, smiling at the dog. He knew better than to attempt to touch him.

'He will be so proud, Momposhe, I mean Marcus.'

'Who will?'

'Your father. The first Maasai lawyer in the whole world.'

'Don't be silly, *Enkiti*,' he said. 'I have a long way to go.'

But she could see he was pleased.

'What about you?' he asked. 'Have you decided what you want to be?'

'A hunter.'

He shook his head in disapproval. 'Still thinking like a child.'

His condescension was beginning to annoy her. 'And what's wrong with being a hunter?' she asked indignantly.

'Nothing, if you are a man.'

'Being a man has nothing to do with it. I can stalk, I can shoot.'

'A few gazelle here and there.'

'I bagged an eland a few weeks ago.'

'A big gazelle.'

She didn't want to defend herself with the truth — that her father forbade her hunting anything other than table meat.

Wonder lifted himself from his repose and pricked his ears. The hackles on his back rose, and before Jessie could speak or make a move to stop him, he had bolted towards the house *shamba*, a guttural growl emanating from deep in his chest. He charged through a gap in the fence rails, knocking one loose with the bulk of his shoulders.

'Still ugly and still senseless,' Marcus said, shaking his head.

Was there nothing that Mr Smarty-Pants-Marcus-the-Lawyer approved of? 'It's probably the baboons in Papa's tomato patch again,' she said, more annoyed with Marcus than the dog.

'One day that old man baboon will stand against him, then just watch out,' he said.

Jessie preferred not to dwell on it. 'What will you do now?' she asked, looking down at his hand beside hers on the log, and noticing again the contrast in their skin colours. When she was a child she was fascinated by his warm brown skin that simply shone when he raised a sweat. And his eyes — they twinkled like black pools. She thought he was the most exotic creature in the world, and would slyly follow him around the farm, watching him work beside his father in the *shamba* weeding the spinach and the potatoes, or in the yard shucking maize cobs.

'Now? Now I must pay my respects to your father.'

'I mean, what will you do these next few weeks before returning to school?'

'I know what you mean, *Enkiti*, but it is not for me to say. Your father has already been too kind sending me to college. I will do what he asks.'

He stood and headed towards the *banda* where Bruce Dalton would be penning the calves before the chill of the evening descended. She watched him go, walking tall and straight. His

long arms swung easily by his side in a slow-motion lope —
what Jessie privately called his *morani* walk.

Marcus had changed. He seemed to have acquired a sense of
place, of knowing where he was in his world and in his life. It
could be said that he had learned to be proud, but that would
imply that it displaced the wonderful kindness and sensitivity he
always showed towards any other — man or beast — that
crossed his path. It was an unassuming pride, more of an
awareness of who Momposhe, or Marcus Ole Matipe, really
was.

Jessie sighed. Momposhe — Marcus — was no longer the
slim bean-pole of a Maasai boy who had turned her world
upside-down when he arrived, years ago, with his stories of
warriors' wars and Maasai magic. Being seven years older than
she, he had not joined in her childish games, but had taken her
to another world, where Maasai legends and heroic characters
dominated their days. In the last two years, it seemed he had
become a man — not a Maasai man, but a man like any other
in Londiani or Nakuru. She wondered where the Maasai in him
went.

Bruce Dalton sat on the veranda, which faced west into the
setting sun. A mist was rising in the cooler air of late afternoon,
guiding golden shafts of light into the long shadows in the
valley. But he wasn't watching the setting sun in all its glorious
wet-season colour. He was whittling a piece of camphor —
whittling without any plans to make something useful from it,
but simply as a means to expel his frustrations.

Dalton was annoyed because he had two things on his mind.
Two important things. Both of them concerned Momposhe, and
when he raised them, as he must, they would make the young
man feel estranged and cheated. To make matters worse,
Momposhe had done nothing wrong; he could not be blamed
for the situation Dalton now found himself in.

The camphor was whittled almost to a nub. He threw it away
and snatched up another piece. No, he had to admit, both
blunders were entirely of his making — a combination of
misguided generosity and neglect of his duty as a father.

Dalton had never considered himself to be sentimental or overly generous, so it was out of character for him to continue to pay for Momposhe's education. He'd always had a deep respect for what he termed 'the learning'. His own formal education had been limited, but as he progressed through life he had picked up knowledge as if it were treasure.

Jessie showed no interest in furthering her education. Everyone he knew said it was a waste of time and money anyway; girls needed to know how to sew, how to cook and how to raise babies. Anything else was superfluous. Dalton would have encouraged her if the desire was there, but it wasn't.

The problem with the promise to Marefu was the question of where an education ended. Primary school was not an issue, but for some reason Dalton had carried the responsibility into college education, and the costs were becoming a concern. With the farm struggling to survive the lean years, and hardly thriving in the rare good year, the truth was he really couldn't afford even the modest fees the Mission College in Mombasa charged. On some chilly Londiani nights, when sleep eluded him and — like a dripping tap — the yip of jackals and the whooping snigger of hyenas kept him awake, he would try to answer the question of why he paid school fees long after the point where any reasonably minded person would say he had done enough. Ultimately, he would be forced to admit he liked the boy — had liked him since he came in looking like a half-starved cattle dog at his father's side, with inquisitive, intelligent eyes as large as saucers. Yes, Dalton liked the Maasai boy, and secretly delighted in the almost reverential respect he paid him in gratitude for his kindness. And Dalton also had to admit he perhaps saw in Momposhe the son he would never have.

It was at times like these that he really needed his dear wife, Marie, beside him. He sighed. It was true that Marie could have given him the moral courage, but only he, Dalton, could speak of it with Momposhe, because it was he who had raised Momposhe's sights to what could be achieved by an education. But the farm was in a parlous state. The bank was becoming impatient. He might be forced to take Momposhe out of college.

If anything, the second problem was even more difficult for him.

Jessie was his baby, his cherished daughter, and Momposhe was a healthy young man. Jessie was becoming of an age where Dalton knew she would soon be taking an interest in boys. The pair had been innocent childhood friends since Momposhe and Marefu had arrived at the farm. Indeed, he had no reason to suspect it was now otherwise, but Jessie had grown quickly in the last year or so and was now beginning to look like a young woman. God only knew what schemes might blossom in that pretty head, and her infatuation with Momposhe was obvious. Dalton had that afternoon seen her galloping across the home paddock to rush to Momposhe's arms.

Yes, if Marie were alive she could certainly help in tackling such delicate topics. Dalton knew he was not good at that kind of thing at all. But, as always, he would do what must be done.

'Sit, sit.' Bruce Dalton indicated the best of the other three chairs in the part of their simple dwelling that resembled a sitting room. Marcus perched on the rickety chair's edge, not quite able to trust his weight against its back.

'So it's Marcus now, eh?' Dalton said, testing the name for the first time. He tamped tobacco into the bowl of his pipe and lit it. It was not uncommon for the natives to adopt Christian-sounding names for their children, but it was unusual for one to make the change himself. He decided to let it go. There were more important matters to raise — matters that had prompted him to ask Marcus to come into the house in the first place.

Dalton puffed the pipe into life and watched as the blue smoke wafted towards the ceiling. He was stalling, trying to find the words. He didn't have much time. Jessie would soon return from the errand he had invented to get her out of the house. It wouldn't be fair to Marcus to have her present while he discussed personal matters with him. He decided to tackle the other matter, about Jessie, first. He straightened in his chair and put the pipe on the table in front of him. 'Jessie,' he began, then realised he had nowhere to go with such a sentence opening.

'Yes?' Marcus said, smiling a little uncertainly.

'She's, you know, grown. Don't you think?'

'Hmm,' Marcus answered noncommittally.

The reply made Dalton nervous, and he picked up his pipe again. 'You've been friends a long time, you two,' he began, trying another tack.

'Yes.' Marcus paused, perhaps sensing that something more was expected from him. 'Since I was quite young,' he added.

'Exactly.' Dalton nodded. 'And I see that the two of you are still teasing and play-fighting when you meet.'

'Yes, it is embarrassing.'

'It is?' It was not the reaction Dalton had expected.

'She is such a child,' Marcus said, shaking his head. 'You know —' He stopped abruptly, dropping his eyes to his hands. 'I'm sorry, Mr Bruce, it is not for me to speak so about your daughter.'

'No, you can ... I mean, it's just that I thought you agreed with me that she was growing up?'

'I cannot disagree with my father.' It was a term of respect he often used when referring to Dalton. 'But I also must be truthful when you ask. She is my sister, and I worry about her.'

'And why is that ... exactly?'

'Well ...' The young man hesitated.

'Yes, go on.'

Marcus sighed, trying to gather his thoughts. 'She is such a child. She says she wants to be a hunter when she is grown. She has no idea of the importance of education.'

'Well, Marcus ... an education ... I mean, not everyone can have a good education.'

'But you have told me since I was a child that to complete an education is the most important thing for anyone, man or woman, black or white.'

'Well, yes ... that's so. But not for everyone.' Here was his opportunity. He could raise any one of the reasons he had constructed to ease Marcus's disappointment. Such as why it was not as important for a black man to have an education as it was for whites, because a person like Marcus could learn much of what was needed for his life from his father and other

Maasai. 'Desirable, yes, if at all possible. But not essential.' He thought a less confronting example might help him into the matter. 'A woman, for example. A woman can be educated in different ways. She must learn to cook and to sew and to prepare for marriage.'

'But ... that is how the Maasai think about their women.' Marcus scratched his head. 'I thought the *wazungu* were different.'

Dalton began to get flustered. Damn, he thought. Marcus never forgot a thing. He needed another way to get his point across.

'Don't you understand, Marcus? For a woman that *is* education. It's what she was born to, and that is what she will study.'

'Will that be enough for Jessie?'

'What do you mean, *enough*?'

Again the young man dropped his eyes to his hands. 'I am sorry, Mr Bruce, I have made you angry with my stupid talk about Jessie. It is not for me to say she is childish, or that she should listen to your advice about education.'

Dalton chastised himself. He had always taught Marcus to speak his mind, and in particular not to be brow-beaten by a man because of his position or merely because he was white.

'No, I am not angry, Marcus,' he said, taking a deep breath. 'What I really wanted to raise with you was *your* education. It's been years now. I suppose you're getting tired of all that book-learning.'

Marcus's eyes widened in surprise. 'Oh, no! Not at all, Mr Bruce. I thank you so much for what you are doing. Maybe you don't understand. Without this education, I would be nothing. It will change my life!' Perhaps surprised by his own fervour, Marcus lowered his voice. 'What I mean is, you have given me a chance to be somebody. Somebody special.' His eyes were misting and glistened in the lamp light. 'I can never thank you enough.'

Dalton was taken aback. He had no idea it meant so much to him. 'I ... I'm glad you're finding it, uh, useful,' Dalton stammered, and then found himself lost for words. Marcus sat attentively waiting for him to go on, but he now found it impossible to continue. 'Thank you, Marcus. You can go now.'

'Thank you, Mr Bruce.' At the door he said, 'Good night, Mr Bruce.'

'Yes, good night, Marcus.'

As the door closed behind the young Maasai, Dalton ran a hand across his brow. The evening hadn't been a complete disaster. At least his imagined problem of Jessie and Marcus becoming romantically attached turned out to be nothing. But, the financial issue of Marcus's education had now reached another level. Having seen the fire he had kindled in Marcus, and the importance the young Maasai attached to his continuing education, how could he now tell him he could no longer support that ambition? In Marcus's eyes it would be a massive betrayal.

Dalton again ran through the imminent financial demands of the farm — they were never far from his mind. He felt he might be able to squeeze a few items in anticipation of a better year ahead. With luck, he thought he might be able to carry the school fees for another term.

Dalton shook his head resignedly. If not, he would just have to find the courage to break the young man's heart.

CHAPTER 29

Candlelight flickered as the waiters moved around the long dining table, clearing a plate or replenishing a glass. All those in the gathering were formally dressed — the dozen men wore black ties on starched collars, and the women, who numbered five fewer, were wearing what had become known as Edwardian fashion: high collars, long darted or gored skirts — some of which flared below the knee to form the 'mermaid look' — and corsets that forced their wearer's bosom forward and her posterior outward to form the alluring 'S-curve' — so prized in the pages of fashion publications.

Grogan slid back his chair and rose from the table as the men prepared to depart for the veranda. Leaning over his wife, he gave her a peck on the cheek. 'Shan't be long, my darling,' he said.

Gertrude turned to him to whisper, 'Oh, Ewart, I thought we could escape these tiresome rituals here in the tropics.'

'Not so long as the Protectorate is populated by peers of the realm, my dear.'

'Peers? Unwelcome second sons, more like it,' she said with a smile, 'sent here to avoid scandal at home.'

'It's mandatory cigars and brandy, sorry.'

'Boring.'

'Quite right, my darling. I can think of something else I would rather be doing.'

Gertrude raised her fan to hide her smile. 'Ewart, please ...' she whispered from behind it, but he had moved away from the table.

The men gathered in the so-called Sportsman's Bar and Major Ringer handed around a cigar box. Two waiters followed him with a decanter and brandy snifters. Lord Delamere joined them wearing an absurdly large pith helmet that covered his bald pate but allowed his long ginger hair to flap freely about his shoulders.

'What's that for, D?' someone asked. 'The midnight sun a bit strong for you?'

An undercurrent of mirth ran around the group.

'Habit, my good man. And a bloody good one to have. If you'd had the case of sunstroke I had years ago in Somaliland, you'd wear a hat like this too.'

When Grogan had been first introduced to Hugh Cholmondeley, the third Baron Delamere, he had assumed from the old woollen cardigan, untidy appearance and unkempt hair that Delamere was a tramp. Shorter and more solidly built than Grogan, the peer had an imposing personality, and an obsession with keeping his balding head from the sun. Grogan had heard that Delamere let his hair grow long to protect his neck and back in the same way.

'You buggers don't appreciate the deleterious effects of the tropical sun,' Delamere went on. 'Scrambles the brain. Anyway, I wanted to get my revolver.' He patted the handgun tucked into his cummerbund.

'The sun's already got to him, I'm afraid,' said Tommy Woods, a member, as was Grogan, of the Municipal Committee.

The starchy formality of the earlier part of the evening dissolved amid light-hearted chatter.

'Gentlemen,' said Captain Sanderson, the town clerk, above the babble of conversation. 'If you please.' He let it peter out before continuing. 'I didn't want to bore the ladies with business during dinner, but many of you will be interested to know of some recent developments in the Municipal Committee. Recognising the hour, and knowing that the young blades among you will probably want to have another rickshaw race down Government Road, I'll be brief.'

The noise level arose again, but Sanderson reined it in.

'It appears that the engineers and doctors who have been carping on to the Commissioner that Nairobi is unhealthy and ill-chosen and should be moved have been ignored.'

A few cheered, while others chorused 'Hear, hear!'

'This makes the subject of Tommy Woods' Municipality Ordinances Working Party all the more important. On that point I should say that the working party has a new member. You have all met Mr Ewart Grogan, I'm sure.' He raised his hand in Grogan's direction. 'Mr Grogan has recently decided to settle in Nairobi with his lovely wife, Gertrude, and he's the type that this town needs if it is to become the commercial centre we all hope it will be.'

Polite applause rippled around the group. Grogan nodded his appreciation.

'I'm sure his expertise will be of great benefit to Tommy's group,' Sanderson went on.

'Can't you stop your blathering?' Delamere's high-pitched voice intruded. 'I've a fiver to say I can out-shoot you again. Drunk or sober.'

'Steady on, D.' Sanderson held a finger up to Delamere to silence him. 'Give me a moment, will you?' Turning back to the gathering, he said, 'One more thing. Don't forget to make early bookings for the Christmas Racing Carnival Ball. We plan to make it an extra special event this year.' Then the town clerk pulled a revolver from his pocket and waved it in the direction of the bar. 'Now, your Lordship, would you prefer to start on the top or the bottom shelf tonight?'

'What was all that noise earlier tonight, Ewart?' Gertrude had a grip on the velvet back of the bedroom chair, while behind her Grogan was unlacing her corset ties. 'It sounded like we were at war.'

'In a manner of speaking we were, my dear. Lord Delamere and Captain Sanderson were doing battle with the bottles in the Sportsman's Bar.' He released the cord around the final loop. 'Ah, there you are.'

'Childish nonsense.' Gertrude sighed and rolled her shoulders, relieving the tension in her back. She so disliked the newer corsets, which were more rigid than the earlier ones. 'You boys are all alike. You should be ashamed of yourselves.'

Grogan was struggling with his tie. 'Darling, could you help me out of this blasted thing? Damn near choking me.'

'You've pulled the knot too tight,' she said. 'Let me see.'

As she prised at the neck tie, Grogan slipped his hands behind her and began to tease her camisole from the waistband of her petticoat, working his way to the front. Her skin tingled as he slipped a hand under the loose cotton garment and found her full breasts.

'Ewart, if you don't stop that, I'll never get this tie undone.'

He was rolling his thumb over one of her nipples. 'Then I'll have to ravish you fully clothed.'

Her throaty chuckle ruined her fake severity.

'I love that little laugh of yours.' She had loosened the tie and he nuzzled her neck. 'So earthy.'

She put a hand on the back of his head, and ran a fingernail down the long muscles of his neck to his collar.

His hands roamed all over her, from her breasts, down her spine, then he slipped a hand beneath her petticoats and bloomers and gripped her buttocks, pulling her towards him. She felt the bulge in the front of his trousers and her hand went there, seizing his erection through the material.

Ewart mumbled something into her hair and led her backwards to the bed, where he sat on its edge to remove the remainder of her undergarments.

Gertrude became overcome with pleasure as he planted kisses on her belly and down to the top of her thighs. She ran her fingers into his hair and gripped him there, holding her breath as his tongue slipped into the moisture of her body. She wanted him inside her, but couldn't resist the surge of pleasure his tongue gave her. Finally she forced him away and drew him across the bed towards her. She tore open his trousers, and smothered kisses on his rigid penis before climbing on top of him.

*　　*　　*

The early morning light was brilliant, bouncing from the puddles and wet grass as Grogan and Gertrude strolled from the Norfolk towards the ridge above the swamp. They had eaten an early breakfast, and Gertrude had suggested that they take a stroll as the entirely predictable afternoon rains had kept them confined indoors for the previous few days.

'Ewart,' she said, giving his arm a tug.

'Yes, my love?'

'Can we please make this a leisurely walk rather than one of your forced marches?'

'Sorry, wasn't thinking.'

'Thinking too much is more like it,' she replied. 'Whenever you've got something on your mind, you go charging about like a wild animal. I'll look a positive fright by the time we get to the tea house.'

'Not possible, you look delicious.' She was wearing an outfit he hadn't seen before, and a broad bonnet with a cocked brim. 'Ostrich farming is another venture we could look at, Gertie,' he said, reminded of it by the feathers on her hat. 'There's a few doing quite well at it down on the Athi Plains.'

'So it's business that's taking you away from me again? Well, if it's anything to do with ladies' fashion you'd better take care, Ewart. Feathers are sure to be out of favour one day. Fashion is changing every few years. Take this dress, for instance: it's by Paul Poiret — one of the new Parisian designers. Who would have thought we ladies would wear such soft pastel colours and have a waistline sitting so high?'

'Perhaps you're right, but it's taking a hell of a time to find land in the centre of town — which is my first priority. I feel like I'm standing still while everyone else is rushing by.'

'I don't think I can ever imagine you *standing still*. Your problem, my darling, is quite the reverse. You'll find something. Just be patient.'

Patience was not a virtue he had in abundance. To Grogan it appeared that the whole Protectorate was moving forward apace, that all the good business opportunities had been snapped up, and all the best land in the town had already been taken by the Asians, many of whom had been in East Africa for generations.

They had seen the opportunities in the fledgling settlement and bought up most of the town's centre in the early days.

Gertrude tugged his arm again. 'Perhaps we could have a short rest here and enjoy this wonderful panorama.' They were at the point where the rise in the path allowed a view of the swamp and the putrid Nairobi River, neither of them visible from Government Road.

Gertrude's sarcasm was lost on Grogan, whose mind wandered as his eye followed the papyrus stands around the edge of the swamp. Here and there were the paths worn by animals heading to the usually reliable waters of the swamp. From past excursions along its edge, Grogan knew the tracks would be covered with a large number of spore including buffalo, lion and many of the plains antelope and zebra. From where they stood, he noticed that these animal paths converged at a point on the town side of the water.

'A natural hub,' he said.

'What's that, darling?'

He had been exploring an idea and uttered his conclusion without realising it.

'A natural hub,' he repeated. 'This land, the swamp, is a natural hub for the animals. They converge here and then continue on their way, in all directions.'

Gertrude looked perplexed. 'So ... what is it you're thinking?'

'I've looked at this swamp so many times, never realising it's the centre of the plains that Nairobi sits in. Every moving thing, from an elephant to a field mouse subconsciously moves along the line of least resistance. This is it. Nature cannot support waste. This swamp has been the natural hub for every animal for centuries — for thousands, perhaps hundreds of thousands, of years.'

Gertrude continued to look confused.

'Can't you see, my love? We are looking at Nairobi's heart. The person who owns this land controls the centre of commerce of the town.' He swept her into his arms and gave her a kiss. 'I think I'm going to buy the swamp.'

CHAPTER 30

The Lunatic Express clawed its way up the slopes beyond Dagoretti, eight miles from Nairobi, wrapping itself into the land's contours like a python around a snake-charmer's body. Following a fold in the tortured terrain, it would then, a mile or so later, leave it to tackle the next, higher hurdle.

Shortly after leaving Kikuyu station, the train jerked and bucked like an unbroken horse. From Grogan's carriage he could hear the expiration of steam, and a roar from the funnel as the driving wheels lost their grip on the wet rails. There were a few false starts when the locomotive briefly gained purchase, but then a loud hissing came from beneath the carriage and the vacuum brakes decided the matter — they were stalled until the fireman could raise another head of steam.

In the interim, as the engine driver walked down the train, hitting the sand boxes with a hammer, Grogan was reminded of Henry Labouchere — the British parliamentarian — and his many barbs fired at the Salisbury Government about the exorbitant cost of building what he termed 'the lunatic line' across Africa. Labouchere had composed a very amusing poem that Grogan had quite forgotten, but the title Lunatic Express had stuck. Looking out of his carriage window, Grogan could not understand what the fuss was all about. He had travelled over three hundred miles on this railway, more than half its entire length, in his journey from Mombasa and there was nothing, apart from its sheer remoteness, that could explain the enormous expense of the project. Certainly the terrain here at Kikuyu made the climb difficult, but in his experience of railway lines in other places in the world, it was not exceptional.

Eventually the train got under way again, and began to gather some speed as it crested the Kikuyu Escarpment. Grogan was gazing idly out the window as the line rounded a stand of trees and broke free of the persistent mist that had accompanied them during most of the climb. Suddenly, the world seemed to open beneath him. The earth fell away for two thousand feet in two or three mighty bounds, and landed on a sun-dappled plain that ran, yellow and brown, for some thirty or forty miles before hitting the western escarpment in the heat-hazed distance. He was staggered at the immensity of it, and by the stark contrast between the heavily wooded heights and the golden grassland below. It was as though he had departed East Africa at some point on the Kikuyu Escarpment and entered an alien place — alien, but beautiful in its own way.

Below them was the yawning crater of ancient Longonot, a wisp of smoke — or was it mist? — clinging to its rim. The train again entered the snaking curves of the contours, crossing gossamer trellises of steel that hovered out in space over the Great Rift Valley one moment and huddled into the rock face of the escarpment the next. But they were in an inexorable descent to the floor of the valley, brake shoes screeching and the hot oil of the axle boxes filling the carriage with pungent fumes. The metallic clatter of wheels on rail bounced from the rock face,

At Naivasha, as the gradient eased, they passed the sparkling blue expanse of a lake, with its verdant ribbon of papyrus and squadrons of water birds. A handful of houses and small shops, or *dukas*, hugged the railway line. Golden fields of maize and wheat and a variety of leafy green crops clung to the slopes, while others spread towards the lake shore like a patchwork quilt.

The train made good time across the floor of the valley, sidling along the ridge of a volcanic outcrop here, skirting another there. It was rugged country, but at every turn was a small flock of goats or herd of cattle attended by a solitary red-robed man, often leaning on his staff and perched on one leg like a crane.

Lake Elmenteita appeared, nestled into the protective folds of its volcanic neighbours, and then Lake Nakuru, circled by a wide green swathe of grasses, and inside that, the vivid pink ribbon of a million flamingoes.

Ahead rose the western escarpment, obscured by a heat haze. Grogan began to reconsider his earlier dismissal of the construction task that had faced Preston and his men, and the criticism of faraway politicians as to its cost and complexity. Here was an engineering accomplishment to rival anything in the world.

At each station, Grogan left his compartment to stretch his legs and observe the people alighting from or joining the train. He heard accents made familiar to him during his travels: the self-assured drawl of an American; the harsh, back-of-the-throat brogue of a Scot; the guttural bark of a Boer; the nasally twang of an Australian. People were on the move — not many at present — but the word was spreading that land in British East Africa was there for the taking.

Two years ago, in South Africa, he'd had discussions with Sir Charles Eliot, the British East Africa Commissioner, who had come to South Africa to promote the benefits of BEA. In those discussions he had learned that the British Government would avail every opportunity to 'the right type' to take up land holdings along the railway. When Grogan told Eliot he and his South African partners, led by Fredrick Lingham, the Canadian 'Lumber King' of the Transvaal, were interested in securing a major forestry lease for the purpose of providing the Johannesburg mines with tunnel posts, the Commissioner was most enthusiastic. He said it was precisely the type of project that the Protectorate needed if it were to pay its way. He encouraged Grogan to go to British East Africa and find something suitable. If he did, Eliot agreed to consider a generous forestry concession for him and his partners.

Soon after the train left Nakuru, it began its painful, slow climb up the valley's western barrier. From his study of the map, Grogan knew the Mau Escarpment was an even more formidable climb than that on the eastern side. By the time he reached his destination — Londiani — the line would have started its descent after reaching its maximum height of over eight thousand feet above sea level.

As the train slowed to a walk on the steep gradient, he noticed they had entered the remnants of a forest. The trees had obviously been felled in their thousands for the construction of the railway, its buildings and the many viaducts and bridges.

The train gave a gasp of relief when it arrived at Mau Summit after more than an hour's twisting climb. Grogan was equally glad to plant his feet on something solid, and to gaze out over a landscape not hidden by the folded terrain of the escarpment. He felt he had been transported back to the moors of England. The wind — an icy sliver of steel — cut through his clothing and made his eyes water. The grass stubble seemed to cling to the earth for dear life. There was not a tree, man or beast in sight. Grogan knew he was near Londiani, and if the outlook there was similarly bleak, then he had been badly misled.

Soon after the train started its descent from the Mau summit, the landscape changed dramatically. Among the stumps of numerous felled trees, the grass grew thick and lush for miles, until, in the distance, the blue haze of a forest clothed the hills. By the time they reached Londiani, the impression of England persisted, but this time it was of English woodland. Grogan's high spirits returned, and he was impatient to begin his work.

Preston had advised him that the township of Londiani was adequately provided with animals and conveyances for hire and people to guide him, but upon looking around the station, he found only one white man.

'Afternoon,' Grogan said to the man, who was dragging a bag of flour out of the freight carriage.

The man spluttered a greeting in return. He was solidly built, a little on the portly side, and was, Grogan thought, about fifty years old.

'Sorry to startle you,' he apologised.

'Not startled, just a little surprised. We don't get many visitors to Londiani.'

'I see. My name's Grogan. Ewart Grogan.'

The man wiped his hands on his trousers and took his hand. 'How do you do? I'm Bruce Dalton.' He had thick freckled arms, and unruly, straight ginger hair. Got a place up there.' He nodded towards the wooded hills, broken by stretches of cleared grassland. 'What brings you to Londiani, Mr Grogan?'

'I have, ah ... an interest in the area.' Seeing that Dalton was expecting more, he added, 'An interest in some land.' He had already attracted unwanted interest in Nairobi by his various enquiries. He didn't want a trainload of speculators traipsing behind him as he searched for forestry land.

'Plenty about,' Dalton said. 'There's a three hundred acre plot next to mine but one.'

'That's interesting, but I'm here to have a general look around. Want to get a good idea of what's available.'

'Of course, you'd be a fool not to. You can't rush these things.'

'What sort of farming are you in, Mr Dalton?'

'Cattle mostly, a few sheep. Some wheat, maize and potatoes. I keep a *shamba* for house vegetables, of course.'

'Cattle ... Can't say I know much about cattle.'

'Nor do I,' Dalton answered.

Grogan gave him a questioning look.

'Everyone else seemed to be doing well with them. When all the cedar was gone there was plenty of grass if I cared to try my hand, but I wasn't too sure. Anyway I gave it a try — without luck, at first. Then one day an old fellow, who I reckon knows more about cattle than any man alive, came to the farm.'

'Now you're raising cattle?'

Dalton smiled. 'Wouldn't be without old Marefu. I tell you, he not only knows how to raise cattle, he knows when they need a tonic. And if one does fall ill, he makes up this jungle juice and sings to them.'

'Sings to them?'

'Yes, I suppose you'd call it a kind of a chant. He says hardly a word otherwise. Before long, the cow's well again.'

'How do you find an expert like that?'

'Came to me from out of the blue. A Maasai. That's his young fellow over there at the cart.'

Grogan glanced at the tall young man lifting a drum of paraffin onto a mule cart. He wore a sleeveless checked shirt over a traditional red Maasai *shuka*.

'I understand the Maasai are expert cattlemen.'

'Aye. That they are.' Dalton fell silent, appraising Grogan for a few moments. There was something on his mind. Finally he said, 'There's not much by way of accommodation in Londiani. You're welcome to stay at my place while you look around.'

'Why, that's very decent of you, Mr Dalton. I'd appreciate that.'

'It'll be good to have some company, and get some news from Nairobi. I'll warn you though, the house's not much, but it's ... well, it's home.'

'I assure you, I've had my fair share of rough digs in my day. I'm sure your farm is a bed of roses by comparison.'

Dalton gave him a sceptical smile, perhaps doubting that Grogan had seen a day's discomfort in all his life.

Dalton's farm was in a grassy glade embraced by rolling wooded hills. They had passed through a number of similarly lush valleys in their short journey from the station, bringing again to Grogan's mind Preston's description of a landscape not unlike the English countryside. When the mule cart crested the last rise and dropped into the long shadows of late afternoon, Grogan felt a chill in the air that penetrated his shirt. He was thankful for the light jacket he had brought. The Maasai youth, wearing only his *shuka*, seemed unaffected.

'Before the railway came through, there was no one here,' Dalton said. 'Not even natives. Neither the Maasai on one side nor the Kipsigis on the other stayed too long in these parts. Too cold.'

He continued with similar commentary during the thirty minutes it took to reach his farm, pointing out various landmarks and remarking upon the success or otherwise of each of his neighbours' crops and herds. The Maasai boy, Marcus, surprised Grogan with his active participation — answering Dalton's questions and, when invited, making a contribution to the discussion. Most of the Maasai Grogan had met couldn't speak English, and those who could string a few words together were a rather shy, withdrawn lot.

The farmhouse was fashioned from rough materials, but was generally well-made and, with a good cooking fire going, comfortably warm.

Grogan met the fat Kikuyu nanny, Bernase, and Dalton's daughter, Jessie. The young girl had almost nothing in common with her father. Her skin was light brown, as if she'd spent her life in the sun, which may have been the case, although Grogan suspected her colouring was more likely her birthright. Her hair was honey-coloured and shimmered under the golden light of the lamp. Where her father would carefully consider a point before ponderously speaking, his daughter was spontaneous, uninhibited, and, when she allowed herself, her laugh was light and catching. About the only trait she shared with Dalton were her hazel eyes, which in her case held all the excitement and anticipation of youth. She seemed to hang on Grogan's every word.

After their simple meal, Grogan shared a pipe with Dalton while Jessie propped an elbow on the table and, resting her chin in her hand, quietly listened to the men talk about crops and weather and the land.

Grogan felt a rapport with Dalton, and in the friendly atmosphere of the kitchen decided to lower his guard and share with him his real reasons for being there. He needed help if he was going to be able to survey the countryside north of Londiani.

'Timber, is it?' Dalton said after Grogan had confessed his interest.

'I was told the cedar runs far to the north of here.'

'Aye, there's plenty.'

'How much is in private hands?'

'None. I have one neighbour to the north, but he only runs a few cattle nowadays.'

'No timber-cutting?'

'Not since the railway passed. Most people reckon the timber's too difficult to get out. Hard enough in the dry — no labour to speak of for the cutting and hauling. In the wet it's impossible.'

'What do you make of the country further north? How's the going?'

'I believe it's rough, but I've not been more'n twenty miles thence. There's trouble up that way.'

'What trouble would that be?' The Governor in Mombasa had warned Grogan, but he wanted to obtain a local's interpretation.

'The Nandi have never forgiven the British for building a railway across their land without so much as a by-your-leave.'

'But I understood that the army defeated them a few years ago.' Again, Grogan had been informed of the enforced, but shaky peace, this time by Lieutenant Meinertzhagen of the 3rd African Rifles, whom he'd met on the train. The lieutenant's opinion was that the Nandi were the most formidable enemy faced in East Africa and, contrary to the official view, were far from subdued.

'Aye, that's what they say. I say — and plenty more around these parts will tell you — the Nandi have other ideas. It's a godforsaken place out there towards Uasin Gishu. Men have clean disappeared, never to be seen again.'

'I am not one to be discouraged by a few excited natives, Mr Dalton.'

Dalton nodded, studying Grogan as he puffed his pipe. 'Aye, I can see that, Mr Grogan. But you asked me about the country up there, and all I can say is what I know.'

'Of course, and I appreciate your candour, but given that I am here, and determined to complete my mission, what can you suggest?'

'You will have no chance without a good guide.'

'And can you suggest where I might find such a man?'

'It would be a rare person to take on such a task.'

'I am willing to pay as much as five pounds for the service.'

Dalton's ginger eyebrows raised imperceptibly. 'As I say, haven't been there myself. Not sure I'd go even if I had the chance.' He puffed his pipe. 'But five pounds is a lot of money for some people. There's only one man I know who knows that country, but I don't believe he'd agree. You'd have to talk to him yourself.'

'I am happy to do the negotiations. If you tell me where he lives, I'll ride out tomorrow and speak with him directly.'

'No need to travel far, Mr Grogan. You met him this evening.'

It was Grogan's turn to look surprised. 'I only met your herdsman ...'

Dalton nodded. 'Marefu.'

'But if, as you say, he's your man, surely you can speak for him?'

'That's the reason I can't ask him myself, Mr Grogan. Marefu is very loyal, and he'd go if I asked, but there's a story I think I should tell you before you speak to him.' Dalton glanced at his daughter, who was hanging on his every word. 'Marefu knows the north very well. He comes from the Uasin Gishu plateau, about seventy miles north of here. Until about, let me see, it must be about nine, ten years ago, he was friendly with a Boer farmer near Sixty-Four.'

'Sixty-Four?'

'Plot Sixty-Four. I suppose they'll get round to giving the town a real name one of these days. Now Sixty-Four is between Maasai and Nandi territory. They've been fighting over that rich grazing area up there for I don't know how long — centuries, I suppose. Anyway, a Nandi raiding party was on its way to deal with a section of the Maasai. They went through the Boer's farm and tried to steal a few of his stock. All hell broke loose. The result was that he, and his family of six, were killed. The Nandi retreated into their hills, taking their dead and injured with them. In the inquiry that followed, it was decided that the Maasai were the culprits as a band of Maasai *moran* were seen in the area about the same time — probably in pursuit of the Nandi. Marefu was known to be some kind of leader of the Maasai, and he was charged as an accomplice and sentenced to two years. It was a lenient sentence because the magistrate said he had already been punished by the death of his wife in the same raid.'

Dalton tapped his pipe out on the table and brushed the tobacco charcoal into his hand. 'As you can imagine, Marefu hates and fears the Nandi.' He stood and walked to the wood stove where he brushed the ash from his hands into the coals. He turned back to Grogan. 'If Marefu agrees to take you, you should be mindful that he might want to start another Nandi–Maasai war if he's given the chance.'

Jessie could not take her gaze off the man with the beautiful eyes. All night, as he sat at their dining table and told his enthralling stories in his wonderful voice, he held her captivated.

He was so interesting; had done so much in his life. He had been to San Francisco, Paris, London. And other places that she had never heard of, like Melbourne, Auckland and Santiago, but she was afraid to interrupt in case the flow of spellbinding words came to an end. She learned about the Islanders' habit of touching noses in greeting, of the Japanese's fondness for raw fish, and places where men, with their bare hands, could scratch chunks of gold from the dirt.

She was enthralled by his voice, his stories, but it was his face, his eyes, that held the magic. There had never been such eyes. They were almost frighteningly intense when he became engrossed in one of his stories of danger or wrongdoing, but then incredibly tender when he spoke of people and friendship and the ice blue melted into the warm colour of the late-afternoon sky.

Too soon, he changed the subject and began asking her father questions about Londiani and Uasin Gishu and Sixty-Four. Jessie ignored most of the detail, concentrating instead on the way Mr Grogan's mouth moved when he spoke; how it curled and made almost invisible dimples when he smiled. She did, however, pick up on the fact that, if Marefu agreed to be his guide, he would leave as soon as he could arrange a line of porters. He and her father discussed where porters might be recruited, and where Mr Grogan could buy the provisions he needed. It sounded as though he would be ready to leave in three days. *Three days!*

When her father insisted she go to bed, Mr Grogan smiled at her pout. He offered her his hand in a good-night gesture, and it was firm and warm — just as she knew it would be.

In bed, unable to sleep, she tried to imagine her life when she was married to Mr Ewart Grogan.

CHAPTER 31

The rickshaw boy ploughed straight through the puddles, mindless of the mud splattering onto the short *kikoi* that flapped around his skinny legs. He dodged around the carts and carriages, and challenged other rickshaw boys for right of way.

Gertrude sat unperturbed by the commotion in Government Road, demurely fluttering her fan and enjoying the ride. The morning was fine following a late afternoon storm the previous day. It was the reason she'd decided to make her calls sooner rather than later in the day. The short rains had been a nuisance during the last few weeks while she made plans for their house, but she was able to arrange her day around them.

The shopfront was unadorned, except for a sign painted on the panel beside the door with the words: 'R O Preston. Estate and House Agent' and on the opposite side: 'Firearms and Sporting Goods'. An odd combination, Gertrude thought, but she appreciated the fact that Preston's shop, unlike those of his neighbours, which proclaimed all manner of amazing goods and offers on fluttering banners and signboards that impeded traffic, had some dignity.

She dropped a coin in the rickshaw boy's grubby hand and stepped from the sunlight into the darker interior of the shop.

A man she assumed was Ronald Preston was serving a customer — a bearded man in work overalls. Preston gave her a discreet appraising glance, and nodded he would attend to her shortly.

Gertrude strolled around the shop. There were display cabinets with handguns and rifles under glass. Boxes of cartridges were stacked on a shelf nearby. On the walls were photographs of various trains and long lines of workmen beside a railway track. As she sauntered, she was half-listening to the dialogue between Preston and his customer.

'But I want the English bicycle,' the man in overalls said, pointing to a machine hanging on a wall rack.

'Well, you can have the English bicycle if you have the extra ten shillings.'

'But I told you, I don't have the ten shillings.'

'And I told you, Hamish ... I said take the Indian one.' Preston's exasperation was showing. 'It's a better price.'

The man turned his back on the Indian bicycle held by Preston and stood beneath the bicycle on the wall.

Gertrude returned to study the old photographs. There were about a dozen in all, none of which seemed to have anything to do with houses, sporting goods or guns. One showed a strangely built train carriage rearing up on tall front stilts on rails that sloped steeply down a hill. A number of men were proudly perched on top, posing for the camera.

'This is a very fine bicycle,' the man said.

'Then come back when you have ten shillings more,' Preston said dismissively.

'But how will I get to Machakos on Sunday?'

'How will you get to Machakos?' Preston repeated. 'You want to know how will you get to Machakos? You buy the bloody Indian bicycle is how you get to Machakos, Hamish.'

Gertrude turned away to hide her smile.

'You know what, Preston?' the man said. 'You're no help at all.' With that he stomped out the door.

She heard Preston sigh as he joined her at the wall of photographs. 'That's Flo and me at Voi,' he said. 'We'd been on the road for nearly two years by then.'

'Hello, I'm Gertrude Grogan,' she said, turning to him.

'Ronald Preston, pleased to meet you. And that one's at the top of the Kikuyu Escarpment. Built that special carrier so we didn't have to wait for the construction gang to get us down into the Rift Valley. Did you say Grogan?'

'I did.'

'Then I know your husband.'

'Yes, he told me you'd met.'

'Indeed we have.' His attention returned to the photographs. 'That's Flo again, hammering home the last key at Kisumu — or Port Florence as they called it in those days. And that's my gang — railhead platelayers.' He pointed to a line of men in *dhotis* and turbans.

'It must have been an exciting job, Mr Preston.'

'Exciting? Hard to say. It's the only job I know.'

'Was it difficult to make the change from railway engineer to storekeeper?'

He dragged his attention from the photographs and let his eyes drift around the store with ill-concealed distaste, pausing at the display cabinets before continuing along the shelves. He studied every wall, every bench, as if he were seeing them for the first time. He appeared about to answer her question, then said instead, 'How can I help you today, Mrs Grogan?'

'Ewart, my husband, has told me what a fine job you've done arranging contacts and business connections for him.'

He nodded. 'I know most people in the town. And I know the good ones from those you wouldn't waste a rupee on. Like Hamish there.' He nodded towards the door, indicating the workman who had just departed. 'He's a carpenter, but I wouldn't recommend him to build you a hen-house. The man's a damn fool.'

'I see. Well, it's not a carpenter I'm looking for, Mr Preston, although I will be needing one of them soon enough. It's land.'

'Would that be in addition to what I'm after for your husband?'

'Yes. This is a plot — here in Nairobi — where we can build a house. For our family.'

'Land, eh? Well, I have a few plots on my books. How much land are you after? And where?'

Gertrude wandered away a few steps, thinking as she ran her finger along a display cabinet. 'I expect we will need quite a lot. Plenty of room for our children to play, and their pets. They will probably have ponies. And there's the garden, of course.' Under the glass beneath her hand was a rifle labelled 'Express .470. Good condition'.

'That double Express used to belong to young Billy Judd,' Preston said, following her gaze. 'Shot his father when he tripped and fell while loading it. The bull elephant they were stalking turned on them, grabbed the boy in his trunk while he was still crying over his father's dead body and threw him to the ground.'

'How awful,' Gertrude said, lifting her hand from the display cabinet. 'Was he badly hurt?'

'Killed him,' he said with a shrug of finality. 'The elephant put his foot on his face. Crushed it.'

Gertrude walked to the serving counter, determined to get the conversation back on track. 'Land,' she said, settling herself on the stool, forcing Preston to join her on the other side.

'Patel has a few plots on the other side of the river,' he offered.

'How big are they?'

'Oh, I think they're ten and twenty acres. But old George Hull has some smaller plots beside the Nairobi Club, on the hill.'

'Somewhere on one of the hills out there past the Norfolk would be suitable, I think.'

'Out west is good, healthy red soil, none of the black cotton muck we have here in town — like granite in the dry, and a stinking glue-pot in the wet. On the western slopes you're talking about Parklands. I have a place out there myself, Floette Villa, but land's not cheap there any more. These days you can pay twenty to twenty-five pounds an acre.'

Gertrude gave a determined nod. 'About fifty acres should do.'

'Fifty acres? Neither you nor your husband do things by half, Mrs Grogan.'

'I should certainly hope not, Mr Preston. So do you have anything that might suit me?'

'Matter of fact, I think I have.'

Gertrude paused at the doorway leading from the cool interior of the Norfolk's entrance foyer to the open front veranda. She felt a moment of light-headedness, but blamed the late morning warmth and the splash of brilliant sunlight that bounced from the white balustrades.

Major Ringer was standing at the veranda rail with another, well-dressed gentleman. When Ringer caught sight of her, he immediately came over and took her outstretched hand, which he gallantly kissed. 'Mrs Grogan,' he said. 'You look radiant as usual.'

'Thank you, Major Ringer,' she said, with a smile of appreciation.

'Have you met Mr John Ainsworth, the Sub-Commissioner?' He indicated the man who had come from the balustrade to join them.

Gertrude gave the gentleman a smile. 'I don't think so.'

Ainsworth clasped her hand. 'I believe we have met previously, although only briefly as you passed through Mombasa, ma'am.'

'Really? Oh, it seems so long ago now.'

'It was at the Commissioner's office. I was happy to hear you wanted to see me as I have been negligent for not welcoming you personally to Nairobi.'

'Everyone here has been wonderful, especially Major Ringer and his staff. And thank you for kindly accepting my request to meet this morning.'

'My pleasure.'

'Perhaps we should take tea?' Ringer suggested. 'Mrs Grogan, would you like a table here or in the dining room?'

Gertrude ran her eye around the tables and found one sheltered from the glare of the road by a drooping peppercorn tree. 'That one behind the tree looks cool enough,' she said, fluttering her embroidered fan.

Ringer indicated she should lead the way.

John Ainsworth held her chair as she sat. Gertrude had heard a lot about Ainsworth who was, like Ewart, a man of action.

The locals called him Gumtree Johnnie after he enthusiastically planted large numbers of Australian eucalypts around Nairobi. In his dual capacity as land officer he had also been very helpful during Ewart's search for town land, which was the reason Gertrude had asked to see him that morning.

When they were all seated, Ringer ordered tea.

'I do so like to watch the passing parade, don't you?' Gertrude said, fanning the air that seemed so much warmer than usual. 'So many interesting characters.'

'Interesting is one word for them, Mrs Grogan,' Ainsworth said. 'Downright barmy is another.'

'I like to think of them as curiously quaint,' she replied.

He smiled with her.

'Mr Ainsworth, Ewart has said you've been of great assistance to him.'

'It's been my pleasure, and no more than my duty, Mrs Grogan. If we are to attract and keep valuable new settlers such as yourselves, we must ensure you receive all the help you need to get started.'

'You've certainly been helpful in that regard, Mr Ainsworth. And I believe Ewart is quite pleased with progress on the transfers of the Kabete and Ngong titles.'

Ainsworth accepted the compliment with a modest nod.

The tea arrived, and Ringer waved the waiter away, preferring to pour the tea himself. 'Sugar and cream, Mrs Grogan?'

'Oh, dear,' she said, fanning herself in agitation. 'You did ask if I wanted tea, didn't you, Major? I'm sorry, but I suddenly feel quite ... well, warm. May I possibly have a cool drink?'

'Certainly you may.' Ringer gestured to the head waiter who took the order and hurried off.

'Where were we?' Gertrude said, a little flustered. 'Oh yes, land titles.' She thought for a moment before saying, 'We have made a good start, but we're not settled, Mr Ainsworth.'

Ainsworth frowned, trying to catch her meaning.

'You have helped us to get started, but now I would like to get settled.' When Ainsworth seemed little the wiser, she continued, 'I'm sorry, I'm not quite myself this morning. Let me make myself clear. Ewart is very busy finding investment and business opportunities. Even now he is up country on another venture and goodness knows when I'll see him again. What I would like to do, have in fact already begun, is to find us a town plot where we can build our house. A place where we can settle.'

'Ah ... I see. To be *settled* as well as *started*. Now I get your meaning.'

'Exactly. A home for our children who are presently stuck in England.' For some unaccountable reason she felt on the verge of tears. Startled, she blinked them away. 'And I have found a beautiful plot. Why, I believe it is just past your house, Mr Ainsworth.'

'Really?'

'And I was wondering ...'

'Yes,' Ainsworth said encouragingly.

'I was wondering if ...' She suddenly felt weak. A hot wind rose from the road and swirled around under the veranda. In the same instant she felt a constriction in her chest as if her bodice had tightened. She tried to focus on the passers-by on Government Road, but she found herself staring at a man mounted on a zebra. 'Oh, dear,' she said.

'Is there anything wrong, Mrs Grogan?' Ainsworth asked, a frown of concern on his face.

'Waiter!' she heard Ringer call from what seemed like a long distance. 'Bring some cold water.'

The man on the zebra was bearded, heavy-set and very well-dressed in a three-piece pin-striped suit. The zebra ambled along, staring into the dust of Government Road. Someone called to the man on the zebra: 'Dr Ribeiro! Please come.' It was Ringer, or Ainsworth — she could not be sure. The man in the pin-striped suit drew his bizarre mount to a halt.

Gertrude felt she had fallen down Alice's rabbit hole. Where was the line between reality and fantasy? In Nairobi, was there anything to distinguish between them?

The morning's brightness waned, her head spun. Then came darkness.

The portly bearded man leaning over her looked strangely familiar.

'Are you in a certain condition, my dear?' His voice was friendly, matter of fact.

Gertrude looked around her. She was in her bedroom at the Norfolk — with a strange man. 'Who ... who are you?' she demanded.

'I am Rosendo Ribeiro, Mrs Grogan. At your service.'

His calm tone went some way to reduce her alarm. 'What are you doing here? In my bedroom.'

'Why, I'm examining you, my dear.'

'What for?' She made to sit up and the bearded man tried to assist her. 'I am quite capable of doing this myself, thank you,' she said haughtily.

'As you wish, madam.' He gave a stiff bow which was in keeping with the vaguely foreign accent and name.

She pulled a pillow across her chest, not at all sure she had fully recovered from her faintness. 'What did you say your name was?'

'Rosendo Ribeiro. *Doctor* Rosendo Ribeiro.'

'A doctor?' She only then noticed the stethoscope around his neck

'Amongst other things, yes.'

'And what did you just ask me?'

'I believe I asked if you were in a certain condition.'

'By that do you mean am I pregnant?'

'I find that many English ladies are coy about using such terminology.'

'Well, I'm not. And I'm not. Not pregnant, I mean.' She thought for a moment. 'Am I?'

He smiled, revealing an irregular set of white teeth. 'Quite possibly. Do you have other children?'

'Yes, two. They're in England with their nanny until we become settled.' A recollection of the veranda with Major Ringer and Mr Ainsworth returned. 'Good heavens, I must have fainted, right in front of the Commissioner.'

'No need to worry yourself about those gentlemen, although they are a little worried about you. They're waiting outside for some word on your condition.'

'Then you mustn't tell them.'

'If you wish.' His professional tone revealed nothing, but the owl-like expression behind his thick eye-glasses conveyed his surprise, 'I presume your husband is near to hand?'

'No, my husband is —' Another thought jumped into her head. 'The zebra. Was it real? Was that you riding a zebra?'

'Yes. That was Mr Zoot, my trusty steed.'

Satisfied, she returned to her previous line of thought, which included the fact that she really *was* acting strangely. 'I just don't want them to know about the pregnancy.'

'So you believe you *are* pregnant?'

'Apparently. I mean, probably. Now that I come to think of it. By my recent behaviour, almost certainly. It's just that my husband doesn't know about it yet.'

'Please do not concern yourself, Mrs Grogan. I had no intention of informing the gentlemen outside that you were, or were not, pregnant. I would merely have told them something to ease their concern.'

'Oh dear,' she said as the realisation struck home.

'Yes?'

She had been looking for a plot for their house, and for the first time since arriving had been feeling optimistic about their future in Africa. A tear glistened in her eye at the thought of it. 'If I'm having a baby, I'll have to go back to England.'

CHAPTER 32

Four days after arriving in Londiani, Grogan led the small caravan, consisting of nine porters, Marefu and Marcus, out of the Daltons' farm. The number of porters was less than Grogan wanted, but more than he could easily recruit — even at the inflated prices he was prepared to pay for the three-week safari. The Maasai would not stoop to being used as beasts of burden, and the Tuken, who had seen enough of the Nandi's savagery over recent years, declined to venture deliberately into their midst. He was only able to lure those itinerant Kikuyu who were either so desperate for food or ignorant of the Nandi situation to accept.

The whole area knew about the 'Nairobi chap's' safari. It wasn't often that a safari set off from Londiani. Indeed, it was the first one that anyone could recall, and many turned out to see it off from Dalton's home allotment. It was almost a festive occasion. Buggies had been spruced up for the outing, and the ladies wore their best hats. Dalton strolled around chatting to his acquaintances, as if he were a ring-master keeping the patrons distracted while the circus performers made ready for their acts.

Jessie appeared wearing a dress, but she seemed glum. Grogan chided her, but couldn't elicit a reason.

The restricted number of porters obligated Grogan to travel lighter than he'd planned. He had always intended to steer clear of items considered by many to be essential to comfort, including a tent, a bath and an adequate supply of good whisky, but now he trimmed his list further, limiting it to food supplies, basic equipment, and two rifles.

Another crowd was waiting at Dalton's neighbour's farm — the unfortunately named Major Drought. Grogan smiled at the thought of Sir Charles Eliot's reaction, after spending so much energy encouraging settlers to his 'land of milk and honey', at having Major Drought as his first significant landowner. He could well imagine how fervently Eliot had wished the major had reached any other rank during his illustrious career.

When the caravan was finally on its way and free of the carnival atmosphere, Grogan looked back over his men. The porters were in good spirits; as well they might be, having received half their pay in advance. They marched along carrying their sixty-pound parcels on their heads, humming one of their tribal songs.

Marefu was in the middle of the column, silent as always, and walking with the regal bearing characteristic of his tribe. He had initially resisted the job of guide. Even the enormous sum of five pounds — a year's wages for him — could not sway him, but something had changed his mind during the day for he'd returned that night to nod his agreement to the offer. Grogan had intended to make the journey without the old Maasai if necessary, but with Marefu as guide he knew they were less likely to stumble into trouble. Either way, Grogan was grateful to him, and also grateful to Dalton, who had initially said he wouldn't coerce Marefu into accepting the role, but who in the end had effectively done just that by keeping his silence.

Marcus had pleaded to join them, and when Marefu made no sign of objection, Grogan agreed, particularly when Marcus pointed out he could act as interpreter.

At the top of the cleared hills that represented the boundary of Drought's farm, Grogan's breath caught in his throat. Ahead lay an endless undulating expanse of forest. There were towering pin-needled cedars — some easily over a hundred feet tall and twelve feet in girth at shoulder height; podocarpus — many ancient and lichen-covered; and juniper. It was impossible to say how far the forest ran, but Grogan knew he must learn everything possible about the next fifty or so miles, not only about the prospects for timber, but for other land uses that could subsidise the enormous investment he and his partners were contemplating. There were roads and mills to build. Drays, bullocks, mules and horses would be needed for the transport. Hundreds of men must be employed before they could sell a matchstick. Eventually they would need a spur line from the Uganda Railway. He had assured Lingham and his backers that he could convince the Governor to extend the spur at government expense.

But that was a task for another day. For the moment, he had a forest to conquer.

Dawn, and the ritual of the safari began again. Grogan had been up for an hour, coaxing and, as necessary, kicking the porters into action. After they'd sullenly drunk a mug of tea or coffee, they packed their bed rolls, which would be slung over their shoulders together with their water canister and *posho* sack. They then hoisted their loads onto their heads and trudged between ten and twenty miles before making camp again. The ritual had been repeated for twelve days.

Their route had been a meandering one as Grogan followed many promising wooded valleys to assess the quality and extent of the timber, and the difficulty in extracting it. The forests were strangely quiet. They had not seen another human being in eleven days. This seemed to unsettle the Kikuyu, who were more familiar with the bustle of densely populated Kikuyuland, nearer to Nairobi.

Even game was scarce, or, more correctly, too well concealed in the forest to be easily seen, although there were many times when a thunder of hooves told of a fleeing herd of buffalo or antelope. At night, they were made aware that their passage had not gone unobserved by the predators, with the coughing grumble of lions and the titter of hyenas coming from barely beyond the circle of campfire light.

Of the Nandi, there had been no sign, but Grogan noticed Marefu had become particularly vigilant, taking great pains to search the surrounding forest before giving Grogan his all-clear to make camp. A number of times Grogan had awoken in the dead of night to find Marefu standing with his back to the fire, peering into the darkness with his heavy-bladed spear in hand.

Grogan was not at all concerned at the absence of tribesmen. It meant he didn't have to waste time paying his respects to resident potentates and dealing out the *hongo* expected in exchange for the courtesy of letting the caravan cross their land.

The morning's walk proceeded much as it had on other days, but later, as Grogan was considering calling the midday rest break, Marefu abruptly stopped. Grogan took his rifle from Marcus and the pair of them moved to join Marefu at the head of the column. Grogan strained to find the reason for Marefu's intense concentration, but could see nothing. After a long pause, Marefu indicated the three of them should move forward leaving the porters behind.

They stalked through the forest. Still Grogan found no reason to arouse concern. He was about to ask Marcus for some explanation from his father, when they came to the edge of a circle of rough huts concealed within the jungle. They were empty, but there were a number of hints that the place had not been abandoned for long. A cooking fire had cold ash in it, but had not been disturbed by weather or the small animals that were inclined to root around in old campfires for food scraps and charcoal. There were scuff marks outside the huts and inside one were the remains of a meal.

When he had satisfied himself with his reading of the situation, Marefu finally answered his son's questions. Yes, he nodded, it was a Nandi camp. Probably belonging to a raiding party as there was no sign that women had been present. No sign that pots had been used or maize meal prepared. The raiding party was travelling light and fast. Where they might be headed, or who they were pursuing, Marcus said his father could not guess.

For the first time on the safari they did not pause for a midday rest, but pressed on until they found a suitable site at least ten miles from the Nandi's camp. The porters were unaware of what Marefu had found in the jungle, and arrived at the end of a long, hot and trying march irritable and showing signs of revolt. They grumbled among themselves and refused to set the camp. They wouldn't listen to Marcus, whose task it was to supervise the positioning of tents and cooking fire, and sat in a group demanding that he inform the *bwana* of their grievances.

'They say they need meat,' Marcus told Grogan. 'And that they cannot march in the heat of the day.'

Grogan nodded patiently as Marcus rolled off a list of demands.

'They also want more money,' he added.

'All right, all right. I think I've got the gist of it,' Grogan said. 'Come with me while I straighten this out.'

Grogan marched up to the porters, who seemed to stiffen as a group at his approach. He spent a few minutes strolling along their line, daring any one of them to meet his gaze. Then he took a position at the front and centre of their ranks.

'Tell them this,' he said to Marcus. 'There will be no more money.'

Marcus translated into Kikuyu.

The men kept their heads lowered, although some glanced sideways at others.

'And when I say we march, we march. Until they drop, if required.'

When this reached them, the men's shoulders seemed to slump a little further.

'But let them know I will bring them meat. Soon. Now tell them to get to work or I'll put the *kiboko* whip to them.'

Before Marcus had completed his translation Grogan strode off. As he expected, the porters' voices lifted at the unexpected victory about the meat.

It was no more than they deserved. It was generally accepted practice that the porters' regular fare of maize-meal *posho* would be regularly supplemented with fresh game meat. This had been relatively easy in the broken country earlier in their trek, but the heavy forest cover in the valleys they had followed during the last four days had made hunting difficult. And now that a Nandi raiding party was in the neighbourhood, Grogan would not risk announcing their position with gunfire.

He would have to manage the men's mood until he felt they were safely in the clear.

There was surely no other sight to compare with it. No matter how Grogan chose to assess the Uasin Gishu plateau, it had boundless treasures.

They had walked ten miles to find a vantage point, and here, with the waving grasslands running golden to the northern horizon, Grogan was able to make his judgement. The plateau was an upland extension of the Great Rift Valley, cradled between the Elgeyo and Nandi escarpments — a fertile forty-mile-wide spread, laden with flavours for all tastes.

The grass was ideal pasture — the Maasai had used it as alternative grazing land when the Laikipia grasses were thin. Cattle were the obvious choice, but sheep would also relish the drier conditions up there on the tableland.

A crushed handful of the rich soil ran through his fingers like warm honey. There could be no limit to the grains, the legumes and pulses able to be harvested from that fecund earth.

Finally, there was game — a hunter's paradise. Jackson's hartebeest in herds of three to five hundred strong; a herd of at least two hundred eland; the largest and, some said, the finest eating, of the antelope. Thousands of zebra. Surely there were a hundred thousand animals across the Uasin Gishu plateau. It was beyond comprehension that any number of dedicated hunters could make an impact on that population.

Here was the centrepiece of Grogan's plans to develop the cedar forest. Farmers, pastoralists and hunters would soon swarm into Uasin Gishu to pluck its fruit. With them would come the traders, the storekeepers, the builders, the craftsmen. There would be a heavy demand for transport, and the Uganda Railway was just seventy miles away at Londiani. Here was a natural match between the dreams of the settlers for land and the needs of the government to make a return on their heavy investment in the Protectorate. Meanwhile, Grogan and his partners would load sawn cedar logs onto the freight cars as they passed through the company's 100,000-acre forestry concession.

It was time to return to Nairobi to set the wheels in motion.

CHAPTER 33

Gertrude sat alone in the buggy, smiling at the eighty acres upon which she had decided to build their hopes and their home. It was a gently wooded space sitting between the Nairobi and Kubwa rivers. Between the rivers — it reminded her of a place Ewart had been in his travels. She couldn't remember where it was, but she remembered it was called 'between the rivers' in the local language. It was such a wonderfully evocative word — like the sound of waters mingling and tumbling.

In the mix of emotions that crossed her mind as she sat in the buggy, with butterflies hovering on the grass heads and weaver birds squabbling for territory in the acacias, was an element of uneasiness. In all six years of their marriage she had never made a decision that would affect Ewart without first advising him of it. It wasn't because he was tyrannical — far from it. But he was such an energetic person that he generally anticipated their needs. She seldom had the opportunity to provide any original input. He doted on her; had done since the day they were married, and she'd never had cause to resent it, but it was rarely she was able to place her stamp on matters that determined the direction of their lives. Ewart was the instigator, she the collaborator.

She supposed that it was her lack of practice in making important decisions that made her nervous about this one. Or perhaps it was the ghastly pregnancy condition that seemed to render her incapable of making a decision about anything. Even deciding what to have for dinner was becoming an ordeal. She was reconciled to the fact that her confinement with their third child would mean her return to England, so there was no time to mope about. She would put all her energy into the home project to take her mind off her impending separation from Ewart.

It truly was a beautiful site for their house. She could imagine the children running through the garden; throwing stones in the river; having adventures in the bush. She picked up the reins and gave the mule a flick with them.

Ewart wasn't happy being a mere inheritor of wealth. As the oldest sibling, he had control of the sizeable Grogan estates, and now, through his marriage to Gertrude, would also be a beneficiary of her even more substantial inheritance. But this did not satisfy Ewart. He considered his present comfortable financial position to be no more than a launching place. He wanted to expand on his family's estate for the benefit of all his siblings, and to amass a fortune sufficient to impress even Gertrude's imperturbable stepfather. He had spent years searching the world for opportunities, so he'd known within a few weeks of arriving in British East Africa that it had all the possibilities he needed. Being the most successful businessman in all of British East Africa would achieve both his ambitions.

As far as Gertrude was concerned, this place between the rivers was what she had been looking for. Ewart would always need a larger world in which to expend his considerable energy, but Gertrude needed a house — their house, not the Grogan mansion in West Sussex or the flat in London — to mark the real beginning of their married life together.

By the third day after leaving the Uasin Gishu plateau on their return journey, the caravan was again in the thick of the forest. They had fed well on the bounty of the Uasin Gishu, but now Grogan decided to replenish the larder, hopeful he could find sufficient meat to last until Londiani.

In the late afternoon, when the camp had been set, he took Marcus and four men, leaving Marefu in charge, and headed back into a clearing they had passed earlier that had promising signs of game.

He had already had a number of hunting sessions using Marcus as gun-bearer and guide. A successful hunting partnership required good rapport; without it the hunt would be unsuccessful and, at worst, dangerous. Grogan had been doubtful that such an understanding could exist between himself and the young Maasai, but he had few choices — the partnership required communication on a number of levels, including dialogue, and Marcus was one of the few in camp who could speak English with any fluency. Grogan had been surprised to find that they worked well together, resulting in a number of successful hunts where they bagged bushbuck and gazelle. The rapport between them grew and developed into a comfortable working relationship.

Grogan posted the four men at the edge of the forest, telling them they were to follow only if they heard gunfire. Their task would then be to butcher the kill and carry the meat to camp.

After almost an hour, the only spoor he and Marcus had come upon was a lone buffalo — probably a bull — and from the fresh scat, it was not far away. The buffalo was not an ideal quarry under the circumstances. They were following a stream through tall grass in a clearing between the trees. This was country that favoured the buffalo if it chose to stand and fight for its territory.

Grogan's neck-hairs bristled. His sixth sense seldom failed him, and he had learned to trust it, regardless of the inner voice of good sense that chided him for his superstition. There was nothing in their immediate vicinity to concern him, but he decided to abandon the stalk and signalled to Marcus they should return to the camp.

The sun dipped behind a distant hill, bringing an immediate reprieve from the scalding heat. The valley sighed with relief, sending a wave of cooler air rippling through the grass. It carried their scent downwind to the buffalo. Before they had taken more than a dozen steps, a rumbled grunt came from the tall grass behind them.

Without taking his eyes from the direction of the buffalo's

grunt, Grogan showed Marcus his hand. His gun-bearer placed the .404 into it, keeping the .303 in reserve.

The buffalo was no more than fifty paces from them and had obviously caught their trace. Grogan knew their choices were now limited by the buffalo's mood — a notoriously unpredictable affair. If the buffalo chose to charge, it would be invisible until the closing strides, giving Grogan perhaps only one good chance at a kill shot. He prayed the bull would just walk away.

Another grunt from the tall grass, then the thunder of hooves and splintering undergrowth. Grogan was now fairly sure the beast was galloping towards them, but had only a rough idea of its position.

A bellow shook the valley.

Grogan went down on one knee to get a view beneath the thick grass stems and seed heads. He could feel the hard earth pounding as three-quarters of a ton of buffalo charged towards them.

A black flash through the parting grasses gave Grogan his first glimpse. He fired the left barrel at where he thought the chest would be. The buffalo's head appeared through the grass ten yards away, the extremities of its huge spread of horns lost in the cover of undergrowth. Grogan took aim below the boss at the butt of its horns and went for the brain shot.

The next instant was a blur. He was high above the grass heads — the buffalo and Marcus far below. He hit the dirt hard, and as he fell into oblivion, the last sound he heard was the thundering hooves of the buffalo continuing to come after him.

Grogan's consciousness came from a dark place where the thunder of buffalo hooves were his last thoughts and his first memory. He forced himself to emerge into painful daylight. The sun had painted the horizon blood-red. Above him stood Marcus, trembling. The .303 dangled loosely in his hands.

Grogan got shakily to his feet. A pace away lay the huge mass of the buffalo, a wound to its forehead beneath the heavy boss at the butt of its horns, and another — a massive hole — between its ribs.

He felt the warmth of the .303's barrel as he took it from Marcus's limp fingers. Marcus looked at him, his eyes wide with shock.

'He lost you in the grasses. I fired before he could find you.'

'I'm glad. You fired well.'

'He didn't see me until I fired. Then he came at me.' His hands went to his face and he scrubbed his cheeks as if they had suddenly turned cold. 'But he dropped there,' he said, gesturing with his chin towards the huge beast, 'before he reached us.'

'The soft-nose did a good job,' Grogan said.

'You went flying through the air.' The thought seemed to amuse the Maasai. 'Like a bird,' he added, smiling.

The tension was broken. Grogan moved his shoulder, provoking a stab of pain. He winced then smiled. 'Landed like one too — a bloody ostrich!'

Marcus laughed.

'Come, let's sit,' Grogan said. 'The men will be here shortly.' The glazed eye of the buffalo glared at him on his approach. 'At least we have a good supply of meat from this big boy.'

'I hope those ignorant Kikuyu appreciate it,' Marcus said with unconcealed disdain.

Grogan used his good arm to lower himself to the buffalo carcass. The beast's rear end was firm and warm. 'Tell me, Marcus,' he said, 'how old are you?'

'I don't know for sure. I think about twenty-two.'

'Where did you get your education?'

Marcus squatted on his haunches. 'I went to the village school in Londiani for two years. After that I spent three years in boarding school at Nakuru. Then Mr Bruce sent me to Mombasa to study at the Mission College.'

'Is it a school for natives?'

'No, there are many Indians and Swahilis. Only a few from the tribes. I am the only Maasai.'

'Who pays for your schooling?'

'Mr Bruce. He pays for everything, even for the train. I make some money sweeping and preparing the rooms for the schoolmaster. It helps with books and some food, which is not good at the school.'

Grogan wondered how Dalton could afford such payments. He knew that small farms did little better than sustain a modest living.

Marcus went on. 'It is the reason why my father said he would be your guide into the Nandi hills.' He plucked at a strand of grass. 'He wants to make a contribution with the five pounds.'

'I see ...'

'But he also hopes to find the Nandi.'

'Dalton told me about your mother's death. I'm sorry.'

'I was a boy then, and I don't know everything that happened, because I escaped before it was done. All I know is that when the Nandi had killed the Boer family and had tied up my father, they tried to take my mother with them. She refused and cursed their ancestors and made terrible insults. She wouldn't stop, although my father demanded that she be silent. The Nandi became very angry. They beat my father, and they tied my mother to the ground in front of him. One warrior took out a long spear and stood between my mother's legs. The others gathered around to see what he would do. That was when I escaped into the fields.' He stripped the dry husk from the grass strand and examined it. He swallowed hard before continuing. 'I ran and ran, until I could hear my mother's screams no more.'

Silence fell around them. Grogan could hear the soft rustlings of a small animal in the grass, probably attracted by the scent of the buffalo's blood. From one side of the valley came the braying cries of a trumpeter hornbill, answered immediately by another from the opposite side, less than a half-mile away. There was also the *hoo-hoo-hu* from a wood owl deep in the darkening jungle.

Finally Grogan spoke. 'It must have been hard for you — a boy at the time — to forget.'

'I find it hard to forget her cries. But it is worse for my father. He has seldom spoken since that day. He says nothing about his time in the Fort Ternan jail, but it changed him. I think he would have died there if he didn't escape. After that we had to run away from our *enkang*.'

'That's a shame. Leaving family, and everyone you knew.'

'My father would not have stayed anyway. He has turned his back on all our family, all the Maasai.'

'Dalton told me he had an important position within the tribe.'

'Yes. He is a respected elder. The *wazungu* would call him a medicine man, but my father is more. He is the healer, but also the one who keeps the Maasai beliefs strong. He has our tribe's history in his head. They cried when he left the Uasin Gishu. But he will not go back.'

'Why?'

'Because they abandoned him. When the soldiers came to take him away, they did not defend his innocence. And when they put him into jail, they did not fight to release him. They abandoned him, and he cannot forgive them.'

'But surely there was nothing they could do to help.'

'He believes they should have, if they respected him as their leader, and their healer.' Marcus threw the grass stalk forcibly back into the thicket. 'To him, that is all that matters.'

CHAPTER 34

Jessie told her father not to worry about the leopard that had been troubling the cattle, because she and Wonder would find it and settle the matter.

Her father told her she would do no such thing, especially not with that daft dog who would only make a bad thing worse.

'But, Papa,' she pleaded, 'I'm only trying to do my share. How can you do everything while Marefu and Marcus are away?'

'I can manage. And I'll move the herd into the home paddock until I get the time to run that leopard to ground. In the meantime, Jessica, you stay out of trouble, young lady.'

Whenever her father used her formal name she knew he meant business, but she took a risk and pressed the matter further. 'Anyone would think I'm just a child. I can look after myself, and Wonder won't get into any mischief — he'll just sniff it out for me.'

'The only thing that dog is good at sniffing out is trouble. Anyway, I've told you, you're only to hunt for the table. That means no cats, and no buffalo for that matter. Nothing bigger than a gazelle.' He swung into his mule's saddle, and headed towards the *shamba*, trying to persuade it into a trot.

Jessie stood pouting for a moment, then climbed onto her bay pony's back. She looked down at the dog, who was trying to take advantage of the shade of a fencepost. 'C'mon, Wonder.'

The big yellow dog lurched to his feet and shook the dust from his coat.

'We're going hunting for leopard, and we're not going to tell Papa.'

Jessie tied the bay to a tree and unshouldered her rifle. She reached down and ruffled Wonder's ears. 'Be good, Wonder. Stay close.' The dog licked her hand and then trotted off towards the *kopje,* sniffing at rocks and cocking a leg on one.

The *kopje* rose gradually at first, dotted here and there with stunted shrubs, then abruptly came to a bare peak. Jessie had always considered it an eerie place, but was unsure if this was her imagination playing on visions of the Maasai assembling to conduct their mysterious rites under cover of darkness, or some trick of the landscape that made a breeze come up where none existed and then sent it searching between the rocks, making a sound like a distant moan.

Jessie's heart leapt to her throat as a small animal hurtled past. Wonder followed with a bark of delight. It was a rock hyrax. The small rodent-like animal was too quick for Wonder and disappeared into a hiding place, leaving the dog whimpering in frustration.

Jessie's nerves were now on edge. She hadn't seen the hyrax until it was on top of her. If it had been the leopard, she would be dead. She put thoughts of Maasai magic from her mind and concentrated upon the tumble of rocks in her immediate vicinity. There weren't many places a leopard could conceal itself, but she approached each one with great caution.

Wonder had rejoined her and was sniffing at every rock and cavity. 'Good boy, Wonder. Sniff him out. That-a-boy. Sniff out that nasty old leopard.'

Jessie glanced back down the incline to check on her pony. She was still there, nuzzling at the meagre vegetation. It surprised her to see that they had already come halfway to the top of the rocky hill.

Wonder's low growl brought her attention back with a start. His hackles were up, but he wasn't fixated on the rocks as Jessie expected; he was glaring up at the summit instead. Jessie followed his eyes.

A group of about ten men were standing on the peak. They had white ash on their faces, which were framed with feathers — ostrich feathers. They were silent, unarmed; a long walking stick was all each had in his hands. All wore the traditional piece of red cloth.

Jessie was calmed by the men's serenity, but puzzled. The Maasai hadn't come to this *kopje* for many, many years. Why were they here now?

Marcus was near the head of the caravan. Grogan was in the rear to keep an eye on the porters, his damaged shoulder in a make-shift sling that Marcus had made from the bolt of *mericani* cloth in the trade goods supplies.

The porters were again in a fractious mood. It seemed to Marcus that the more they received the more they wanted. For three days the going had been easy while they reconnoitred Uasin Gishu. Grogan told him they were being difficult because they were not professional porters. It was not simply a matter of lugging sixty pounds of supplies or trade goods all over the countryside. A good porter took pride in his ability to complete the journey safely, efficiently and without creating a fuss. This crew showed every sign they would have already bolted for home if it hadn't been for Grogan's constant vigilance.

Grogan had told him it would not be the first time he had seen it happen. A few minor problems arose, men started to grumble among themselves, making a mountain out of a molehill, and then it was mass desertion. Grogan said he was legally able to force the men to finish their contract, and he would do so armed if necessary. Marcus didn't doubt him. He quite admired the tall white man, and they had become close during the times they hunted together, but when aroused — as Grogan had been when the men started to threaten a revolt over the scarcity of fresh meat — his gaze held all the menace of an enraged lion. He needed do little more than turn those green-fire eyes on the men, and they fell into surly silence.

The wooded country they were passing through was more densely covered than it had been over the last day or so. He'd lost sight of his father, who was leading the caravan, on a number of occasions. Marefu was quite capable of defending himself against anything in the bush, but Marcus was concerned because his father had begun to act strangely since they found the Nandi camp.

It still worried him that Marefu had made him lie to Grogan about the nature of the camp. The Nandi were part of the same Nilo-Hamitic group and followed similar age-set traditions as the Maasai. So Marcus had a good idea of what the young Nandi acolytes were up to. They were not raiders, but young men on a bachelors' camp in preparation for their rite of passage into manhood.

It worried him too that Marefu was not sleeping, but patrolling the camp at all hours of the night, with his spear half-cocked, ready to be hurled. What Marefu sensed was out there Marcus had no idea. It was not a son's position to question his father in such matters.

The undergrowth thinned and Marcus could see his father fifty paces ahead. He stood motionless, caught in a half-stride, his spear at the ready and a hand on the scabbard of his *simi*, the short stabbing sword used for close combat. There was no sign of danger. Marcus felt sick at heart to see his father acting like a confused old man, lost in a fantasy of ancient wars.

Then a bush parted and three Nandi warriors appeared.

Jessie was unsure of what to do. The Maasai paid her no notice. Motionless, they stared out over the land from their vantage point on the crest of the *kopje*. Even Wonder was silent, except for an uncharacteristic whine.

'Shh, Wonder,' she said, patting him. 'It's all right. They won't harm us.'

The low moan of the wind came again and grew more penetrating. Wonder acted very agitated, at first sitting, then lying with his head on his paws, then standing and whimpering in distress. Jessie realised it was not the wind in the rocks, but the Maasai, making the sound by chanting a mournful dirge.

The notes of the doleful song resonated in her head and in her chest until it seemed they were part of her; as if it was her song they were singing.

A new voice, deep and rich, joined in. And another. It filled her until she felt her head spin with the intensity of the song. Wonder began a long drawn-out moan of his own, lifting his head to howl like a wolf.

The song was now more than her body could contain. It filled her and carried part of her spirit with it out over the farm, over Drought's farm too, and into the hills to the north. She sensed it flying over the dense jungles, high above the trees, with the strength to reach all the way to the Uasin Gishu plateau and the forests that surrounded it.

Where there had been three, there were now many. Marcus suddenly realised there were a dozen Nandi warriors scattered in the jungle immediately ahead. If they had intended to attack they could have done so, and with great effect, but they were passive, almost friendly. But his father stood like an avenging angel, his spear now at the ready.

'Father,' he called, as calmly as he could, 'put down your spear.' He spoke in the Maa language. 'They will not do us harm.'

Grogan came from the back of the caravan to stand beside Marcus. 'What's happening?' he whispered. He held his rifle in the crook of his left arm, his right arm still in its sling.

'I don't know. Suddenly the Nandi were just there.'

Grogan levered a cartridge into the .303's chamber. 'Maybe they're the raiding party.'

'No.' Marcus didn't want to expose his father's earlier lie, but he felt that the situation could be diffused if the Nandi were allowed to speak. He moved towards his father, a step at a time. To his horror, he saw Marefu unsheathe his *simi*. It made a slicing sound as it came out of the hardened leather scabbard.

The Nandi were unmoved, apparently uncertain of what the Maasai elder was doing.

Marefu let loose a maniacal shriek and flung his spear at the nearest Nandi. It pierced his body and protruded beyond. He then charged into the bush, flaying his *simi* indiscriminately, slicing branches off the bushes as the Nandi warriors took evasive action. They they too raised their weapons.

Marcus charged forward to defend his father who was now in hand to hand combat with the Nandi. A bullet buzzed past him and he felt the explosion of Grogan's rifle from close behind. The Nandi nearest his father was flung aside.

Another shot from Grogan, and another warrior dropped beside Marefu.

Marcus was only yards from his father when he saw the raised stabbing sword of the Nandi warrior fall to his father's chest.

'No-o-o-o!' he screamed.

The heifer looked to be in good health, but she was down and nothing Dalton was able to do could persuade her to get to her feet. Wonder edged forward and took a sniff at the animal. The heifer ignored him as she did Dalton.

'Back, Wonder,' Jessie said to him. 'Good boy.' The dog did as he was ordered, his thick tail whipping the air as he licked her hand.

In a moment of vengeful spite Dalton's inclination was to leave the heifer there for the leopard that had been terrorising the herd. But good sense prevailed and he again tried to roll her over her legs.

'Maybe she's pregnant,' Jessie said, trying to be helpful.

'No, Jessie, I don't think so,' her father said, glaring at the heifer. He stepped back and hitched up his trousers as he ran his eyes around the hills. Dark clouds towered over the Aberdare Ranges. There would be heavy rain later in the day. The Maasai were still there on the *kopje*, about a half-mile away.

'What the hell are they waiting for?' he said, more to himself than to his daughter. 'Been there for a week now.'

'I don't know,' Jessie answered. 'But at least they've stopped that dreadful chanting.'

Dalton's attention returned to the heifer. 'What am I going to do with you, girl?'

'If Marefu was here he'd know what to do.'

'There's a lot Marefu could do at the moment, my darling, but he's not here, so we'll just have to work it out ourselves, won't we?'

It had been a difficult month. Dalton had been unable to recruit enough labour to harvest the maize. Then the rains came, which in itself was not a particular setback, but an unseasonable wind came out of the north, flattening most of the maize still in the field. If Marefu, or even Marcus, had been there to take charge of the cattle, he could have attended to a dozen other problems, including the leopard, which continued to harass and occasionally take one of the stock. He had lost five hens, two goats and a cow that, although not killed by the predator, was so badly mauled she had to be put down. If it hadn't been for the dog, which had charged out into the paddock, bellowing like a buffalo, more stock would have fallen that night. Now some of the cows were about to throw calves. The leopard had to be stopped.

Wonder barked — a resonant sound from deep in his chest — and pricked his ears towards the north.

'What is it, boy?' Jessie said.

The dog remained rigid.

Dalton followed the dog's gaze to the line of hills. He could see nothing. The dog barked again, this time a little louder.

'Did you hear that, Papa?' Jessie had a hand cupped at her ear.

'No, what?'

'I thought I heard something.'

'No, I heard nothing.' He ran a hand across his brow. 'Why don't you ride back to where the men are bagging the maize and get Wanjiru and ... what's that other fellow's name? Thomas. Tell them to come straightaway. Maybe the three of us can get this stubborn animal on her feet before the rain comes.'

Jessie swung herself onto her pony in a single action and gave the reins a tug, turning the bay towards the farmhouse. 'C'mon, Wonder,' she said. The dog was making a grumbling, guttural sound.

'There it is again!' Jessie said, turning towards the Drought farm. 'Wonder hears it too.'

The Maasai on the *kopje* were also looking to the north.

This time Dalton heard it — a chorus of male voices coming faintly over the hills as the breeze caught it. Both he and his daughter remained motionless, their eyes fixed on the last line of hills before the land dipped into the valley towards Jack Drought's place.

'Look!' Jessie was standing in the stirrups, a finger pointed at the crest of the hill. The Kikuyu's song came more strongly now, a single raised voice calling the question, followed by the resonating answer of joined bass voices.

'It's Mr Grogan and the caravan,' Jessie said excitedly.

Dalton released a sigh of relief. 'Thank God,' he said. 'Help at last.'

CHAPTER 35

Dalton poured two full measures of whisky and handed one to Grogan, who sat, elbows on knees, beside the open fireplace. He took the whisky and nodded his thanks.

Dalton took a seat on the other side of the fire and studied Grogan, who was staring into the flames. The man seemed genuinely upset by Marefu's passing, which made Dalton's concerns about how he could continue to run the farm as before petty and selfish. He had been initially shocked and greatly saddened by the news. He and Marefu had worked side by side for nine years. While the old man seemed to prefer his self-imposed detachment, the camaraderie that grows between men sharing toil had bridged the gulf between them. When the realisation that the difficult times of the last month would continue, Dalton felt a wave of self-pity. It was an emotion he seldom entertained, and coming as it did as a result of Marefu's death, it disgusted him.

Knowing a little about Grogan's circumstances, Dalton wondered if he'd ever had a day's concern about where tomorrow's living would come from. He knew Grogan had a family; indeed, he had made it known he had a wife in Nairobi, and two children who were with their nanny in West Sussex. Dalton tried to imagine what kind of life the man had in England, and found it difficult. He could barely recall his own family's modest existence in India, where his father had made a reasonable salary running the rubber plantation. It was time long gone.

'Mr Grogan,' Dalton said, 'how is your house back there in West Sussex?'

Grogan seemed a little surprised by the question. 'It's enough for us,' he answered cautiously.

'I suppose it's grand, your house. Gardens and such.'

Grogan nodded. 'It's been in my family for years. Yes, I suppose you could call it grand.'

'Gardeners and servants,' Dalton said, staring into the fire.

Grogan rested his cigar on the wood pile. 'Why do you ask?' he said, taking a sip of his whisky.

'It must be wonderful to not have a care about money. When I left school I had enough education to win a junior position in the Public Service. I tired of it, of course, and against my dear old mother's wishes went abroad as a deckhand on a ship working the ports of Africa and Asia. In those twenty years I learned a lot. Learned it the hard way.

'After I married, I brought my wife, Marie, to Africa to try my hand at the rubber. But she died of the blackwater fever before Jessie was a year old.' Dalton took a mouthful of whisky and coughed. 'It was a stupid, stupid thing to do, Mr Grogan. Very stupid. Those steaming jungles down there on the coast ... no place for a woman with child. I should have sent her home like the well-off do. People like you, Mr Grogan, I should think.' He made the observation without rancour. 'Sent her home to England to have the baby. Ah, but that's daft — there was no money for that.' He was silent for a moment. 'I buried Marie there, and gave up the rubber and moved here, to what everyone said was the healthy air of the highlands. I suppose it is. Just like England, they say.' He turned to Grogan. 'West Sussex too, probably.'

'I am sorry for your loss, Mr Dalton.'

Dalton nodded and studied him. Grogan had seemed a hard nut when he first arrived, with his cold eyes and calculating mind, asking the price of this and that. Now Dalton was forming second thoughts.

'I'm sorry, Mr Grogan, these are old burdens and not for you to concern yourself with. Marefu's death has made some situations more difficult for me. I can survive, and my daughter will not go wanting, but I had promised him I would take care of his son, and I unwisely promised to send him to school.'

'And now?'

'I hoped I could manage for another year or so, but this last year has been bad. Very bad.'

'I should have been more mindful of what you told me about Marefu,' Grogan said. 'As you say, he wanted to wage a war of revenge. The Nandi were peaceful —'

'Who could know what was going on in that head? Never a word did I have from him. At least it's settled the matter. I'll have to tell Marcus in the morning.'

Grogan threw the butt of his cigar into the fire. 'It need not end.'

Dalton was puzzled. 'What do you mean?'

'I mean, I'm responsible for Marefu's death. I was the caravan leader. There is no dodging that responsibility and I intended to make a decent offering of compensation. The consequences of Marefu's death, as you've just explained, give an obvious answer. I will continue where you left off.'

Dalton stared at Grogan, for a moment unable to grasp his meaning. When it dawned that the man was suggesting he hand over his solemn responsibilities, he was dumbfounded. Grogan was a visitor in his house, and now he dared to offer charity and attempt to solve his problems. He was about to protest; to tell Grogan that these were private matters, and he should not presume that his wealth and position allowed him to intrude into another's personal financial affairs. But then he realised wealth and position was exactly what Marcus needed if he was to complete his education. Dalton recognised it was only his pride that was offended, and his selfishness that would deny Marcus his future.

'That's a . . . very generous offer, Mr Grogan,' he said at last.

'I think it only fair, under the circumstances.'

But Dalton's gratitude and relief were clouded with regret. Marcus had been his concern since he had arrived on the farm as a mere boy. Dalton had watched him grow physically and intellectually under his guiding hand. He had been as close as a son. It would be a terrible wrench to lose him, as he expected he would once Grogan became responsible for his wellbeing.

He knew the financial burden was unlikely to be an issue for Grogan, but Dalton needed assurance that Marcus would not be put in college and forgotten. 'You need to know there's a lot more to it than the fees. There're things like living arrangements, travel. He needs support. Are you sure you want to do this?'

'Yes, quite sure, but there's a further condition.'

'Yes?'

'I owe you compensation too.'

This was too much for Dalton's already wounded pride. 'Thank you, Mr Grogan, but I can take care of me and mine.'

'Are you sure? I gather your arrangement with Marefu was a very convenient one, requiring no cash outlay other than Marcus's schooling. But you'll still need a herdsman, and I doubt you'll find one on such favourable terms as Marefu.'

'I'll manage.'

'Listen to me, Dalton, you've got your pride, I accept that, but so do I. Do you think I can walk away with this on my conscience? I've lost men on caravans before this, but I have never shirked my responsibilities.'

'And I tell you, Mr Grogan, I don't need your help. Other than Marcus's schooling, for which I am grateful.'

'Then you're a —' Grogan shut his mouth. After a moment's thought he resumed. 'If not for you, what about your daughter?'

'She's not the schoolin' type.'

'Who says?'

Dalton hesitated, recalling his conversation with Marcus about Jessie's lack of education.

Grogan seized the initiative. 'She may not be the schooling type, but what about her coming out?'

'Her what?'

'When she wants to be socialising, joining society. Even out here a girl needs to find a husband. Without a mother, how's she going to learn all those things?'

Dalton was silent. Grogan had touched a nerve. Raising a daughter alone alarmed him for just these reasons — he had no idea about matters such as 'coming out'. And Jessie was already growing, changing. He felt lost.

Grogan pressed his point. 'She's a healthy-looking lass, but she could certainly do with some polish.'

'What do you mean?'

'The overalls, the boy's shirts. Come on, Dalton, you don't think any likely lad will look twice at someone who doesn't know how to dress?'

'W-what do people do about those sort of things?'

'There are schools. In Mombasa. Even in Nairobi.' Grogan leaned forward in his chair. 'Here's my proposal: I'll arrange a bursary for your daughter somewhere in Nairobi. When the time comes, I'll leave it to you to make the decision about when, or if, she attends.'

'And if I decide against it?' he asked suspiciously.

'You can inform the school and they can refund my money.'

Dalton stared at him. In a single conversation he had lost responsibility for Marcus, and been confronted with the vision of his daughter becoming a grown woman and seeking a life of her own.

It had taken the death of a Maasai herdsman to make him confront his own vulnerabilities.

The moon was in its third quarter, and the storm clouds of earlier in the evening had cleared. Marcus headed towards the *kopje* with an easy stride.

A cackle from a lone hyena seized his attention just as a jackal darted from its hide in a hollow beneath an old cedar stump. There were ominous movements in the tall grass, but he pressed on. He could have borrowed Dalton's .303, but that would have required an explanation and he didn't want to lie to him.

He had left the farm in a hurry, even forgetting to bring a spear, but the elders had signalled they wanted to speak with him when he passed the *kopje* that afternoon. He couldn't stop then without raising questions from Mr Grogan. Now that he was so late, he was afraid that the leaders of his section would take it as a great discourtesy.

They were huddled in silence around a small fire, their eyes glowing in the flickering light, their faces showing the ravages of time and a life spent suffering under the effects of drought, pestilence and scarcity. But it was this same experience, and their collective wisdom, that qualified them for their position of leaders. On their word, the clan would abandon the land and a village they might have lived in for years and move far away to where the elders decreed would be better for the cattle, and therefore for the section. It was only on their agreement that the section could conduct the ceremonies that were essential to the community's viability — circumcision, naming of children, marriage, the transition from one social status to the next.

No heads turned towards him as Marcus entered the circle of light and took a seat among them.

'You have come from the home of the *iloridaa enjekat*,' one said after a silence of some minutes.

Iloridaa enjekat was the Maa expression for Europeans, or in fact anyone who wore trousers. It meant 'he who confines his farts'.

'Yes, Father. I have answered your summons. Forgive me for my disgraceful behaviour, but there was much to be said and much to be done following the death of my father.'

The elders showed no surprise at the news.

'We have spent these last six days entreating *Enkai* for his safe passage to the after life,' the old one said. 'And to take you back with us, so you can bless us with the healing wisdom you have learned from your father. You will also complete the ritual of circumcision so you can be inducted into the warriorhood.'

'I thank you, Father, but I cannot accept this great honour.'

'But you are the son of Marefu, our healer. There is no question of not accepting the honour. It is your duty. The clan's prosperity, its life, depends upon you. Haven't we suffered enough these nine years without your father's presence?'

'As you know, my father refused to stay in the *enkang*, and I must also refuse.'

The elders exchanged glances. Murmured comments rolled around the campfire.

'What is more important than being Maasai?' one asked.

Marcus searched for a plausible lie — something that the elders would understand — but found his mind blank except for the truth. 'I have a chance to be educated.'

At this there was general confusion. The elders engaged in animated discussion before the spokesman lifted his hand to demand silence.

'Why must you be educated? Is it not enough that you have learned our customs and our history at the feet of your father? It only remains that you learn how to behave as a man and a warrior at your *eunoto* ceremony. How dare you take our customs and cast them aside in this way?'

Marcus dropped his head, as much to think as to avert his eyes from the fierce old man and his righteous indignation. 'My father was accused of a crime he did not commit.' Marcus raised his head to meet the old man's gaze. 'The white man's law would say that two years' jail for aiding a murder is a lenient punishment, but you would know — all of you — how cruel it is to rob a Maasai man of his freedom to walk his land, to attend to his cattle.' Marcus's ire was rising with the recollection of his father's bitter memories of betrayal. 'And you, who knew the truth of the matter, that it was the Nandi and not the Maasai killed the Boer family, did nothing.'

'You are correct,' the old man replied. 'We did nothing — as we had been commanded. Did not the Great Laibon, Mbatian, warn us not to fight the white man?'

'Yes, but he said nothing about defending your age-mate in the face of an injustice.'

'You speak forcibly for one so young.'

Marcus could have added that his father had asked that the tribe come forward to show it was a Nandi spear and not a Maasai one found in the Boer's back, but it was only his rage that made him speak at all. 'Please forgive me. My father's death hangs heavy over me.' He tightened his lips and decided to say no more. No good could come of it.

The old man nodded, as if in forgiveness, saying, 'I feel your pain, but you have spoken strongly and yet not answered my question.'

Marcus looked at him, trying to recall the discussion before he lost his temper.

'Why do you want this education?' the old man repeated.

Again he struggled to find the words that would explain his craving for the power that knowledge could bring. 'If I can understand the white man's law, I can prevent injustice of the kind that took my father's life from him.'

CHAPTER 36

Nairobi was booming — of that there was no doubt. Grogan could see a number of new buildings rising from the baked grey earth, and when his train pulled into the station, it seemed even more bustling that it had been just a month before, when he went to Londiani in search of the cedar. There seemed to be a driving impatience about the town, as if it had somewhere to go and too little time to get there.

He strode through the maddening press of people to where the rickshaw boys stood, but then decided a buggy would be quicker. Ali Khan was there beside his mule cart — in riding breeches, leather-gaitered, and long whip at the slope.

'Afternoon, Ali,' he said, throwing his bag into the cart. 'To the Norfolk, please.'

'Certainly, Mr Grogan.'

Grogan was surprised Ali knew his name as they had never actually met. On the other hand, everyone knew Ali — the most reliable cab driver and horse hirer in Nairobi.

'How was your safari to Londiani?' Ali asked as they rumbled down Government Road.

'Fine. Thank you.' Grogan was no longer offended by Nairobi's blatant disregard of people's privacy, as gossip was like a cottage industry in the town. But he was eager to be home and didn't want to get into a conversation. He stonewalled all the way to the Norfolk. Ali was apparently oblivious to it, because when Grogan alighted and paid his fee, Ali said he had enjoyed their chat and wished Grogan a good day. He then gave the mules a flick of his whip and headed back to the station.

Grogan caught sight of Gertrude in the quadrangle garden between the rows of hotel rooms. He took his bag back from the hotel porter and dismissed him. He wanted to be alone with her when they were reunited.

She was reaching a hand towards a startlingly blue butterfly as Grogan put his arms around her waist from behind.

'Ohh!' she said, turning into his embrace.

Grogan covered her mouth with his and pulled her to him.

'Ewart! Darling!' she gasped. 'You're back.'

Grogan kissed her again.

Gertrude pressed her hands gently against his chest. 'Ewart, behave. We're in a public place!'

'Then let's go somewhere where we can be alone,' he said, taking her hand and leading her to their suite.

Gertrude lay beside her husband, listening to his deep breathing. Outside the sun had dropped behind the row of rooms on the west side of the garden quadrangle, reducing the light that peeped through the gap between their bedroom curtains to a subdued golden glow. Her body was still mildly tingling from Ewart's vigorous love-making. He had hungered for her body, but caressed her, and held himself in check, waiting for the moment that she was on the verge of her intense climax before releasing himself.

'Over-engined' was a description used by one of his friends to describe Ewart when nobody knew she was in earshot. Over-engined. It described Ewart's sexual drive very well. It could also be used in another connotation — to describe his lust for life and living. A 'thruster', was a description her father often used approvingly, even in the days before he was convinced it was prudent to allow Grogan to marry his stepdaughter.

Ewart stirred beside her and lifted her hand to place a gentle kiss on her fingertips.

'Ewart?'

'Hmm?'

'Ewart, are you awake?' She had been waiting for an opportunity to tell him about the land she wanted to have for the family home.

'I am, my darling,' he said drowsily. 'Do you want more?'

She chuckled. 'Presently, my sweet. But I wanted to tell you that I met Mr Ainsworth.'

'Ainsworth ...'

'Yes, Major Ringer introduced me.' She plumped up her pillows and turned to face him. 'I wanted to get his assistance in a matter of a title for some interesting land I found up near Parklands.'

'Some land?' Ewart opened his eyes and blinked at her.

'Yes, some land.' She was barely able to keep the excitement from her voice. 'It's the most beautiful sloping ground between the two rivers. There's a road nearby — quite a good one by Nairobi standards — and it's large enough for a few horses for the children, and a vegetable garden of course, and we could perhaps build a coop and keep some —'

'It sounds wonderful, darling. How many acres?'

'Eighty.'

'Eighty ... I see you have also caught the habit of making big plans.'

'Isn't that what you're always saying? "Our grandchildren will do things that will amaze us." '

'I am indeed. That's wonderful. But why didn't you tell me you were planning such big things? I could have helped you.'

'Of course you could have, Ewart my darling, but I wanted to make a contribution too. For our future.'

He leaned over and kissed her on the nose. 'And you have done very well at it. When do we see it?'

'Now. Oh blast! It's getting too late. Tomorrow morning. First thing.'

'Very well, tomorrow it is.' He smiled, and she was thrilled and relieved to see he didn't resent her intrusion into what had traditionally been his domain.

'And what did Ainsworth say about the title?' he asked.

'Ainsworth? Oh, I didn't get the chance to ask.'

'Why not?'

'I ... um, fainted.'

'You what?'

She felt herself redden, realising she had made a slip that would inevitably lead to revealing the other secret that she was planning to divulge at another time.

'So, I suppose this is the right time to tell you my other little piece of news ...'

'Mr Grogan!' It was Preston, waving to him from the veranda of the Stanley Hotel.

The Stanley had been recently rebuilt following a disastrous fire which gutted most of Victoria Street, where the hotel had originally stood. The new hotel was apparently a great improvement on the older version, although Grogan preferred to hold his informal meetings over drinks at the Norfolk or Tommy Woods' Victoria Hotel.

Grogan crossed Government Road towards him. 'Mr Preston, good to see you again,' he said.

'And yourself. Would you care to join me for a drink?'

Grogan hesitated. Preston had been of some assistance in his early days in Nairobi, but now he dealt directly with the Administration and the larger land owners.

Preston added, 'I know someone who may be able to help you with the land you are interested in.'

Grogan had not had any dealings with Preston on land matters for months.

'The swamp,' Preston said in a lowered voice.

Intrigued at Preston's knowledge of a matter he had spoken to no one about, Grogan walked cautiously to his table and took a seat. 'What do you mean "the land I am interested in at the swamp"?'

Preston raised his eyebrows in simulated surprise. 'Am I misinformed? I had it on good authority that you were interested.' He must have sensed Grogan was not amused, for he added, 'Fear not, Mr Grogan, my information comes from personal observation and simple deduction. I noticed you and Mrs Grogan on the hillside above the swamp the other day. I became interested when you dashed down and prowled the swamp like one of the lions some folk have seen there. I just guessed you were up to something interesting.'

'Indeed? Your detective abilities are quite remarkable.'

'Hardly. I just put two and two together. What I don't understand is why you would be interested in the swamp.'

'It could be that everything else is either too expensive or too far from the commercial heart.'

'Aye, that's a fact, and the reason there are so many Boers living out there at Tentfontein.' He referred to the tented settlement the South Africans had set up across the river. 'But supposing you were interested in the swamp, what would you do with it?'

Grogan was tired of Preston's interference and felt inclined to tell him to mind his own business, but said instead, 'It looks like good soil for market gardening.'

'Mr Grogan, I know the present owner of eighteen acres of it, but ... well, frankly, I think you should reconsider. The reason that gentleman is selling is that none of his vegetables did well. That black soil swallowed everything. What the black cotton didn't take, the frogs — or some other creatures in that dreadful swamp — did.'

Grogan nodded, impressed that Preston had more concern for the hypothetical vegetable garden than for his commission, but again wondered how the ex-engineer survived in a business that required a lot more imaginative salesmanship than he seemed to possess. 'Thank you for your advice, Mr Preston, but I have already bought John Cross's eighteen acres, as well as Pa Bennet's eighty, so as you can imagine, I have a few ideas that might defeat the frogs and other beasties.'

Preston, obviously stunned at the revelation, blinked in surprise. 'You own ninety-eight acres of the swamp?'

'Actually, I own over two hundred acres of the swamp — went into partnership with a fellow the other day to buy a further hundred and twenty-one.'

Grogan was pleased his secret plans for the swamp had passed the ultimate test. He was also enjoying Preston's horror upon discovering the breakdown in his intelligence network. Grogan had been working on his plans for the swamp for months. It was only when he found a prospective partner that he felt confident he could implement them. Now that the final piece of his Nairobi empire was in place, he could afford to be generous in sharing his exciting news with Preston. By the end of the day it would be public knowledge anyhow — he was on his way to sign the title papers before John Ainsworth.

'There will soon be no swamp to worry about,' Grogan said to the stupefied Preston. 'You'll see building plots, shops, roads. Nairobi will be transformed when that swamp is pushed into the river.'

'H-how?'

'Because within a few months, I'll drain it.'

'Why ... that's amazing,' Preston stammered. 'That's a major engineering job, Mr Grogan. Pardon my asking, but do you know anything about drainage and pumps?'

Grogan had studied drainage projects in New Zealand and Egypt. He was by no means an expert, but felt confident about the feasibility of it. 'Enough,' he answered with a dismissive wave of his hand. 'Tell me, Mr Preston, are you familiar with the Jeevanjee family?'

'Jeevanjee?' Preston's brow creased. 'The *Mahindi?*' Preston used the Kiswahili word for anyone from the Asian subcontinent. 'I've heard of him. From Mombasa, isn't he? But I've never had anything to do with him of course.'

'Why ... do you not approve of doing business with Indians, Mr Preston?'

'No, I don't mind them. I was boss of seven thousand of them back in my railway days. I knew scores of them well — some of whom I'd rather have not known; others I could have called friends. But, as I say, I've never done business with them.'

'The Jeevanjee family have been in business on the coast for some time. I've been discussing arragements that will increase his involvement here in Nairobi.' Grogan couldn't resist the extra taunt.

'There're not many folk, particularly among the Settlers, who will thank you for encouraging the *Mahindi* to set up business in Nairobi, Mr Grogan.'

'So long as they're honest, I don't mind.' Grogan was aware of the prejudice and fear about the 'Indian invasion' of Nairobi, particularly among some members of the Administration and the Municipal Committee. But he didn't have the luxury to indulge in such fears — even if he shared them. His cash reserves had dwindled due to a number of sizeable investments: twenty thousand acres with a six-mile frontage to Lake Naivasha, two farms near Limuru where he planned to cultivate black wattle for the tannin industry, and his most recent and most ambitious undertaking — the float of his Kilindini Harbour, Wharves and Estates Company in Mombasa.

He stood. 'Well, I must be going, Mr Preston. Good to see you again.'

Preston shook his outstretched hand. 'Mr Grogan,' he said. 'One more thing before you go.'

'Yes?' He had been patient with Preston's intrusions, but now he wanted to be gone.

'From my knowledge of the engineering involved in draining a swamp of that size, you'll need some heavy equipment and heavier expenditure. I wish you good luck with it.'

'Mr Preston, it's not a question of luck. When I put my mind to something, it's only Judgement Day that will stop me.'

Preston nodded, but Grogan was already on his way down Government Road, the implications of the ex-engineer's words forgotten. He knew it would require a large amount of capital, which, in his straitened circumstances, was a large risk to take, but he had spent his whole life taking exactly that kind of risk. He was not about to baulk at another one when it materially assisted his overall plans to become a leader of British East Africa's commercial world.

CHAPTER 37

Alibhai Mulla Jeevanjee couldn't read or write English. Neither could he read or write in his native Gujarati — the language of his home near Karachi — but to say that he was illiterate implied he did not have a sharp eye for business and had a disinclination to learn the ways of the great European merchants. Both were untrue, although when he arrived in British East Africa as a relatively young man, he had little more behind him than an aborted business venture in Australia to attest it.

Jeevanjee was born in 1856, the year of the great famine in India, and also the year that Burton and Speke set out from Zanzibar in search of the source of the Nile. But Africa, which was to become the dominating influence in Jeevanjee's life, was far from his mind in his early years.

In common with most of their countrymen, the Jeevanjees had a shop. In fact they had four, for they were a large family. Unfortunately, they were grain merchants and the famine nearly wiped them out. It was many years before they were able to recover. Young Alibhai's prospects were grim, and at the age of twenty-five he left Karachi to make his own way in life.

Even in Karachi, people were aware of the many riches in Australia. If you could dig a hole you could find your fortune. So the young Indian man, who could not speak a word of English, set off for Melbourne.

Melbourne in 1881 was a town with an urge to hasten. Not inelegantly, for Melbourne was nothing if not elegant. It was the most elegant city Jeevanjee had ever seen. Fine ladies sailed along the board walks in trailing gowns, or sat regally in polished wooden carriages pulled down Collins Street by high stepping horses. Everywhere, the wide boulevards, magnificent buildings and sophisticated people extolled the wealth of the city — a wealth won from the mines not a hundred miles away, in the richest gold rush the world had ever seen.

But it wasn't for gold that Jeevanjee came to Melbourne. The young Indian's eyes were focused on a far more enduring wealth than what could be scratched from the ground. When all the gold was won, and when all the French champagne had been quaffed in celebration, people would still need basic household items, and Jeevanjee planned to be there to provide them.

It was not long before he became established. With a few crates of cooking items, bolts of cloth and household gadgets by the score, he searched the city for a suitable venue to set up his stall.

It was easy to find. The city had built a magnificent structure to house the Melbourne International Exhibition of 1880–81. Nowhere was the sophistication and wealth of the city more amply demonstrated than in the imposing Exhibition Building. It was a massive construction: a Florentine dome with a promenade deck soaring two-hundred feet above the surrounding gardens, flagpoled towers on the corners, and high arched entrances. There was nothing like it in all Karachi, nor in all of India as far as Jeevanjee knew.

He set up his stall, which consisted of a push-barrow, an umbrella and a small stool, at the foot of the fountain in the Carlton Gardens, which had a grand view of the building's deeply arched main entrance and its forty-feet wide fanlight. There were scores of people flocking to see the exhibition, but not so many interested in buying a cooking pot, a pan or one of his new one-twist can-openers. Sales were slow, but it made Jeevanjee feel elevated simply to be within sight of that magnificent building.

A very friendly policeman stopped at his stall a couple of days after he arrived. He chatted for a few minutes, Jeevanjee understood not a word, and the policeman moved on without purchasing.

A day later Jeevanjee was in jail.

It was a terrible mix-up. The magistrate became very impatient with him, and when a Punjabi clerk with a very rudimentary grasp of Gujarati arrived, Jeevanjee learned he would have to pay a fine or stay in jail for fourteen more days. He had seen the Melbourne jail. Compared to the berth on the ship that had brought him to Australia, it was a palace, so he chose it rather than run down his meagre cash reserves. But his days beside the beautiful fountain, with its naked fish-ladies, and its spouting cherubs, were over.

Jeevanjee hit the road to Bendigo — the gold town to the north — passing small settlements like Diggers Rest and Woodend, where he made good sales. Within a year he had established a warehouse on the Yarra River, from where he dispatched his Indian merchandise to a number of stores up and down the goldfields' roads. Business was good.

The letters from Karachi grew insistent, however. His family wanted him back to assist with the resuscitated business. They had found him a suitable wife, and it was time to return home to marry and begin his family.

Jeevanjee told them he would only agree if one of his uncles came to Melbourne to mind his business until he returned with his new wife. Uncle Akbar arrived as planned, and a month after Jeevanjee sailed home to India, Akbar sold the thriving business and followed Jeevanjee on the next boat for Karachi.

While Jeevanjee had been thwarted in his attempt to make his own way and his own fortune, he was not done. His ancestors had been plying their wares down the east coast of Africa for centuries, and in 1890 he boarded the swift *bagala* and was swept away from Karachi, his family and his newly born son to make a fresh start in Africa. When the *kazkazi* — the trade winds from the north-east — carried the sleek *bagala*, with its beautifully raked bow and white triangular sails, into the old port of Mombasa, Jeevanjee planned to continue the trade that the merchants of his Daudi Bohra sect had been doing for centuries.

In that year of 1890, Sir William Mackinnon, the Scottish shipowner, needed manpower for his newly established Imperial British East Africa Company. With the assistance of his family's connections on the wharves of Karachi, Jeevanjee succeeded in recruiting three hundred Indian labourers for the IBEAC where others had found the restrictions imposed by the Emigrant Act of India impenetrable.

Mackinnon's dream of introducing the African heathen to the mesmerising allure of capitalism failed, and the company went into bankruptcy in 1895. But Jeevanjee's energetic mind found another opportunity.

The 'Scramble for Africa' had been settled by the Berlin Conference of 1884–5 and the partition of eastern Africa was thereby complete. In 1895 Britain embarked upon the momentous task of harvesting the spoils of its share of the continent by building a railway line from the Indian Ocean at Mombasa to the great inland sea of Lake Victoria. Jeevanjee was ideally placed and won the business of finding contracted labour for the Uganda Railway. When he was asked to supply rations and boots to the twenty-five thousand coolies, he moved his headquarters to Nairobi — the town that the railway determined, *de facto,* to be the capital of the British territory. Later, he went on to erect the station and other buildings for them.

When Grogan became aware of the firm of A M Jeevanjee and Company in 1906, they held a sizeable property portfolio, including nearly all the commercial sites in Nairobi. They ran stevedoring services in Mombasa and Karachi, making it difficult for others to compete in the India trade. Jeevanjee owned the purple and yellow Jeevanjee Market on Stewart Street — the only building not constructed of corrugated iron when he built it in 1904. It boasted a clock tower and a balcony from which could be seen the snow-capped mountains of Mount Kilimanjaro one hundred and forty miles to the south, and Mount Kenia seventy-five miles to the north.

Jeevanjee donated one of his Nairobi plots to be used as a park for all its citizens. Subsequently, all the Protectorate's important dignitaries assembled in his Jeevanjee Gardens for the unveiling of another of his gifts — a statue of Queen Victoria, which would stand forever in Nairobi's very heart.

The gardens and Queen Victoria's likeness were not the only philanthropic ventures undertaken by Jeevanjee, but Grogan knew they did little to appease European animosity. It was hard to ignore it, particularly when people like Delamere pressured him into joining the Settlers' virulent fight against Jeevanjee and what Delamere called 'his kind'. Grogan was astute enough to sidestep those overtures while he made his tentative foray into the country's expanding business world.

It was not only Jeevanjee who had agitated the otherwise still waters of the European residents of the Protectorate. The Settlers — British in the main but also the Boers — could not compete with Indian firms, who had made the best of an early start in the country.

The Protectorate's leaders, energised by their European constituency and, in most cases, by their personal aversion to Indians, legislated to limit the Indians' access to markets and land.

Earlier on, Sir Charles Eliot, the first Commissioner of the Protectorate, having sent a delegation to South Africa with the promise of a five thousand acre plot for any new settler wishing to seize the opportunity, was swayed by Lord Delamere, the President of the Colonists' Association, to exclude Indians from the purchase of large plots in the White Highlands. Although the Indians were overwhelmingly greater in number than the European population, Sir Charles Eliot, and his successors, strongly opposed them gaining appointment to a position on any of the governing bodies. With this prejudicial disfavour assured, the Settlers hoped to turn the tide against the Indian businessmen.

So far as business was concerned, Ewart Grogan had no such prejudices. He recognised at an early stage that he must deal with Indians if he were to achieve his ambitious objectives, so he bided his time and watched the battle from the sidelines.

Jeevanjee's house was a modest, rambling affair on Forest Road. It was an unusual building for Nairobi due to the gentler slope of its roofline, large windows and generous, shading verandas. The house overlooked the Nairobi River, and appeared to have started its life as a modest bungalow, but had grown like a vine as rooms were added to each end to accommodate the arrival of various Jeevanjee offspring and a stream of Bohra relatives from Karachi.

A servant opened the door to Grogan's rap on the brass knocker, and immediately behind him loomed the huge shape of Jeevanjee. The Indian businessman was not wearing his usual skullcap, revealing his baldness to Grogan for the first time. He wore a grey buttoned waistcoat under a draping black jacket, and his pale blue tie peeped out beneath his full, greying beard.

The men exchanged handshakes and greetings, then Grogan followed Jeevanjee through a cosy sitting room into a paved patio where a fountain trickled water into a small pool. The patio and surrounding garden were well shaded by vines and appeared to be intended as a retreat where the adults could enjoy drinks in the quiet shade of afternoon, but when Grogan and Jeevanjee arrived it was populated by at least a half-dozen children. However, his host clapped his hands and the children scurried out of sight.

'A delightful house, Mr Jeevanjee,' Grogan said, noting the tidy flower gardens and trellises that carried pink climbing roses to the fine timber scalloped edging of the eaves. 'It reminds me of places I've seen in Australia.'

'Yes, I copied a few of the Australian ideas. I think it better suits the climate than the English architectural style that most people favour here.' Jeevanjee indicated a chair. 'Please take a seat, Mr Grogan. Tea will be here presently.'

'Thank you. It also has a pleasant outlook, if you can call a view of Nairobi pleasant. When did you buy the plot?'

'Well, it's an interesting story,' Jeevanjee said with a smile. 'I'm sure you know Mr John Ainsworth very well, Mr Grogan.'

Grogan nodded.

'Well then, you will surely know he is ... what shall I say? A little unconventional?'

Again, Grogan nodded, this time smiling at the memory of some of Ainsworth's antics when he found himself among friends and considered himself off duty.

'It was shortly after Mr Ainsworth became Sub-Commissioner, I believe,' Jeevanjee continued. 'It must have been about seven or eight years ago, and I think he imagined I could be useful in getting the new town of Nairobi started. In return for me providing all the buildings he needed for his Administration, he offered me all the town plots that my coachman could pass running full speed until he could run no more.'

'Your coachman?' Grogan had been driven to Jeevanjee's house by the elderly, and rather portly, servant.

'The very same,' Jeevanjee nodded, his huge belly beginning to wobble with suppressed laughter. 'Now, as you are probably aware, Mr Grogan, town land in those days was virtually worthless. Nobody wanted to live in a wasteland, but our arrangement was that the government would guarantee me a ten-year lease on the buildings I put up for them, so I thought, why not?

'I remember it very well. It was a hot February day. The grass rains had not arrived and the humidity was terrible. Everybody in the town — mind you, there weren't so many in those days — turned out. Ainsworth, that is Mr Ainsworth, was the starter. Lala Pathan was to start at Ainsworth Bridge. I instructed him to run as hard as he could towards the station, and if at all possible to reach it. Then he could rest.'

'That must be nearly three miles!'

'Indeed. And with that tummy of his ...' Jeevanjee's own girth was now shaking with delight. 'Not as great as mine, but had I known of the challenge, I would have starved him for a month.'

'And was he successful?' Grogan was trying to calculate the present value of those properties.

'No. Of course not. Poor Lala tried hard, but he collapsed at the corner of Bazaar Street and Government Road.'

'Hmm, not bad,' Grogan said, enjoying the story. That the coachman had made it nearly halfway was a surprise.

'Ah, the tea,' Jeevanjee said, wiping the tears from his eyes with a silk handkerchief.

A beautiful young woman arrived with a teapot and two cups.

'My daughter, Atiya,' Jeevanjee said with unconcealed pride. 'Home from Mombasa for the term break.'

She nodded and bobbed a shallow curtsy, then placed a cup before each of them on the small garden table and poured the tea. She wore a spotless white sari and a yellow silk shawl and head veil that did nothing to conceal her flowing black hair. Her smile was as bright as the pearl she wore around her slender neck.

'What college does your daughter attend?' Grogan asked.

'Oh, a very fine one, Mr Grogan. Atiya is under private tuition at the Mission College — one of the finest in the country — but lives with her aunt.'

'Is that so? A young man of my acquaintance also attends that college. Do you know a Maasai lad by the name of Marcus, sometimes called Momposhe, my dear?'

The young woman shook her head and continued pouring the tea. 'No, sir.'

'No, no. Most certainly, Mr Grogan. Atiya is a very quiet girl and, as I said, is under a private tutor. She doesn't mix with other students, and keeps to her studies.'

'A delightful young lady,' Grogan commented to Jeevanjee after she had departed with the teapot.

'Thank you, Mr Grogan. She is just sixteen. Her mother's image at a similar age.'

'And is Mrs Jeevanjee here today?'

'No. She will be home tomorrow, but she spends most of her time in Mombasa. She doesn't like what she considers to be Nairobi's cold nights, and quite a few of her family are there in Mombasa.'

'You must miss her, surely?'

'I do. It is why I so much enjoy it when Atiya comes to stay. She spoils her old father and is the light of my life. As her name implies — a gift. After four boisterous boys, it is a joy to have a daughter. She has been attending the Mission College because at the moment there is no special school for us Bohras anywhere in the country. But at least the Mission College is a suitable one for young ladies. Thank the virtues she has only one more year, and can soon be here with me to soften the discomfort of my old age.'

Grogan nodded, and took a sip of tea.

'Now, Mr Grogan, on the matter of the swamp ...'

As the two men worked through their partnership agreement, Grogan came to understand why Jeevanjee was considered one of the most astute businessmen in Nairobi. He was not surprised the man had the lion's share of the property, and was thankful that his coachman, Lala Pathan, had not been fleeter of foot, otherwise the Indian might have owned all of Nairobi.

Atiya placed the large open water bowl, swimming with orchids, bougainvillea and frangipani flowers, in the centre of the table, and took her seat opposite her brother, Amir. Her three other brothers were in Mombasa, on family business. All was in readiness for the evening meal. The four of them had washed and then completed prayers. Like most of the Bohras, the Jeevanjees were pragmatic. Prayer times were more flexibly arranged. They seldom attended mosque together except for the Sabbath. Distances, and the danger of attack by wild animals after dark, were more important than dogma in Africa.

'Dayambai, my dear,' Jeevanjee said, passing the bread platter to his wife. It was the signal to commence eating and talking.

Amir wanted to tell his father about an American called Henry Ford who had made a cheap automobile. Amir suggested they buy one of these new T-models and mount a crane on it to move small loads on the wharf. It immediately captured Jeevanjee's attention, until Dayambai began to fidget and Jeevanjee said they should talk about such matters away from the table.

'Better we should make more plans for Atiya's future,' Dayambai said.

Atiya cowered inside. He mother had been making repeated hints to her father that he should start making arrangements with a suitable family to find Atiya a husband. So far she had managed to divert them from it, but each time it arose, her parents became more insistent.

'You're right, my dear. We've been talking about this for some time.'

'Not yet, Papa. I'm not ready for that,'

'Nonsense,' her father said. 'Your mother and I were already married when she was your age. Sixteen already. I have been neglecting my duty as a father.'

'No! I mean, you haven't.'

'Atiya ...' he warned, glaring at her with the expression he used when he had been patient but she was pushing him too far.

'I would ask you to please not choose for me,' she pleaded. 'I want to be the one who decides who I marry.'

Jeevanjee placed both hands on the table — another signal: this time that she had gone too far. 'What nonsense is this?' he growled.

'It is Mission School thinking,' said Dayambai with a sigh. 'The sooner we form our own Daudi Bohra school the better, Alibhai.'

But Jeevanjee would not be distracted. His temper was rising. 'I'll not hear of this, Atiya. You may choose, yes. But we are your parents. It will be us, and the parents of eligible young men in our community, who will decide on your choices.'

Atiya realised she may make matters worse by forcing the issue. She decided to change her tactics. 'I understand that, Papa. But what about my education? I still have three years to go. At least let me finish my education. Haven't you always told me what a disadvantage it is to be unable to read or write?'

'Don't be silly, girl. You can already read and write.'

'Yes, but imagine if you had gone further, Papa. What a business we would have if you had had my opportunities.'

Jeevanjee patted his wide girth, thinking.

'Just three more years, Papa.'

Atiya saw her mother sit upright in her chair. If she spoke before Atiya won some concession from Jeevanjee, her argument would be lost forever. He would never override his wife in the presence of her children. She scuttled about her mind for a clinching point.

'Think of how much more attractive I will be as a wife — not only the daughter of the very successful A M Jeevanjee, but with a full education guaranteed to help her new husband in his own business.'

He was wavering.

'And not only that, people will sit up and take notice of you. What a progressive thinker is Jeevanjee, they will say. He is a devoted Bohra, but is not afraid to try some of the modern ways. And who else in East Africa has done so well that he needn't rush to get his daughter off his hands?'

Jeevanjee was nodding, considering the points she had raised. Atiya knew her father well. He couldn't resist the allure of further prestige within his beloved Bohra community.

CHAPTER 38

The short rains had finished. From dawn to dusk the sun poured life-giving energy into the soil, which responded in a proliferation of growth, making Nairobi greener and cleaner than at any time in the seven months that Grogan and Gertrude had been there.

It was nowhere greener than on the Grogans' property between the rivers, where Ewart stood with a protective arm around Gertrude's waist, watching the men begin work on their new house on the slopes above Nairobi. Gertrude was now five months' pregnant, and it was becoming apparent in the thickening of her waist and the fullness of her breasts. She was relieved when the fainting spells and sickness left her early in the pregnancy, as they had done when she carried Edmund and Nicholas.

In three weeks she would sail for Venters, the house in West Sussex that had been Ewart's family home for three generations before he inherited it on the death of his father, fifteen years ago. Their children and Nanny Redwood had been there since leaving South Africa at the beginning of the year. She desperately missed the boys, and seeing them was the one saving grace to look forward to after leaving Ewart behind.

'Will you miss me when I'm gone, Ewart?'

He lifted her hand to his lips and, looking into her eyes, kissed each fingertip in turn. 'You know I will.'

She smiled and took his hand to her lips and kissed the back of it. She loved his strong brown hands. She ran hers over his to feel their texture.

Her attention returned to the building site. 'What are they digging there?'

'They're the foundation trenches for the walls, Gertrude. See?' His pointed finger traced an imaginary line around the perimeter. 'There's the outline of the main body of the house, there are the outhouses — the kitchen, stables and garden shed. They'll pour concrete into them and then begin the stonework.' His hands hovered in the space above the trenches as if painting the scene for her. 'Then, up there, they'll erect timber trusses on the stonework for the roof.'

'Tell me again what we're going to call our house.'

'Chiromo.'

'Ah, yes, Chiromo — between the rivers. Can't you just hear the waters tumbling and churning together? Such a beautiful name. Will it be ready for us when I return with the children?' she asked.

'In seven months? I should think so. Ready for your creative hand to be applied to the decorating, my darling. As you know, I have no skills in that department.'

The thought of her husband so far away brought on a feeling of desolation. How would he manage day to day without her? Meanwhile, she would be far away in cold and damp West Sussex. After a long silence, she asked, 'What will you do while I'm gone?'

'You mean apart from pining for your return?' He was smiling at her.

'Seriously, Ewart.'

'I'm sorry, my love, but you look as though you're getting yourself into a state.'

'I worry that you won't take care of yourself, and you'll overwork — as you usually do if I'm not around to bully you into eating. How will you manage all your new business interests and the building too?'

'Philip will be coming up in a few weeks, probably just after you leave, and he's going to manage the house. With my oversight, of course.'

Philip was Ewart's younger brother — the oldest of his seven siblings — and had been in a business partnership with Ewart in Johannesburg. He was a conscientious and honest assistant, but Gertrude felt he lived in Ewart's shadow. Philip would not be capable of making decisions on Ewart's behalf, and would be in constant need of guidance, thereby negating the help.

He patted her hand. 'Now please don't fret, Gertrude. I've been in a few scrapes in my time. Hard work is not going to kill me.'

'How can you say that, Ewart? You had an attack of the fever just last month.'

'Well, that's gone. You just enjoy the sea air and the journey home.'

Gertrude was not fond of sea travel, and seldom found a kindred spirit on board to distract her from the vague feeling of nausea that usually haunted her entire voyage. She felt it unlikely the young Maasai fellow from Londiani, also making the journey, would prove to be the conversationalist she needed.

'By the way, have you decided where you will send the Maasai boy?' she asked.

'Yes. I've made arrangements to send him to Garethbridge. My sister in Buckingham can help him find a place somewhere. If he's as clever as I've been led to believe, a good pass mark there will get him into Oxford.'

'Oxford? That's rather ambitious, isn't it?'

'Well, it's not ideal for law, I suppose — would have rather sent him to my old turf at Cambridge — but it will give him a good start. And I have a few friends in Oxford who can keep an eye on him.'

'But law ... surely there's little call for a law graduate in a Maasai village?'

'I'm not sure what his intentions are, I'm afraid. He has some idea about *helping people*. Young and idealistic, I suppose. Anyway, a university education is not wasted on a young and inquisitive mind. And he certainly has that.'

Gertrude's thoughts wandered back to the building works. There were about a dozen labourers under the eye of an Indian supervisor. She tried to imagine the building from the plans she'd seen: high gables, divided light windows with chequerboard muntins, colonnaded veranda, towering chimneys. It didn't seem to fit in the lush, warm forest of unfamiliar trees that would surround it. She decided that it didn't really matter how the house appeared; it would be theirs to raise their family in however it evolved. She looked forward to decorating it and arranging the nursery for their newborn.

'This one will be a girl, Ewart.'

He smiled down at her and kissed the top of her head. 'I would love a daughter, but first and foremost I want you and our child to return safely here to Chiromo.'

Marcus indicated the log under the pepper tree in the home paddock where Jessie should sit. When she did, he joined her.

'Now,' he began, 'what is it you must know?'

'Why, everything,' Jessie answered. 'I can't believe it. Your poor father ... murdered.'

'There is no need to feel pity for him. He died as he wished — in battle, avenging my mother's death.'

'How did it happen?'

'A group of Nandi initiates — young men newly admitted into warriorhood. I don't know what they wanted, but my father struck one and there was a fight.' He didn't want to go into details that the young Nandi were probably just full of bluster, demanding a show of respect for their recently won majority, and that their elders in their company had called them off the battle as soon as they saw Marefu fall. 'My father died courageously in battle. It was a good death for him.'

'And where did it happen? Did you bury your father in the forest?'

'Yes. He rests in the forest. I buried him in the proper manner for a distinguished elder. His spirit will pass.'

'A distinguished elder? What does that mean?'

'A leader. A healer. My father held the position within our clan, before we left the village.'

Jessie nodded her understanding. 'Did Papa tell you about the Maasai who stayed on the north hill for a week?'

'Yes. And I saw them as we arrived back.'

'Do you know why they were here? Was it because of your father?'

'You have many questions, *Enkiti*. Unfortunately, I have no answers.'

'Now you have less than me.'

'What do you mean?'

'When you came here, I was glad you only had a father. Everyone else at school had a father and a mother. Somehow, having you here, also without a mother, made me feel better.'

'How do you feel now?'

'Frightened.'

'Because my father died?'

'No. Frightened in case my father dies. I'd be alone, except for Wonder. Aren't you frightened to be all alone?'

'No.'

'What will you do now, Marcus?' There was apprehension in her voice, as if she were afraid to hear the answer.

'Nothing. I will stay here and work for your father until Mr Grogan calls me to Nairobi.'

'Why must you see Mr Grogan?'

'I am not sure, but he and Mr Bruce say I am going to school in England.'

'England!' Jessie said. 'But that's ... that's so far! I'll never see you. How will we keep in touch?'

Marcus smiled. 'Have you already lost faith in the bush telegraph?'

'You will write, won't you, Marcus?' Jessie asked, looking pleadingly into his eyes.

'Of course I will,' he said.

They were standing beside the train on the siding that constituted Londiani's station. Her father was supervising the loading of some potatoes that he had sold to a merchant in Nairobi. Marcus would organise the delivery when he reached the town.

'Oh, I don't know why I bother,' she said. 'You never do. And I write once a month. At least!'

'I will write, but I don't know how long it will take for the letters to reach you. England is a long way from Londiani.'

'How can you bear to go so far, and do so much study? I hate school.'

'It is not a matter of liking or not liking. I must do it — it is my duty.'

'Did your father make you promise to complete school?'

'No, it was not my father.'

'Then who?'

'Only me. My people, my clan, wanted me to go back to being the way I was in the *enkang*, the village, but now I know I cannot go back. I have come too far already. I cannot unlearn what I know. And now I know there is more to life than raising cattle and killing lions. So although I cannot return to carry on my father's duties, I must give them something in exchange. I will make the clan stronger by knowledge. Knowledge of the law. The British have taken the Great Rift Valley from us, now there is talk that they want our highland lands too.'

Jessie didn't understand about Maasai land, but there was no doubting his passion. 'When will you come back?' she asked in a small voice.

Marcus patted her on the shoulder. 'When I know enough.'

'And when will that be?' she wailed, but the station master blew his whistle. 'All aboard!' he called.

Bruce Dalton appeared beside them. After pausing for a moment, he threw his arms around Marcus and hugged him. Releasing him, he said, 'I want you to know that ...' He paused, a frown of concentration on his brow. 'Marcus, you are ... What I wanted to say was ... well, good luck.' He blinked and forced a thin smile.

The train's whistle gave a breathy screech as a shaft of steam billowed from beneath the oversized steel wheels, which made a convulsive lurch, paused, then engaged with the rails.

Marcus swung onto the bottom carriage step. 'Goodbye, my father,' he said, waving to Dalton. To Jessie, who had taken a few steps in pursuit of the departing train, he said, 'Goodbye, *Enkiti*. Next time I see you, I expect you to be wearing a dress.'

CHAPTER 39

Sitting on the veranda seat, Jessie checked her *kikapu* again. In the woven bag she had a flask of water, a few pieces of biltong for lunch, and a handful of spare cartridges. She picked it up and headed towards her pony.

Her heart wasn't in the hunt. She was making the effort simply because they needed the meat. In the three weeks since Marcus left for Nairobi, and England, she had felt lost and alone. She tried to convince herself it was not very different to him going to Mission College, but she knew it would be otherwise. He would be gone for years, and being so far away made it seem much worse. Her eyes filled at the thought of it, but she hardened her heart, and put it from her mind.

'Here, Wonder. Here, boy,' Jessie called, slapping her thigh.

There was no need to call him — the big yellow dog had clambered to his feet the instant Jessie made a move. He trotted to where she was standing by her pony, tying on the *kikapu*. His pink and black tongue hung from one corner of his grinning mouth and globs of drool fell from it to the dirt.

Jessie pulled a piece of biltong from the *kikapu* and Wonder's heavy tail whipped the air. 'Here you go, Wonder. This will keep up your strength.' She waited while the dog took the meat from her hand, then she patted his chest, making a sound like a drum on his ribs. 'We're going hunting.'

The pink and black tongue chased her hand as she ruffled his ears, and his vigorously slashing tail threw his rear end into a waggle. Wonder loved hunting. In these, his older years, Jessie felt it was the only thing that truly enlivened him. As soon as they were out the home paddock gate, the killer in him returned. He would be alert — ears pricked, tail erect, and head bobbing above the grass to keep a watchful eye on any birds that might be flushed out by their approach. When a game animal came on scent he would whimper with excitement, and Jessie would have to shush him.

Wonder somehow knew when an animal was not suitable for the table, and he invariably made a charge at it, sending it off in a panic. He seldom caught anything these days, but if he managed to bale up an animal he would not take a backward step until it was dead. Once he even challenged a bemused elephant, and it was only Jessie's repeated commands that drew him off.

When he wasn't hunting, he seemed content to sit in the shade and watch her, only moving when she did, and taking his time at that too, with laboured steps and lolling tongue.

Jessie swung the pony's head around and gave her a gentle nudge in the flanks. After a couple of miles, she eased her mount to a walk as Wonder started to fall behind. By then they were into the grassy hills above her father's farm where she could see all the way to Londiani. Below them the cattle ambled about in the rich pasture.

She turned back to Wonder who was panting heavily. 'C'mon, lazybones. First we'll get something for the pot, and then maybe we'll go looking for that old leopard.' She thought a little excitement might lift her mood.

The dog rallied to her voice and quickened his pace. He had lost some of the enthusiasm he had shown at the outset, but he wagged his tail to indicate he was ready for any action.

After another fifteen minutes they arrived at the *kopje* where Jessie decided to take a rest in the shade of a small acacia nestled among the rocks. She tied the pony to the tree and took her *kikapu* into the shade where she poured water into her cupped hand. Wonder lapped it up thirstily. Jessie took a long swallow from the flask and rested her back against a rock, gazing over the distant wooded hills.

The cedar trees made her thoughts drift to Ewart Grogan, the man with the mane of fair hair, charming smile and amazing eyes. He had patted her on the head and kissed her forehead when he left Londiani. She was spellbound under his touch. When he was present there was electricity in the air. When he left, she felt like the sun had gone down behind the hills. The farm returned to what it had been before he arrived — a big space, scattered with insignificant features, but not quite empty. That happened when Marcus left too. Now there was no one but Wonder to occupy her day and her attention.

A low growl came from deep in Wonder's chest. He lifted his head from his paws and his nostrils flared as he moved his head to catch the ephemeral scent that had aroused him from his nap. The rumble in his chest came again.

'What is it, Wonder?' Jessie asked, scanning the *kopje*. She could see nothing, but Wonder had come slowly to his feet; he was as tense as a bowstring and his hackles rose into a thick orange mat.

'What do you have, boy?'

Now his growl came stronger and surer as he took a pace towards the up slope of the *kopje*. He sniffed and took a few more steps.

'Wonder, wait. Wait for me to get my rifle.' Jessie hurried to her pony and fumbled with the cords holding her .303. When she turned back, Wonder was already among the rocks, his head alternately down, sniffing the ground, then up, searching for the elusive telltale scent.

'Wonder! Come back. Wait for me.' But the dog disappeared into the tumble of rocks on the hillside.

Jessie hurried after him, now sure it was the leopard. The last time she had a definite spoor he'd acted the same way, but on that occasion the leopard had outsmarted them. This time it was on the *kopje* and was unlikely to risk an escape over the open ground surrounding them. It would make its stand where the terrain gave it an advantage over the less agile dog.

As she scrambled over the rocks after Wonder, she caught glimpses of the rust-coloured coat ahead of her. Several minutes later, a ferocious growl brought her to a stop. Wonder was about a hundred yards ahead of her, where the *kopje* started to flatten out into a gentler climb. Half that distance further again was the leopard, which snarled at its tormentor in defiance.

The leopard was a magnificent beast. Its gold and black coat shone in the sunlight, and its sleek muscles rippled as it tensed into an aggressive pose. It had a low rise of rock in front of it and a boulder behind — a perfect place to make its stand.

Jessie screamed to the dog to *come*, but Wonder was a tight knot of fury, enraged by the leopard's audacity. He scrambled upwards, clearly tired by his efforts but undaunted by the sight of the leopard snarling from its position in the rocks.

Jessie dashed onwards, the heat beating on her back and sweat streaming down her cheeks. She dropped her rifle, which clattered down the rock face, and wasted precious moments retrieving it. The leopard was less than a hundred yards away now, but Wonder was almost on to it. Her tongue had swollen in her mouth. When she tried to command the dog to come back, her call came out as a breathless sob.

Wonder made a feint as if to tackle the big cat from the side, but then charged the leopard's position from front-on.

The leopard reared, took a vicious swipe at Wonder, then fell back, tensed and again prepared to leap into the attack. Its fangs flashed as it snarled a fearsome warning.

The two fighters sized each other up for mortal combat.

Jessie realised she must shoot to save her dog, but the rock in front of them obscured her view. She scrambled up a boulder and was now able to get a line on the leopard, fifty yards away.

She took aim. A line of perspiration stung her eye. She quickly rubbed it away and again found the leopard's chest in the V-notch of her sights. She squeezed the trigger, and as the jolt from the exploding cartridge hit her shoulder, Wonder sprang into the fray. Both animals were lost in a cloud of dust. She couldn't believe she had missed!

Combat raged for a few moments until the antagonists again separated to gauge their next strategy.

The dust quickly dispersed on the breeze and Jessie again had a perfect sight of the leopard's flank. She squeezed off the .303 bullet and the leopard reared, screamed and fell dead.

Jessie let out a whoop of delight and rushed towards Wonder.

The old dog, hackles still flared, stood over the dead leopard, his fangs bared in a final show of victory. As Jessie reached the battleground, Wonder fell at the leopard's side.

'No! Wonder!' she cried, unable to believe that the leopard could have caused enough damage in that short time. But the dog was dead.

She ran a hand over his flank and found a small hole. Rolling the dog onto his other side, she found a dreadful wound, the size of a fist, where the soft-point bullet had exited.

There was a hollowness in the middle of her chest, as if her heart had been torn from it. No tears came. She was numb, holding her breath for something terrible to happen to her, something so enormously painful it would swamp her unforgivable error.

The bullet that had torn through Wonder's body was the first one she had fired. It had destroyed Wonder's big heart, and should have killed him instantly, but it couldn't overcome his indomitable will to win.

Marcus stood at the bottom of the gangway, staring up at the passenger deck where people had gathered to wave self-consciously at family and friends on the wharf below. Above them was the towering bridge. A deafening blast from the horn made him flinch. The sound was a signal for all remaining passengers to become agitated, to make last-minute promises with hurried kisses, and to gather their belongings together.

He studied those nearest him. There was kissing and hugging and tears. The Grogans, standing towards the back of the throng, were in an embrace. Mrs Grogan would be crying. He had noticed her dabbing at her eyes every now and then since leaving Nairobi.

He had allowed them their privacy when they arrived at the wharf, taking himself off to the bottom of the gangway to wait alone. He knew what it was like to leave a loved one behind.

He envied them being able to make their farewells on the wharf rather than in the manner he was forced to use — meeting in the alleyways of Nairobi's sordid bazaar, creeping into the Parklands forest like a thief, stealing kisses in darkened doorways.

His hand went to the pocket where her note was concealed. He didn't need to read it again. *Farewell, my love. I will never forget you, and I will wait for your return, no matter how long. Forever and ever, I love you.*

He had no doubts about her promises, because they were deeply, madly in love. The sensation amazed him. At one moment it made him soar with exhilaration, at the next he was consumed by an aching despair to be with her when he knew it was impossible.

He had few other regrets about leaving Africa for what might be many years. He would miss Jessie and life on the farm. When he thought about it, the Daltons, to some extent the Grogans, and one or two friends at the Mission School were his very small tribe. He imagined it would be worse had there been many.

When he and his father left their Purko section of the Maasai behind, Marcus had found the wrench very painful. He felt part of a strong community where everything was well-ordered and secure. He imagined his grief in separating from his people was how his mother must have felt when his father had abducted her from her Kikuyu village. She had eventually found the love of his father to be her consolation. While he had his sweetheart in his life, no matter how surreptitiously, it made his life complete too. Without her it would be very difficult — the more so for being in a strange land, with strange customs, and among a people he was yet to understand.

He glanced back at the Grogans, who were still holding one another, and decided to board ahead of Mrs Grogan. He picked up his woven *chiondo* stuffed with his few possessions and shuffled along with the ascending crowd.

Here was the point of no return. If he had any doubts, he could still turn back, forget about his passion to learn and return to Londiani — his home, even though his father was now gone. But apart from his own desire to achieve his education, if he were alive, what would his father say if he quit?

In his own way, Marefu had been a very progressive Maasai. If he hadn't been keen to learn new ways of doing things, Marcus's mother would still be alive, because it was daring to try the Boer's method of treating cattle for ticks that had led to her death. But Marefu had never regretted his decision to learn.

Nor would Marcus.

From the railing high above the wharf, Ewart looked diminutive — too small to be the man she knew. They had been married for six years. This would be their first real separation.

Marcus stood a small distance away at the railing. He too stared down at the crowd, but what a different situation he had, Gertrude thought. He was heading to an exciting new beginning, whereas she was retreating, leaving her new world behind. It might have been more tolerable had she been more settled in her mind before leaving. Apart from the sea voyage — she was already feeling slightly unwell — there were a number of other concerns.

Ewart was making marvellous progress on the business conglomerate he wanted to build. It was always biggest and best for Ewart. He could not be satisfied with playing second fiddle to anyone. British East Africa favoured the brave, and Ewart's driving ambition fitted that climate perfectly. If he had a fault, it was that at times he could be dangerously impetuous. Gertrude lacked the killer instinct that was the essential ingredient in turning a profit in the rugged business climate of BEA, but her voice of moderation often prevented Ewart from extending their finances too far, too fast. She had no illusions about her influence in that regard. It was her contributory capital, and the even more substantial sum loaned by her stepfather, that gave her the seat at the table, but she also felt that Ewart respected her input. Together, they had done well, although they were presently stretched to the limit. She hoped he could remain patient until their cash flow improved. She did worry about it, however. When Ewart saw something he wanted, he seized it with both hands.

This brought to mind her other faint concern. She imagined it was a worry common to every woman who must leave a handsome, virile, well-to-do man alone in the predatory environment of other women. Ewart's magnetic personality never failed to draw people to him. He was the life of any social gathering. He could charm a crowd within a minute of joining it. Women, in particular, were drawn by his powerful presence. Gertrude had started to notice a few who seemed more than merely convivial. Ewart could not possibly be unaware of it, but, up until then, Gertrude had felt no real concern about her husband's fidelity. Her nagging concern now, however, was that these women might take the opportunity to demonstrate how considerate they could be by sympathising with Ewart's loneliness while his wife was off giving birth in faraway London.

She shook off her worries as the baby inside her stirred. It would be a girl. Ewart wanted a girl.

PART 3

CHAPTER 40

1911

Ewart Grogan produced a large silver coin and showed it to the dozen children sitting enthralled on the veranda steps. Their eyes shone in anticipation as he held it aloft, turning it front to back and moving it from side to side so that it caught the sunlight.

His own four children sat together on the lowest step. Although they had seen their father's conjuring tricks many times, they never tired of them. Even two-year-old Sarah was attentive, taking her cue from Emma — her older sister by two years — which she tended to do in all matters.

Of the two boys, Nicholas — whose birthday they were celebrating — was the undeniable inheritor of Grogan's strong good looks. His hair was fairer than his father's, but, as he reached his eighth year, it had begun to darken slightly. His green, sometimes blue eyes were clearly his father's, and he was equally capable of showing his temper when aroused — which was seldom, for he was a sociable child until unreasonably provoked.

At ten, Edmund was the oldest and the quietest of the children. Of the two boys, Gertrude felt he had been most affected by his parents' extended absences when they were searching for a place to settle. He was ungracefully tall, awkward, and his reddish hair looked like an unmade bed.

Nothing his mother did could tame it, although she often fussed over him at family gatherings or social occasions, licking her finger and patting into place any loose strand that escaped.

The silver coin moved from hand to hand, occasionally disappearing and magically reappearing from an ear or a pocket.

The pale stonework of Chiromo's high Cape Dutch gables, and the solid mahogany door, loaned a dramatic backdrop to the performance. The children sat on the veranda steps between two tall spiky plants that Gertrude had placed there as sentinels for the mansion's impressive entrance, and which now added an exotic atmosphere for Ewart's magic show.

Although Ewart had done his best to describe Chiromo in great detail before construction began, Gertrude had had no real image of it in her mind and certainly had no idea of its grandeur. The house had been a delightful surprise for her when she returned to Nairobi with baby Emma in her arms. Ewart stood her before the house and proudly called her attention to the leadlight panel with the initials ESG above the mahogany doors, which, when opened, revealed an expansive entrance hall with floors finished in Canadian pinewood. Reception rooms ran off to right and left, and overhead were huge beams bearing the stamp 'Grogan'. It was a palace — something to rival her stepfather's home in the Napa Valley. But the servants had a better name for it: they called it *shamba ya bwana simba* — the lion's den.

Ewart's conjuring tricks were accompanied by his tinny interpretation of a music-hall orchestra: *ra-ta-ta-dah, ta-ra-ta-dah*. He punctuated the prattle with vocalised cymbal crashes at appropriate high points, which made the audience giggle. Gertrude stood at Ewart's side, handing him his props as required; and in the wings — at the edge of the garden and the ends of the veranda — were congregated Chiromo's substantial staff.

Ewart tried to keep his routine interesting by introducing new tricks, but his visits to London's magicians' shops were constrained by the infrequency of his business trips. However, there was one trick remaining from the visit he had made almost a year ago, when he went to Oxford for Marcus's graduation.

He waved the magician's wand to indicate the end of the disappearing coin act and, with a flourish, it transformed into a bunch of flowers, which he offered to Gertrude with a doff of his black top hat.

The children's applause was loud and enthusiastic. Nicholas stood and proudly accepted the congratulations of his friends as if it were he who had performed the magic. Then he suggested they play hide and seek, and all the children disappeared into the garden, except for Edmund and little Sarah.

Gertrude lifted Sarah into her arms and planted a kiss on her cheek. 'Wasn't Papa clever, Sarah?' she asked.

The child's cheeks dimpled with her smile and a finger found its way into her mouth.

At Gertrude's insistence, Sarah had been born in Nairobi. The pregnancy and birth had gone well, confirming Gertrude's wish to have more children since it meant she wouldn't have to travel to England each time.

'Now don't suck your finger, darling,' Gertrude said, but she had an eye on Ewart, who was in deep conversation with Edmund, a hand resting on his shoulder. She handed the child to the ever-hovering Nanny Redwood, before strolling towards her husband and son. As she approached she heard the end of Ewart's conversation. Edmund turned and headed into the garden, his head lowered and his feet scuffing the dirt.

Her heart went out to the boy. He seemed unable to please his father no matter how hard he tried. The pity of it was that she felt Ewart was unaware of his efforts, and single-mindedly continued to pressure the boy in a manner that only made him obstinate and resentful.

'An excellent performance, Maestro,' she said.

'Thank you, my dear. They seemed to enjoy it.'

'Where is Edmund going?'

Ewart sighed. 'To the garden to join the other children, I hope.'

'We've talked about forcing him to do things he doesn't like doing, Ewart. Can't you see you're only making matters worse?'

'Gertrude, I am not *forcing* Edmund to do anything. I simply suggested that since it's his brother's birthday, he might like to join him in the games in the garden for a change.'

It was Gertrude's turn to sigh. 'He's not like Nicholas. He has other interests. Just because he's the son of Cape-to-Cairo Grogan is no reason he must embrace the outdoors in quite the same way as you and Nicholas.'

'That's enough, Gertrude. I'm simply trying to see that he has a balanced upbringing.'

'And exactly what do you mean by "balanced"?'

'I mean that if you didn't mollycoddle him so much, he might have a chance to toughen up.'

'It's not a matter of toughening him up. As you well know, he's had some ill-health. He needs to find outlets that are more suitable to one of a less robust constitution.'

'That's what the blasted doctors told my mother too. There was no feebler child than I at his age, and a few years later I nearly died from the complications of measles. But did I believe the quacks that said I should spend my days in West Sussex? No, I climbed the Matterhorn at age nineteen, and two years later I set off for Africa.'

'For goodness sake, not everyone can be a Ewart Scott Grogan. Let the boy find his own mark, and support him in whatever that might prove to be.'

The eyes that led the staff to call him *Bwana Simba* — Master Lion — blazed. 'This is a man's world, Gertie. It will not make allowance for one of a "less robust constitution", as you put it. I love all of my children. The girls you may raise as you please, and I have no cause for complaint in what I've seen. But for my boys, I won't see them advance into their adult life without knowing precisely how to act like a man.'

The stone walls of Chiromo were warmed by the golden light of dusk. The day was drawing to a close and with it, Nicholas's birthday party. Many of the children had departed and the remaining few, who were allowed to stay over as a special treat, were indoors.

Grogan sat on the veranda with his brother, Philip, both men puffing on cigars. Their conversation had been on business matters, particularly the Naivasha sheep farm, which was having difficulties.

'Pater James says he has the answer,' Ewart said, referring irreverently to his father-in-law. He admired the old man for his energy and business acumen, but was extremely conscious that Jim Coleman had the wood over him. His outstanding loan — a loan that was well overdue — hung like a sword over his head. Both Grogan and his father-in-law knew that at any time he could call in that loan and bankrupt him. Grogan hated being in that position, and hated feeling obliged to listen to Coleman's proclamations. Gertrude told him her stepfahter would never do it, and Grogan was inclined to agree, but the situation was a constant weight on his mind. 'He says this new chap he's sending is one of the best farm managers in California,' he went on to Philip.

'California, for goodness' sake,' Philip responded. 'Isn't there anyone in South Africa, or even here, who can manage a few stupid sheep? How difficult can it be?'

'Not very, you'd think, but sheep are different. I'd say there are few in Africa who can make any sense of a sheep's obscure logic. Anyway, I need to make sure I have someone knowledgeable in place when the merino rams arrive from Australia. I expect it will be tricky cross-breeding them with the local flock. My father-in-law can be pig-headed about getting his own way. No, let me just say he presents a strong case to at least try his suggestions.'

Philip chuckled. 'Same thing. Did you two ever get along?'

'I think he regarded me well enough, but it was always a battle of wills with him. Even as I was leaving California I don't believe I had convinced him I would walk Africa.'

As the Watt children's stepfather, Coleman took his role of guardian seriously. He made no secret of the fact that he was suspicious of Grogan's intentions. He'd said he thought little of a young man who spent his time and annuity aimlessly travelling the world. Coleman politely suggested Grogan continue on his travels and return, if he was seriously interested in his stepdaughter, when he had proven his mettle.

When Grogan had defended himself, stating his intention was to walk the length of Africa, Coleman had stared at him for a moment before saying, 'I can only presume that you are trying to be funny, young man. If so, I do not appreciate it.'

To disagree with James Coleman was not a task to be undertaken lightly, but Grogan had politely informed Coleman he was quite serious, and accepted his offer to return when he succeeded.

'Big Jim Coleman just couldn't accept I might be family one day,' he went on to his brother.

'Speaking of families,' Philip said, tapping his cigar ash over the balustrade, then leaning back in his chair, 'have you heard from our little brother Quentin?' Philip was two years younger than Ewart, and they had always been the closest pair in the family, whereas Ewart and Quentin, separated by nine years, were often at odds.

'Nothing since he went hunting elephant in the Lado Enclave,' Ewart said.

'That's a no-man's-land these days, isn't it?'

'Yes. Always was. When I passed through there back in '99 it was still under the Belgians. Even then there were countless elephants. If he doesn't get himself killed, and he can shoot as well as he can talk, he'll make a tidy parcel from the ivory.'

'At least he's out of harm's way so far as the ladies are concerned.'

Philip was referring to their brother's apparent attraction towards the opposite sex, and vice versa, which ended his naval career when he was found in a compromising position with an admiral's wife.

'I don't think his heart was in the navy,' Ewart said. 'After the defeat of the Boers there didn't appear to be any prospects for active service. "An alarming outbreak of peace", he used to say. I should think he acted a little hastily. The latest news from home convinces me we have a war coming with Germany.'

'Do you really think so?'

'Absolutely. The question is merely when?'

'Then it'll be back home for us,' said Philip, drawing on his cigar. 'There'll be bugger all for us to do out here.'

'What makes you think that?' Ewart replied. 'This war, when it comes, will be all about territory. Don't forget our neighbour: German East Africa. With a bit of luck, we'll have our chance to be in the thick of it right here in British EA.'

Gertrude leapt out of the carriage almost before William had drawn it to a halt in front of the house. 'Come,' she commanded Edmund, who was slow in joining her at the foot of the stairs. 'Hurry along.' She wasn't angry with her son, just anxious to get him back into his bed. Doctor Ribeiro had diagnosed an infected eardrum and prescribed rest and hot milk.

Before Gertrude could reach the front door, the ample form of Nanny Redwood appeared in the doorway. 'Ma'am?' she said, but her eyes were on young Edmund.

'Another infected ear,' Gertrude answered. 'Doctor says he —'

'Bed and warm milk,' Nanny Redwood said, and swept the boy indoors.

Gertrude went upstairs to her bedroom, and plucked her gloves free before dropping them on the huge bed that she and Ewart shared. The bed dominated the room. Bright sunlight splashed through the window behind the iron bedhead, making a shadow pattern of bars on the floral coverlet. She stared at it for a while, then picked up her gloves, and put them on her dresser before leaving the room.

In the warmth of the veranda she began to pace. It usually helped when she felt stressed. Edmund's illness troubled her, but at the same time she was perversely relieved to know it was not merely her imagination. Ewart would have chided her if Dr Ribeiro had found nothing wrong with Edmund. He would also have probably referred to her 'umbilical cord syndrome', again.

Nicholas never seemed to fall ill. If he did, maybe Edmund would not appear so different, and his father would not be able to make critical comparisons. Now she berated herself as she paced. She felt mean — wishing Nicholas to fall ill for the petty reason of diminishing his sibling's uncertain health. She wrung her hands, sat on the chair at the occasional table, and immediately stood again to resume her pacing.

Why was Ewart at the Norfolk with that woman?

There — she had done it. Although she had cautioned herself to resist it, she had allowed the vision of her husband — having a completely innocent conversation with a woman — to invade her thoughts.

She had spotted him entering the hotel as she was returning from the doctor's rooms. It may not even have been Ewart — the doorway was in heavy shade.

It was simply Edmund's health, and not that she was at all concerned that Ewart was chatting to an attractive young woman, that had upset her.

She bumped into the bentwood chair and irritably righted it.

And really, what was so significant about his behaviour? He was always very gallant and charming with women of their acquaintance. Didn't her friends constantly comment on Ewart's charm and impeccable manners?

She came back to the chair and repositioned it. Then she moved it a quarter-circle and pushed the other chair to sit opposite it. It didn't look right. She began to push them back to their original positions before abandoning the exercise.

And what if it was a day he had told her he was going to spend in Naivasha and would not be home until tomorrow? He had obviously changed his plans, and she would no doubt see him that evening as usual.

That night, with candlelight on the table, and the children early in bed, she dined alone.

CHAPTER 41

Jeevanjee gritted his teeth, closed the accounts book and leaned back in his chair. His youngest brother sat opposite him looking agitated and annoyed.

Young Tayabali had been an ill-fitting wheel in the machinery of A M Jeevanjee and Company for many years, and Jeevanjee had called him up from Mombasa to again remind him of his responsibilities. He referred to his youngest brother as Young Tayabali because he was only a youth having difficulty growing a beard when Jeevanjee had gone off to Australia in his twenties to find new opportunities for the family business. Now, all these years later, Young Tayabali still had the disposition of a beardless youth, although he was nearly forty years of age.

Jeevanjee tried to avoid using his brother's nickname in his presence because he was liable to take it as yet another admonishment. In fact, the so-called admonishments were Jeevanjee's efforts to educate Tayabali in the finer points of the business. Unfortunately, his brother's naturally aggressive nature almost always led to conflict between them.

Not that Jeevanjee didn't have a temper of his own, but he was usually able to keep it under a tight rein, although his brother was now pressing the boundaries of his patience.

With Tayabali again in Nairobi to receive a dressing-down for his behaviour, Jeevanjee wondered if running the stevedoring operation was the correct placement for his headstrong brother. On the Mbaraki wharf they had several hundred men on call who would be employed on an as-needed basis. There were many Moslems in that number, but not nearly enough to cover all their manpower requirements. As a consequence, Tayabali had recruited other Indians to meet their requirements, mainly Hindus and Jaines. But it was the martial races, the Pathans, Punjabis and Sikhs, originally employed by the Uganda Railway — hard men accustomed to hard work — who created the difficulties for him.

As a young man, Jeevanjee had managed stevedores in Karachi. He knew, or had quickly learned, the skills needed to manage men. Tayabali had no idea. He didn't have the temperament to handle them. Jeevanjee believed in firm discipline among his workers, but there were times when a manager had to listen. When conflict arose, as it inevitably did on the wharf, Tayabali reacted rather than reflected; he would always respond with aggression when conciliation might be the wiser course.

Jeevanjee leaned back in the worn chair that had served him from the first days of his East African empire and plucked irritably at the feathered edges of the leather padding on the armrest. 'You say you don't disagree with the coolie's account?' he asked.

'No. He was an insolent Baluchi. So I had him thrown off the waterfront.'

Jeevanjee had seen Tayabali's 'men'. They were members of the thuggee sect, given easy jobs in return for acting as his brother's personal bodyguard. The thuggees, or thugs, were a cult of professional murderers who killed as an act of worship to the goddess Kali. They were hereditary killers drawn from all regions of India, and were united by their devotion to the goddess and the act of strangulation.

'I see,' Jeevanjee said, looking down at the armrest, which he had made worse by his attempts to tidy it. Annoyed with himself, he slapped at the frayed edges.

Tayabali took his brother's gesture to be anger directed at himself. 'Would you have me let the matter go?' he snapped. 'The man had defied my orders and was indolent. Am I to be treated like a fool by these ignorant coolies?'

'I am not making judgement on the matter, Tayabali,' Jeevanjee said, but he had made his own enquiries. The man had been forced to work a double shift in the steaming hold of a cargo ship bringing cattle from Bombay. He complained to his foreman when he found the water container empty. Tayabali overheard him and chose to make an issue of it. He thrashed the man and then sacked him. 'I have become involved merely because one of his friends — a senior man — pointed out the matter to me when I was last in Mombasa. He said the man nearly drowned when you threw him overboard.'

'Ach! Give me the name of the informer and I'll see to it he keeps his tongue inside his head from now on. Anyway, the coolies pulled him out. He was unhurt.'

'Perhaps, but I have warned you about using physical violence on the wharf. I will not have it, Tayabali.'

'You will not have it?' He spluttered a derisive laugh. 'You would let them run away with our business.'

The use of the collective pronoun in connection with the business irritated Jeevanjee. Tayabali had been arguing for some time that A M Jeevanjee and Company was a family partnership. His other brothers had made no such claim, so it was obviously only Tayabali who thought he should share what Jeevanjee had built by his own sweat and blood over the years, but Jeevanjee had already had that dispute many times with his brother. On this occasion he let it rest. Instead, he said, 'If you would like to exchange your position here with one in Karachi, I'm sure I could persuade one of your brothers to take your place. And it would give you a chance to find a wife.'

'I don't want Karachi and I don't want a wife!' he snarled. 'I want my share of the business so I can run it as I please and not have my big soft brother counting my mistakes every minute of the day.'

Tayabali stormed from the office, slamming the door behind him.

Jeevanjee was forming a sharp retort, but just shook his head. *Soft*? He had never considered himself soft. Even when Governor Sir Percy Girouard recently called him a low-caste coolie, he ignored it, when a weaker man might have raved about prejudice and racism. And when he was granted a lease on five unused acres of the Uganda Railway's land for the purposes of building a grand hotel, there was general uproar — not from competitors like Tommy Woods and Major Ringer of the Norfolk — but from the landed gentry of the White Highlands, the Settlers. One of them implied it was favouritism and that the concession came as a result of a bribe. The Governor of the day examined the allegations and declared Jeevanjee innocent — as he most decidedly was — and the grant of the land was allowed to proceed.

Jeevanjee had plans drawn up for a two-storey hotel incorporating one of the new-fangled electric lifts, and arranged the delivery of all materials to the Nairobi building site, only to find that the railway said they had made a mistake and that in fact they needed the land for their own purposes after all.

Soft? No, a man had to be strong to face such outright injustice.

He looked down at the armrest of his chair. The leather edging was shredded, exposing the kapok stuffing.

Atiya sat opposite her father and mother at the circular table. All four of her brothers were in residence — a rare occurrence. The family seemed to have surrounded her.

The evening meal was completed, but Jeevanjee, who had been agitated all day, made no sign that anyone could leave the table. Atiya sensed there was to be a family conference. She dreaded what might be raised.

Her father cleared his throat. 'So, Atiya, have you given any thought to the Adamjees' invitation?'

Atiya groaned inwardly. The Adamjees had made a formal approach to her parents to consider their son, Choleim, as a suitable partner for their daughter. 'Papa, I don't need to give thought to it. I don't want to marry Choleim.'

'And why not?' Jeevanjee spluttered. 'Isn't he a fine young Bhora man? Good family. They run one of the best general merchadise stores in Nairobi, and another in Nakuru. What more can a girl ask?'

'I can ask what I have always asked, Papa — to be given the opportunity to choose my husband.'

Her mother tutted.

Jeevanjee looked stern. 'I have been very patient, Atiya.'

'But why should I be the first to marry? Even Amir is not married!'

Amir, her oldest brother, made no comment, but Jeevanjee said, 'Amir is betrothed, and when his fiancée is older, they will marry. But I am not discussing Amir and do not be distracting me. If you will not accept Choleim Adamjee, then you will take Asgher Gulumdar for your husband.'

Atiya began to panic. She felt the room closing in around her. Hostile faces surrounded her. She didn't want either man. Even if they were attractive and successful and witty and wise, she woudn't want them. She had already met the man she wanted to marry.

'I need more time,' she implored.

'You have had time. Didn't I give you time to complete your education as you asked me? Even more than that? You are now twenty-one years old. Who will take a woman older than twenty-one? It is impossible.'

Atiya grasped for straws. She had one more card to play. She put on her sweetest, most childlike face and pleaded, 'I need another year, Papa. I have won an education, that's true, but what is that without experience?'

'Experience?' Jeevanjee's brow wrinkled.

'Real experience. Not just from books. To be ready to help my new husband to run his business don't I have to get out into the world, as you did, and learn what business is about? Didn't you always say it was not schooling that makes for a successful businessman, but cunning and brains?'

'Yes ... but —'

'And what better place than beside you? Think of how much more valuable I will be to my husband, having studied at the feet of the most successful Indian businessman in British East Africa.'

Jeevanjee patted his belly and turned down the corners of his mouth to conceal his proud smile.

She pressed her advantage. 'I can be your personal assistant, and by helping you in the office for a year or two, I will have the best education possible — working with the best.'

'A year or two? Out of the question!' her father protested. 'By then you'll be twenty-three! Too old for anyone eligible to be interested in you.'

'Then just a year.'

'No! Six months. And not a day more.'

'Yes, Papa,' she said, dropping her eyes to the table in a show of respect.

Jeevanjee smiled.

Atiya kept her eyes down to conceal her own smile of triumph. She would have accepted three months. By then she would have introduced her father to the man she had found all by herself.

CHAPTER 42

Jessie stood at her dressing table mirror wearing only her drawers with the gathered ankles and drawstring waist. She piled her long fair hair on top of her head, revealing her full breasts and the tiny white scar beside her left nipple that she'd earned in a mock spear fight with Marcus long before they developed their form. She turned from left to right, studying the style, unsure if it would better suit the evening to wear it up or down. She allowed the bundle to drop, and the yellow light of the lantern brought out its honey colour, making it shine and bounce as she swished it this way and that. It settled over her breasts again, leaving a peephole for each rosebud nipple.

She reached for her bust supporter, or brassiere as they were now called, and tied it on. Then she lifted her breasts and brought them together to assess the effect that the brassiere and her new dress would have on her cleavage. She nodded to herself in the mirror. She was not as full-busted as she would like to be, but her shape suited the loose clothing and natural waist look that was the latest fashion, even for evening wear. She was glad Mrs Hanlon allowed her girls a choice between corsets and camisoles or brassieres. The Methodist Missionary School for Girls, although not a finishing school like Mrs Hanlon's, insisted all their girls wear the dreadful straight-fronted corsets to formal occasions. They made Jessie's back ache.

Mrs Hanlon's School for Young Ladies offered more liberties than the Methodists. The girls were encouraged to attend social functions, and were allowed to be escorted by young men provided they arranged a suitable chaperone. And as it was a smaller establishment, each girl had her own private room.

The formal functions, like the ball she was attending that evening, were what Jessie referred to as husband and wife bazaars. 'Bizarre' was more apt. The young ladies paraded and the men gawked. She realised she shouldn't be so critical. It had taken her all of the first six months to overcome the near-terminal shyness she suffered upon first arriving in Nairobi, but a more brainless bunch of immature bachelors she had yet to see. They were almost exclusively the sons of wealthy settlers — all very eligible according to Mrs Hanlon — but, by and large, gormless.

One or two had taken her eye, but each time she thought she had found someone slightly appealing, Ewart Grogan would reappear in her life and their shortcomings became all too apparent.

Not that she actually spoke to Grogan. She might be enjoying a day at the races, and he would be there on the members' lawn, sipping champagne with a group of friends. Or she would be in Sixth Avenue, promenading with a girlfriend, and he would be across the road in discussion with a couple of business acquaintances. She once saw him on the station with his wife and children — they must have been his children because one or two were his spitting image — and had been struck by a great sense of emptiness that she wasn't in that picture. Whatever it was, his presence and his personality — or the memory of it — cut all other men down to nothing.

On one occasion, at the Commissioner's Grand Ball, Ewart went waltzing by with a stunning young woman in his arms and their eyes met. In the time it took for her heart to skip and for the dancing couples to spin past each other, Jessie felt she saw a flicker of awareness in those commanding eyes of his. It could have been a spark of interest in her as a woman, rather than his recollection of a fifteen-year-old girl, for he turned again to follow her passage before her partner twirled her away and out of his sight. For the remainder of the night she kept one eye on him in the hope that he would seek her out for a dance. She prepared a number of witty remarks and little games she would play to tease him while he tried to recall where they had met. He would ask had it been at the Governor's tea party in May? And she would reply that yes, she had attended, but he was too busy showering his attentions on the dazzling lady in a red dress, and hadn't noticed her. But the night ended without him ever glancing her way again.

She wondered if it was wrong to feel as she did. Ewart Grogan was a married man. But although he was charming to all in his orbit, with her acute attention to his every gesture, and a woman's intuition, Jessie believed he was a man inclined to have a roving eye. She realised she had sensed this upon meeting him as a young girl in Londiani. Maybe it was the reason she had always considered him available, and was the cause of her occasional restless nights.

It was the reason she had agreed to attend Mrs Hanlon's School for Young Ladies when her father told her, more than a year ago, about Ewart Grogan's generous bursary. By then she had realised she had the looks to win his attention, but knew she needed something more to win his heart.

Grogan came out the front door and stood on the top step that led down to Chiromo's spacious gardens. He stretched his arms above his head, feeling the welcome warmth of the feeble morning sun on his chest.

Marcus was walking wearily up the gravel path, wearing the navy suit he'd had on when he arrived at Mombasa from Oxford. Grogan had originally thought it was a case of him trying to look his best for his homecoming, but he later found that Marcus preferred the suit to other, more practical clothes. Grogan found it curious. Perhaps the young man wore it as a badge of honour — a Maasai in a Drury Lane suit was certainly a unique sight.

'Ah! There you are, young Marcus!' Grogan said. 'We thought you were coming on yesterday's train.'

'I *was* on yesterday's train. Unfortunately, it didn't arrive until today. Sorry for the inconvenience.'

'Is that the best a budding lawyer can do in his own defence?' Grogan asked, smiling, and indicating the small coffee table on the veranda. 'Come, sit with me. William is bringing tea. How is everything in Londiani?'

'Not bad. Mr Dalton started to sow the maize, and then took ill, so he wants to wait for a week or so.'

'Old Bruce, eh? I haven't asked about him and little Jessie. How are they? It must be five years. About the time you went off to Oxford.'

'Mr Dalton is finding the farm more difficult these days, and Jessie … well, Jessie is no longer a little girl. She becomes twenty-one next month, and Mr Dalton is coming down to Nairobi to see her.'

'Twenty-one! I can't imagine it.' Grogan remembered her as a scruffy child when he stayed at her father's farm at Londiani. Her only saving grace had been her beautiful olive skin and long fair hair. 'Did you say she's here in Nairobi?'

'Yes, she's been attending Mrs Hanlon's school this past year.'

'Mrs Hanlon's school? The finishing school, or whatever it's called?' He remembered arranging the bursary on her behalf.

'Yes, Mrs Hanlon's School for Young Ladies.'

'Well, why didn't she come to visit?'

Marcus looked uncomfortable. 'I don't know. Maybe she felt strange about it.'

Grogan couldn't imagine why. 'Anyway, I must write to Bruce. Maybe I can arrange a little party for the girl.' He imagined convincing Dalton to accept his offer wouldn't be easy. 'How is the farm business going?' He felt a vague sense of guilt for not having called into Londiani in all that time, but he found visiting his forest concession was easier from Molo — a station a few miles short of Londiani.

'He went through one very bad year while I was away in Oxford, but he's been able to sell some potatoes and a few heifers lately.'

'And there's only the three of you running the place?'

'He hired another old Maasai man to help with the cattle. I said I could do it, but he refused. You will remember what he's like. He said I had to be off doing my lawyer's job.'

'And are you? Off doing your lawyer's job?'

'Well, in a way. I am down here to speak to one of the elders of the Purko section who is worried about some changes to the Maasai land resettlement agreement.'

'Land resettlement agreement? You mean the plan to reunite the two parts of the Maasai tribe in one place?'

'Yes. The government wants to move all the clans from north of the railway, around Laikipia, to the south.'

'Isn't that what your chief, Lenana, wants?'

'I'm not sure. I will be meeting with the elder, Ole Gilisho, and Lenana at Ngong.'

Grogan had succeeded Delamere as President of the Colonists' Association, and in this capacity had spoken to the Governor, Sir Percy Girouard, about the northern land. There were many among the Settlers who said that giving the good grazing land of the Laikipia Plateau to the Maasai back in 1904 had been a huge mistake.

'I believe the Maasai need to be in one place,' Grogan said. 'How can Lenana govern them if they are spread all over the countryside?'

Marcus fiddled with his teacup. 'It is not really about governing. The *laibon* is more like a prophet. His role is to make decisions about ceremonies, to advise on matters about our teachings and our culture. He heals the sick and arranges the rainfall. He doesn't rule us in the same way as the chiefs of other tribes do.'

'Well, from what I've heard, the northern group are causing quite a bit of trouble up there in the Laikipia region. If they all go south, it will be easier to manage them.'

Marcus carefully replaced his cup. 'I had better get changed for breakfast.'

Grogan patted Marcus on the back as he passed and said with a smile, 'Yes, old boy, you look totally fagged. If you're going to keep up these night-time activities, you need your rest.'

Marcus walked inside without comment.

William drove Grogan past the gardens that Jeevanjee had donated to the town and where his life-size statue of Her Majesty Queen Victoria now stood. Government Road seemed to grow busier every day, Grogan thought, and the buildings more substantial. William drew the carriage to a halt outside the offices of A M Jeevanjee and Company.

Grogan appraised the building as he stepped down. Double-fronted, like so many of the more modern establishments, but with just a touch of Victorian-era nostalgia in the filigreed cast iron lining the veranda and a vestige of stained glass on the panelled door.

He entered into an antechamber, which looked very much like every room in any type of Indian business premises, be it a cloth merchant, a spice dealer or a businessman's office — an identical mix of austerity and efficiency. For some strange reason, they all smelled of a mixture of curry and incense.

Jeevanjee's office furniture was Spartan and the floor bare, except for a small rug. Half-closed holland blinds obscured the light through the windows, making the interior uncomfortably dim, and although there were connections for the notoriously unreliable electric lighting, none were turned on.

The antechamber was empty, but Jeevanjee must have heard him enter, as his wide and very stout frame appeared in the doorway to the adjoining office.

'Ah, Mr Grogan,' he said.

'Morning, Mr Jeevanjee,' Grogan answered.

'Come in, please.'

They shook hands and Jeevanjee stood aside to allow Grogan to enter his office first. A battered old swivel chair sat behind a large but simple desk under the window. 'Please,' Jeevanjee said, indicating the visitor's chair, which was equally old but in better condition than his own. He waited until Grogan was seated before taking his seat on the other side of the desk.

'Thank you for coming, Mr Grogan. As I said in my note, I'd like to discuss arrangements whereby we can profitably combine our resources at your wharf at Mbaraki.'

Grogan nodded. He had been doing battle with the government over access to a further tranche of land in Mbaraki for his deep-water port, and he appeared to be on the verge of winning considerable expanded capacity. Jeevanjee's stevedoring operation at the existing wharf would be an excellent match with his plans.

Since the days of their swamp project, Grogan had respected the Indian's business brain. For an uneducated man, he was remarkably astute in finding ways to make money. But it was not just any business opportunity that he chose. Like Grogan, he knew there were dozens of good prospects in British East Africa for the right kind of entrepreneur. What Grogan most admired about Jeevanjee was his interest in the new and innovative business opportunity. Once a business was established and had proved its profit-making capabilities, it lost most of its appeal for Jeevanjee; Grogan felt the same way.

Although stevedoring was not a new or innovative enterprise, Jeevanjee planned to use it in an innovative way to gain leverage from their combined operations. He'd said to Grogan preparatory to their meeting: 'What is a ship without a port? And what is a port without stevedores?' Grogan immediately understood what he had in mind.

Traffic through the government wharves had been moribund since inception — strangled by myriad independent operators clamouring for business. By closely linking wharfing and stevedoring, Jeevanjee could schedule his men to meet ships arriving at Grogan's wharf and obtain maximum throughput — the basis of Grogan's revenue. The flow of material through the docks would be streamlined to mutual advantage. Grogan was quietly enthusiastic. Kilindini Harbour, Wharves and Estates Company Ltd and A M Jeevanjee and Company would be an excellent business mix.

An hour later, the two men had substantially agreed on all the major issues and Grogan drafted papers to capture it. Jeevanjee seemed pleased, and suggested they toast to their renewed association.

Grogan raised an eyebrow. 'By "toast", do you mean alcohol, Mr Jeevanjee?'

The big man smiled expansively, 'Is there any other kind, Mr Grogan?' and lumbered through his office door.

From the antechamber office Grogan could hear loud clattering as Jeevanjee rifled through all possible storage places.

His voice — sounding as if it emanated from a cupboard — drifted back to Grogan, apologising for having no assistant to attend to such matters, and what a pity it was that he had not planned more adequately for the occasion. Finally he returned, looking flushed, carrying two glasses and a half-bottle of whisky.

'To our new enterprise,' he said, raising his glass to Grogan who saluted him in return. 'May it be as profitable as the swamp.'

They clinked glasses, sipped their whisky and chatted amiably.

'I understand your brother runs the Mombasa side of your business?' Grogan said.

'For the time being, Mr Grogan. His name is Tayabali, but I am sending two of my sons to join him presently. They will help with the stevedoring side of the business. You will meet them all when you go to Mombasa to inspect our operations.'

'I look forward to it.'

Jeevanjee had told him he had several cousins, aunts and uncles on the Karachi side of the operations. It was a family affair.

'And how are the rest of the family?' Grogan asked, trying a more comfortable position on his straight-backed chair. 'Your charming young daughter ... where is she these days?'

'Atiya has finished college and is helping me here in the office, although, as you can see, not today. She was not well this morning. And your family? I hope they are all in good health.'

'Well enough, although my oldest, who is ten, is suffering from some slight ailment at the moment.'

'I'm sorry to hear that.' Jeevanjee nodded, looking sad.

They sipped their whisky in silence for a moment before Jeevanjee said, 'Children can be a worry at times, isn't that so, Mr Grogan?'

'Indeed.'

'My Atiya is now twenty-one years of age, and still not married. I try to introduce her to some of the nice young Bohra men, but she turns up her nose.'

'Surely there are plenty of young Indian fellows who would make for an ideal match?'

'Oh, but they are not all Bohras. It must be a Bohra for her to marry.'

'Well, I can understand that might be the ideal situation, but surely a countryman is close enough?'

'No-no. Oh, no. We may all appear alike to you, Mr Grogan, but we would no sooner marry outside our sect than you Englishmen would marry a ... an African.'

'Surely not! Not even another Moslem?'

'Not even another Moslem, although that would not be so bad as a Hindu, a Jain or a Sikh.'

'Then I don't envy you your task of finding her a husband.'

'I wish I could say it will happen if God wishes, but I suspect it might be out of even God's hands.'

'How so?'

'My Atiya has been acting very strangely these days. She mopes around, is not eating her meals. She is also often unwell, as is the case this very day.' He paused to take a rather large mouthful of his whisky, which caused him to choke. He coughed and dabbed at his eyes with a silk kerchief before continuing. 'I do believe she has a boyfriend, Mr Grogan.' His expression was one of wretched misery. 'I swear by almighty God, it would kill me if it were someone outside the Bohra community.'

The figure clung to the tree line, its moon shadows cloaking his cautious progress along the dirt track that was Forest Road. He froze, immobilised by a rustle in the long grass beside the track. After a moment he let his breath escape as a mongoose scurried into darkness.

Before moving on he checked the landmarks to confirm his position, for although he knew the house by daylight, this was the first time he had attempted to find it at night.

Behind him was Ainsworth Bridge. On the rise across the river he picked out the flagpole on the new hospital building silhouetted against the blue-black sky. A few plots further along was the Norfolk Hotel, another imposing shape. Satisfied that he was now quite close to his target, he moved on, but with extreme caution.

The Jeevanjee house appeared through a clutter of low shrubs. It was in total darkness except for a dim light from a shuttered window the next but one from Atiya's room. He crouched in the darkness, listening to the pounding of his heart and scanning every corner of the building for a movement that would indicate a trap.

He tried to regain control of himself. His hands shook, and his breathing was shallow, causing him to swallow and take a deep breath to regain his composure. Even when hunting lion he had never been so fearful, but in this hunt it was more than his life at stake — if he was discovered lurking around the Jeevanjee house after dark, he would never see the love of his life again.

The light behind the shuttered window went out.

He waited a full ten minutes more before he crept forward, across the open courtyard in the full light of the moon, and into the relative safety of the shadows of the house. He took a deep, silent breath, and slowly let it expire.

On his haunches beneath a window, he checked the instructions she had given him — *the second window on the left-hand side of the house*. The window above him was the second window, but with a rush of panic he realised he was unsure if it was the second window from the entrance or from the end. He cursed himself for not clarifying it when they'd made their plans. There was no way he could be sure it was Atiya's window or that of one of her fierce brothers.

He scratched at the shutter.

After a moment he heard a click and the shutter opened. His heart was in his mouth until Atiya's hand reached out and touched him on the cheek. He stood and they embraced through the open shutters. When her lips touched his, he felt the same electric excitement that had swept him into heady ecstasy the first time they had kissed. It was a totally unknown sensation for him. The Maasai never kiss, and although his opportunities with Maasai girls had been few, it was a thrill he would not have experienced if he hadn't met Atiya. Since she had introduced him to that wonderful foreign custom he'd dreamed of her lips, day and night.

When they separated from their embrace, Atiya drew Marcus into her bedroom.

CHAPTER 43

'My dear Gertie,' Quentin said as Gertrude swept into the room with an armful of flowers, 'if you don't stop fussing around with these decorations I shall be forced to do something silly, like assist you.'

Gertrude laughed. 'And that would simply be too much for the likes of Mr Quentin Grogan, would it not?'

'Indeed, so come away from this scene of mindless chaos,' he indicated by a sweep of his arm the workers and servants busying themselves in the ballroom, 'and arrange something for a man to drink. I'm perishingly thirsty.'

'Oh, you poor dear,' Gertrude said, in a voice thick with sarcasm. 'Would that be tea, or are you great white hunters permitted to take something stronger before sundown?' But she handed the flowers to one of the servants, and took him by the arm to lead him towards the drawing room.

'Somewhere on one of His Majesty's ships, the sun is over the yardarm,' he said.

'May I remind you, dear brother-in-law, you are no longer with His Majesty's navy.'

'Irrelevant, and thank God for that. There's more money to be made in ivory.'

The afternoon sun streamed through the drawing room's white muslin drapes bringing vibrancy to the terracotta-coloured walls — Gertrude's only serious departure from the architect's suggestions. He had wanted modern pastel colours, but Gertrude insisted on a more traditional finish for the drawing room, where she also retained the traditional floral frieze beneath elaborate plaster cornices. She particularly wanted the drawing room to reflect the comforts of England, for although she considered herself an American by adoption, like all well-bred colonists she still called the mother country home.

Gertrude went to the rosewood sideboard that filled the alcove opposite the marble fireplace. 'Rum?' she enquired.

'As a matter of fact, do you have a gin? I seem to have developed a liking for it upcountry.'

She uncorked the Gilbeys and poured a portion into a crystal tumbler, then, remembering Quentin's tastes, added another splash. 'I have no lime twists here. Would you like me to call for some from the kitchen?'

'No need, my dear.' He took the glass from her. 'You're not joining me?'

'No. A little early for me, but I will take a glass of tonic water.'

She carried her glass to the Queen Anne suite; he stood at his chair until she sat on the serpentine-backed sofa opposite him.

Gertrude always felt relaxed with Quentin. While awaiting Ewart's arrival in England from his Cape-to-Cairo trek, she had established a kinship with Ewart's youngest brother within the large household of more staid family members, many of whom were adult children of their father's first marriage. Being just a few years older, Gertrude grew quite close to Quentin, and found they shared an irreverence for prim Victorian conventions. Hers was born from a life spent far from the influence of the British upper classes, and Quentin's by his rebellious nature.

'The outdoor life seems to have agreed with you,' she said. At twenty-eight, Quentin still had the Grogans' fresh-faced appearance.

Quentin took a sip of his gin and tonic. 'Bloody hard work for the most of it.'

'And will you go back?'

'I don't think so, Gertie. There're almost as many hunters up there as there are elephant these days. I'm thinking about

Ewart's suggestion that I join him and Philip here in Nairobi. What do you think?'

'There's certainly plenty to do. Sir Percy Girouard appears prepared to open new land concessions up north and —'

'You know what I mean, Gertie. I'm not sure I can work too closely with Ewart. I love my brother dearly, but you know what he's like. He insists everything must be done his way. I'm not at all sure I can operate like that.'

'I know what you mean, Quentin, but you just need to adjust.'

She poured more tonic into her glass before offering the bottle to him. He raised his hand, declining.

'In my stepfather's words,' she continued, 'Ewart is a thruster. I've never seen or heard of a man who has more self-confidence, sense of purpose or love of a challenge than Ewart.'

'All of which are no doubt essential to survive in Africa — in business as well as in any other pursuit,' Quentin said. 'And you could add to that list. Individualism and ambition come to mind.'

'Yes.' Gertrude nodded, looking through the window where the breeze gently stirred the drapes. Her husband was certainly a complex person. Even now she found aspects of his personality that she'd little suspected were there at the time of their marriage. 'I sometimes think Ewart has no real need for the support and intimacy of others,' she said wistfully, and then realised she had spoken her private thoughts aloud. She laughed self-consciously. 'But you are making too much of this, dear Quentin. I'm sure there are positions within Ewart's domain where you will have free rein to apply your talents — so long as it's not anything to do with motor cars.' She alluded to his last position in England with a motoring firm, where he was sacked for driving at what Clement Talbot referred to as 'break-neck speed'.

He smiled with her. 'Gertie, there's no chance of reaching forty-five miles per hour on these roads, I can assure you.'

'I'll take your word for that. Another drink?'

'Please.' He handed her his empty glass. 'Now, tell me about this little lady who's having her twenty-first celebrations here tonight.'

323

'She's Miss Jessica Dalton. Ewart met the family years ago during his first excursion up in the north-west.'

'What is she like?'

'I have no idea. Even Ewart hasn't seen her in over five years. He brought her father over here yesterday for tea, but Jessica was being fitted for her gown and we shan't see her until this evening, at the party.' She paused while opening the gin bottle to say, 'Why do you ask?' She tried to conceal her smile, knowing full well the answer.

'I've found that women between the ages of ten and thirty are very rare in British East Africa.'

'Really?' She popped the tonic water and added it to the gin in his glass. 'I hadn't noticed.'

'I sometimes think it's as if their families want to hide them from me.'

Quentin Grogan was known to have an eye for the ladies. It was another trait he shared with his brother. Always one with a wandering eye, Ewart seemed lately to be paying more attention to some of the women of their acquaintance, Gertrude thought. She loved him, and she knew he loved her, but a man of Ewart's energy was hard to keep from temptation.

The tonic water overflowed the rim of the glass into a fizzing puddle on the rosewood sideboard.

Grogan stood before the bedroom mirror, studying his appearance in preparation to going downstairs with Gertrude to await the arrival of the Daltons and their other guests.

The occasion had grown from a dinner party with the Daltons and a few close friends to celebrate Jessica's majority to a grand party with a guest list of sixty, few of whom had even heard of the Daltons but all of whom were close friends of the Grogans. The exception was the Charles Hamiltons, whom Grogan knew from business dealings in Thika, but whom Gertrude had not previously met. Hamilton's wife, Louise, was a stunning redhead. Grogan had kept an eye on her over recent weeks, finding her discreet flirtatiousness quite exciting. He looked forward to the evening with anticipation.

He turned his head from side to side, checking his hair was

in place. The part, just left of centre, was perfect, but a few loose strands of fair hair had drifted free. He patted them into place, and gave the knot of his bow tie a final tug. It turned askew.

'Damn!' he said, annoyed that he couldn't leave well enough alone. 'Gertrude!' he called over his shoulder. 'Darling, are you there?'

'In a minute,' came her voice from her dressing room.

Grogan gave the tie another tweak. It went sideways. 'Damn the bloody thing to hell!' he spluttered.

'What is it, Ewart?' Gertrude said calmly as she entered their bedroom.

'It's this bloody tie! What fool could invent such a contraption?'

'You're just out of practice, dear. Here, let me see it.'

'Never was any bloody good at ties. Abominations, the lot of them. I'm going to buy one of those fake bow ties — the ones with the ready-made knot and strings.'

'You had one of those years ago, don't you remember? You threw it away because it looked cheap.'

'Did I?' he asked. 'Hmm.'

'There,' she said, stepping back to study it. 'That's better. Now leave it be.'

'All right, all right.' He forced his hands away from his collar. 'Come. Let's go down and have a drink before the herd arrives.'

He offered his arm at the top of the curving staircase and slowly led the way.

Philip stood as Gertrude entered the parlour, nodding a greeting. He had been talking to Quentin, who was leaning against the marble mantel, a cigarette in one hand.

'Evening, Gertie,' Quentin said.

'I see you've started without us,' Ewart said, referring to Quentin's gin.

'In your absence, I received fraternal permission from my other big brother,' he said with an impish grin.

'You did no such thing!' Philip protested.

'It's all right, Philip,' said Gertrude. 'Quentin is only joking. Ewart doesn't mind if his brothers have a little drink, do you dear.' It was a statement more than a question.

'Humph,' Ewart muttered, heading towards the sideboard and its row of crystal decanters. 'And what about you, my dear — a sherry?'

'No, thank you, darling. The guests will be arriving soon, but you go ahead.'

'The guests won't be here for another hour, but I've asked Dalton to bring young Jessica around to meet us a little earlier.'

'While we have a chance, Ewart,' Philip said, moving to where his brother stood at the sideboard, 'I was wondering how your discussions with Governor Sir Percy —'

'You're not going to talk business again, are you Philip?' Gertrude reminded him.

Ewart liked Philip's diligence. 'It's all right, Gertrude,' he said. 'We have a little time. After all, we're all family.'

Philip gave Gertrude an apologetic smile before continuing. 'Are there any further developments on the Uasin Gishu plots?'

Grogan had extended his forestry concession by a further sixty thousand acres, stretching his finances in the process, but the viability still relied on the government agreeing to run a railway spur from Londiani through the forest. They were only ever likely to do that if the Uasin Gishu, and, preferably the Laikipia plateau too, were opened up to intensive farming.

'I think I've persuaded him to that way of thinking, but his problem is how to renegotiate the land agreements with the Maasai.'

'Wasn't all that land business settled years ago?' Gertrude asked, becoming involved despite her objections to what she called 'shop talk' before dinner.

'There was an agreement, of sorts, reached in 1904 to move the Maasai out of the Great Rift Valley,' Ewart said. 'We — that is, the government — had to recoup the investment on the railway, you know, so we decided to open up the Rift Valley to farming and grazing. Half of the Maasai went north, into the Laikipia region, and the other half went south, around Narok.'

'Were they agreeable to that?' she asked.

'I'm sure I don't know, but their chief agreed at the time.'

'So, if they agreed to the present situation in 1904, why would they want to change it again?'

'Well, I'm not at all sure they do, my love, but the Governor believes he can persuade the chiefs.' He carried his glass to a chair. 'And I hope he can, because if that spur line doesn't go through, Lingham and the South Africans will be after my blood.' He said it with a smile on his face, but he was only partly joking.

'We used to call it gunship diplomacy in the navy,' Quentin offered.

Ewart glared at him.

'Excuse me, sir.' The Luo doorman was at the parlour entrance. 'Mr and Miss Dalton are here.'

Grogan nodded. 'Show them in, William.'

The young woman who preceded Bruce Dalton into the parlour was beautiful. It took Grogan a moment to realise it was Jessie.

Gertrude stepped forward. 'Mr Dalton. I'm Gertrude Grogan. Welcome to Chiromo.'

Dalton took her offered hand and bowed stiffly. 'Mrs Grogan. Pleased to meet you. This is my daughter, Jessie.'

Ewart recovered sufficiently to laugh and splutter apologies for his bad manners. 'It's just that I never expected Jessica — Jessie — to be so ... to have grown into such a fine young lady. And Bruce, so good to see you again.' They shook hands. 'You're looking well.'

In fact, Bruce Dalton looked anything but well. The square jaw and unruly red hair were still recognisable, but his solid frame and corpulent belly seemed to have deflated. What remained was a shell of the man Grogan had met in Londiani five years ago.

The young woman had also been transformed over the five years, but in her case it was into an angel. She had grown from a short square girl in overalls into this statuesque woman in a sweeping gown with a nipped waist and boned undergarment that lifted her full breasts beneath her lacy bodice.

Jessie caught Ewart's admiring eye and smiled at him. He was about to speak when Gertrude, now caught in the role of host due to her husband's earlier stupefaction, took Jessie by the arm to meet Quentin and Philip.

Dalton looked awkward in his suit, and remained with Grogan. He was clearly uncomfortable in the unfamiliar atmosphere. Grogan would have preferred to follow the ladies, but listened half-heartedly as Dalton tried to make polite conversation to fill the void. Grogan nodded as he spoke, trying to maintain his concentration. Dalton nervously prattled on with uncharacteristic verbosity; he had always been a man who kept his thoughts to himself, but he gave Grogan no opportunity to rejoin the other party. He sensed Jessie was aware of his gaze, as she entered into animated conversation with his brothers, fluttering her fan and flashing her radiant smile.

When he finally extricated himself from Bruce Dalton's clutches, he found Jessie being escorted from the room by Quentin. Grogan turned to Gertrude with a questioning look.

'Quentin's showing Jessie the gardens, dear,' she said. 'Why don't you take Mr Dalton and show him the rooms we've made up for them in the south wing.'

'I . . .' he began as Quentin and Jessie disappeared from sight. 'I'd be delighted. Follow me, old boy,' he said, leading Dalton from the room, but his searching eyes went beyond him to the window, through which he could see Quentin offering his arm to the enchanting Jessie.

Gertrude took a moment to appraise the gathering. The guests were now all present and filled Chiromo's ballroom. The stringed quartet, who were a rare find by Gertrude, were a gathering of Nairobi enthusiasts — the cellist coming from as far afield as Channon Bridge. Their chamber music was just perfect for the occasion. The servants and hired staff swept through the gathering serving drinks and chef's famous *eu dervs*. There was a buzz of conversation and a pattering of laughter. Everything was perfect.

Holding court near the ballroom's entrance was Ewart, surrounded by more than half a dozen guests. Gertrude was accustomed to Ewart's magnetic effect on people — both men and women. They gravitated towards him, and why not? He had charm, wit, he was a captivating speaker and his eyes engaged everyone in his orbit. She was also accustomed to at least one female in a gathering who was more than merely entertained by Ewart's repartee. She soon revealed herself by appearing

328

particularly amused by his jokes and more than usually fascinated by his stories, and by being the first to encourage him to continue when he appeared to be about to move away.

Gertrude knew these women were as she had been, and still remained — obsessed by the obvious power of the man — but in their case, they wanted to possess it for themselves. This Gertrude could not allow.

Unfortunately, Ewart luxuriated in the attention. She sensed he was an eager accomplice in a game in which he staked the risk of being discovered against the thrill of a brief encounter. For that was what they invariably were — brief, meaningless encounters after which, having conquered the willing prey, he tired of the game and returned to his life with Gertrude.

Regrettably, Gertrude knew about all the affairs — at least she assumed it was all of them — because Nairobi was too small a town to keep anything a secret for long. Women friends — probably jealous that they were not the successful seductresses — would hint at this or that sighting of Ewart with an attractive companion. Pieces came together and soon Gertrude would have the whole story. She sometimes wondered how she and Ewart had arrived at the situation where he could blithely succumb to a seductive female, then return to her apparently unburdened by guilt.

Ewart was the supreme individualist. She greatly admired his unwavering self-confidence and sense of purpose, but it had its disadvantages. Sadly for Gertrude, it meant he had no inherent need of her support, nor that of anyone else, and the intimacy that she needed from him was not reciprocated. She had no doubt that Ewart still loved her. He could be very demonstrative in his love-making, kind and attentive, and there were occasions when they could recapture the same tumultuous passion that had been so much a part of their lives just a few years ago.

She also sometimes wondered how she could tolerate such infidelity, but she knew the answer, no matter how distasteful it was. She was still as madly and deeply in love with Ewart Scott Grogan as she had been when he'd conquered all Africa for her.

Louise Hamilton's laugh was soft and throaty. Grogan was aware of her presence in the circle of guests he was attempting to entertain with stories of his times in the gold fields of California. When next she laughed, she placed a hand on his forearm — a subtle, but significant gesture.

At that point he would normally promote conversation within the circle and, in a confidential aside, suggest to the lady that she might like to join him on the veranda for a breath of cool night air. But that night he had been greatly distracted by Quentin and his shameful monopolisation of Jessie Dalton's time. He had been talking to her almost constantly since she had arrived that evening. Grogan thought it most inconsiderate of him — he should allow her to circulate amongst the other guests. After all, it was a party to celebrate her twenty-first birthday.

The pair were at the fireside, he leaning on the mantel and she sitting with her hands folded in her lap. Quentin leaned over her, whispered something to her, and Jessie laughed — not the throaty confident sound of Louise Hamilton, but the merry, unpretentious chuckle of one genuinely enjoying the conversation.

Grogan intended to put a stop to it. He would soon interrupt them to suggest that Jessie should allow him to introduce her to the other guests.

Jessie felt completely at ease with Quentin. She seemed to have spent most of the party in his company, and while Mrs Hanlon had taught her to overcome much of the shyness she'd suffered when she arrived at her school as a bumbling hayseed, she had still to learn the art of mixing with people as important as the Grogans' guests appeared to be. The house was filled with very rich men and peers of the realm, and although Quentin dismissed them as the jetsam of an overburdened House of Lords, she was in awe of them.

Talking to Quentin was fun. He enjoyed a fair share of the famous Grogan charm, and some might even think he was more handsome than his older brother.

Jessie thought Quentin handsome enough, but the older man, with the touch of silver at his temples, had something extra, something intangible that made him stand apart from any other man she had ever met. If the twenty-one-year-old had been pressed for an explanation, she would describe it as the irresistible appeal of strength, for there was no doubt Ewart Grogan was a potently powerful man. It was definable by his bearing. He carried himself like a man who was exactly where he desired to be in his life. He had faced challenges that would make a lesser man quake, and he had enjoyed the experiences. She felt that when he entered a room people became instantly aware of his presence as if they were in a jungle, alone, and the roar of a lion commanded their attention.

She had no idea what she wanted of him. He was married, and one of Nairobi's most influential men. Perhaps, for the moment, she could be content with nothing more from him than an acknowledgement of her existence.

She watched now as she had done all evening — covertly — while trying to pay attention to Quentin's conversation. Once or twice Ewart almost caught her looking at him, but she had deflected her gaze in the nick of time. Now he was excusing himself from his circle of friends, probably to have words in private with the redhead he had been chatting to for most of the evening, or perhaps to speak with his wife, who was in another group.

His tread was graceful and balanced. As he proceeded across the room she realised with a shock he was heading in her direction. She felt an inexplicable panic. She had envied the women in his company, but now that he was headed in her direction she had the bizarre urge to flee. She got to her feet, taking Quentin by surprise, but explaining that her leg had gone numb and she needed to stretch it.

To escape she at first thought she could ask Quentin to spirit her away, perhaps to show her the gun collection in the billiard room, which he had alluded to earlier, but it was too late. She stood, frozen like a gazelle under the gaze of a leopard. Ewart's progress was relentless. He was smiling at her as he approached.

Quentin interrupted his story to enquire if there was anything wrong. She said no, everything was quite all right but she had to go; she had to go somewhere — to her room for a moment. She fled, leaving the two brothers staring after her.

CHAPTER 44

Jessie came out of the house after lunch, and found Marcus sitting on the bench seat under Chiromo's huge podocarpus tree.

'Where were you, Marcus?' she said, joining him on the seat. 'I looked everywhere for you last night and you were nowhere about.' Jessie tried her best to imitate the hurt-feelings voice she'd used as a girl, but as usual Marcus ignored her pretence.

'I was with your father for some time, then he went to bed, not feeling well.'

'Not well? I didn't realise.'

'If you paid more attention to those close to you, and less to those who flatter you, you might have noticed.'

'I was busy. And after Papa went to bed, where did you go?'

'I was there, but you had so many admirers you ignored me.'

'I did not!' she said, before noticing he was teasing. 'Well, I did have one admirer ... for most of the time.'

'Mister Quentin Grogan, I think.'

'Yes ... I suppose it was,' she said nonchalantly.

'He seemed pleased with your very polite manners. I should tell him what you were like when you were a girl, when you used to gallop all over the hills in Londiani, shooting, shooting.'

'I did nothing of the kind, and you'll tell him no such thing.'

'Oh-ho ... so you are serious about him?'

She thought about it for a moment. 'I'm not so sure.'

'Why not? He has the Grogan good looks and the Grogan ... what do you call it? Charm.'

'Yes, he's quite handsome, I suppose, but perhaps he's a bit too young.'

'Too young! He must be ten years older than you.'

'Seven, actually. But a man should be at least fifteen years older than the woman he intends to marry.'

'Oh no, now you're getting married.'

'Don't be silly, Marcus. I'm just stating what everyone says about people's ages.'

'And *everyone* being ...?' He folded his arms, looking down his nose at her.

'Stop acting like a lawyer. And anyway, where were you last night?'

'I was around.'

'No, you weren't. I went looking for you, and the servants told me you had disappeared out the door around ten.'

'Well ... I had someone who was expecting me.'

'You have a secret lover, don't you?' she said with mounting excitement. 'Tell me about her.'

'What do you know about love, *Enkiti*? Just because you wear a gown in place of your cover-alls doesn't suddenly make you a woman.'

She fluttered an imaginary fan under her chin. 'You might be surprised,' she said, batting her long lashes. 'So tell me, who is she?' She gave him a coquettish smile. 'Tell me everything. Is she a Maasai girl?'

'No.'

'Well, what then?'

Marcus stood, agitated. 'Really, Jessie. You're such a child. Twenty-one years old and still playing childish games.'

He strode off into the spacious Chiromo gardens with his hands in his pockets and his shoulders up around his ears.

'Ah! There you are,' Ewart said cheerfully as he approached.

'Oh, Mr Grogan!' Jessie said, startled.

'I'm sorry, my dear. Didn't mean to surprise you.'

'No, you didn't, I was just ... just sitting.' She winced inwardly at her foolishness.

'So you are.'

His smile was probably the most wonderful thing in the world.

'Do call me Ewart. You make me sound like your grandfather. Do you mind if I join you?'

'No.' It sounded too abrupt. 'I mean, please do.' Now she sounded too forward.

'I saw you from the window,' he went on. 'Alone at last, I thought.'

She felt the colour rise to her cheeks.

'I mean, I thought it was about time I broke the ice. You know, you are a very difficult young lady to find alone.'

'I am?' She wondered if he was referring to her rudeness of the previous night when she'd virtually bolted from the room at his approach, leaving both him and his brother in, she imagined, stunned disbelief at her bad manners. She felt she would die of embarrassment if he raised it with her in the full light of day.

'Just thought it time for a chat, you and I. Do you mind if I smoke?'

'Not at all.' That was better. Mature, measured, and certainly not overwhelmed by him being on the same garden seat with her.

'Twenty-one,' he said, sucking his pipe into life and then extinguishing the match with a puff. 'What are your plans now that you've become a grown woman?'

He wore that half-smile she remembered from Londiani. In those days she'd never quite known if he was teasing or trying to be conversational. She decided on this occasion to treat it as the former.

'Oh, I don't know ... maybe I'll become a White Hunter and make my fortune hunting ivory.'

Ewart stopped puffing his pipe and stared at her for a moment, before bursting into uproarious laughter. 'I don't know where you get that sense of humour.' His eyes sparkled with mirth. 'I can't say I see it in your father. But seriously now, what is it you are after in life?'

She couldn't now bear to admit that she wasn't entirely joking about her desire to go hunting. She and Quentin had spoken of it at her party the previous evening, and found they shared a love of the sport. 'Oh, it's difficult to say. Perhaps I'll go back to the farm. Papa can always use some help.'

'I spoke to Bruce briefly about you last night.'

'You did?'

'Yes, I asked him how he felt about you staying up there on the farm now that you are of an age to be making your way in the world, and he said it was a matter for you.'

'Papa said that?'

'Well, not precisely. Your father is a man of few words — as I'm sure you know — but he did give me the distinct impression that he wouldn't insist on you remaining on the farm if there was something on offer that you would prefer.'

'Then it's settled. I will remain on the farm for I have no skills that would suit me to any other position. Thanks to Mrs Hanlon, I know how to set a table for eight, the correct form of address for an archbishop, and a dozen different stitches to decorate a doily, but not much else.'

'You can read and write, I suppose.'

'Of course I can.' She frowned at him, annoyed that she had given him the impression that she was a simpleton. 'And do arithmetic and book-keeping.'

'Excellent! Then you have a job. You can assist Philip in keeping the books.' He studied her expression, which was one of bewilderment. 'If you wish.'

'I ... I'm ...'

'No need to make a decision at this moment. Think about it, and of course you'll have to discuss it with your father.'

Nairobi, and all its excitement, compared to the tedious monotony of Londiani came into stark contrast. In Nairobi she might mix with interesting people like those she'd met at her party; she could make new friends; she could buy just about anything in Nairobi's many stores. The changes that a position in Nairobi could make to her life made her head spin. She could spend time with the two most exciting men she could imagine.

Ewart was smiling at her, nodding his reassurance. 'Are you interested?'

'Yes! But, um, as you say, I need to think about it a little more.'

Atiya lay with her head on Marcus's bare chest. Sunlight fell through the tree above them in dappled patches. The diaphanous folds of her white sari were draped loosely across her naked body, not to keep away the chill — they were both gleaming with perspiration — but because when the height of passion had passed, she felt curiously in need of modesty.

Marcus seemed to have no such concerns. He lay on his back, naked, his manhood lying thick and limp across his belly, and his chest rising and falling in sleep.

Atiya felt deliciously wicked. Marcus's body elicited a behaviour from her that shocked and amazed her. Never in her wildest dreams could she have imagined lying naked with a man in the bush. Lying naked with a black man was inconceivable. She wondered how she could have changed so much since she had fallen in love with him. Her perceived wickedness unashamedly excited her. The illicit acts between a man and a woman had always intrigued her. Some of the girls in the Mission College were experienced — or said they were. They would whisper secrets to one another within Atiya's hearing. What she heard caused a warmth to spread through her thighs to forbidden places. At night, alone, she would try to imagine how it might feel as a man entered her body.

The sight of Marcus's member also excited her. She found it endlessly fascinating. Already large, it became enormous when he was aroused by their petting and fondling. She watched it grow with fascination. When he made love to her, it was divine — the more so now that she had learned to enjoy it, and to explore her own pleasurable feelings.

She reached a hand to touch it, and gently ran a finger along its soft roundness. Marcus stirred. She knew him well enough now to know that he was already acutely awake, remaining still in observance of some instinct, while his senses absorbed the world around him. After a moment more he put his arm around her.

'Mmm,' he said, kissing her on the top of her head.

'You slept,' she said.

'I'm sorry. I was very tired. I haven't slept well for some time.'

'Is something troubling you?'

He thought for a moment. 'Yes,' he replied.

She waited for him to proceed, but when he remained silent she lifted her head from his chest and looked into his eyes. 'Marcus? Won't you tell me?'

'It is too much to concern you. I try to understand it, but at times it's just too much for me too.'

'If you tell me, maybe it will help you to understand too.'

He looked at her for a moment, and then sat up, drawing her to him to rest his back against the tree.

'I told you I have been speaking with some of my people about the meeting they will have with the Governor,' he said.

'About the land resettlement?'

'Yes. It troubles me. Some of the elders disagree with what is proposed and want our leader to be strong. They say we were tricked into agreeing in 1904. Now the British want to push us harder. The young men — the *moran* — want to fight.'

'Fight the government?'

'Yes. But many of the elders are saying we cannot defeat the British in war, and that we must again talk.'

'You said that some disagreed with the first resettlement plans in 1904. Then why did your chief sign it in the first place?'

Marcus's chest rose in a deep breath. 'It is difficult to explain. You will find it strange, but the Maasai do not have a chief, or the so-called Paramount Chief of the Maasai as Lenana is called. Before the British arrived, the Maasai had no such title. We Maasai follow the advice of different councils. Some deal with matters concerning the age-set. Others work as councils of war. The Maasai are guided by the *laibon* when it comes to healing and matters of timing for the important ceremonies in our lives; for instance, when we can be circumcised, and when we can become a warrior.

'Now that I have become familiar with their ways, I understand what the British had in mind by making Lenana the

Paramount Chief — it's a title that makes administration easier for them. You see, the British have no way of dealing with a tribe that has more than one spokesman.'

'Why did they choose Lenana over all the other elders?' she asked.

'Lenana is a *laibon*, but also the son of the Great Laibon, Mbatian. The Great Laibon was said to have been able to see the future, and predicted the coming of the white man and their diseases. I don't know Lenana, but maybe the British also thought that they could more easily get agreement from him than any other. Maybe he had been friendly to them. But there are some who doubt Lenana's ability to guide us well in this matter.'

'Do you think Lenana will do what must be done?'

He thought about it for a while, and decided he had been too long away from his people to know how Lenana might react. 'I'm not sure,' he said.

'What about you, Marcus? What are you going to do about it?'

'This is a very important matter for me — for all the Maasai. I must help where I can. This type of situation is exactly the reason I studied the law. The Maasai cannot beat the British at their own game. Not without guidance. The elders need someone they can trust to interpret the law and to guide them in their decisions. I must be involved somehow.'

'And if you lose?'

'If I lose?' He smiled. 'If I lose it won't be the first time a great injustice has won the day for the British.' His smile faded and his dark brown eyes found hers. 'But the thought of soldiers driving ten thousand of my people, and over a million of their stock, across the Great Rift Valley ... it terrifies me.'

A driving rain added to the despondent atmosphere of the *enkang*. Brooding above the Maasai village were the Ngong Hills, wreathed in low clouds that were spasmodically tossed about by the strong breeze from the Great Rift Valley.

Ole Gilisho came out of his hut to Marcus, who was sheltering under an umbrella to protect his suit from the rain.

Placing a hand on Marcus's bowed head, the old man gave his blessing. '*Sopa*,' he said.

'*Hepa*,' Marcus replied, adding the traditional greeting, 'I hope your cattle are well.'

'You have come,' the old man said in Maa.

'As you wished it,' Marcus answered.

Ole Gilisho was of the Purko section of the Maasai — the section that Marcus used to belong to — and held the important position of *olaiguenani*, or spokesman, for his age-set. Ole Gilisho was of the age-set that were the last to see the days of immense Maasai power. It was before the rinderpest took the cattle, leaving a multitude of starving tribesmen to squabble for food scraps, and before the smallpox swept away more than half of those who remained.

'And you, my son?' It was an invitation to Marcus to formally introduce himself.

'I am Momposhe Ole Matipe of the Purko section, but I have not joined my age-set.'

The elder showed his surprise. 'What do you mean? How can you leave your people?'

'My father was forsaken by the clan when they left him in jail for a crime he did not commit.' Marcus went on to explain the circumstances.

Ole Gilisho was saddened by the story. 'In those days the Maasai did not understand the white man's ways. They would not know how to raise the injustice of the matter with them.'

'He felt they should have taken him from the British by force.'

Ole Gilisho sighed. 'In the days when your father and I were the *moran*, yes, we could have driven the British away. But now we are weak. Even the Kikuyu show contempt towards us.' He spat in the dirt. 'The *moran* in our war parties are too few. These days we must talk, when in the past we would fight.'

The old man's mind seemed to wander off, for he was silent for some time. Finally, he said, 'This is the matter I wish to discuss with you, my son. I am troubled by it, and ashamed to admit that we are forced to again talk with the British about our land.'

Ole Gilisho led Marcus into the smoky interior of his hut, where he gave him his account of what the British called the 1904 Maasai Land Settlement Agreement, but what the Maasai referred to as the time the British took their land.

When he had finished, Marcus said, 'The government will want Lenana's signature on any new agreement. Surely he will refuse it?'

The elder slowly shook his head. 'I do not know what Lenana will do.'

'Then we must speak to him before we can do anything else. I thought he would be with you, my father. Where is he?'

'Come. He is nearby. You can see him yourself.'

The elder led him from the smoky hut into the bright afternoon sunlight, and onwards up the slopes of the Ngong Hills. After a short walk they approached a tree where a small boy perched in one of its branches. When they were only a few yards away, and Marcus realised the tree was their destination, he noticed that what he'd thought was a boy was in fact an old man, shrivelled with age, wearing an elder's leather cap, or *enkaranda*.

Marcus waited for Ole Gilisho to speak, but he simply stood there, staring at the old man in the tree. Marcus realised he was looking at the *laibon*, the Paramount Chief, the man who would defend the Maasai's rights against the might of the British legal system.

CHAPTER 45

The ball at the Nairobi Club was the best evening that Jessie could ever remember. Quentin had been her escort, and Gertrude Grogan had acted as her chaperone in the absence of Ewart, who was in Mombasa on business.

At the end of the evening, as Gertrude was saying her farewells, Quentin whisked Jessie out from under her nose and into one of Ali Khan's carriages before she could protest. 'Don't worry, Gertie, I'll see Jessie home,' he called as the carriage rumbled out the gate into Ngong Road.

Gertrude shook a fist at him in mock outrage. Jessie and Quentin laughed.

It was a short ride to Mrs Hanlon's boarding house on the other side of Nairobi Hill, but Quentin told Ali Khan to go slow, and be careful not to shake the carriage as he had a delicate heart.

'It's you who have damaged my heart, lovely Jessie,' he whispered into her ear.

The brush of his lips on her neck, and the pressure of his thigh against hers, sent a ripple of pleasure down her spine. 'Have I just?' she said, trying to control the quaver in her voice. 'And how, sir, could that be?'

'It's been strained by my constant efforts to win your affection.'

'Surely not,' she said, letting him take her hand in his. 'You are a big strong man and, from all accounts, a great white hunter.' Jessie started to relax and enjoy the game he was playing with her. 'Maybe you've been hiding behind false assertions all these years,' she teased.

'I may have once been a great hunter, but these days I can't capture the most elusive quarry — the most important in my life.'

'H-how so?' she asked, watching his lips go to her fingertips and gently kiss them.

'I have been hunting for the most beautiful young woman in Nairobi.' His kisses advanced to her wrist.

'Really?'

'And each time I get close, she draws away.'

'That sounds so cruel.'

'Indeed. But I may have her at a disadvantage now,' he said, drawing closer to her lips.

She opened her mouth to speak, but he pressed his lips against hers and she nearly fainted with the unbelievable pleasure of it.

Gertrude was in the parlour when she heard William bring the horses to a halt outside the front entrance. Ewart had reached the veranda by the time she arrived to greet him.

'Hello, my darling,' he said, drawing her to him and covering her mouth with his. He held her to him with a firm hand on her lower back. She could feel the shape of him as he pressed into her through her loose, unboned tea-gown. She was quite sure that Ewart was unaware of this habit of his, but it always excited her. She enjoyed a moment imagining her body beneath him.

'Hello, my love,' she said, leaning back and looking into his smiling eyes. 'How was your trip to Mombasa?'

'Wretched. As usual. And the heat! To make matters worse, I had a touch of the old malaria while I was there.'

'Oh, no. It's a sign you're driving yourself too hard. You must take it easy, or your liver abscess will flare again. You know what it's like.'

'Yes, yes, now don't go getting panicky, I'll be —'

'Papa! Papa!' Nicholas and Emma ran to him, followed by Mrs Redwood carrying little Sarah. Four-year-old Emma wrapped her arms around her father's legs. Ewart bent down and gathered both of them into his arms, kissing and hugging each in turn. He stood and took Sarah from her nanny, and although the baby tried to hide herself from him in her shyness, he lifted her chubby fingers from her eyes and kissed her tenderly on the cheek.

Edmund joined them. 'Hello, father,' he said. 'Welcome home.'

'Thank you, Edmund,' Ewart said, extending a hand to his oldest child, before kissing him on the cheek.

Gertrude didn't approve of these manly greetings between father and son. She felt it further distanced Edmund from his father, and only emphasised the difference between the boy and the other children. He was still only ten years old, but Ewart had decided it was time to treat his elder son as a man. 'It will instil some independence into Edmund', he'd said, and that it would help his son 'come out of himself'. Gertrude could not agree. Her assessment of the situation was that Ewart was applying his own extremely high standards to his two boys, and in the case of Edmund had found him wanting. His response to this was to bring his considerable will to bear on his son to help him 'improve'.

But for Ewart's occasional flaws as a parent, he also had great strengths. He seldom refused his children his time — even when under strong pressure from his many business ventures. And now, returning from his absence in Mombasa, he again sat with them, giving each his full attention while they recounted the important events that had occurred while he was away on business.

Finally, when Rachel — the short, pleasant-faced Kamba maid — brought tea, Ewart told them to go and play outside while he and their mother talked.

Their conversation drifted from family to domestic matters, and then to issues outside the house. Gertrude was keen to hear how Ewart's work with the Jeevanjee interests was progressing. Ewart said it was going well, and that all arrangements for docking Jeevanjee's shipping line had been put in place at Mombasa during his visit.

'I discussed the stevedoring side with Jeevanjee's brother.' He scratched his chin for a moment. 'Strange fellow. Anyway, it appears everything is moving along quite nicely, if a little slowly for my liking.'

'I'm sure Papa will be patient about the loan.' Gertrude was well aware that Ewart was worried about meeting his agreement with her stepfather.

'Maybe so, but I don't want to go to him to ask for an extension.'

'Then let me do it.'

'It's not that. You know what I mean. I don't want to give him any reason to doubt what I'm doing.'

'Yes, I understand what you mean. How is it at the bank?'

He snorted a laugh. 'Grim. They're prepared to take another mortgage over the Naivasha farm, but the terms are savage.'

He looked drawn and tired. The malaria was totally unsympathetic to stress.

'Let's change the subject, shall we?' he said, and reached for his cup, pausing with it at his lips to ask, 'What about our guests, the Daltons? How are they?'

'Mr Dalton went back to Londiani about a week ago. I don't think he is quite well. It was a few days after you left for Mombasa.'

'I see. And what about Jessie?' he asked, offhandedly.

'She's still in Nairobi. Back on the Hill with Mrs Hanlon. Do you recall her husband was taken by the blackwater fever a few weeks ago? Well, she needs a little company at the moment, and Jessie is staying with her for a while.'

'I see,' he said, eventually taking a sip of his tea. 'And how is she, young Jessie?'

'She looks well. We've seen quite a deal of her of late — in Quentin's company.'

'You have?' He replaced his cup on the saucer with a clatter.

'Yes, Quentin's been to see her; checking on her from time to time; making sure she isn't marooned up there, in his words. Just an excuse to see more of her I suspect. He occasionally brings her down here for a luncheon. I must say, she's a charming young lady, don't you think?'

Ewart didn't appear to hear her last words. 'Quentin,' he said, with exasperation. 'Now that he's discovered it, he seems to be enjoying Nairobi's social life.' He shook his head in disapproval. 'It's about time he went back home or got into something useful.'

'I'm not sure Jessie would be happy about that. She seems quite taken with your dashing young brother.'

'With Quentin? Surely not!'

'Unless I'm terribly mistaken, I'd say they are quite fond of one another.'

'Aren't you the least bit worried about the girl, Gertrude?'

'Should I be?'

'Well, for goodness' sake, you know what Quentin's like.'

'They're a couple of young people. Perhaps they're in love. You do remember about being in love, don't you, Ewart?'

Grogan snorted something unintelligible. He reached for his cup and sipped his tea in silence.

Atiya entered the sitting room for the third time that morning. Her father was in the same place — in his favourite, overstuffed chair. He seemed to be brooding, with his chin on his chest and his folded hands resting on his enormous belly. The newspaper and an empty teacup sat on the table at his side.

On each visit, Atiya had entered the room with the resolve to broach the subject of her love for Marcus, and their intention — no, their desire — to marry. But on each occasion she had failed to find her father alone.

On her last visit, she arrived at the room to find her brother reading the newspaper to him. This was always a time-consuming process as her father would interrogate Amir until he was satisfied that he had understood all the nuances of the report. To Amir's great annoyance, he often found himself the focus of his father's ire should a news article enrage him. Atiya had heard many such interjections as she passed the sitting room door that morning. It made it even more difficult for her to bolster her courage. But she had promised Marcus, and herself, that it would be done that day.

She studied her father's pose now in an attempt to decipher his mood and concluded it was not good. He had not noticed her enter, so after waiting for a few moments she lost her nerve and decided to come back later when he might be in a better mood.

Jeevanjee caught sight of her as she retreated from the room, and called her back. 'Come, my little dove. Come in, come in.' He waved her to the sofa opposite him. 'You came to see your papa about something?'

Atiya opened her mouth to reply that, yes, she had a small matter to raise with him, but the words would not come. Her vocal chords seemed to have shrunk and she gaped like a landed fish. But her father's eyes had returned to the side table, and that day's edition of *The Chronicle* sitting on it, before he could notice her anxiety. He snatched up the newspaper, and jabbing an angular finger at the page said, 'Ah, that Amir! Your brother is a lummox. Here, Atiya, read this story to me — the one about the Governor.'

Her father's illiteracy demanded the constant attendance of a secretarial assistant — a shadow, who sat at Jeevanjee's elbow, often even during business meetings. It was Amir's primary responsibility within the company, but Atiya filled in for him from time to time.

Atiya took the newspaper with a shaking hand. She realised she had come very close to raising the matter of her marriage with her father, and it alarmed her to discover how frightening the prospect was. Could it be that she was so in awe of her father — the father who had always shown her so much affection — that she was afraid even to speak of a matter so important to her future?

Under the thrusting finger she found an article headed: *Town Plots for Whites Only*. Her head still reeling, she began to read: '*The sixty town plots that your correspondent advised his readership would go up for auction at the end of this month have been declared by the Governor, Sir Percy Girouard, to be for the exclusive bidding of white residents of BEA only.*

'*The plots are in the north-east quadrant of Nairobi town.*

'*The Governor was quoted as saying he felt the Indian Question had been neglected for too long, and —*'

'The Indian Question!' her father squawked. 'What does he mean, *the Indian Question*?'

But even Atiya had heard the expression. It referred to the Europeans' concern that the Indians were monopolising the country's commerce — a position that even the Indians could not dispute.

'The only Indian Question the Governor needs to worry about,' Jeevanjee continued, 'is how will he raise revenues for the city, for British East Africa, if the Indians are not here to pay their very high taxes?'

He waved his hand in agitation indicating she should continue, but before she could, he added, 'Does he ever speak of the Missionary Question? No! Or the African Question? No!'

He chewed the inside of his cheek, then waved her on again.

Atiya found her place and resumed reading. *'The Governor was quoted as saying he felt the Indian Question had been neglected for too long, and he felt it was necessary to reassure the European population that the British Government was firmly behind the white population and would not surrender to the wave of emigrants now flooding these shores.*

'The Governor, Sir Percy Girouard, has made a number of representations to London and been a strong advocate for —'

'Sir Percy Girouard!' her father burst in again. 'What a strutting peacock that man is, with his monocle and his ribbons and medals. Representations to London is right! He's always over there, mixing with his aristocratic friends. Parties and such, no doubt. You know, Atiya, a man like Girouard has no ... no understanding of the ordinary person. Not like John Ainsworth. There was a man you could talk to. Gumtree Johnnie they called him. A plain-speaking man, but he had a lot of common sense. Not so much of the college education as the likes of Girouard, but common sense. He understood business, and he was a fair man.' He brooded in silence then waved her on again.

'The Governor, Sir Percy Girouard, has made a number of representations to London and been a strong advocate for the Settlers whose rights he has so staunchly defended in the face of this unsanitary, disease-ridden tide of human —'

'Enough!' Jeevanjee raised his hand, then placed it on hers in a mollifying gesture for his outburst. 'Enough, my dear. It seems the news is unchanged. It is as bad when you read it as it was when Amir did.'

'I'm sorry, Papa.'

'No need to be sorry, my little dove. I know it's not your fault. Or Amir's.' He shook his head in frustration. 'Can you see how this is turning out, little one? The British are marshalling us into pens, like sheep.' He pointed both hands to the left. 'Here are the British and Europeans: administration and agricultural development.' Directing his hands to the centre, he said, 'Here are the Indians: trade and craftsmanship. And here,' he pointed to his right, 'are the Africans, cheap labour. Do you see how we Indians are in the middle?'

Atiya nodded although she was not at all sure she followed him.

'The British want us to be the middlemen to the Africans, while here ...' he waved his hands around the imaginary Africans, '... are the missionaries — making sure the millions remain uneducated, God-fearing labourers for the white races. Do you understand what I'm saying, my little one?'

'Yes, Papa.'

'Yes, and so do all the other Indians. We are not sitting still for this ... oh, no. We are organising. We are protesting very soon. You'll see.' He sat nodding to himself for a few moments. 'So, Atiya, what was it you were wanting me for?'

Atiya's hands were in a tight ball in her lap. They felt sweaty and cold. She tried to smile, but it felt wrong, as if she were about to be ill.

'And another thing ...' Her father had obviously not yet finished speaking his mind. 'Do you think the black man will take this for much longer? No. He will also protest to the whites. And he is in greater numbers even than us.' He raised an admonishing finger. 'Make no mistake, Atiya, there is a class war coming. The Indians will start it, but the Africans will end it.' The finger shook. 'We Indians must band together. There must be no backsliding, as some would have it, to make the African our comrade. No. Never. We must hold our precious Bohra community together; all Moslems; all Indians. We must never let the enemy within.'

He nodded, satisfied he had covered all points.

'Now, my dove. Tell me, what is it you came to see me for?'

CHAPTER 46

Tayabali resented staying in his brother's house when he came to Nairobi on business. He felt it would be more fitting, and certainly more relaxed, to stay at the Stanley or the Norfolk Hotel, but his brother, who controlled all the finances on such matters, absolutely refused to budge.

'What do you need fancy hotels for?' he'd say. 'Didn't I sleep on the ground while I was in Australia? Surrounded by people from all lands. Never knowing when I might get a knife to my throat or lose all my stock. Hotels ... it's out of the question.' And he would hear no more on the matter.

At least Tayabali had the house to himself that day, and time to spare. Jeevanjee was in his town office for a meeting, and the rest of the family were not at home. He sipped the tall rum he had poured for himself from his brother's miserly drinks cabinet. No gin, no whisky — the man had no idea of how to enjoy himself, he mused. If he were master of Jeevanjee and Company there would be plenty to drink. Parties too, for all the best people in town.

From his refuge in the heavy shadows of the creeper-covered veranda, he gazed out into the shimmering midday heat of Forest Road. It was barely more than a track, leading to the town in one direction and to the small farming settlement of Channon Bridge, sometimes called Thika, in the other.

Beyond Jeevanjee's house was the town boundary and the forest, these days called Parklands, in anticipation of an expansion of Nairobi's residential acreage. The forest was known to be home to many dangerous animals, making the proposed housing estate something of a joke to Nairobi's entire population. Jeevanjee warned all his family to stay out of the forest, and kept an ancient shotgun in his wardrobe in case of emergencies.

A noise from the other end of the veranda startled him. He had thought he was alone, but his brother's spoilt daughter was standing in the shadows at the other end of the long veranda. She had not given his corner a glance, for she was peering intently towards the road, as if expecting someone to come walking up the path at any moment. He wondered what she was looking for, then she quickly ran to the gate, and, instead of heading towards the town, disappeared behind the house towards the forest.

Tayabali could not care less for Atiya's safety — she could do what she pleased as far as he was concerned — but for the girl to be so flagrantly disobedient to her father's orders regarding the forest, she was obviously up to some mischief. He waited a couple of minutes and then, for a joke, followed her.

The undergrowth soon became quite thick and he lost sight of her. Just as he was beginning to reconsider the wisdom of tackling the wild animals of the forest for idle amusement, he heard a low whistle coming from directly ahead. An answering call came from deeper into the forest.

He crept forward, taking care to keep enough foliage between him and Atiya, who was now picking her way towards the answering call. At times she disappeared in dense cover, then she would reappear.

The answering whistle was quite close, and she stopped in a small clearing in anticipation of the other's arrival. Tayabali stopped too.

The undergrowth shook and parted. Tayabali dropped to his haunches behind a bush. When he thought it was safe to lift his head, his brother's darling daughter was locked in an embrace with the stranger who had come from the forest. Tayabali felt a surge of vengeful delight — he had found a flaw within his perfect brother's world. For once, he would have the delicious opportunity to take revenge for all the times he had suffered ignominiously at his brother's hands.

Atiya and the man broke from their passionate embrace. Tayabali couldn't believe his eyes. Where he had at first been delighted to have found something to use to tease and annoy his brother, seeing her with a black man so scandalised him it shook all other thoughts from his mind.

Slowly his imagination began to return to the possibilities this new-found information presented. Such an enormous humiliation went beyond mere annoyance; here was an outlet for all his hate — a chance to inflict untold suffering upon his brother, and to completely annihilate his reputation.

Secure in the shadowy isolation of the Parklands forest, Atiya rested her head against Marcus's shoulder and looked through the dappled light of late afternoon. A Superb Starling hopped among the grass tufts, sending bolts of colour from the iridescent feathers of its wings. Soon another starling, attracted by its display, joined it, and the two birds danced one final act, before the setting sun drew the curtain on their performance.

She and Marcus had also been engaged in a dance of the imagination, as they often did when discussing their future together. On this occasion she had been describing her wedding dress and the wonderful wedding reception they would have. They had both fallen silent as they again faced the reality that they still had not overcome the first obstacle in reaching that future — they had been unable to find a way to get Atiya's father's agreement, much less his blessing, to their union.

'When will we go to see him?' Marcus asked from the silence.

Atiya had pondered the matter numerous times. Her father was not a strictly religious man, and although he often attended mosque, and said his prayers five times a day when he was at home, he had adopted many western practices. He had even been known to drink alcohol on special occasions. Her heart refused to accept what her head knew — that her father would never allow her to marry a non-Moslem.

'I don't know. Oh, how I wish I could be strong like you, but I just can't seem to find a way to let him know. I'm sure he cannot agree to see me married outside the Bohras.'

'Is it because I am not of your faith, Atiya, or because I am African?'

It was a question he had never raised before. 'Oh, no,' she quickly replied, not at all sure if she was speaking the truth. 'Papa hates prejudice. He is always saying how unfair it is to us Indians.'

'And does he ever defend Africans against the same kind of prejudices?'

'But ... is it the same?' She knew that the Africans were often poorly treated, but it had never occurred to her it might also be as a result of prejudice.

'Of course it is.'

'Papa says we Indians can't get more than two places on the Legislative Council although we outnumber the whites ten to one.'

'Atiya, we, the majority, have none.'

'Oh.'

'And isn't it prejudice when the government forces Africans to leave their cattle and farms to become labourers so they can earn enough rupees to pay the hut tax? And the *kipende* papers that only we natives must carry to prove who we are.'

'Oh, Marcus!' Her hand went to her mouth with the realisation she had completely missed the fact that her father's hatred of prejudice was entirely self-centred. It was only Indians he perceived to be the sufferers of the government's poisonous attitude. He didn't seem to care about the Africans. Worse — it had never entered her mind to question his one-sided view. Of course, Marcus was right. If her father was truly fighting inequalities imposed by the government, he should have been defending the Africans with equal zeal. She was ashamed to stand before the man she loved, a collaborator, although an unwitting one, in a monstrous injustice against him and his people. 'I'm sorry, Marcus. I never ... I don't understand any of these things.' In that moment she couldn't face him, and buried her head in his chest while she struggled with her embarrassment and confusion. Finally, she forced herself to look into his eyes and run her hand down his cheek. She kissed him. 'I only know I want us to be together.'

He returned her kiss. 'Me too, but come, my love, it's time you went home.'

Leaving Marcus always made her feel depressed, but with the added weight that she had somehow forsaken him by her ignorance, she felt worse. To make amends, she decided to strengthen her resolve. It had already been too long. 'I'll do something about it,' she said, as if unburdened by a terrible load. 'I'll tell him! This time I'll just go to Papa and tell him we are in love and we want to marry.'

He lifted her chin and laid a gentle kiss on her lips.

'I will,' she said. 'I really will.'

Tayabali could scarcely concentrate on the wages sheet. His mind was in a whirl. He had hatched so many schemes to take advantage of the delicious piece of scandal he had found out about Atiya that there was hardly a moment in the day that didn't bring forth another, even more embarrassing way to use the story. His brother's shame would be excruciating. But he was in no great hurry to reveal his niece's disgrace. Timing was the essence of his success.

He savoured the imagined scene in the Jeevanjee household. The entire family would be assembled, even visiting relatives and temporary house guests. Jeevanjee would be holding forth, as he usually did, on the need for all family members to be careful to uphold Bohra civility and good manners. His precious daughter would be sitting beside him, a picture of virginal beauty. Tayabali would stand and point to her and describe the scene in the jungle — a scene of lust and utmost depravity, rutting like an animal with her black lover. It would be sublime.

But no, he thought — this was such a priceless piece of information he could not squander it by exposing it to only the immediate family. Far better to expose it to a large gathering of the Bohra people, perhaps at a *majlis*, where most would be in attendance. His imagination ran away with him. He could see his brother's mortification intensifying as more and more people knew of his family's shame.

Everyone must know; his business partners, of course, and the entire East African business community. Then there was the family in Karachi, and other parts of India. Nobody would want to know Alibhai Mulla Jeevanjee by the time Tayabali's story had spread.

A cloud of uncertainty descended to dampen his reverie. How would this landslide of shame escape the confines of the family home, or even the Bohra community? They were all so protective of their brethren; when it came to a person like Jeevanjee, whom the community admired, they would be even more likely to try to conceal it. Tayabali's frustration soared. Here was a stumbling block to his great plan to destroy his brother.

He pushed the wages sheet to the edge of his desk and rubbed at his pounding temples. There must be a way to let the whole world know of Jeevanjee's shame. He must think.

He put his elbows on his desk and dropped his face into his hands, searching for the solution. He was too close to success to let it trickle away.

He ran his hands down his face and found himself staring through the office window towards the wharf. Two of his men were harassing one of the stevedores. The thuggees had been one of his best ideas. They made his job in Mombasa so much easier.

As he stared at the scene developing on the wharf, the beginning of a wonderful plan began to take shape in his mind. What if the leaking of Atiya's shameful affair was followed by the murder of her lover? It would be a matter too outrageous to be concealed from the world.

The whites were always intrigued, and sometimes titillated, by the goings-on of the Indian community, by their strange customs and religious ceremonies. It would not surprise any of them to hear of an outraged father arranging the murder of a man who had sullied his daughter's reputation. It was the kind of story that newspaper editors loved. And if the person who arranged such a killing was also a very successful man, much admired and very much envied by the newspaper's readership, it was certain to get extensive coverage.

CHAPTER 47

'I suppose you'll have a gin,' Grogan said.

'You're most kind,' Quentin said, smiling, with no attempt to conceal his sarcasm. But his remark was not intended — as they often weren't — to be provocative. His brother Ewart was always stern when they were together, and Quentin continually attempted to lighten the mood, or tease him into relinquishing for a moment his terse role of father figure. It was an aspect of his brother's personality he had observed with no one else, although he suspected it also occurred with his next brother in line, Archibald. It was obvious that Ewart and Philip had no such formality between them; indeed, they acted just as brothers should. Quentin realised he had always resented Philip, and his other older brother, Norman, for this privilege.

He understood its genesis. Quentin was quite young when their father died and Ewart had taken his place as the male head of the household. This became outright on the death of their mother four years later.

The nine years that separated him and Ewart meant they were never children together; never shared boys' games in their childhood. In later years, Quentin never knew Ewart as anything but the disciplinarian he needed to be to keep control of his seven younger siblings while trying to manage the family estates.

Ewart put the gin on the occasional table between them. Quentin noted that Ewart had also poured himself a gin and tonic.

'Cheers,' Quentin said, raising his glass.

'Cheers,' his brother replied with little enthusiasm.

'So, what's up?' Quentin said, seizing the initiative.

'Why should anything be, as you say, up?'

'Well, let's just say that I seldom get summoned to Chiromo unless I am going to get a dressing down about something or other.'

'For God's sake, Quentin, I did not *summon* you. I sent what I think was a reasonably courteous note to your hotel inviting you over for a chat. And why do you insist on staying at that dreadful Stanley Hotel anyway? You know Gertrude and I would be happy for you to stay here at Chiromo.'

Quentin had made the choice to keep his distance from his brother so as to avoid the possible incidences of friction between them. 'Space,' he said. 'Breathing space, brother. It's nothing personal, mind, just need to spread my feathers a bit.'

'Humph,' Ewart said, and seemed about to launch into one of his tiresome lectures on behaviour and family name, but changed his mind, for he said, 'Anyway, the reason I asked you over was to see if you have changed your mind about joining us in the family enterprises. Are you interested?'

'Could be. What did you have in mind for me?'

'I have a six thousand acre farm at Eldama Ravine up on the Mau Escarpment. Next door is a homestead, a sawmill and twenty thousand acres of forest concession that I need someone to help me bring into production. The government has indicated they might be inclined to extend a spur line from the railway so I can get at another hundred thousand acres of timber. It's an exciting opportunity for a young man with experience in the African bush. I think you're the man to drive it through.'

Quentin was only vaguely aware of Ewart's many business interests, but he did know of his highlands properties, and if he were to join his brother, it would be this and similar positions that would be of most interest. However, Quentin didn't want to appear too keen otherwise he would lose any advantage he might have in negotiating the terms of his appointment. He particularly wanted to spend as much time in Nairobi as possible. An itinerant manager's position across a number of properties was what he had in mind.

'That's very kind of you, Ewart,' he said, 'but to tell you the truth, I haven't given it much thought.'

'Well, perhaps you should. You can't go squandering your life doing nothing.'

'Far from it. I've been quite busy these last few weeks.'

'So I've heard,' Ewart snorted. 'I should think you would be a little more circumspect when it comes to courting the under-age daughters of family friends.'

'What do you mean *under-age*?' Quentin said, raising his eyebrows. 'If you're referring to my friendship with Miss Dalton, as you well know, she is now twenty-one. And as far as being the daughter of a family friend ... how many times have you seen the Dalton family in the last five or six years?'

'Beside the point. You're making a spectacle of yourself, and embarrassing the rest of the family.'

Quentin considered not arguing the point, but he realised his brother was on one of his vendettas and would not be diverted until he had re-established his dominance within the family pecking order. 'Quite obviously, my social activities and personal life are no business of yours,' Quentin said, placing his glass on the table between them.

Ewart's eyes blazed with barely concealed fury. 'They are, for so long as it affects the family's interests, and clearly they do.'

'Then clearly,' Quentin said, standing, 'I have no place in your little empire.'

He got up and stormed out of the house.

He was still cursing as he galloped his horse past the Norfolk, before hauling cruelly on the reins and dragging the blowing horse back to the hitching rail outside the Norfolk's terrace. By the time he had consumed his third gin, he had made up his mind. The Lado Enclave looked a lot better now than it had an hour ago. It would be ivory, not cedar, that he would harvest.

Marcus squatted on the track and untied his black leather shoes. He had bought them in Bond Street at a time when he really couldn't afford them, and was usually more careful than to wear them out in the bush at night, but he had been in a hurry to be with Atiya and had forgotten to change them. Dinner had been an extended affair to celebrate Ewart's appointment to the Legislative Council, but in particular the sterling speech he delivered which brought the entire Council to their feet — supporters and opponents alike.

Marcus had found that the Parklands forest provided the safest route to the Jeevanjee house, especially at night. It was uncommon to see a person at large in Forest Road after dark, and on foot. The locals knew better than to take their chances with the wildlife. Nairobi's cemetery had more than one headstone marked: *Taken by lion.* However, it was not lion that concerned Marcus, but the attention he would draw if found in Forest Road, particularly if found by one of the Jeevanjees.

He carried the shoes in one hand, and fended off overhanging branches with the other. Soon he slipped into an easy gait.

Maybe it was in response to walking in bare feet, but he had unconsciously adopted a stalking tread, sensing the forest floor with his toes, and instinctively adjusting his footfalls to avoid snapping a twig with his weight. There was no real need for stealth, the house was a further quarter-mile away, but he had been taught to listen to his instincts and he did so now, slowing his pace and probing the dark void surrounding him with his highly tuned senses.

Shadows danced in the understorey. He glanced up at the night sky. Above the tree canopy the silver disc of the moon slid between clouds scudding across the star-speckled sky. When it disappeared into a cloudbank, the forest went from shadowy to near-total darkness.

The sensation swept quickly over him. He couldn't say how he knew, but every fibre of his being told him that something was in the darkness with him.

He sensed a movement to his right. He swung towards it, preparing to do battle. A sliver of white flew from the darkness to his left and wrapped itself around his throat before he could react. His windpipe was pinched shut and he gasped at night air that wouldn't come. He dropped his shoes and struggled for a finger-grip under the band of silk that had cut into his flesh. A blood-red haze formed at the edges of his vision. He clawed at the cord, tearing at his skin, knowing he would soon pass out if he couldn't lever the strangler's weapon loose.

He swung his arms in vain and was forced to his knees by the strangler. The darkness began to smother him; he clawed at the ground and found a very solid English brogue. He grabbed it by the heel and with his last scrap of energy, drove it over his shoulder, toe-first, into the eye of his attacker.

He heard a reassuring screech of pain. The silk cord softened into a diaphanous veil which he ripped from his neck.

The second man came at him from the darkness. Marcus swung the shoe again, and bolted through the undergrowth.

Jessie flicked at the horse with the buggy's reins. The mare, startled, put her ears back and dashed down the Sixth Avenue hill at full pace. It had been years since she had driven a buggy so hard and it exhilarated her. The wind tore her cloth cap from her head and whipped her long golden hair into a liquid glistening stream behind her. As she flew into Connaught Road, the buggy's wheels protested, throwing up a pall of dust in her wake.

It had taken many hours for her anger to rise to the point of explosion. When Quentin told her he was leaving Nairobi and going back to the Lado Enclave, she assumed he was making a brief hunting trip for more ivory. It had saddened her to lose him for a few weeks, but when she heard his whole story — that he was leaving Nairobi forever — she was bereft, and through tears asked him why.

It was a kind of relief to find it wasn't because he didn't love her, but because his brother had made it impossible for him to stay.

They parted, with Jessie promising to see him off on the evening train to Kisumu.

For hours she seethed over the matter, finally concluding that Ewart had constructed the whole affair to keep them apart. She sensed he had disapproved of their relationship from the start.

By Salisbury Road the horse was tiring, but she flogged her into the final quarter-mile. When she leapt from the seat at

Chiromo, she felt a moment's pity for the mare, wide-mouthed, gasping and covered in foam, but she charged up the steps and banged once on the door, before flinging it open and storming inside.

Grogan was coming from the parlour, a bemused expression on his face. 'Jessie! What in —'

'Why did you do it?' she demanded.

'Why did I ... Jessie, you're distraught. Come into —'

'Was it because we were happy together?'

His conciliatory smile waned. 'What on earth ... What has Quentin been telling you?'

'Is it because you can't bear to see two young people in love?' Tears welled in her eyes. She hated to hate him, but he was trying to destroy her happiness for his own selfish reasons.

'This has absolutely nothing to do with you and Quentin.'

'Liar!'

'It's entirely a private matter between Quentin and me.'

'Was it because he loved me?'

'Love! What would you know of love? As for Quentin, he's been *in love* more times than he's had —'

'Was it because he loved me? And you couldn't?'

Ewart stopped short. 'What?' he asked.

'I said ... Oh, never mind! I wish I'd never set eyes on you.'

She turned and hurried down the hall, flew down the steps, past the horse, and down the carriageway to the road. She now knew what she must do. Never one to take a setback to heart, she decided she would seize the initiative.

Grogan followed Jessie into the hall, arriving at the open front door in time to see her disappear down the track towards the front gate. For a moment he considered chasing after her, but immediately decided against it.

His *syce* was standing at the buggy, unsure of what to do with the sweating, distressed horse. Grogan stepped onto the veranda and indicated to the young man that he should take the mare to the stables and tend to her.

He took a seat beside the bentwood table on the veranda. He was stirred as much by Jessie's temper as by the splendour of her rage. She was like a wild and beautiful animal; a predator in full charge, eyes blazing. A sleek, wind-torn dweller of the plains.

She had accused him of trying to spoil her happiness — a preposterous accusation. Why, he had nothing but best wishes for her happiness.

As for interfering in her love affair with Quentin, well, it was for her own good. Quentin was an immature drifter, never able to make any commitments, be they to the defence of his country, his family or those he claimed to love. Quentin was unworthy of a woman like Jessie. He had no right to sweep her off her feet the moment she stepped out into society.

Jessie needed time — time to become accustomed to the ways of life; the ways of love. She didn't realise how immensely important it was to learn passion through a shared love experience, rather than from a one-sided infatuation.

He drummed his fingers on the table.

Worst of all, she had accused him of these imagined acts of sabotage because she thought he was in love with her. The girl had no idea about such matters. He would never fall in love with anyone else. It would be totally unfair to Gertrude. He simply would not allow it.

Grogan wrestled with the dilemma for two days, and continued to do so over lunch at the Norfolk with Philip. Finally, Philip convinced him to go up to Mrs Hanlon's house and apologise to Jessie for being a boor.

Halfway up Sixth Avenue's hill, Grogan berated himself for taking a rickshaw. The boys were barely making headway, so he got out to finish the last half-mile on foot.

By the time he reached the Hanlon house, hot and sweaty, he was cursing himself roundly for not remembering that the journey took a steep climb near the end. One of Ali's carriages would have been far better, and given him a much-needed boost to his dignity, which he expected would get a beating as he tried to smooth the waters with Jessie. Trying to compose himself on the doorstep, he rapped the knocker.

He heard light footsteps approaching, and prepared his opening spiel, which was going to be bright and breezy; nothing too formal or grovelling.

His smile faded as Mrs Hanlon's face appeared at the door.

'Ah, Mrs Hanlon,' he said, wiping the sweat from his brow. 'So nice to see you. I, ah, was in the neighbourhood and, ah, thought I should just pop in to see how she — to see how you are.'

Mrs Hanlon looked stunned. She remained silent.

'So ... ah, how are you, Mrs Hanlon?'

'She's gone, Mr Grogan,' she exclaimed finally. 'So help me God, gone.'

'Jessie? Jessie's gone?' He tried to maintain his buoyant manner, but the old widow's expression worried him. 'She's gone ...?'

'To Kisumu. On yesterday's train,' she wailed. 'Oh, Mr Grogan, I should have sent word to you, but I was so shocked by it. I thought she was such a very nice young lady, and now look what she's gone and done — run off to Kisumu with your brother!'

CHAPTER 48

It was dangerous for them to meet in daylight, and even more dangerous to meet in the Indian bazaar, but when Marcus saw Atiya in the crowd and saw the look of despondency on her face, he had to comfort her. He drew her into a gap between the *dukas* and asked what was wrong.

'I failed again,' she said, no longer able to hold back the tears. 'I was just too frightened to tell Papa about us.'

'There, there,' he said, glancing around to see if they were concealed from the market crowd. The corrugated iron on the rear of one *duka* protected them from the prying eyes of Bazaar Street, but the *dukawhaller* in the neighbouring one could see them through his boxes and sacks of curries and spices. 'Shh, it's all right. We'll find another time. Another way to tell him.'

'But I'm a coward, Marcus. Of all things, I should be able to stand up to my father about the man I love. And I failed.' A tear ran down her cheek, along the line of her jaw, and dropped to her breast.

Marcus caught the next tear as it reached her chin, and licked it from his finger. 'Don't cry, my darling.' He looked at the *dukawhaller*, who was trying to conceal his fascination at seeing an Indian girl with a black man, but without success. 'We shouldn't be here, it's unsafe. We'll meet later and talk about it,'

'Yes, I need you.'

'But I can't make it until tomorrow night. I must go to Ngong again.'

'Oh, no. But you didn't come last night as we planned.'

'I'm sorry. I had a big problem last night — I was attacked by two or three men on my way to your house.' He told her about his lucky escape from the man with the silk scarf. 'I don't know how many there were in the bush. I thought they could be part of a big gang.'

The *dukawhaller* was hovering near them, and Marcus gave him a stern look. 'Atiya, we can't talk here.'

'I know. I'll go,' she said, and took his hand in hers. 'I'm sorry I failed you, Marcus.'

'Don't be sad. When I come back we'll make some plans to see your father together.'

'Oh, Marcus.'

'It's the best way. I hate to see you suffering this alone.' He could see she had brightened at the hope he had given her. 'We'll talk.' He kissed her forehead. 'Soon.'

'Goodbye, my darling,' she said.

He quickly kissed her on the lips, and slipped out through the lane and disappeared among the piles of rotting fruit, fly-blown meat scraps and market filth.

The train ride west to Kisumu lacked the exhilaration of Jessie's eastward journey to Nairobi just a few weeks before, and it worried her. She felt she should have been unbelievably excited; after all, she was eloping with a dashing young man, on her way to spend her honeymoon hunting elephant in the Lado Enclave.

Quentin was softly snoring, his head resting against his window, his unfinished gin in the curl of his hand.

Her enthusiasm had waned as soon as the train began its slow climb up towards the Mau Summit. Now, on the approach to her hometown, she started to reflect upon the recent events that had turned her life upside-down.

As the train emerged from a cutting, and took its breath before gathering its strength for the last climb into Londiani, she caught sight of the distant *kopje* that marked the boundary of her father's farm. The farmhouse was in the valley and not visible, but Jessie didn't need to see it to imagine how it looked. At that time of the afternoon there would be a light mist hanging over the house, mixing with the wisp of smoke that rose from the slightly crooked chimney. The farmhouse would already be closed up against the chill of approaching evening, but the lanterns would not yet be lit so as to save on the paraffin. Her father would be in the barn, bedding down the smallest and weakest of the animals, and somewhere in the hills their old Maasai herdsman would be patrolling the herd, with his walking stick in the crook of one arm and his spear hanging loosely in the curled fingers of the other hand.

The *kopje* disappeared behind the rise of hills, but the memory it had evoked did not. She could see her old dog, Wonder, in those ancient rounded boulders, his tongue lolling from the side of his mouth like a pink and black slab of meat, and his big brown sad eyes gazing at her in adoration. They were frozen in death the last time she'd looked into them, and the old body had lain still, finally conceding to the inevitable outcome of a life spent defying the odds.

Jessie wondered about her odds, and her chance at happiness. She glanced across at the sleeping Quentin. He was such a handsome man, with the Grogans' wide forehead and intelligent eyes.

The comparison led her to Ewart Grogan — a place she'd been so many times in her thoughts. Ewart's eyes were the most commanding aspect of him, and were what had first drawn her attention to him. Intelligent, touched with humour, or ablaze with anger, depending upon his mood. She now knew the mood could change in an instant. But that was the Ewart of today — not of six years ago. Six years ago he was an entertaining stranger that filled a young girl's heart with unbidden dreams. Forbidden dreams.

Quentin awoke when the train stopped for the usual fuel and water pick-up at Londiani. He looked out the window and then around the cabin. His eyes paused briefly when they met hers, as if he was recalling the hectic events of earlier that day when they dashed together to the departing train. He smiled at her before settling himself into the headrest and going back to sleep.

The train would remain at Londiani station until sufficient fuel and water were loaded on to carry them all the way to Kisumu. Jessie knew this because she used to play at the station while her father collected stock feed and supplies from Nairobi, so far away.

Her childhood — when going to Nairobi had been an impossible dream — now felt so distant. Nairobi had come and gone in what seemed a moment. But she had been there long enough to know her childhood dreram had been correct. Nairobi was where she wanted to be. The man she had loved for so long — six years — was there, but now she was leaving it, and him, perhaps forever. How could all her plans have changed in such a short time?

With a start, she realised she had been dreaming about the wrong Grogan. She glanced at Quentin. His mouth hung open, and a bead of drool clung to his bottom lip.

The station was buzzing with ineffectual activity. Faces she vaguely recalled from childhood were still there; the same people sweeping, loading, refuelling, collecting baggage. She could almost see her father among the crowd, and Marcus helping with the loads.

What would Marcus think about her impulsive elopement? She could imagine him shaking his head in resigned acceptance of another foolish *enkiti*-like exploit.

What would her father think? Would he support her in her defiant independence as he usually did, turning his nose up at convention? Or would he say he had hoped for more from his one and only child?

Marcus had said her father was ill. She hadn't thought any more about it since that day after the party. She hadn't seen him off at the station either, being too busy with Quentin at the time. She searched among the few faces on the platform, hoping she had missed him on her first search. If only she could see him for a moment, she could go on to Kisumu in peace. But he wasn't there.

She had known every nook and cranny of Londiani station, and she wanted to share her childhood memories with Quentin, but she didn't want to wake him. Anyhow, the details had faded, as had the dreams of the girl who had farewelled another Grogan from Londiani station all those years ago.

In the last few days, the village of Ngong had grown from a well-ordered circle of dung-covered huts and a scattering of small Indian *dukas* supplying household and clothing items, into a sprawling squatters' settlement thrumming with colour and activity. Hundreds of visiting Maasai in red *shukas* filled every path and track, making it difficult for Marcus to pick his way through the crowd to find the meeting of the elders.

There were bands of proud young *moran*, strutting like peacocks with their shaved heads gleaming and their painted war shields proclaiming their heroic deeds and age-set affiliations.

The young female residents of Ngong were clustered into groups, giggling and flirting with the visitors.

Dignified old men carrying walking sticks and *orinka* — the short, round-headed clubs without which they would feel improperly dressed — tottered along, accompanied by their most senior wives, whose arms and legs were ringed with the many copper hoops of their *surutya*. Wives both young and old wore multi-coloured, beaded ornaments on their necks and ears.

Most of the crowd were shuffling along with no obvious destination in mind. It was a social occasion for many of them, for it was only the elders who would be participating in the discussions on the proposed Maasai land resettlement agreement. The others were merely attending as part of their elder's entourage.

Sir Percy Girouard and his officials had been pressing the Maasai for a decision, and it was the threat of precipitate action by the British, in the absence of any considered advice from the Maasai, that had brought the elders to Ngong for talks.

After much difficulty, Marcus had found a copy of the 1904 agreement; a brief document but he spent days considering it. He believed he had found a legal issue that might be exploited to prevent the government from forcibly moving the northern Maasai, but Ole Gilisho was not confident he could convince the other elders. He did, however, allow Marcus to return in the hope of persuading Lenana that the Maasai had a legal case.

He found Ole Gilisho in the centre of the *enkang*. He was sitting cross-legged in a circle of elders, many of whom wore *karosses* — the long hyrax-skin cloaks signifying their age and standing within the clans. With them was a young man — a youth not yet elevated into warriorhood. The group were explaining matters to him. Marcus thought it extraordinary that such a young person — a boy of no more than fifteen or so years — was accepted into the company of the elders, let alone being included in their discussions.

He caught Ole Gilisho's eye, and joined him at his beckoning. They exchanged greetings, and made the customary polite small talk that convention decreed must precede serious conversation. Marcus patiently waited for the old man to get to the point.

'The Governor wants a meeting soon,' Ole Gilisho said at last, 'and we cannot reach a decision on the resettlement.' He raised his hands in a sign of resignation. '*Ai, ai.* Everyone must have his chance to speak on all matters, even if he has nothing to say.'

'And who is the *olaiyoni*, the youth?'

'It is Seggi, son of Lenana. He speaks as the *laibon* here.'

'And what of Lenana? When will he come?'

Ole Gilisho shook his head sadly. 'He is just as you saw him when you came here. At times his eyes are clear and he can give us guidance, but then he slips away into the dark place again. We have seen little of him in these gatherings, and he is needed. We go in circles like the dying wildebeest. Soon the British will demand answers.'

'Lenana needs to know more about the ways of the British law. Can I see him, Father?'

Marcus suspected that Ole Gilisho was suspicious of British law, and didn't have much confidence in a Maasai who had turned his back on his culture, but he was as desperate as Marcus to avoid the enforced mass movement of people and stock.

'I seldom find the *laibon*'s spirit with him after the sun has passed the noon, but come, we will see.'

They left the circle of elders, who continued their debate on the finer points of tribal law.

It was a short distance across the crowded *enkang* to Lenana's hut, which was indistinguishable from any other except for the cluster of old women gathered around the entrance.

In the smoky light from the cooking fire it was impossible to see if Lenana was awake or not. The only indication was a softly murmured song that Marcus vaguely recalled as one of the *moran*'s hunting songs. He found the moveable panel in the roof and pushed it aside.

The shaft of light fell directly onto the old *laibon*'s face, causing not a flicker in the glazed eyes. The lips continued to mouth the hunter's song, but it was obvious that Lenana was not yet ready to absorb the intricacies of British law.

The stone idol was obscenely misplaced in the quiet greenery of the forest. Atiya stared at the many-limbed statue in horror. She was not familiar with all the Hindu goddesses, but Kali was unforgettable. The figure exuded menace.

She had come upon it while walking alone in the forest. She could not have been more than five minutes from her home. She wouldn't risk being any deeper in the bush because of the lion attacks that still captured the township's attention and kept the residents on constant alert. The only reason she had ventured out at all was for a respite from the oppressive presence of her uncle, whom her father had called up from Mombasa on some business matter.

What could the image mean here in the bush, she wondered. There were blood-red flowers strewn around the goddess's feet, and some white silk material folded into pads beside her.

Now that she took the time to examine the area, she noticed the ashes of a campfire, a few cooking implements, and the unmistakeable signs of flattened grass where bedrolls had been. She scanned the bush for any sign of the men, then carefully approached the idol.

Kali's bulging eyes held her spellbound. The protruding tongue seemed to drip with blood. She tentatively reached a hand to the white material and lifted it by a corner. The silk unfolded to reveal a long scarf.

At the sound of men's muffled voices coming from the road, she staggered back from the idol in fright and fell over a log beside the cooking fire. Scrambling to her feet, she dashed towards home, remembering at the last moment to fling the silk scarf behind her.

Gertrude watched Ewart pack his valise with the clothes she had neatly folded and placed on the bed for him. 'Surely you're not planning to chase them all the way into Uganda?'

'If necessary, but I suspect they'll be forced to spend a day or so at Kisumu waiting for the boat to Kampala. They may even have stopped off at Londiani on the way.'

'To ask Bruce Dalton for his blessing? I doubt that even your reckless brother would be so indiscreet.'

'You're probably right. Do you know where my walking boots are, Gertie?'

'They're on the floor at your feet. But they left on Monday's train. You've given them three days' start.'

'It was still a better idea to wait for the next train than to follow on foot.'

'It seems like madness to me, Ewart.'

'Maybe to you, my dear, but not to me.'

She wrung her hands, watching as he rolled a shirt into a ball and stuffed it in the side of his bag.

'Ewart, stop.'

He glanced up at her, then resumed stacking his valise. 'No time, Gertrude. The train leaves in an hour.'

She gripped the fingers of one hand in the other. 'I said, stop!'

This time he straightened from his crouch over the bed and gave her a quizzical look. 'What in blazes is —'

'Ewart, you're making a fool of yourself,' she said, holding herself upright and trying to control the quaver in her voice. 'I long ago gave up worrying about you making a fool out of me, but this time you're making a fool of yourself. And I won't allow it. It's madness.'

His expression was guarded as he said, 'I don't know what you're talking about, Gertie.'

'Quentin is not the only Grogan who can't resist the charms of a woman. Any woman. I've known about the others, of course. If I didn't see it for myself, one of the women in town would, and sooner or later someone would find the courage to advise me — "for your own good," as they'd say.'

She couldn't stand the intensity in his eyes and turned to the window to escape them. The breeze played with the flimsy curtains. 'I know you love me, Ewart. Not as much as I love you, of course. You've always been so self-sufficient, and love is, after all, a certain kind of cry for approval. But I always accept your love on whatever terms you are prepared to offer it. Pathetic, I know, but —'

Ewart gently touched her shoulder.

'No!' she said. 'I must get to the end of this, and I can't do it if you take me into your arms.' She touched her silk handkerchief to her nose. 'As I say, pathetic, but there you are.' She took a deep breath and continued. 'This time it is you who are being weak. Jessie Dalton is little more than a girl. The daughter of, if not a friend, an associate. But more to the point, she says she's in love with your brother, and if for no other reason than that, you must take her at her word and let her go. I won't allow you to destroy your relationship with your brother, while also making a damn fool of yourself.'

She had more to say, but felt she couldn't go on without totally losing her composure. The tears were welling behind her eyes and she fought to hold them back.

Ewart cleared his throat. 'Gertie ... um ... Let's talk about this when I get home.'

'No,' she said firmly, her eyes still turned from him.

The lace curtains parted to reveal the foxgloves nodding on the warm breeze in the garden encircled by the carriageway. She was afraid to utter her next words, but realised she had now travelled so far down that dangerous road, she could not turn back.

'If you catch that train to Kisumu, I don't want you back in this house.'

CHAPTER 49

Atiya was in her bedroom when she heard the voices in the garden. She crept to the window and peeped through the curtains. Three men were talking with her uncle. One carried a silk scarf.

She threw a hand over her mouth when she grasped the truth of the situation. The camp she had stumbled upon in the bush was not that of a band of thieves who had attacked Marcus. It belonged to a gang of thugs — the ritualistic assassins who worshipped the goddess Kali. What she now realised was that her Uncle Tayabali was somehow involved with them, and that the next sacrifice to their bloodthirsty goddess would be Marcus.

She had to get a warning to him before he attempted to reach her through the forest on the following night.

Shafts of morning light speared across the Athi Plains, striking a glancing blow to the topmost folds of the Ngong Hills' saddleback ridge. The dawn's warmth melted the remnants of night mist clinging to the peaks, and chased the cloudbanks down the slopes until they had all disappeared and the village was awash in the glow of morning.

Marcus had slept poorly, and had given up trying about an hour before dawn. With a blanket wrapped around him against the cool early morning air, he watched the dawn break and the village stir.

Ole Gilisho appeared from nowhere, his thick hyrax cloak clutched tightly around his shoulders. 'The elders are meeting at Lenana's hut. We have found that the dawn is the best time for him. Maybe he will hear us this morning.'

He turned, and Marcus threw off his blanket and followed.

A woman crouched over a smoky cooking fire in Lenana's hut, stirring a *posho* mix. In the diminishing circle of light sat a number of elders. They studied Marcus as he entered with Ole Gilisho.

'*Sopa*,' he greeted them respectfully.

A muttered chorus of replies followed.

'Who is this one who would speak with the *laibon*?' a wizened elder asked.

'He is Momposhe Ole Matipe, of the Purko section,' answered Ole Gilisho with a touch of brittleness in his tone.

'I know him,' the first speaker continued. 'He is not of the Purko, for he has spurned us.'

Marcus peered into the gloom and recognised one of the elders who had come for him after his father died.

'You are correct,' he responded. 'I have turned my back on my section, as my father did before me. But it was to allow me to continue my studies; studies that I now believe will help you in your fight against the British.'

'Who says we have a fight with the British?' the old man demanded. 'Many of us agree with Lenana, that we have no choice but to move from the Laikipia and rejoin our brothers in the south.'

'But don't you see? The British wanted the Rift Valley because the Maasai's cattle improved the pasture there. Now, they want the Laikipia Plateau. How many times can we Maasai move? Each time we are given worse lands in compensation. The settlers continue to take the best from us.'

A muttering of sympathetic voices arose from the gloom.

'Again, you say "we Maasai", but you stand there with your English clothes and talk about your English studies. What of your Maasai learning? You have chosen to turn your back on that. You have denied your people, your traditions. Speak not of the Maasai as if you are one of us.'

Ole Gilisho interrupted. 'It is true that some of us believe it is in our favour to reunite north and south sections,' he said to the elder. 'Others disagree. What we must know is our *laibon*'s final word on the matter. To make this important decision he should be informed of all the choices open to us, rather than just what the whites tell us.' He indicated Marcus. 'This man says he knows the British law and believes we have been misled. Lenana should know this.'

'Then let him speak with Lenana if he can,' a new voice from the darkness said. 'But see, it is impossible. The *laibon* is still not among us.'

Marcus had noted that the old man had not stirred since the time they had entered the hut. He wore the same vacant expression as he had the day before.

Ole Gilisho sighed. 'You are right; perhaps tomorrow will bring him back to us.' He turned to Marcus. 'Come, my friend, we will leave.'

Ole Gilisho led the way. As Marcus lowered his head to follow him through the door opening, a faint rasping voice came from the bed platform behind him.

'Beware, my son,' it said.

Marcus turned back. Lenana's eyes, now bright and intelligent, reflected the glow of the fire. 'Beware the forest ... The men with death in their hearts.'

Marcus returned to the bed platform and knelt beside it. 'What do you mean, Father?' he asked. 'Who are these men with death in their hearts?'

'The beast stalks the one who is loved.'

Marcus took the old man's hand in his. 'The one I love?' He felt a stab of panic in the pit of his stomach.

The other elders muttered in the darkness, but Lenana's hand went limp in Marcus's grasp.

'What did he mean?' he asked Ole Gilisho.

'He is an old man. Who knows what old men see in dreams?'

The words tumbled through Marcus's head. 'Lenana said, "The beast stalks the one who is loved."' He looked at Ole Gilisho with eyes widening in fear. 'Atiya,' he said, and burst through the hut's opening into the blinding light of morning.

As he walked quickly across the *enkang* his mind conjured all manner of accidents that could befall Atiya. He thought of cholera and plague — diseases common to Nairobi, and chillingly effective killers. Or lion. There were many in the Parklands forest.

The incident in the forest with the men who had tried to strangle him returned to mind. Could they be the ones who posed the threat? He quickened his pace. He had thought the attempted robbery odd at the time. He had managed to glimpse his assailant and recognised him as an Asian. Why would an Asian want to rob an African? Now it occurred to him that perhaps he had stumbled into a larger plot. Maybe they were planning to attack Atiya's house? After all, Jeevanjee was a wealthy man. He began to trot through the pressing crowds inside the compound, bumping into indignant *moran* and angry women.

At the *enkang's* entrance, he plucked a spear from a collection that were planted at the gate and began to jog. He gathered speed as he passed through the village, causing people to stare and wonder.

Lenana's words surged through his mind and his imagination carried them into visions of Atiya under threat from machete-wielding murderers. As he joined the road towards Nairobi, suit coat flapping behind him, he felt he had precious little time to reach her.

Jeevanjee felt his cheeks burning with aggravation. The market was humming with gossip. Filthy gossip! He could ignore it no longer, and had to fight to control the urge to turn on the sniggering faces and scream his retaliation. *No! My daughter would never do such a disgusting thing!* But it would not silence them. He would need to find the proof and shove it under their noses. Then he could have his revenge at their expense.

He had heard the rumour, at first delicately conveyed to him, but it grew until all the Bohra seemed to be whispering it among themselves. Other Indians — outsiders — were hard-pressed to conceal their delight. They were the same types who, hearing that one of his ships had run aground in Kilindini Harbour, would almost have had a heart attack in their dash to be the first to break the sad news to him.

He couldn't stand the humiliation any longer. He stormed up Bazaar Street and headed for home.

Atiya left the house mid-morning, giving the impression she was going shopping. Her Uncle Tayabali had been watching her like a hawk, and as soon as she reached Forest Road, heading ostensibly towards the town, the three thugs appeared in her wake and remained determinably within sight. It was obvious they were hoping she would lead them to Marcus, so she returned home, for the moment, at least, defeated in her plans to reach Chiromo and warn him of the plot.

To make matters worse, her uncle kept a close eye on her for the remainder of the morning. Atiya became anxious that she would not be able to steal away from the house before dark, before Marcus came to see her as he had promised. By then it would be too late.

Her opportunity came during lunch when the servants bailed up one of the thugs who had been spotted lurking around the house. Brandishing carving knives and garden implements, they surrounded him and raised the cry for Tayabali to come and seize the suspected felon. When her uncle went to calm the affray, Atiya quickly checked the garden and made a dash for the bush. But her father, his face dark with anger, caught her at the gate.

'Daughter!' he said. 'Where are you going?'

'I ... I'm off to the market, Papa.' She knew how explosive his anger could be, particularly if family matters went awry, and she had never seen such a look of pure fury as he wore at that moment.

'Without a shopping bag, or even a hat for your head?'

'Oh, I was only going to —'

'Come inside with me. There's a serious matter we need to discuss.'

'But Father, I —'

'*Now!*' he commanded, and took her by the arm.

Tayabali and the thug were in the garden, surrounded by the house staff.

'What is this?' Jeevanjee demanded.

'Nothing to worry about, brother,' Tayabali said. 'A little misunderstanding.'

'I know you,' Jeevanjee said to the thug. 'What are you doing here?'

'I am sorry for your trouble, Mr Jeevanjee Mulla.' He glanced at Tayabali. 'My master sent for me.'

'Did he?' Jeevanjee turned to his brother. 'How dare you have men such as these around my house?'

Tayabali's ire immediately rose to meet his brother's. 'Am I a dog to sit and wait your attendance? I have business to conduct as well as you. My men go with me wherever I need them.'

'What possible dealings can you have for brutal assassins? I am a respected businessman, and we run a respectable business here. There is no place for their likes around here.'

'Respectable, is it?' Tayabali sneered.

Atiya was reminded of a cobra about to strike.

'Since you are so ignorant of what is going on under your own roof,' Tayabali continued, 'I shall tell you why my men are here. They are to protect the honour of this family!'

Atiya felt a tremble of dread.

'What are you saying?' her father said, but he shot a quick glance towards Atiya. His anger was suffused with fear — the terrible fear one feels when one's worst nightmares are about to be proven real. Her heart missed a beat.

'This one,' Tayabali said, with ill-concealed disgust, 'has taken a lover.'

In the moment it took her father to respond, a host of thoughts stormed shrieking through Atiya's head. She would stand no tawdry slurs on their love. She would defy any demands to end it. She would stand up to her father and fight for her love as she had promised Marcus she would.

In the verbal mêlée that followed she heard little of the detail. Her father was on the point of explosion. Her uncle was needling and taunting. When she thought it could get no worse, her uncle unleashed what he had obviously kept as his most savoured and vilest condemnation.

'And a black lover, to boot!' Tayabali crowed.

378

That was when her father struck his brother with the back of his hand — a loud crack that hung in the air for a heartbeat, silencing Tayabali for only a moment before his vitriolic tongue wove lurid descriptions of what he had seen in the jungle: '... writhing like two snakes ... his black body sliding over her ... her mouth on his black cock ...'

In all of this Jeevanjee had not dared look at his daughter, containing his anger and humiliation like a volcano on the point of bursting. When he could control himself no longer, he turned on Atiya, his face contorted with rage, his shirt collar threatening to strangle him, and demanded she deny all these filthy lies. But she could see in his face that he already knew the terrible truth of it.

Atiya staggered back under his fierce appearance. The man before her, with murder in his eyes, was not her father. His wrath was so overwhelming that for one shameful moment Atiya contemplated denial, but she found a courage she had not imagined she had. Summoning all her strength, she said, 'Yes, and I love him, and we are to be married!'

'You ungrateful slut!' Her father's words whipped her like a lash. She could scarcely believe he could use such language against her, but he stood before her, his chest puffed out and his eyes burning with disgust and revulsion. It was worse than if he had assaulted her. Her fear turned to anger, and at that moment she had never hated anything so much in her whole life. She screamed at him in blind rage, calling him names without thinking what she was saying.

He struck her.

Her head rang with it, and she looked at him in horror. Instead of regret and remorse, she saw only loathing. It was the final, terrible blow.

She had nowhere to retreat. She fled from her father's sight.

Jeevanjee was blinded by the red cloud of anger. He tugged at his collar to give himself air. There was a burning pain in his chest.

Atiya was gone, but the blinding, maddening pain remained.

Tayabali's face, smiling, gloating, was before him. He said no more, but his smug expression spoke volumes.

There was nothing to be said. His daughter — the love of his life, the person he would have given everything for — had stabbed him in the heart. She had turned his concern for her happiness into a blade to rip him apart. Instead of accepting his kind words of encouragement to take a Bohra husband, she had deliberately turned against him, inflicting a humiliation that would taunt him for the rest of his days.

His daughter was the spawn of the devil. She was evil.

'You!' he commanded the thug. 'Go! Get that creature that would shame our family.'

The thug glanced at Tayabali before replying. 'What do you want us to do with her?' he asked cautiously.

'Just do what you do.'

CHAPTER 50

Within an hour of Ngong, Marcus had already discarded his tie and suit coat. It pained him to toss away the smart navy blue jacket like a useless rag, but the sun was hot and he was streaming with perspiration. He had persevered for as long as he could, for the coat, and in fact the whole suit — trousers, coat, shirt and tie — were important to him. They represented hard-earned cash, but more than that, his clothes were symbolic of his new life. It was his lawyer's uniform, as he so often joked to Atiya.

As he ran, he'd had time to reflect upon Lenana's vision. The more he thought about it, the more he was convinced it was a portent of danger. Lenana's reputation as a prophet was unequalled. The connection of his words and the eerie feeling Marcus felt as he uttered them left him in no doubt that he had to reach Atiya urgently. There was no time to wait for the coach to return for his homeward journey.

After another hour Marcus had fallen into a relentless trot. Head down, shoulders slumped, he carried his spear in one hand and let the other arm swing loosely to conserve his strength. His shirt was gone, and he had sliced the legs from his trousers with his spear.

The hard surface of Ngong Road had blistered his feet, and by ten o'clock he had thrown off his shoes, and ran on in stockinged feet until the wool shredded and fell away.

He stumbled into the Maasai village at Dagoretti Corner, a few miles from the outskirts of town, and begged for water. He was weak and his heart beat like a drum in his chest. He had to fight the desire to simply lie down in the shade and let his exhaustion claim him.

The cool water poured over his face and body revived him a little, and he gratefully accepted a little fresh milk mixed with cow's blood. He left the village without his cut-down trousers, but with a *moran*'s short, red *shuka*. The water, and the freedom given by the loose garment, gave him renewed energy.

He was now no more than an hour from Atiya. And he was ready to do battle with whatever manner of danger she faced.

Atiya stumbled through the bush, hoping she was on the rough track Marcus took on his cross-country excursions from Chiromo. At times she was uncertain if she was on the path or not, and thought she had got lost a number of occasions. *Only a Maasai could follow this*, she thought in despair.

A monkey screeched in the branches above her, sending her heart racing in fear. She watched it swing through the trees, protesting her invasion until it was long out of sight. It had been hours since she had last seen Forest Road, and even if she felt inclined to retrace her steps and attempt to reach Marcus another way, she was now unsure she could find her way back.

Strange sounds surrounded her. All manner of cries came from hidden places — of birds or animals she was not sure. Where the path had previously wound through bush with sections of relatively open grassy patches, the tree canopy now seemed to close out the sky above her, throwing the forest into a kind of twilight of soft shadows and indistinct shapes. Thick vines conspired to weave an impenetrable wall across her path, forcing her from it and into another diversion.

A sharp branch caught her sari and tore a piece from it, nicking her thigh at the same time and drawing a trickle of blood. Much to her distress, a pitiable whimper escaped her lips before she could bite it back. She collected her resolve and pressed on.

Through the thick undergrowth up ahead, there appeared to be an opening. She caught a glimpse of sky. Although she felt she still had some further distance to travel, the thought of breaking free of the grasping forest into open grasslands lifted her spirits. She hurried to the edge of the open veldt and paused to fill her chest with warm, grass-scented air. The sun unleashed all its searing strength on the cheeks of her uplifted face, but she didn't care. It was a welcoming beacon in the unbelievable blue of the sky.

She picked up her pace, moving from the heavy cover of the forest with new energy in her step. The stultifying heat and the enfolding curtain of dense foliage conspired to deaden every sound. Atiya felt the press of silence as she did in the mosque when there was no one around. Such a silence had the ability to raise the tiny fine hairs on her arms.

The air was like a thick blanket that snuffed out everything that made an attempt to reach through it, leaving an eerie emptiness. It was almost too much to bear. She stopped, listening, daring a sound to break the stillness. She needed a sign to say that the world was still spinning in its orbit, that life still went on somewhere out there.

She heard a grunt — an exclamation of surprise. It came from directly ahead. About fifty yards away, among the shadows of a tall thin bush standing in the grassy clearing, a black-maned lion had lifted its head from his quiet repose beside its three lionesses.

Atiya had already reached her emotional boundary that day. Nothing further could affect her. With a calm that she dredged from an exhausted spirit, she stood totally still in that dreadful silence and stared at the four sleepy lions.

Jeevanjee had ranted and raved through the house, sending servants scurrying for somewhere to hide until his mood subsided. When he came storming outdoors again, still fuming, and saw his brother once more — his supercilious smile still fixed to his face — he disappeared, returning a moment later with his ancient shotgun in his hands. Tayabali backed away, and retreated down Forest Road towards the town.

Jeevanjee was still not subdued and raged about the house, loudly slamming doors behind him. He retreated to the parlour, unable to stem the streaming tears of anger that fell into his beard.

After the best part of an hour he went to the mahogany sideboard where he kept his meagre store of alcohol. There was no whisky. He grabbed a near-empty bottle of rum and drained it into a glass.

He picked it up and was about to swallow it all — a unique deed for him, an abstemious drinker — but replaced it on the table to pace the room. After a few minutes he had calmed sufficiently to return to his rum. He again lifted it to his lips.

It was then that the full import of what he had done struck him.

The thugs.

He slammed his drink to the table, shattering the glass, and dashed from the house.

Atiya kept her eye on the lions as she slowly backed away.

The three lionesses were sprawled in the grass. Only an occasional flick of a tail or a twitch of an ear indicated any sign of life, but the black-maned male was half-awake, sitting up and blinking its golden eyes in what appeared to be an attempt to focus on the yellow sari that shimmered in midday sunlight in front of it.

She tested each backward step in advance. Instinctively, she tried to keep her profile small and her actions slow. A stumble would surely disturb the lion's daydreams, and bring it and its harem down on her.

Slowly. Step by step.

She was amazed at her composure. Soon she had almost retreated to the shade at the edge of the clearing. The lions were now only an indistinct blur in the grass. She felt safe enough to turn her head away; to retrace her steps to find another path to Chiromo.

The thug's eyes locked onto hers the instant she faced him. His two comrades were behind him, a dozen paces apart. Their eyes, too, were fiercely fixed on her, as if by the mere intensity of their gaze they could immobilise her where she stood — cold now in the bold sunlight. Like performers on a stage, they approached in unison, each step calculated to enthral her with its poetry. She felt the macabre fascination she once had as a child, watching a spider wrap its wretched prey in its web.

Her assassin's gaze was as cold as the lion's — calculating and cold, as if assessing his prey. There was no sign of passion on his swarthy features. The act he was about to commit was part of a well-rehearsed play. He drew nearer, taking each step as he would in a dance. He wore an almost serene expression, dreamlike. A fleck of spittle formed at the edge of his mouth. He licked his lips and it was lost.

As he pulled the flowing white silk scarf from his belt, his face finally became animated, alive with joy. He was about to honour his goddess Kali in the ancient manner.

Marcus had departed the road that led towards the town and taken what he had hoped would be a quicker, more direct route, cross-country. Now he found himself whipped and torn by vines and branches. His tongue had swollen in his throat from dehydration, and he was almost at the end of his strength. He stumbled on through a fog of exhaustion and pain. It was only the vision of Atiya that drove him on, blindly thrusting through the bush that tore at his bloodied and aching body.

He had lost track of time. The dense foliage of the forest blocked his view of the sun. He thought it must be about midday. He had been running for nearly five hours.

His falls were more frequent, but he repeatedly dragged himself to his feet. Each time the effort took a heavier toll. A demon of doubt crept in to whisper that he could not make it before the disaster — whatever its nature — struck. He began to rage at himself, driving himself onward.

He fell again, this time into a pool of sunlight. As he struggled to raise himself from the dirt, he noticed he was in grass — a wide open expanse of short grass. The sun glinted into his eyes as he strained to find a landmark. The clearing was only about three or four hundred yards wide. It looked like the veldt halfway from Chiromo to Atiya's house.

A movement caught his eye at the distant line between forest and grass. A large male lion with a full black mane was strutting across its territory — a picture of power and arrogance. It was moving on an oblique line to Marcus's path to Atiya's house. Marcus tested the reassuring weight of his spear. A mere lion would not stop him. He moved forward, keeping an eye on the lion as he made his way across the clearing.

The lion was aware of him, but was keeping resolutely to its path. Three lionesses stopped some distance off, a little more nervous about the presence of the Maasai. The black-mane increased its speed and hunkered into a running crouch, suggesting it was approaching its chosen prey.

Marcus followed the line of the lion's gaze and saw something in the grass. His heart leapt in his chest as he recognised Atiya's yellow sari, and her long black hair spread around her, beautifully awry.

'Atiya!' he called. It was a pitiful effort from his dry throat. He forced his useless legs into a staggering gallop. 'Atiya!'

The lion was closing quickly. Marcus made a mighty effort to bridge the gap. His breath came in sobs as he crashed through the grass. Suddenly, the lion recognised him as a threat and swung to face the oncoming Maasai with a snarl, coiling its limbs beneath it in preparation for a charge.

Marcus braced himself behind his spear and met the oncoming lion as it surged through the air. He caught the beast front-on, and the impact sent him backwards to the ground. The lion's momentum carried it forward, and it fell dead beside Marcus in the grass, the full length of the iron blade buried in its chest.

'Atiya! Atiya!' Marcus cried, stumbling forward on hands and knees until he was beside her inert body. He slipped his arms under her and drew her to him, but her body was limp, and her head hung at an obscene angle. Her dark, unblinking eyes stared into the sun.

He held her and sobbed over her, sheltering her face from the burning sun with his. When he lowered her carefully back to the ground, he found a white silk scarf in the grass.

He cried for Atiya and he cried for himself. He had sacrificed everything to find completeness in the sophisticated life of an educated Englishman. There were times when he had felt he had made a bad choice, denying his culture for the promise of this new life — then he found Atiya, and happiness. Now, instead of paradise, he was in a bereft and desolate place. What price sophistication when his life could be destroyed by a single savage act?

He lay across her body, letting waves of self-pity wash over him, abandoning himself to a convulsion of sobs.

There was no way to escape the agony, and when all the tears he possessed had been shed, he stood, lifted the cool body in the yellow sari into his arms, and headed towards the Jeevanjee household.

There was a long jagged rip below one knee of Jeevanjee's fitted white trousers, and his beige tunic was spotted with flecks of mud and stained by the sap of torn vines. He had lost his gold embroidered cap somewhere on the trail, if it was a trail, for at times it seemed to disappear altogether.

The dying sun flung brief bursts of light into the small clearings he passed through, before he again plunged into the gloom of the forest — a brooding, shadowy place that reflected his dismal mood. There was a haziness on the periphery of his vision, tinting the jungle blood-red, and his breath came in painful bursts. His only thought was to find his daughter before the thugs did.

He caught a glimpse of yellow and his hopes soared. And then it became clearer to him, and he was struck as if by a powerful body blow. Out of the gloom came a red-robed Maasai warrior carrying an inert figure in a yellow sari.

A limp arm flapped from a yellow sleeve. Her head hung across the black man's forearm, bobbing like a rag doll's. Jeevanjee wanted to protest at the discomfort of it, but there was something terribly wrong with the image: Atiya should not be in the embrace of a red-robed warrior; she should not be so still in his arms; and now that he was nearer, she should not have such a tinge of blue on her soft, full lips. Behind it all was the thought that the life should not be gone from that sweet face — the face he had adored since she was first placed in his arms twenty-one years ago.

He dragged his eyes from his daughter's staring dark pools to those of the black man, ready to scream — in anger or grief, he could not say — but there was nothing behind those African eyes. The man was somewhere else, perhaps in a place where he could do what had to be done without the agony of awareness.

He stopped in front of Jeevanjee, who reached to take his daughter's body from him. But the Maasai did not offer it. He stood there as if silently proclaiming his proprietary right. Jeevanjee was indignant at the gesture, but the young man held firm, neither offering, nor aggressively resisting the request of Jeevanjee's extended arms.

When the Maasai turned to him with that unrelenting gaze, Jeevanjee dropped his arms by his side, surrendering his demands, for it was he, Jeevanjee, who had killed his daughter. What right had he to ask for the honour to carry her back to her family?

The man in the red robes stepped around him.

Jeevanjee followed.

CHAPTER 51

The driving wheels spun on the rails, and the pistons pumped furiously, before the engineer eased back on the throttle. The big wheels re-engaged, the carriage couplings clanked, and the locomotive eased out of Londiani station towards the Mau Summit and, beyond it, to Kisumu and Lake Victoria.

The brief stop at Londiani had given Grogan time to reflect upon Jessie, and Gertrude's harsh words to him.

He'd known Jessie as a girl of fifteen — all limbs, teeth and bumbling awkwardness. That person had nothing in common with the fair-haired beauty who appeared in his life to celebrate her twenty-first year. She was now a woman, an irresistible jewel, and a very different person to the child he knew. So he couldn't be accused of stealing a young girl from her father's arms, as Gertrude so ridiculously implied.

He was not overly concerned about intruding into his brother's love affair. He knew Quentin well enough to suspect he would tire of the race once it had been run. He would be exaggerating if he said Quentin was likely to abandon Jessie somewhere in the wilds of Uganda, for his brother was not a cad. But Quentin had a long history of failed love affairs and broken promises.

He blamed himself for Quentin's character. The boy had always had the expectation that he would get everything his heart desired, and on many occasions Ewart had acquiesced, taking pity on the youngest of his charges. Deprived of his mother's love at a tender age, and then thrust into his brother's rough care, the youngster deserved special consideration, Ewart felt. But his patience with Quentin had long ago been exhausted. He was certain that intervening in the elopement was the correct course of action.

Grogan's remaining worry was Gertrude. He'd had no idea she was aware of his occasional affairs. While he hadn't been obsessed with secrecy, in his heart he realised he perhaps could have been more discreet.

He had his needs — to some extent, every man needed the allurement of other women in their life. It was a natural thing; part of the drive that made the human race such a successful species. But as for love, that was an entirely different matter. And to threaten him with banishment from his own home was just too much.

He went back over the scene as he left Chiromo — he'd stormed from the house in a fit of anger, feeling Gertrude's eyes on him from the bedroom window. He'd had no response to make to her accusations, and had thought better of attempting anything while she was in that odd frame of mind. He remembered her curious, stinging words: *I know you love me, Ewart. But not as much as I love you.*

How could she know how much he did, or didn't, love her? Even he didn't know such things. It wasn't until his mother died that he realised how much he had loved her, but had never told her. It was regret as much as grief that brought forth his tears at her deathbed.

In normal circumstances, feelings such as love were unknowable. They were too deeply buried. Wasn't that true of everyone? And what had she meant by the odd comment that love is a cry for approval? It was nonsense. He needed no approval — certainly not through love.

Perhaps love was only measurable by its loss. How much had he loved Gertrude when they were first together? It must have been great — enough to motivate him to risk his life conquering a continent.

Over the years he had felt the passion ebb away. At first, it was time that inevitably quenched their ardour, but he felt sure his love for her remained somewhere deep in his being. It was his need for excitement that drove him into the arms of others. His life had always been that way. It was what made him the person he was.

Kisumu station had none of the qualities that Grogan thought appropriate for the final stop on a grand line like the Uganda Railway. And from where he sat — in a rickshaw taking him to the wharf — Lake Victoria was nowhere near as impressive as some of the other great lakes of the Great Rift Valley, like Tanganyika, Kivu, or even Lake Albert Edward. Having been no closer to Victoria Nyansa than about two hundred miles during his long trek, he had always felt that it would make a greater impact upon him when he eventually cast eyes upon it. But it didn't.

He was also unhappy about the late arrival of the train. When he enquired about the next boat for Uganda, however, he was informed that sir had plenty of time, because the *Kampala Princess* was not leaving for another hour. He was relieved to find he had not missed the boat, but the news did nothing to ease the discomfort that had hounded him throughout his long journey from Nairobi.

Having made his grand gesture of defiance against Gertrude's ultimatum, he now felt faintly uncertain about how to proceed. He had to convince Jessie into reconsidering her headstrong act of rebellion, and if she and Quentin were also on the *Kampala Princess*, it gave him precious little time to do so.

The rickshaw pulled into the mêlée that was the passenger boarding area on the wharf. He was momentarily lost in a swirl of sweaty bodies and loose items of baggage. In the midst of this, he spotted Quentin at the head of the gangway, shaking hands with the captain and being patted on the back by one of the officers. He was in his element — a navy man on board a ship that could well command the high seas.

Suddenly, Ewart felt out of his depth. Why was he so doggedly chasing this obsession? In a moment of uncharacteristic self-doubt, he realised he had no idea how Jessie felt about him. In his pride he had assumed that she, like all the others, would fall at his feet. The evidence so far had been quite the reverse. And back in Nairobi there was a woman whose loyalty, love and honesty deserved better from him.

Grogan tried to find Jessie in the crowd to savour one last glimpse of that gorgeous face, then turned to retrace his steps to Kisumu station, and home.

Marcus stood on the low bluff overlooking Bruce Dalton's farm. It was, of course, familiar to him, but now, in a strange and slightly frightening way, felt quite alien.

A few enormous juniper and cedar trees studded the bluff, giving it some shelter from the harsh dry highland winds that came from a cloudless and intensely blue north-eastern sky. Why had these particular trees been spared the axe? Perhaps it was the bluff that made the felling a little more difficult, or perhaps hauling the timber off the rise to the railway line, a mile or so away, was not worth the trouble — there were a million more trees further up the line.

The trees on the bluff were like a memorial to what once had been a great forest, before the voracious needs of the white man's railway prevailed. After all the years as a boy on a white man's farm, when felling trees had been every settler's bounden duty, he wondered why he thought of them that way now — a memorial.

It had been a week since Atiya's burial. He had waited until her family had left the grave to find a time when he knew he could kneel there alone.

He envied Atiya's family. They could console one another in their grief. Marcus only had his memories, and they were not comfort enough. He wanted, selfishly, to stand with her father and other members of the family because, of all human emotions, he felt that grief was best shared with others. But he knew that to do so would mean forcing her father, and the family, to again confront the reason Atiya was dead. The graveside was not the place to publicly announce his love. So he waited until the cemetery was empty, and the cool night cocooned him in his grief.

He had been on the bluff for too long, and had to admit he was stalling. Something about the farmhouse intimidated him, as if it were home to ghosts. It was there he had harboured dreams of becoming an honorary white man. He had planned to achieve this by means of an education and a navy blue suit. Now the suit had been replaced by a traditional red *shuka*, and the education had been found wanting when it was most needed.

The recollection of the land resettlement agreement reminded him that his arrival at Londiani was the beginning, not the end, to his journey. He walked down from the bluff and slowly crossed the short grass stubble of the home allotment. It was only then that he realised how empty the property seemed. It was mid-morning, yet Bruce and his Maasai herdsman were nowhere to be seen.

He rapped on the door.

Silence from behind the rough-sawn timber.

Presently the door opened a crack, and Jessie peered at him. She flung the door open and threw herself into his arms. He felt her warm tears run down his chest.

'Jessie, what is it? What's happened?' he asked as he stroked the top of her head.

She couldn't speak, but sobbed as if her heart would break.

'Is it your father?' he asked softly.

Her head nodded on his chest.

The admission seemed to give her strength, for she found a handkerchief somewhere in the sleeve of her blouse and blew her nose.

'Last week,' she said in a thick voice. 'We buried him last Tuesday. You were right, he was ill in Nairobi. Much worse than he let be known.'

'Jessie ... I'm sorry.' He was becoming familiar with the pain of helplessness. It stabbed at his gut. He remembered Bruce Dalton as a silent, kind man who had taken him and his father in when they had nowhere else to run. 'I had no idea he was so unwell.'

'Neither did I,' she said. 'He wouldn't admit to anyone he was sick.'

'Then how did you know to come home? I didn't expect to find you here. You were going to stay in Nairobi for some time.'

'Yes, I ... I was travelling to Kisumu, but had a change of heart.'

'Kisumu? Why?'

She looked into his eyes as if about to begin a long story, but dropped her gaze. 'Nothing important,' she said, studying the knuckles on the hand that clenched her handkerchief.

She lifted her head to him again and forced a smile. 'Seems like coincidences are common. I arrive just as Papa ... and here you are. What are you doing in Londiani?'

Now he had a long story to tell, but perhaps, like Jessie, he had no courage to tell it. 'I am going home,' he said simply.

'To ...?' Her forehead creased in perplexity.

'To my people. Somewhere out there on the Uasin Gishu.' He indicated a faraway place beyond the forested hills that rose in steps towards the horizon. 'I know I always said that the Maasai were not my people, but that's a lie. To be Maasai is not just to be a member of a tribe. It's a place in your mind.' He smiled at her puzzled expression. 'What I'm saying is, I'm going home. My people will need me very soon.'

'W-when will I see you?'

He thought about the task that awaited him when he reached his section's *enkang*, and the long journey that would follow. 'I don't know.'

Jessie hugged him fiercely, and when she released him, she put her hands to his face, clasping his cheeks. 'Be safe,' she said.

He smiled. '*Kwaheri, Enkiti*,' he said, taking a hand from his cheek and kissing it.

'*Kwaheri*, Marcus,' she said as he stepped from the veranda onto the gravel path.

He turned back to her. She had an arm wrapped around the veranda post. Wearing a pair of overalls, she could have been the wild child he had teased many years before. 'I'm not Marcus any more,' he said. 'I'm Momposhe again.' He gave her a small smile. 'Marcus is dead.'

Having searched the Uasin Gishu for days, Marcus came upon the village unexpectedly. It had taken him five days to find it, crossing and recrossing the plateau from one escarpment to the other.

He sat in the tall grass on the slopes leading to the shallow valley where the *enkang* lay. He was tired — tired from carrying so much sorrow. His life to that point had been spared all but a few traumatic events. Now he felt a lifetime of grief had been loaded onto his shoulders in a matter of days.

If his sorrow needed company, it had been found at Londiani. But although suffering her own deep grief, Jessie's strength had roused him from his self-pity. He knew there would soon be more suffering, which would begin when he walked down the grassy slope to inform his people about the new British laws concerning their land.

Marcus suspected that his Maasai section had been wandering the Uasin Gishu plateau in search of better grazing for their stock, and from the look of the lush hills surrounding them, and the newness of their huts, they had only recently found what they had been looking for.

He was surprised that the Maasai village seemed so well organised so soon after settling. The women were sitting in circles, laughing and gossiping while they sewed or combed hides. Herd boys threw playful stones at one another while keeping an eye on their goats and long-tailed sheep. On the nearby hills and, unusually, within sight of the *enkang,* the older boys and elders stood among the grazing cattle. It was only in the early days of a new *enkang* that the tribe could enjoy such a luxury. In time, the distance the herdsmen had to cover to find water and good grazing for the cattle became so great it was necessary to again move the whole village for the sake of the herd.

Marcus stood, stretched his long frame, and walked down the slope towards the *enkang.* He was wearing his *shuka* and carried only his spear.

Immediately upon his appearance, a call went up that a stranger was approaching. He knew the tribe would not be comfortable with his presence until they knew exactly who he was.

As he neared the *enkang,* the old men came from the hills, leaving the *olaiyoni* boys to mind the herd. The young *moran,* visiting the *enkang* from their *manyatta,* or bachelors' village, strolled out through the *boma* gate, spears in hand, eyeing the newcomer with barely disguised antagonism. It was their way.

Marcus was unsure of his welcome. He was a social misfit. An uncircumcised, uninitiated man with no status, no cattle and no family. But he was coming home — not to the village, because the village changed with the seasons — but to his people.

If they admitted him at all, he would find it difficult to adapt to the old traditional ways. But he had more than assimilation ahead of him. It was his task to tell his people that having so recently found this very pleasant site for their village, they would have to leave it almost immediately. He must tell them, too, that the British not only wanted them away from this valley, and away from the Uasin Gishu, but they must take all they owned — cattle, sheep, goats and personal possessions — and leave their northern homeland forever, to resettle somewhere on the far inferior land of the southern reserve. He would have to explain that the men who had written into the 1904 agreement that this land was for the Maasai 'for so long as they existed as a people' had changed their mind. Now they wanted the land for themselves.

A small crowd followed him to the *enkang* in silence, studying him, and perhaps wondering at the purpose of his visit.

An elder met him at the thorn-bush gate, standing erect, his head held in the pose of one accustomed to respect. He waited for the newcomer to speak.

'I am Momposhe Ole Matipe,' he said. 'An uninitiated boy, formerly of the Purko Maasai.'

PART 4

CHAPTER 52

1914

The breeze wafted gently up the Great Rift Valley from the south-east, forming tiny wavelets that caught the sun and made the surface of Lake Naivasha sparkle and crackle like wildfire on a dry season wind. Overhead a squadron of pelicans wheeled into formation before coming to a synchronised landing on the surface among a herd of bellowing hippopotamus.

The day was perfect for sailing, and Gertrude was content to let Ewart skipper the little skiff in and around the inlets with no particular destination in mind.

It was seldom that she and Ewart were able to spend time alone together. Edmund was in England attending school, Nicholas was camping with friends a little further up the valley at Lake Elmenteita, and the girls were staying overnight with family acquaintances on the other side of Naivasha to help celebrate their daughter's birthday. Gertrude was particularly pleased that she had managed her sailing coup without the need to bully Ewart into it. So often he was too busy for such frivolity, but today she had manoeuvred him as skilfully as he now manoeuvred the little craft into the beach at the outlet of a small creek.

'Time to stretch the legs and take a pee,' Grogan said as the yacht bumped into the sandy bottom.

'Ewart, don't be crude. You'll spoil the mood,' she protested.

'What mood, my love? Have I missed something?'

She shot him a glance, but he was smiling.

'You know very well what I mean. This is the first time we've been alone for ages. And it's such a divine day.'

'God is in His heaven, etcetera, etcetera,' he said. 'But I'm sure He won't mind if I take a pee.' He disappeared into the long grass that formed a fringe on the sandy shore.

'Be careful of crocodiles,' she yelled after him, but he was already gone.

Gertrude hitched up her skirt and waded to shore, her shoes in hand. The sand was hot and rough on her bare feet. She sat on a rock and wriggled her toes. It was curiously erotic — the warm sand between her toes — or perhaps it was the isolation of the place that made her feel that she and Ewart could do absolutely anything they chose without fear of discovery.

Their love life had been reduced to near zero in the last few years. Ewart was always too busy or absent for days on end. Many times she suspected he was with his latest dalliance, but he had been more discreet since her explosion of anger when he had so shamelessly rushed off to Kisumu in pursuit of the Dalton girl.

In the days after threatening to end it, she lived in an agony of indecision, vacillating between her resolve to force her husband to respect her and his vows, and the utter dread that he would take her at her word and never return.

As soon as she voiced it, she knew her warning was hollow. Ewart was a man impervious to emotional blackmail. He seemed to have no need for an emotional connection with any other human being. Even when newlyweds, she had sensed this about him. He was a passionate and demonstrative lover, but had no need of anything in return.

'Ah, that's better,' he said, coming from the papyrus.

'Why don't we rest here a while,' Gertrude said, pushing her toes through the sand.

'Very well, my love,' he said and lowered himself to the rock beside her. 'It's your day.'

Gertrude was first to break the long silence. 'Why don't we do this more often, Ewart?'

'Do what, Gertie? You mean go sailing?'

'Not necessarily sailing. Just be alone together. Anywhere.'

'Hmm, it would be nice, wouldn't it?'

'We're always entertaining someone or other. Your business associates, or the PC, the DC or some other so-called dignitary. The ADC. We need time alone.'

Grogan took her hand and kissed it. 'I'm all yours, my sweet,' he said.

'If only that were true.'

'What do you mean by that?' The smile faded on his lips.

She had let the words slip without thinking because the sentiment had been on her mind for a long time. Ewart had become increasingly involved with business to the point of becoming quite distant from her.

'I mean we are seldom together these days.'

'Why that's nonsense, Gertrude. I'm always home, except for the odd business trip.'

There were times when Ewart would be gone for days, and occasionally for weeks when he had to visit England. During his absences — even those of only one night — her imagination, abetted by painful experience, nearly drove her insane with jealousy and fear.

'I mean, like this. Alone, and without the distractions that call you away at all times of the day and night.'

'Some things are urgent, Gertrude, and can't wait for a more convenient moment to deal with them.' He got up from the rock and shoved his hands deep into his trouser pockets. 'Apart from business things, there's all the Legislative Council nonsense to contend with.'

'You've always wanted to be the biggest player in the field. Even when we were first married and just arrived in BEA, you had that ambition, but we still had time to make love.'

He gave her a sidewise glance and frowned. 'You know how things are, Gertie. I'm stretched as thin as a string. Cash flow — that's what I need. I've been back to Lingham three times for extensions on our line of credit. The South Africans have only so much patience.'

'Then sell some of your assets.'

'And lose my advantage? Never. I'll get through it, but it needs constant attention. All in all, I'm a little distracted at times.'

'Yes, but by whom is a question never far from my mind.' She bit her lip, hating herself for letting old wounds ruin their day, but it was out and she couldn't retrieve it.

'For goodness' sake, Gertrude, you make it sound as if I'm jumping into bed with every woman I meet.'

'For the life of me I try to forget, but it's happened too many times. Each time we drift further apart. Can't you see that?' She suddenly felt drained, as she did each time these issues were raised. Releasing her pent-up tension in a long, slow breath she said, 'I have loved you more than you could know, Ewart. I can say that with great confidence, because I know you have a very limited capacity in that regard.'

He opened his mouth to protest, but she raised her hand, silencing him.

'I once heard you described as *over-engined*. I never quite knew what that meant. At first I thought it meant that you were very passionate, and I have seen that side of you, but now I think it means you have all power and no soul. No heart to give.'

She stood and retrieved her shoes from beside the rock. She let the sand trickle from one, then the other. 'At this moment I feel I have given you almost all the love I have. I think the next blow will kill what little remains. And as much as I might pray it would be otherwise, I don't think I could go on without it.'

Five miles from Nairobi, the Uganda Railway met a long straight section on the ridge above the Empakasi Plains. It gathered some speed there, testing its puff for the three hundred and twenty mile journey to Mombasa.

Alone in his first-class carriage, Grogan settled back in his seat, and idly watched a herd of zebra and wildebeest gallop away from the side of the track, flicking their tails and kicking their heels and causing a late afternoon golden cloud to form with their dust.

The journey east would take them through rolling grasslands, beneath the brows of high wooded hills, across a cruel thorn-bush desert, over bridges spanning rivers and ravines, through dense littoral forests, before arriving at Mombasa on the following day — some five and a half thousand feet below on the Indian Ocean. He knew the journey well, having made it many times to attend to matters to do with his Kilindini wharf.

The *East African Standard* was folded on the seat beside him. Its front page drew his eye, but he had already read the main story: *Indians Ready to Pounce*. It was a warning to the Settlers that the Indian political machinery was again stirring trouble for them, this time advocating that the White Highlands land should be open to all comers. Grogan knew the story because he had provided the journalist with most of the facts — had virtually written it for him. He found it a useful method of getting the philosophy of the Association of Colonists into the public domain. Some of the detail was a little exaggerated, but that was seldom a concern for the Nairobi newspaper men. On this occasion he had planted the thought that the East African Indian National Congress was planning to assist in the mass immigration of unskilled, uneducated coolies. They would land in their boatloads, bringing all the usual cases of disease. Mombasa was still on edge following a recent outbreak of cholera. There had already been an uproar in the Legislative Council about imposing a moratorium on immigrants, and demands for quarantine. There would be pressure on the Governor for action.

Being President of the Association of Colonists had strained a number of Grogan's earlier business connections with Indians, particularly Alibhai Jeevanjee, who was at a loss to understand Grogan's animosity. This surprised Grogan, because Jeevanjee, of all people, must know that business and political alliances had to change to suit the circumstances. In Jeevanjee's case, it was forced upon him by the judicial inquiry following his daughter's death. In Grogan's case, it was to align himself with his stronger connections to the Settlers' group and Lord Delamere.

He knew that Jeevanjee and the others might find it difficult to understand his changed situation and hence his changed allegiances, as did minions like Ronald Preston and others he had met on his road to the top. There were times in both business and friendships when people went through a period of being useful, and then circumstances changed, and new alliances must be made. It was an evolutionary process: survival of the fittest; it happened in life, as well as in nature.

The train began the first wide sweep approaching Athi River. Grogan checked his timepiece. They were on schedule.

Each individual first-class carriage, no more than twenty feet in length, had a porter, who had his own small compartment with a connecting door to the carriage, and one to the outside. He would purchase refreshments for his passengers at stations along the way, and, if required, would make up a bed on one of the two longitudinally fitted seats. Grogan got to his feet and opened the door to the porter's compartment.

'I'll call if I need you,' he said. 'In the meantime, keep this door closed.'

The Indian porter nodded. 'Certainly, *sahib*.'

Grogan closed the door and engaged the catch.

He sometimes thought it a shame that innovative men like Jeevanjee could not be incorporated in the Association's plans, but to include one was to open the floodgates to all, which would defeat the purpose. Grogan and people like Delamere knew that the Indians would find a place in the new colony when it was proclaimed — and he had no doubt that it soon would be — but that place would be a closely controlled niche. It was the Indians' position to form the bridge between Africans and whites. They would introduce the concept of capitalism at the workshop and *duka* level, where small enterprises would import or produce basic commodities. These industries would be owned and managed by the people who had most expertise in such matters — the whites.

Without exception, the blacks would be the major consumers and providers of labour. Grogan didn't go as far as some, who said that educating the natives only led to dissatisfaction and unrest and therefore should be avoided, but he did believe that people like Marcus were an anomaly. There was no place for a highly educated black in BEA, or Kenia, as it would soon be called. His personal reason for educating Marcus was an entirely different matter, and anyhow, it had been a waste of time as subsequent events had proved.

The train began to slow and Grogan drew all the window shades save one from where he could observe the people at the Athi River station.

Jessie suddenly came to mind, as she sometimes did. He wondered where she was, and if she had yet tired of Quentin. The Lado Enclave was no place for a woman, especially if she was with a man as selfish and immature as his brother. He shrugged. It was probably for the best that he hadn't found them together. There would have been a scene, and, he had to admit, Gertrude's threat had shaken him. He still loved her, and in his own way was faithful to her. There was no one who could take him away from her because his little affairs always remained just so. And he had learned to be discreet. He had a separate life where he lived exotically and dangerously, enjoying the thrill of the chase and the satisfaction of victory, but by keeping it apart, he avoided it intruding upon his life with Gertrude and his family.

Grogan's carriage crept down the platform, coming slowly to a stop about twenty yards from where Mrs Tessie Norris stood, the young wife of a successful Athi River estate owner. She looked splendid in a long pale green skirt with a darker green cutaway frock coat. Her blouse was made of gauzy white fabric trimmed with lace. Gertrude had told him they were the latest style, called 'pneumonia blouses', and had set tongues wagging when they first appeared in Nairobi. Her hat was a frivolous concoction with sweeping feathers.

Grogan flicked a spot of cinder from his sleeve and went to his carriage door.

He opened it and Tessie Norris entered. She smiled shyly at first, and then came to him, throwing her arms around his neck and kissing him with passion.

Jessie brought her horse to a halt on the grassy rise below the *kopje* at the high end of her property. Before her was all she owned — five hundred acres of stubble and fifty lean cattle.

She looked up into a pitiless blue sky. This was the time when the rains should have been soaking the farm, but the dry, which had begun in 1912, showed no sign of ending. She wondered how long her herd could survive. Tom Burridge at the bank had suggested she should reduce her risk and sell what stock she could. But there were no buyers for cattle at any price in a drought.

Tom was sweet, but no farmer. If she agreed to his other plan, she would have to give up the farm — sell it if she could — and move to Nakuru. Walking away from the farm was a question she wrestled with almost every day. She was sure that her father wouldn't blame her for it, but it somehow felt disloyal to his memory. She was torn between Tom and what she felt was her duty. If the rains came, she could at least make an objective decision. It was difficult to give an answer to a proposal of marriage when all that occupied her mind was the loss of the family farm.

Marriage to Tom would also mean an end to another enduring hunger. Her infatuation with Ewart Grogan would have to come to an end. In her rational moments she thought this would not be difficult, but there were times when the haunting memories of him drove all such sensible resolutions from her mind.

She was trapped between conflicting options. Decisions were too hard to make in such a climate. What she needed was rain. The old-timers said this was the worst drought in living memory. The more superstitious said it had started when the Maasai were kicked out of the Uasin Gishu.

Jessie had gone up to Mau Summit after she heard about the forced movement of the Maasai and their herds. Those who had seen it said it was like the coming of doomsday — a million cattle converging into the tight forested confines of the Mau; not a blade of grass to be found for fifty miles in any direction. She thought she might find Marcus there, helping with the muster. Instead, she found a thousand carcasses — cattle, sheep and goats in the main, but the desiccated bones of their Maasai herdsmen too.

At the outset, she searched among the dead for a Drury Lane suit and stylish brogues — her most enduring memory of him. Then she recalled he had rejected his civilised exterior and had reverted to his Maasai roots. Every red-robed corpse thereafter looked the same.

CHAPTER 53

Since arriving in British East Africa, Grogan and Gertrude had invested almost their entire capital in the country.

Grogan's financial empire had grown to include his wharf and its surrounding land in Mombasa; a nineteen thousand acre grain farm on the Kapiti Plains near Nairobi; Chiromo — an estate of one hundred and thirteen acres, ensuring no encroachment upon the Grogans' privacy; a sisal plantation near Athi River; the thirty-five thousand acre sheep farm at Naivasha with its six-mile frontage to the lake; a six thousand acre farm at Eldama Ravine, and a further twenty thousand acres at nearby Turi and Molo; a plantation growing black wattle at Limuru, and another growing oranges and coffee; and a variety of Nairobi properties including holdings in the swamp and a large plot in Sadler Street. Finally there were the vast and virtually untapped resources of the forest concession on the Uasin Gishu Plateau.

Although he was rich in assets, Grogan was cash poor. Hardly any of his investments were making money, for they were long-term investments, not expected to become revenue-producing for some time. His financial success lay in his sawmills, for which he had contracts worth many thousands of pounds, but he faced insurmountable difficulties in filling them. It proved impossible to buy enough oxen, recruit enough labour, and feed the saw blades with enough timber to keep the mills running efficiently.

The answer, as he'd always known, was a railway to get the timber from the forest to his mills, and then onto his wharf.

Grogan knew that his neighbour, Delamere, was keen on a spur line to service Equator Ranch, his enormous holding of one hundred thousand acres in the Great Rift Valley to the north of the railway line. To some extent this made the two men competitors, since it was unlikely that the government, or anyone else, would fund two spur lines. The matter remained deadlocked until Grogan had a fresh idea.

'What makes you think the dunderheads in the Colonial Office will want to reopen discussions on the spur line?' Delamere asked, as he and Grogan sat on the Norfolk Hotel's terrace.

'Not a spur line,' Grogan replied. 'Another main line — from Nakuru through the Uasin Gishu to Uganda.'

'What?' Delamere raised his eyebrows, then guffawed. 'I always warned you about not wearing one of these when out in the sun,' he said, tapping his trademark sun helmet on the chair beside him. 'You've gone stark raving mad, Grogan.'

'Not at all, D. Why do you suppose we've had no luck getting our spur lines approved?'

'Because you wouldn't concede mine was the more important,' he answered with a twinkle in his eye.

'Not quite,' Grogan said, smiling. 'It was because even the pen-pushers in the CO knew that we, or at least one of us, would be the principal beneficiary.'

'So ... what's changed? Ah ... here's the drinks.'

Grogan waited for the waiter to leave before continuing. 'What's changed is this: the Uasin Gishu is now full of Boer wheat farmers, and the Trans-Nzoia district further north will soon follow. Just as I always predicted — the country's made for European flocks and crops. Wheat, potatoes, all kind of vegetables.'

Delamere nodded. 'You're right about the settlements up there. And further west there are the banana plantations that Gumtree Johnnie got going when he was DC up that way.'

'Exactly! Can't you see it, D? A new main line, running through both our properties, taking wheat from the Uasin Gishu, bananas from Mumias, and then skirting Lake Victoria to the cotton fields of Uganda. The Colonial Office have to take notice.'

Delamere nodded, tapping a finger to his chin in thought. 'I wonder how much they'll need,' he said.

'A million pounds,' Grogan said without hesitation. Seeing Delamere's surprise, he added, 'I've had Lawley and Paulings make a rough estimate for me.'

'Mile-a-day Lawley, eh? He's certainly got the credentials. That should help with raising the capital with Treasury.'

'Treasury is one option, but it's too important to let this stand or fall on the whim of some jumped-up clerk with a grudge against us colonials.'

'What do you mean?'

'I'm counting on you getting your friends in the House of Lords to lend their support for this, but if not, well . . . we may have to consider going it alone.'

'Go it alone? You mean a private railway? Good God! You're talking a million pounds!'

'Don't get too excited, old man,' Grogan said. 'Let's not cross that bridge until we come to it.'

In reality, a privately owned railway was Grogan's preferred strategy. In that way he could influence where the stations were built to maximise the benefits for his timber operations. He was confident that his old friend, Alfie Lawley, from the Matabele war days, and now the acknowledged expert on railway construction in Africa, would be useful in that regard.

'And,' Grogan added, 'it's probably for the best if we let them think that private finance was their idea. We'll let them hum and haw about the difficulty in raising government funding, and wait for them to toss the ball into our court.'

Delamere took a swig of his gin. 'I can see you've given this quite a bit of thought, Grogan.'

'I have,' he replied. What he didn't say was that his next challenge was to find a new source of capital for his grand plan. He had mortgaged his family estates to the hilt, and significantly drawn down on Gertrude's inheritance.

Grand plans, such as the additional main line, had always been a part of Grogan's character. It had been both the hallmark of his success, and the greatest threat to it. In this regard he had a great deal in common with his old partner in the swamp, A M Jeevanjee, who was having problems of his own.

Alibhai Mulla Jeevanjee climbed the six steps to his house, leaning heavily on the handrail to spread his considerable weight. His breath was coming in short gasps as he approached the door, but his servant, Ali, opened it before he could reach it. Without a word, not even a glance, he ambled past Ali to the courtyard with the odd rolling gait he found relieved some of the pressure on his back. He flopped to his favourite chair and sighed, patting the solid mass of his midriff as he was prone to do when his mind was distracted by problems.

The courtyard was sheltered from the sun by a huddle of palms, and from the curious eyes of his extended family who these days tended to fuss over him too much. Maybe it was because they pitied him after Dayambai had gone back to Karachi to be close to her ailing mother. Jeevanjee could hardly argue with his wife's decision. She had been recently spending more and more time in India, and there was little to keep her in Nairobi these days. In fact, there had been no real life for either of them since Atiya died.

Whether his daughter's tragic death had any connection with the business woes that began at about the same time, he could not say. He had retreated into a grey, tortured place after her burial, and remained there until he was able to finally bury his grief as they had buried Atiya, but it had taken a year. Even now, three years later, there were days when her loss was still as keenly painful, and at such times he had no heart for money matters and again neglected his affairs.

Ali brought him his usual cup of tea liberally laced with sweetened condensed milk. He sipped at it contentedly.

His wife had always been homesick for India, and it was no surprise that she had departed Nairobi in a buoyant mood. As she was boarding the train, Jeevanjee tried to recall when he had seen her so animated. It had been years, but there were joyous times in the early days when they took pleasure in the privileges brought by financial success.

He remembered happy times when they threw race-week parties for all the important members of Nairobi society. Race days were entertaining and exciting, and the Jeevanjee colours were often paraded in the winner's circle. Other owners followed his lead by importing Indian thoroughbreds, which eventually replaced the nuggetty Somali ponies that had previously dominated the East Africa Turf Club events. The Turf Club's President, Ewart Grogan, invited him to join the board, and Jeevanjee had assisted in developing a new racecourse to the north of the station, and donated many trophies and cash prizes over a number of years.

He tried to remember when race week, which was now held twice a year, began to lose its appeal. It was around the time that the rhino ran onto the course during the third race. That was the meeting of July 1911. It was around then that he became actively involved in the political campaign run by the Indian Association. People like Grogan began to avoid him, and race days became a trial as Jeevanjee ran a gauntlet of abuse and sneers on his way to his box in the grandstand — a grandstand that he had built for the racing community.

Far from deterring him, this behaviour convinced him that something had to be done to prevent the spread of anti-Indian sentiment and the discriminatory legislation that began to appear with the arrival of Sir Percy Girouard, the monocled new Governor. Girouard, who was overheard referring to Jeevanjee as a 'low-caste coolie', was eventually pressured to resign following the debacle of the resettlement of the northern Maasai.

The resettlement had been an unmitigated disaster, with many hundreds of Maasai, and tens of thousands of their herds, perishing on the journey south. Whether the Colonial Office had punished Girouard for the loss of life, or for usurping their authority by promising the vacated Maasai land for the exclusive use of white settlers, was uncertain. For three years, Girouard had presided over a Legislative Council that imposed laws such as those forbidding Indians from occupying business premises they owned, while permitting them to rent them to European competitors.

Jeevanjee felt the need to consolidate the many voices calling for full and equal rights for all races in East Africa, and had formed the East African Indian National Congress. The EAINC's initial objectives were three: permission to own land in the White Highlands; the right to trial by jury; and the removal of the prohibition against carrying firearms. There were many other relatively minor issues, like amending the rule that Indian travellers on the Lake steamers were allowed one overnight blanket while white passengers received two, but these were trivial matters.

The Congress did not differentiate along racial lines. Their demands therefore included removal of similarly discriminatory policies against natives. This was too much for the Settlers and they retaliated.

The Association of Colonists — established by Grogan, and presided over by him and Delamere — was intent on furthering the Settlers' cause at all costs. It demanded residential and commercial segregation against the Indians, a maximum of two Indians on Legco — the Protectorate's legislative body — and restrictions on further Indian immigration. But its most vehement demand was that Indians be excluded from the White Highlands, because under the EAINC's non-discriminatory policy, if Indians were allowed to take up holdings in the White Highlands, then every native in East Africa would also be given access.

Jeevanjee's treatment at public gatherings would have been more tolerable had his family, and the Bohra community, remained supportive. But the Indian community — indeed, all of British East Africa — was seething with rumour and innuendo following Atiya's death. There was a formal inquiry, which ran for months. It dissected Alibhai Jeevanjee's life and the lives of all his immediate family. It probed into his business affairs and revealed his previously confidential financial matters.

As the evidence of foul play emerged, a number of witnesses told the court that Atiya Jeevanjee had been seen in the company of a Maasai man, who went missing immediately after the girl's death. The court heard they had been seen in intimate contact amongst the stalls at the Nairobi Market.

The goings-on of the previously reserved Bohra community became bigger news than the murder itself as the colony buzzed with salacious gossip. There were reports circulating that the strangulation was the work of a bizarre oriental cult of devil-worshippers. The Bohra witnesses were reluctant to expose details of their religious ceremonies to a gawking European audience, and their reticence further piqued the white's collective curiosity.

As the family's bonds frayed, two of Jeevanjee's brothers joined Tayabali in claiming part-ownership of A M Jeevanjee and Company, and became vocal critics of what they determined was their brother's 'anti-British' stance. The Bohra community, formerly a model of solidarity, split its support between the bickering parties.

Tayabali found a latent interest in politics, and claimed to represent the portion of the Asian community who were loyal supporters of the Governor. He said his constituency made no claim on land in the highlands, and were content to continue to freely trade in the towns as at present.

Although Tayabali was excluded from membership of the Nairobi Club because of the colour of his skin, senior Administration officials occasionally invited him there. But Alibhai Jeevanjee was the only Indian ever given full membership of the club, and that was because he had built it on credit. On principle, he never entered it.

Jeevanjee lifted his teacup and savoured the last of the thick, sugary brew. Replacing the cup on the small round table with its bowl of rose petals, he patted his great girth, making a reassuring thumping sound in the confines of the courtyard. He hefted himself to his feet and headed inside to his office, where he would again tackle the backlog of legal and commercial dross that had once been the driving interest of his life. Now, his life clouded with family intrigue, beset with huge financial problems, and without the joyful assistance of his daughter, it was an almost unendurable burden.

He wondered how long he could continue.

* * *

Charity functions were a fact of life in Nairobi society. Gertrude attended for the cause rather than for the social outing.

Beatrice Hopper was chairperson of the St Stephen's Building Fund. She claimed Gertrude almost the moment she arrived. 'Gertrude! So good of you to come,' she gushed.

'I wouldn't miss it, Bea. You know St Stephen's has always been one of our favourite charities.'

'Indeed. But where is dear Mr Grogan tonight?'

'He's up at our Kapiti Plains property for a day or so. Some problems with rust on the grain, apparently.'

'Oh, such a shame. But Kapiti you say? I could have sworn I saw him at Naivasha. I said to Mr Hopper, why there's Mr Grogan, I said. But I was mistaken of course. This fellow was with a blonde lady. A little done up for Naivasha, I thought at the time. But there you are. It couldn't have been your husband, now could it?'

Gertrude smiled and agreed that, no, it couldn't. There was little more to say after that, and Beatrice sailed off to corner another victim.

Gertrude forced herself to remain for another hour, then departed for Chiromo. She sat at her dressing table, stared at her reflection in the mirror, and watched as the tears trickled down her cheeks.

CHAPTER 54

Hugh Cholmondeley, the third Baron Delamere, sat astride his horse and, for Grogan's benefit, pointed to distant boundaries that marked his Equator cattle ranch. Surrounding them were the grasslands of the Great Rift Valley, which spread out of sight to faraway escarpments. The thin grass in the sun-drenched valleys and bleak exposed hills had previously fed a multitude of plains animals and the cattle of wandering Maasai, but now Delamere's huge herd grazed there. The few remaining Maasai were Delamere employees, guarding Delamere cattle rather than their own.

Grogan understood why many were envious of the generous concession granted Delamere by Sir Charles Eliot back in 1903, but he had no reason to deny D his good fortune. Both men had gained from the chaos that existed before a proper land policy was developed. The two were members of a very small, elite group who held one-fifth of the alienated land of the Protectorate, and he and Delamere were determined to fight to retain it. The EAINC's call for Indians and others to be given identical privileges to whites had galvanised them.

Heading their mounts downhill to Delamere's farmhouse, they continued to wrestle with the vexatious matter of the Indians' demands.

'I'm worried about Belfield,' Grogan said. 'We all knew he had Indian sympathies when he arrived. Now ... well, you can almost hear the Indians crowing with pleasure, with Jeevanjee writing letters to the *Standard* praising Governor Belfield for this and Governor Belfield for that.'

'We have to win Belfield's ear,' Delamere agreed. 'He's been around — not some Whitehall flunkey sent to the colonies to get him out of the way. He has to understand that agricultural business on this type of land needs large holdings to be profitable.'

'And large capital reserves,' Grogan added. 'I've told him about our proposals for the extension of the rail. He understands the figures, but he was noncommittal.'

'If Belfield lets the Indians and natives into the highlands,' Delamere said, 'it won't matter a damn what the Colonial Office decides about the railway. All those small landholders will go broke before long, and someone will have to pay. There won't be an economic argument for the line.'

They continued in silence for a time. When they dismounted and handed their mounts over to the *syces*, Grogan said, 'It's all a matter of perception, isn't it? I mean, the Governor thinks that Jeevanjee is a very capable fellow, and that he and his ilk have got the country at heart, whereas we all know the Indian is in it for himself.'

'Yes ... what are you getting at?' Delamere asked.

'What if Jeevanjee were not as competent as the Governor believes? What if it became known that he was in financial trouble?'

'What have you heard?'

'There's a bit of gossip in Mombasa about Jeevanjee's shipping line. The legal fellow I have working on my government lease down there happened to mention that there's a smidgen of trouble in the Jeevanjee camp. Family matters.'

'Odd,' Delamere said.

'That he's in financial trouble?'

'Well, that too, but it's odd that any of their family business gets out into the public. They're usually as thick as thieves.'

'True, but this is certainly not public information, although the brother, a chap by the name of Tayabali, has been bad-mouthing Jeevanjee for some time. Ownership of the company is the issue.'

'How will any of this help us?'

'Don't know exactly, but it's worth keeping an eye on it. The Indian business community enjoys the Governor's support because, in his view, they are behaving like proper English gentlemen. But if their hero, Jeevanjee, were to get into a bun fight with his clan, and he gets into financial strife, well, that may make the Governor think twice about the rabble he has been defending.'

Pandit and Pavitt sat opposite Jeevanjee in his Nairobi office. That both partners of the bank had made the journey from Mombasa for the meeting impressed him, but the tedious pleasantries wore on until Jeevanjee was about to suggest they get down to the crux of the matter. Then one of them launched into it.

'The matter we mentioned in our correspondence is entirely grave, Mr Jeevanjee,' Pandit or Pavitt said — Jeevanjee always had difficulty remembering who was who. 'So we must ask, with great respect of course, has there been any resolution to the legal matters that your brother, Mr Tayabali Jeevanjee, has raised through the courts?'

'Nothing further,' Jeevanjee answered, smiling to reassure them. 'But it is progressing. Very satisfactorily.'

'Can we therefore assume from that, Mr Jeevanjee,' the other legal partner — the bald one — said, 'that the order freezing your funds is lifted?'

'Mmm ... not quite. But it is only a matter of time.'

'But if I might be so forthcoming, with even greater respect, Mr Jeevanjee, unless the law suit that your brother has raised can be without delay and most swiftly resolved, we are concerned about your ability to be servicing your loan.'

'Mr ... um ... Pandit —'

'Pavitt.'

'I beg your pardon, Mr Pavitt, the legal issue with my brother Tayabali is a family matter, and you know how these things go. We will sit down and take chapatti and rice ...' he made a gesture as if washing his hands, '... and it will all be cleaned up.'

The partners remained silent.

'Don't worry, gentlemen. The ships that your bank helped to finance will soon be earning money carrying freight and passengers to Mauritius, Bombay and Karachi. Your one hundred thousand pounds are safe.' He looked from one to the other with a broad smile. 'Perfectly safe.'

Amir Jeevanjee was an intense young man. He was athletic, energetic, idealistic and scholarly, and therefore had nothing in common with his father, Alibhai Jeevanjee, except for a strong work ethic directed at preserving the family business.

He knew almost as much as his father did about the business because he was his father's eyes. Jeevanjee had long ago lost patience with learning to read. Everything that his father needed to read, Amir read for him. His task had always been to convey the content of newspapers to him, but after Atiya died, it fell to him to carry the entire load. Amir therefore knew the financial situation of A M Jeevanjee and Company, and it was with that in mind that he summoned his courage and went to his father to advise him about what he had heard around the ports of Mombasa.

Across the desk from him, Jeevanjee raised a hand. 'Not before tea,' he said, signalling to his assistant, Asma, to bring two cups.

His son knew better than to argue. After he'd told his father he needed to talk about serious matters, the tea ceremony was inevitable. Jeevanjee had developed traditions over the years. Taking tea on important occasions was one of them. They made small talk until Asma returned with the steaming cups.

'Now,' Jeevanjee said, nodding and raising an upturned palm to Amir, 'please speak.'

'Father, you have ruffled feathers around this place, you know,' Amir began.

'There are feathers needing ruffling. You should know that, my dear son.'

'Too many this time. And not always the feathers you should be ruffling. I'm talking about financial feathers.'

'Talking, talking, they're always talking. What now?'

'There's talk that our financial people are getting nervous because of the ruckus in our family. They are saying that your fight with Uncle Tayabali is causing our business to suffer. And that because of this distraction, your enemies are waiting to spring a trap on you.'

'That is the pastime of all enemies, my boy. What is new in that?'

'They say there is a squeeze on our credit.'

'A temporary aberration.' Jeevanjee smiled. 'That's not a bad word for an old *dukawhaller*, ah? Aberration — a real lawyer's word.'

Amir's smile was polite. 'Yes, most certainly a lawyer's word. But even if the squeeze is gossip, it could ruin us, couldn't it?'

'Oh, people like to gossip when there is a family squabble going on. There is nothing to worry about.' He leaned forward over his desk and signalled for his son to come closer. 'We are getting very close to agreement with the Germans. Then we shall see the pompous British take notice.'

Jeevanjee had been encouraging discussion in the East African Indian National Congress about the frightful service Indian passengers received on the British shipping lines between Mombasa and India. He had also pointed out that the Germans could manufacture everything the British could, but because every nail and hammer had to come through London or Plymouth, they paid a fortune to tranship small cargoes to Africa. He had been in negotiations with a big German cargo company to ship all their Asian and African trade through India. Importantly, A M Jeevanjee and Company would handle port clearance in Karachi.

'I now have an agreement-in-principle with the Germans,' he said excitedly. 'Oh, yes. And our three ships will soon arrive. We will soon be able to import German goods from our warehouses in Karachi. The shipment costs will be a fraction of what we pay the British.' His eyes were alight with enthusiasm. 'And our people will get passenger service through an Indian firm: A M Jeevanjee and Company.'

'Wonderful news, Father.' Amir sat back with a look of approval on his face. 'Congratulations. When will all this shipping through the Germans start?'

'Very soon. It's all very hush-hush because of the politics, but we are almost ready to start.'

'Excellent.' He got up from his seat and nodded in admiration. 'This is what you do best, Father. Stick to business matters, and forget the family squabbles.'

It had been an unseasonably hot July in Nakuru, and August was heading the same way, but everyone thought Jessie looked beautiful in her lace wedding gown, and Tom, resplendent in top hat and tails, looked far too dashing for a bank manager.

In keeping with the modest nature of the wedding, Jessie and Tom decided to be married on a Thursday. It also allowed people from upcountry to take the late afternoon train back to their farms in Londiani, Fort Ternan and beyond. The plan was for the newlyweds to leave the afternoon reception and join the convoy of coaches to the station, where they would bid their departing guests farewell before proceeding to their honeymoon hotel on the lake.

But the photographer had problems with his plates. It appeared that the heat had affected a few, and he pleaded for a little more time while he dashed back to his studio for more.

'Tom, darling, why don't you tell our friends to go on to the station?' Jessie said. 'If we finish here in time, we'll see them off. Otherwise they may miss the train.'

He took her hand in his and kissed it. 'Wise as well as beautiful, my dear. I'll tell them, although I'm sure we'll be there before they leave. The train stops in Nakuru for tea.'

As it transpired, the photographer was more than the few minutes he promised, and when Jessie and Tom arrived at the station, the train had already been in for twenty minutes. No one was having tea, however. People were clustered together, their guests included, chattering excitedly.

A couple of guests came running to meet their carriage. 'Have you heard?' one asked.

'Heard what?' Tom said.

'We're at war!'

Tom turned to Jessie, a look of amazement on his face. He jumped from their carriage and rushed to see the newspapers, leaving Jessie in the seat, still stunned by the news.

She watched the younger men slap one another on the back, grinning at the prospect of some real excitement that would provide a noble excuse for leaving the drudgery of farm life for a brief lark against the enemy. Even the older men, of Tom's age, seemed invigorated. Tom looked back at her, and waved for her to join him, but Jessie sat tight.

She could see the future roll out ahead of her. She had already lost a father to death, and a friend to his tribal customs. She had fled from the man she had loved, and turned her back on his brother. It seemed as though all the men in her life were destined to disappear in one way or another. Would Tom be the next?

CHAPTER 55

The Times of East Africa arrived at the Turi sawmill just before Grogan rode in with a team of timber jinkers loaded with cedar. By the time he reached his office, there was a small gathering consisting of his Indian foreman and three of his Indian staff around the open newspaper on his desk. His foreman thrust a finger at the newspaper, jabbering incoherently. Grogan threw them out of his office and turned to the front page. The dateline was Tuesday, 4 August 1914 — three days before.

Britain At War! screamed the headline.

He had been expecting it. A month earlier, the accident-prone Archduke Franz Ferdinand had survived two bomb attempts on his life in Sarajevo before a wrong turn by his chauffeur brought him within range of an opportunistic assassin's revolver. Grogan had suspected at the time that it could be the spark to set Europe alight.

He had followed the story over the following weeks. The Germans used the distraction of an Austro–Hungarian attack on Serbia to quickly fulfil their belligerent ambitions towards France. It appeared that for strategic purposes, their latest manoeuvre saw them advance their attack via Belgium, thereby bringing into play a nearly forgotten sixty-year-old treaty that required Britain to go to Belgium's aid.

Suddenly, Great Britain was at war with Germany, and, as a consequence, the British Empire was also at war. *The Times* suggested that the conflagration would soon involve not only Great Britain and Germany, but also France, Belgium, Serbia, Austria–Hungary and Russia.

Grogan caught the train from Turi station and arrived in Nairobi the following morning. By then the train was full of men keen to rush to the aid of Great Britain, regardless of the details.

Nairobi was in a carnival mood. Grogan went directly to his Sixth Avenue rooms. The government's ground floor offices were under siege from hundreds of irregulars demanding to know what they could do to help the war effort. They had come on horseback and mules, bearing weapons ranging from ancient flintlocks to hunting rifles and shotguns, with bandoliers of ammunition around their shoulders.

Old Russel Bowker, with his trailing feathery white moustache and wearing his snarling leopard's-head cap, held a group of men captive at the front door with a rousing address.

Upstairs in his office, Philip looked harassed. 'Thank God you're here,' he said when Grogan arrived. 'The Governor wants to know what we are prepared to offer the war effort. He says Britain needs timber, grain, meat. What are we to do?'

'Calm down, Philip. I don't know yet. I need to speak to some of the others — Delamere and the like.'

'You'll find them at the Muthaiga Club. The Settlers are using it as their headquarters. From what I've heard, it appears that Delamere, and some of the others, are planning to raise their own forces.'

Grogan nodded. 'I'll go out there now. Send someone out to Chiromo to tell Gertrude I'll be home later.'

'What will I tell the Governor's people?' Philip wailed.

'If they come back, stall them,' he answered.

Philip began to protest, but his brother was already out the door.

Muthaiga — the Wakikuyu name for the bark of the greenheart tree used by the Kikuyu to make poison — was situated three miles from the town centre. In 1913, an immensely wealthy visitor established a building fund for the Muthaiga Country

Club, with its whimsical pink stuccoed walls, but had never returned to see the results of his largesse. Many Settlers thought the club too remote, but they preferred it to the Nairobi Club, whose membership was predominantly senior government officials — often their direct opponents in bureaucratic battles.

It was after noon when Grogan reached the Country Club.

Delamere was standing with his back against one of the tall windows, his bald pate catching the western light, and his longish ginger hair looking even more dishevelled than usual. In front of him were gathered a group of men, some seated in plush armchairs, others standing in lines behind them. Indian waiters wearing long white *kanzus* and scarlet cummerbunds moved invisibly among the members, dispensing concoctions of gin, rum and whisky.

'Ah, Grogan,' Delamere said. 'Glad to see you. Have a seat up here.' He indicated a chair at the front of the gathering. 'I was just about to tell everyone about the latest news.'

Grogan bid them all a good day and sat.

'Our dithering Governor's desire to remain neutral is up the spout,' Delamere said, addressing them all. 'Yesterday, our cruisers — the *Pegasus* and *Astraea* — bombarded Dar es Salaam harbour. Gave them the devil of a lashing, apparently. Consequently, the Germans are mobilising on the border near Taveta.'

'What's been Belfield's response?' Grogan asked.

'Nothing yet. But I expect when the Germans retaliate, even our worthy Governor will be forced to act. But we haven't been waiting for him.' He pointed to Berkeley Cole, son of an earl and Delamere's brother-in-law. 'Berkeley's got a couple of hundred Somalis ready to go. He hopes to get a few hundred more. Cole's Scouts, he calls them. And there's young Denis Finch-Hatton's Somali Horse, Bowker's Horse, Arnold's Scouts, the Legion of Frontiersmen. There's even a bunch of Boers from up your way, Ewart, the Plateau South Africans.'

'All ill-equipped and poorly supported,' added Lord Hindlip scathingly. 'They'll get their collective arses kicked down there in Taveta.'

'Well, dammit, Fred,' said Berkeley's brother, Galbraith, 'it's all very well for you to blow into town on an inspection tour, but what options do we have? The KAR are spread all over the north, while our southern border and the railway are totally exposed. If we don't get there, and fast, the Hun will waltz over the border. Next thing we'll be putting up barricades in Government Road.'

'Gentlemen, please,' Delamere said, raising his hands. 'I believe the King's African Rifles are on their way back to Nairobi from up north, and until then your men will fill the void. In time I suspect the irregulars will be incorporated into our formal military response, but in the meantime let's give our boys every encouragement.' He looked around the men who made mumbled words of support.

'Now, a couple more things.' He raised his voice to regain their attention. 'With the imminent commencement of hostilities, every man will have to make a decision on how he intends to respond to the crisis. And be assured, it *is* a crisis.

'Secondly, there is the matter of the women and children. I would advise you to consider sending your loved ones home while it is still possible to reach the coast. Some of you have already made preparations to do so.' He ran his eyes over the gathering. 'Until we teach the Germans a lesson, this is no place for a family. Think seriously about their safety.'

The children were in and around the rotunda when Grogan arrived home just before dark. They ran to him like a herd of long-legged gazelle. He swept the girls — Emma now seven, and Sarah, five — into his outstretched arms while the boys stood by awaiting their turn.

Edmund, at fourteen, had recently come home from London on his school break. During his absence he had become more independent and obstinate, Grogan noticed, now seemingly impervious to his father's chiding whenever he retreated into a book rather than indulging in outdoor sports as his brother, Nicholas, did at every opportunity. Gertrude was his champion and wouldn't allow Grogan to override his interest in improving his education by studying during the school holidays. He stood shyly while his father ruffled his hair and patted his shoulder.

Nicholas, two years younger, was never still, and on this occasion jumped on his father's back when he bent to lower the girls to the ground. He clung there like a monkey until Grogan dislodged him and then indulged in a little roughhouse sparring with him.

'You're home,' Gertrude said as she came down the garden path. She was smiling, but Grogan could tell she was fully aware of the war situation, and was worried about it.

'Indeed I am,' he replied pleasantly, giving her a kiss on the cheek.

'I've been expecting you, but when you didn't arrive immediately after the news came out, I assumed you still hadn't heard.'

'Only got the word yesterday. News travels slowly on the Mau Escarpment.'

'What news, Papa?' asked Emma, raising her freckled face to her father.

'Ah, my little pumpkin scone,' he said, giving one of her plaits a playful tug, 'the news of those flying elephants that live in Uganda.'

'The ones Uncle Quentin is still chasing?'

'Yes,' said Gertrude, 'the very same. Now run off and play while your father and I talk.'

The three younger children bolted towards the rotunda. Edmund followed at a more sedate pace.

'I went out to Muthaiga to find out what Delamere knew of the situation,' he said as they walked towards the house. Grogan was suddenly acutely aware that he and Gertrude seldom held hands as they had in the old days. Perhaps it was the likelihood of his imminent departure that brought it to mind.

'And what *is* the latest? There's nothing meaningful in the press.'

'We're not going to escape it, I'm afraid, my love.'

She dropped her eyes to the ground and kicked at a nut fallen from one of the trees as she walked. 'I suppose this means you'll dash off to enlist?'

He had been thinking about what response he would make to

the call ever since hearing the news. 'I can't sit idly by while all my countrymen march off to war, Gertrude.'

'Why not? You're forty years of age, and you did your duty during the Matabele uprising.'

'That was different. That was Cecil Rhodes' war. This is a threat to Great Britain. To the Empire, and here, to our home.'

Gertrude sighed. 'I had a few days of hope, while waiting for you to arrive, that I'd be wrong and that you'd realise you have a family to protect and stay at home with us.'

He had deferred telling her that he was going to send them all back to England for safety.

'Are you planning to join one of those silly units that are forming up?' she asked. 'What are they? Monica's Own or So-and-so's Horse?'

'No. I don't think my skills lie in charging across the savanna with a rag-tag army. I spoke briefly to Meinertzhagen out at the Muthaiga Club.'

'Meinertzhagen. Colonel Meinertzhagen — isn't he the man known for shooting a Nandi chief while shaking his hand under a flag of truce?'

'That was a long time ago, Gertrude. Who knows what circumstances prompted him to do that.'

'Well, does he have similar tricks planned for you?'

'He wants me to join his Intelligence unit.'

'Intelligence unit. You mean be a spy? Ewart, you'd be shot if they caught you.'

'Gertrude, for God's sake. Don't be so damn theatrical.'

'Theatrical? How dare you dismiss me like that! Look at those four children down there,' she threw a hand towards the rotunda, 'and tell me I'm theatrical to suggest that their father stay home to protect them. If anyone is being theatrical it's you — playing the part of a boy scout at your age.'

She rushed indoors, slamming the heavy door in his face.

Grogan burst through the door behind her, his eyes ablaze with anger. 'Don't you dare slam the door in my face, Gertrude. So long as I'm the head of this household I'll make the decisions in these matters.'

'I accept the fact you're the head of the house. But we used to discuss matters that affect the whole family. Now you speak to your friends at the club and do what you want.'

He was taken aback by her accusation, realising it was true. Rather than mollifying him, it made him angry with himself, worsening his mood.

Gertrude took his silence for repentance. She lowered her voice. 'Ewart, you once walked the length of Africa for me. Can't you at least let me share in decisions affecting our family?'

Grogan was disgusted with himself for being loutish and stupid. His anger boiled up to the point of explosion. 'Hah!' he said, his guffaw a parody of his usual generous laughter. 'Walk the length of Africa for you? Are you serious, Gertrude? You talk about maturity, then you can't understand the simple fact that I walked from the Cape to Cairo for the Queen, for the Empire, and for the sake of Rhodes' great railway plans. In other words, for every other reason than for you.'

He turned and stormed out of the house.

CHAPTER 56

'Again,' Jeevanjee said. 'Read the part about perfidy again.'

Amir, grim-faced, returned to the correspondence page of *The Times of East Africa*. '*As a loyal subject of King George, I cannot in conscience remain —*'

'In conscience!' Jeevanjee spluttered. 'What conscience can such a dog have, knowing our plans were made long before the war was declared?'

Amir, standing in front of his father's desk, remained respectfully silent.

'Go on! Go on!' Jeevanjee said, waving his hand.

'*I cannot in conscience remain silent, given the perfidy I have discovered in my own family. As we loyal Indians stand shoulder to shoulder with our British brothers, we must be vigilant against sympathisers among our ranks and reassure our comrades that we stand with them to defend the Empire from treachery. We will never stoop to profit from dealings with the enemy, no matter how far removed from our shores. I can only pray that by making this matter public, I can convince my brother to return to the bosom of the British Empire.*

'*I am sad to say that Mr Alibhai Jeevanjee has bitten the hand of Empire that fed him.*

'*Sincerely, Mr T (Tayabali) S Jeevanjee. Mombasa.*'

Amir closed the page and put the newspaper back on the table.

Jeevanjee grabbed it and hurled it across the room. 'A snake! A snake in my own house!' he groaned. 'What is he doing to me?'

'I have already drafted a reply, Father, stating we had cancelled our arrangements with the German company immediately war was declared, and had informed our Karachi office to do likewise.'

'Ah, what good is it, these letters? Nobody will believe.'

'We will demand an apology from Uncle Tayabali.'

'Apology, apology,' he said, wringing his hands. 'The damage is done. Who will deal with A M Jeevanjee and Company now, with the sound of war drums in the air?'

'There is more, Father.'

'Oh, no. What is it this time?'

'A threatening letter.'

'From who now?'

'It's anonymous.'

'Read it,' he said grimly.

'*To the traitorous Jeevanjee — beware trouble at sea. A traitor deserves no good luck.*'

'Is that all?'

'Yes.'

Jeevanjee shook his head sadly, again counting the cost in lost cargo. 'What are we to ship on our three fine ships, ah? Three fine five thousand ton ships. Can a man be punished for dealing with a commercial company? Wasn't Britain herself also conducting trade with the Kaiser right up to the declaration of war? Has everyone forgotten this?'

'What will we do, father?' Amir sat opposite Jeevanjee, who had dropped his face into his hands.

Jeevanjee lifted his head and sat straight in his chair. 'We will do what A M Jeevanjee and Company always do — we will trade. We will buy and sell. I want cargoes — many cargoes. From anywhere to anywhere. Mauritius, South Africa, Portuguese East Africa. Anywhere.' His face had brightened at the unexpected challenge. 'The war has been a blow; now we make it an opportunity.'

*   *   *

430

The face was more angular, the body leaner. Grogan spotted him from across the road, leaning against the door jamb of the Volunteer Forces Headquarters; although he had changed, he was unmistakeable.

'Hello, brother,' Quentin said with an easy smile when Ewart stood before him.

'Quentin, I thought it was you. How are you?' He hesitated before offering his hand. His brother clasped it firmly.

'I'm well,' he said, nodding. 'And you?'

'Not bad.' Grogan now noticed his brother had dark rings under his eyes and there was a nasty scar above the angle of his jaw. He realised he had been staring, and turned his attention to the queue of prospective volunteers that reached from the front desk to the door. 'It looks like you've got a long wait,' he said.

Quentin nodded. 'No real need to rush back from the Enclave after all, was there?' he said with a chuckle.

'Why don't you come back later?'

'Good idea, brother. You can buy me a drink if you like.'

Grogan was pleased to see him, and more than interested to know how he was handling married life. 'Come on,' he said, 'let's go to Tommy's place.'

On the walk from Sixth Avenue to Woods' hotel, Ewart asked Quentin how his life was going, expecting to hear about Jessie, but his brother instead went into detail about the ivory trade, and the greatly reduced number of elephants, even in the wildest depths of Africa, and the almost daily skirmishes between hunters and local tribes. In fact he talked of all manner of what Ewart considered trivia, but said not a word about his wife.

Finally, with an ale in his hand, Grogan could hold back no longer. 'So tell me, Quentin, how is your wife?'

Quentin grinned at him. 'What the hell are you talking about, Ewart? What wife?'

'What do you mean, what wife? It's a straight question, man. Jessie, of course.'

'Oh ... Jessie ...' Quentin took a long, slow sip of his whisky, a wistful look in his eye, obviously enjoying the memory. 'Nearly forgot about Jessie. Sweet girl.'

'Yes, dammit, Jessie. Are you trying to be funny with me, because I —'

'Don't get excited, old boy. Didn't realise you'd still remember her. Jessie and I never married. Didn't even go with me to Uganda.'

'No? But you and she . . . So, what happened? Where is she?'

'What happened was she got off the train at Londiani. Changed her mind, I suppose. A woman's prerogative, they say.' He took another sip of whisky. 'Never saw the dear girl again. As for where is she — presumably in Londiani.'

Grogan was dumbstruck, trying to come to grips with the irony of it. He had been within a couple of hours' walk of her in Londiani on a score of occasions while visiting his sawmill and farm in the area. 'Londiani,' he mumbled.

'Yup, Londiani,' Quentin said. 'What a waste. Imagine a beauty like that stuck out there among ignorant farmers' sons, milking cows, or whatever else farmers' daughters do up there. Such a waste.' He shook his head and downed his whisky.

'Yes,' Ewart agreed, staring at the nearby station. A crowd was gathering in anticipation of the incoming train. 'Imagine that.'

The ship's black hull loomed above where the Grogan family clustered together at the barricade guarding the gangway. Around them, men in blue and white striped shirts hastened among the passengers, sorting luggage and whisking it away on handcarts. Uniformed officers checked paperwork and tickets, and ushered first-class passengers on board.

The ship's horn gave an impatient hoot. Emma began to cry.

Grogan lifted his daughter into his arms and she clung to his neck like a limpet. Sarah had been happily sitting on Gertrude's hip, but now began to suck her thumb, and let a tear of sympathy for her sister's distress run down her plump cheek.

'Shh, Emma. There, there,' Grogan said. 'You're going to have such fun on this great big ship, and look — see over there?' He pointed to the pair of Royal Navy corvettes at anchor offshore. 'Those big ships are going to race you all the way to England.'

Emma tried her best to smile, but failed.

'That's my girl. Now, I want you to look after your little sister on the ship. Will you do that for Papa? And be good for Nanny Redwood.'

She nodded.

'I'll speak to your brothers for a little bit, and then I'll give you a kiss, all right, Emma?'

Emma nodded again, and Grogan put her down beside her mother.

In his new blue shorts and vest, Nicholas was trying to be brave, but clung to the tail of Ewart's coat. Grogan took his hand and squatted beside his younger son. Tears welled in the boy's eyes, but he fought them.

'You're a brave soldier, Nick. Papa's so proud of you.' He ruffled the already untidy hair. 'Do you know you'll be going to my old school?'

Nicholas nodded.

'Why, that puts you one up on Edmund then, doesn't it?'

'It does?' he asked with a frown of uncertainly.

'Certainly. Edmund didn't go back home to school in England until he was thirteen. I bet he's jealous.'

Nicholas nodded and smiled, no doubt storing the information away for another time. Grogan knew that Nick's competitive nature would help to distract him.

'Now, Nicholas, give Papa a hug, and go stand with Nanny for a moment.'

He did as he was asked and joined Nanny Redwood, who hovered around their mountain of luggage as the stevedores began trundling it towards the gangway.

Edmund stood a little way off, feigning boredom. Having already made two trips to England for school, he was familiar with the routine, but Grogan could see uncertainty in his eyes. On the last night before leaving Chiromo for Mombasa, Grogan had tried to reach out to Edmund, but at fourteen his son had grown even further away from him. It was a situation that Grogan found impossible to reverse.

He put his hand on Edmund's shoulder and struggled for words to bridge the gap between them. 'Edmund, you're the man of the family now. I know you'll look after your sisters for me. And Nicholas too.'

Edmund nodded, keeping his eyes on his feet.

'Edmund,' he said, and waited for him to meet his eyes. 'I love you, son.'

There was a moment when he thought Edmund might make the response that would allow Grogan to expand on it, but it passed.

'I know,' he said, but his eyes returned to his study of the wharf.

'When this is over, and I come to England, we'll get together you and I.' He drew his son to his chest. 'We'll do some things. Things that you like to do. Anything you want.' He stepped back and lifted Edmund's chin. 'I'd like that. Would you like that, Edmund?' He smiled to emphasise his eagerness.

'Yes,' Edmund said. Then added, 'Very much, Papa.'

Grogan hugged him to his chest and again kissed his forehead. 'Come, it's time to board.'

Grogan caught Gertrude looking at him. Her eyes were red-rimmed and she appeared drained by the ordeal of the last few days. She had reluctantly agreed that it was sensible to repatriate the children, but absolutely refused to leave herself. It must have been a very difficult decision for her, but she stuck to her argument that her place was with her husband — war or no war.

'The voyage will be perfectly safe, Gertrude. Please don't fret,' he said, patting the hand that held Sarah to her. 'And Nanny Redwood will take good care of the children. As usual.'

'I'm not thinking about that, Ewart. I was just thinking that we have recently had so little time together as a family. This is how you used to be — surrounded by your children. They've missed you.'

Grogan gave her a frown to say this was not the time to discuss those tired old issues. He swept Sarah into his arms and kissed her, then placed her in Nanny Redwood's ample arms and gave Emma a hug and a kiss.

The ship's solemn horn bellowed.

Gertrude hurriedly kissed them all again and, blinking away threatening tears, said, 'Come, children, it's time to get onboard.' She searched the crowd at the entrance to the gangway where Nanny Redwood had taken her stand. 'Nanny? Has all their luggage gone up?'

'Yes, mum,' came the reply.

'Give your papa a kiss,' she said to the children, and watched as each gave Grogan another hug and a kiss in turn.

When an officer took the children and Nanny Redwood in hand on the gangway, Gertrude fiercely clutched Grogan's arm.

'They won't be children when we see them again, you know, Ewart. Never again.'

CHAPTER 57

Colonel Richard Meinertzhagen had gathered a few silver hairs at his temples in the ten years since Grogan first met him on the train going west from Nairobi. At that time he had been en route to quell another Nandi uprising, and Grogan was making his first trip to the cedar forests beyond the Mau Escarpment.

They were alone in a room in the Land Titles Office, which Meinertzhagen had commandeered. The colonel had begun by explaining the line of command and other bureaucratic matters pertaining to the Intelligence Unit, which he headed. He then congratulated Captain Grogan on his commission, and they toasted to the success of the unit's work.

'I heard you've turned your house over to be used as a hospital,' Meinertzhagen said as they sat, casually chatting, with a drink in hand.

'Yes, Gertrude and I fit quite snugly into the guests' quarters,' Grogan said. 'There's really no need for all that space in Chiromo now that we've sent the children home.' It still surprised him how easy it was to walk away from the family home of seven or eight years. It was not so for Gertrude, who had spent an age in their bedroom. When he went to find her she was staring at the bed, crying.

'Damn fine gesture, old man. Another?' Meinertzhagen held up the whisky bottle.

Grogan nodded, offering his glass.

'Excuse me for asking, Richard, but what made you take up this position in Intelligence? I understood that your career had been in the field up until now.'

'That's quite so.' Meinertzhagen paused as if considering what answer to give. 'I suppose I could say that Intelligence is an essential role if we are to maximise our winning chances, especially by finding and exploiting the enemy's weaknesses and mistakes. Or I could say that espionage is a legitimate arena of warfare, and in this case requires people like you and me, who know Africa, to do it right.' He nodded and allowed himself a wry smile. 'And you know, Ewart, all of that would be true. But the fact of the matter is, if you have been soldiering all your life, then you find yourself serving under a fool, you have to face some stiff choices. I decided to get out of the field. At least the mistakes I make here will be my own.'

Meinertzhagen had served under General Aitken when whispered condemnation had run through the Muthaiga Club membership that Aitken's eight thousand men of the 29th Punjabis had been seen off by a thousand, mostly black, German troops.

'I heard about Aitken's blunder at Tanga,' Grogan said.

'Blunder? It was a bloody disaster! The Germans don't need allies when they have the arrogance of British generals working in their favour.' The colonel slammed the palm of his hand onto his desk. 'Aitken bragged that he'd beat von Lettow-Vorbeck and his "bunch of ignorant niggers" by Christmas. Well those "niggers", the Chagga and Nyamwezi *askaris,* wiped out three hundred of Aitken's Punjabis before lunch.'

'And, I also heard, managed to capture a huge arsenal when Aitken retreated,' Grogan added.

'Hundreds of rifles, machine guns, and six hundred thousand rounds of ammunition. Can you believe it? Enough to see him fight on even though we have blockaded his supply lines from the sea.' He gave a dismissive wave of his hand. 'Ahh, forget it. Let's not whine about what's done, Captain Grogan, there's more than enough work here for you and me. So, let's get down to it, shall we?'

Meinertzhagen sat back in his chair and clasped his hands behind his head. 'Having allowed von Lettow off the hook in Tanga, the High Command don't like the idea of chasing him all over German East. He's already proved himself to be something of a strategic wizard, and may well tie us up here in Africa for quite a spell unless we do something clever. The sooner we finish his little games, the sooner we can all get into the main event.

'We need the Belgians to enter GEA from the west, and help us squeeze von Lettow's forces from the east. But having got us into this bloody war, it appears the Belgians are a little chary about getting involved themselves over there in the Congo.

'The Colonial Office have been lobbying High Command to leave good enough alone. Seems they have some concerns about Belgium's territorial ambitions beyond what they already have. We know they have their eye on some of the other German colonies, and would dearly love to add Ruanda and Urundi to their collection.'

He took a map from an umbrella stand and unrolled it across his desk. 'Here's the Belgian command's last known location,' the colonel said, indicating a point on the map. 'Now you can see why I asked for you on this assignment.'

The area he indicated was the border country between German East Africa and the Congo, and the point under his finger, indicating the Belgian command's headquarters, was precisely the point where Archie Battersby had made his camp in 1899 while Grogan circumnavigated a new volcano and fought a running battle with cannibals.

Delamere paused while the doorman pushed open the bank's heavy wooden doors, planted his sola topee firmly on his head, and plunged into the liquid heat of Mombasa's morning. He silently cursed the itching spine pad beneath his flannel shirt, and decided to head straight to the club, not a hundred yards away, to await the afternoon's train with a spot of lunch and a cold whisky soda.

He hated Mombasa. The old Arab trading port had an impossible climate, and was full of indolent Swahilis, content to sit beneath a mango tree and wait for the fruit to fall, rather than get up and do something constructive.

As he passed the Indian bazaar, with its cacophony of excited bargaining in full swing, he had to admit that as much as he loathed their ways, the Indians could teach the natives a lesson or two in making a go of nothing.

'Lord Delamere!' a voice called from behind him.

He turned to see an Indian wearing a pin-striped suit and a scarlet turban beckoning as he hurried through the crowd towards him. Delamere ignored him, and continued his brisk walk towards the Mombasa Club, swinging his walking stick with military zeal.

'Lord Delamere, *sahib*,' the man persisted, now a few paces immediately behind him.

Delamere turned without slackening his pace, surprised that a chap so well turned out would be hawking so keenly. 'Be off with you, or I'll take my stick to you,' he said over his shoulder. 'I'm not interested in whatever you've got to sell.'

'But I am not selling, Excellency. I would have a word with you, if you please.'

Obsequiousness, Delamere thought. The most annoying of the Indians' characteristics. If they weren't haranguing the Europeans into buying their shoddy goods, they were bowing and scraping to win a favour. The club doorway was in sight and Delamere tightened his jaw in an effort to prevent his anger from overflowing.

Now at his elbow the irrepressible pest said, 'Lord Delamere, my name is Tayabali Jeevanjee, and there is something you must know.'

The name sounded familiar, but it took a moment for it to register with Delamere. He glanced at the fellow, but continued to stride towards the Mombasa Club, where a cold drink and an overhead fan awaited him in the muted light of the palm-fronded lounge.

'You should know about my brother, Alibhai Jeevanjee, Excellency. It is of very great importance to our war effort, *sah*.'

'What's that you say?' Delamere said. 'War effort? What nonsense is this, man?'

Tayabali was panting. Sweat ran from under his turban and trickled into his full black beard. 'Please *sahib*, if you would be so kind as to hear me out. It will be in your interest to do so.'

Delamere had stopped outside the club's doorway and, against his better judgement, said, 'Well, get on with it, man, it's damn hot out here.'

'Yes, Excellency. Certainly, Excellency. It's about my brother, Jeevanjee.'

'You bloody well said that already.'

'Yes, *sahib*. He is consorting with the enemy, *sahib*.'

'What?' Delamere demanded. 'If you're going to tell me about his shipping arrangements with a German export agency, I know all about it — it was in the bloody papers.'

'Oh no, *sah*, it is not about that. It was I who wrote that letter, *sahib*. But please, let us move from the doorway. You must understand that this is a matter of great shame to my family. But it is my duty to alert someone in authority to his crimes. Someone such as your good self, *sah*.'

Delamere followed Tayabali to the end of the porch. 'Get on with it,' he snapped.

'Thank you, Excellency.' Tayabali bobbed his appreciation. 'Your lordship would be aware that my brother has purchased three ships.'

'I am,' Delamere said cautiously. He was very much aware of Jeevanjee's expansion to his shipping line, as was everyone else in the Protectorate. Even the Governor had made a public comment on how pleased he was to see 'a new vitality in the essential supply lines' to and from the country — another boost to the Indian's influence.

'Well, it is a matter of grievous shame that I must report that he is not using it for the purposes that many believe he should, *sah*. He is not using it to benefit our wonderful country — yours and mine, for I am a loyal subject of His Majesty, *sah*.'

Delamere shot him a warning glance to continue without the palaver. Tayabali lowered his voice and hurried on. 'The Germans, your Lordship.'

'What about the Germans?' Delamere asked, frowning.

'Those rotten Germans, *sah*. He is feeding them. My brother is slipping guns and supplies to those rotters, *sah*.'

The entire community had been stunned by the German commander's ability to avoid capture while running numerous damaging raiding parties across the border into British territory.

'Nonsense,' Delamere said, without showing his interest. 'How could you know this?'

'Are we not family, he and I, Excellency? But such a shameful thing cannot be kept in a loyal household such as ours. And also, does your Excellency not wonder where are his other ships right now? They are not here is where they are not.'

Delamere turned his back on Tayabali and strode to the doorway.

Tayabali trotted behind him and continued his prattle. 'They should be here helping our war efforts. Is that not so, Your Lordship?'

'Be off, you and your stories,' Delamere said, waving a hand in dismissal, 'or else I'll have the doorman give you a clip behind the ear.'

The doorman opened for him and Delamere walked into the serene atmosphere of the Mombasa Club without a backward glance, leaving Tayabali to explain his presence on the doorstep to the towering major domo.

Delamere was not a man to abide rumour-mongering, but the gravity of the remarks made him think it worthwhile to ensure that others around the Mombasa Club heard about it. There were members of the club who would know what was happening on the wharves and shipping lanes. Although all gentlemen, there would be some among them who wouldn't hesitate to use people of their acquaintance to right a wrong, if one had been committed.

Grogan fished for his watch. 'I should have thought everyone would be aboard by now.' He snapped the case shut and slipped the watch into his fob.

'I think it must be running a little late,' Gertrude said.

'Yes, probably.'

The Nairobi station was its usual chaotic scene of passengers, luggage and freight, all vying for priority.

'Why is this so urgent, Ewart? It's so soon after the children leaving.'

'I know it is, Gertie, but Meinertzhagen wants me to start as soon as possible.'

'So soon? Where to?'

Grogan looked about him at the surrounding crowds. 'It's confidential, Gertrude, but it's in country I'm quite familiar with.'

'I see.' Gertrude touched her handkerchief to her eyes. 'Well, you'd best go.'

'No, no. There's still time.' He smiled to reassure her, and noticed her distress. 'Look, Gertie, this is bad timing, I know. Maybe I should catch the next one.'

'That's not until Thursday.'

'Never mind. The men can go up to Kisumu without me. There's work they can do until I arrive. They'll manage.'

She smiled sadly. 'I know what you're like, Ewart. You'll be fretting all the time, wondering if you've done the right thing.'

'I don't want to rush off and leave you like this.'

Gertrude put her arms around him. Grogan hoped she wouldn't cry. He always felt helpless when she cried, which, fortunately for him, was seldom, but she had shed a flood of tears when they had discussed her going to England with the children. Grogan said he expected to spend long periods away from home, and that the country was in real danger of an invasion by the Germans from across the border. But she wouldn't budge, and they'd compromised by sending the children away with Nanny Redwood.

He felt her shoulders lift, and was sure that she was weeping, but when she stepped back, she took a deep breath and composed herself.

She smiled, but her eyes still glistened with tears. 'I love you, Ewart,' she said without emotion. She was almost analytical about it.

He studied her face — her strong jaw; the elegant nose. She had a sad expression — like a person resigned to the loss of a distantly related loved one.

'I love you too, Gertrude,' he said, trying to find the words that would console her, but she reached up, gave him a lingering kiss, then pushed him away.

'Go,' she said.

She was standing in the same place on the platform when he reached his seat. People were waving and throwing kisses to loved ones on the train. Gertrude didn't; she simply smiled a little wistfully, and watched him until the train took him out of sight.

With much pomp and ceremony, Jeevanjee broke a bottle of gin over the bow of the first of his three new ships, the SS *Nairobi*, and sent it on its maiden voyage. He would have liked to use champagne, but there was a war on and he daren't give the press any further reason to chastise him.

Amir had done a good job in pressing what remained of Jeevanjee's supporters on the Indian Congress to attend. He needed a crowd to impress the reporter from *The Times of East Africa* to run a story on it. He was successful. The following morning, Amir read Jeevanjee the story under the headline, *Indian Merchant Prince of Mombasa*. Jeevanjee was pleased.

However, he was not as pleased about the cargo, as the hold was only a quarter filled, and the voyage was not financially viable. But he was determined to prove that A M Jeevanjee and Company were still in business, and hoped it would send a message to his creditors that they had nothing to fear about their investment in the company: it was business as usual, and the cargo was moving.

Three days later, a telegram arrived from Malindi — a mere sixty miles from Mombasa. *SS Nairobi run aground offshore Malindi. Please advise your instructions.*

He chartered a boat to inspect the situation, and found the *Nairobi* undamaged on a sandy reef, with no loss of lives. In fact, he learned from an Indian crewman that the ship had been abandoned in such a leisurely manner, the captain was able to return several times to retrieve forgotten items.

'What happened here?' he demanded of the British captain.

He man shrugged. 'Damned strangest thing,' he said without the slightest conviction. 'That reef must have shifted since my last voyage.'

Although Jeevanjee couldn't read, he could read a chart. The reef was exactly where it had always been.

He returned to Mombasa and demanded a commission of inquiry. He was told by the port commodore, a founding member of the Mombasa Club, that since the *Nairobi* was registered in Bombay, it was a matter for the Indian authorities. That ruling, coming in war time, effectively sank any chance of Jeevanjee finding answers to the mysterious events.

His next problem was to set up a salvage operation. Again, the exigencies of war prevailed. There were no tugs available to conduct the salvage and his boat appeared doomed to spend the war years a half-mile off Malindi's beautiful beach.

Jeevanjee was again in turmoil, rescheduling his other two ships, which were due to arrive in Mombasa within a few weeks. Before either docked in Mombasa, his indistinguishable bankers, Pandit and Pavitt, requested an urgent meeting.

CHAPTER 58

Grogan sent his men on to Kisumu to prepare their camp, and climbed off the train in Londiani where he borrowed a horse. As he crested the rise the wind took his hat. Below him stretched a gentle valley dotted with cattle, with a crooked farmhouse, leaning outhouses and a neglected vegetable garden in the home lot. He reined in his horse, and retrieved his hat as the wind whipped at his trouser legs and threatened to take the hat from his head again.

It had always been like that at Londiani, he remembered. Especially at Dalton's farm, where the dry wind from the Great Rift Valley met the cool, damp air from the Lembus Forest.

He climbed back into the saddle and continued down the hill to the farmhouse, with a number of breezy opening remarks in mind that he could use when he reached the door. Apart from the awkwardness of the initial moment, his next concern was how to explain his long absence, or indeed his belated presence.

He thought he might be able to say he was making a tour of inspection of the most westerly corner of his concession, and being only a couple of hours away from the farm thought he should just drop in to say hello. But he had to dismiss it, as it couldn't explain why he had never done so in all the years since his first visit in 1906.

Then he thought something a little closer to the truth might serve, without divulging army secrets. He could say he was calling in to say hello while on his way west on a military matter. It would be perfectly understandable, even laudable — given the implied peril of army business — to visit old friends before putting his life on the line for the loyal cause.

By the time he reached the farmhouse door he was still undecided, but gave it a gentle rap anyway.

The door swung open, and a total stranger stood on the threshold. 'Yar?' she asked.

Grogan was dumbstruck. He had so effectively steeled himself for a meeting with Jessie, he couldn't force his mouth to function. All possible explanations surged through his head: Bruce had taken a wife; a relative had come to visit; he had mistaken the house — all equally unlikely.

'Can I 'elp you?' she asked, looking a little concerned at the stranger's silence.

'Who is it, Edith?' came a male voice from somewhere within the house.

'It's . . . I don't know,' she replied, turning back to scrutinise Grogan again.

A grey-whiskered bear of a man appeared beside the woman. 'Arrrh?' he asked.

Grogan found his tongue. 'The . . . ah . . . Daltons?' he mumbled.

'What's that ye say?' The man raised a cupped hand to his ear.

'He said *the Daltons*,' the woman advised in a loud voice.

'Yes,' Grogan said. 'I'm looking for the Daltons — Bruce, and his daughter, ah, Jessie.'

'Oh, the Daltons,' the man said, nodding. 'Oh . . . too bad. Passed away.' He shook his head.

'A few years back,' his wife added, looking sad.

'What? I can't . . . Bruce *and* Jessie?' Grogan asked incredulously.

'Yar, that was 'is name orright. Bruce. Water on the lungs I think they said. We bought the farm orf his daughter. What was 'er name, Edith?'

'Jessie,' she replied, using the same loud voice.

'Arrh, yar, Jessie.'

'So Jessie is not . . . dead?'

'No! Not that I know of,' the man said, scratching his whiskers.

'I 'eard she had a wee baby,' Edith said.

'Did she now?' said her husband. 'I didn't know that. Well, I'll be damned. Didn't she marry old what's-'is-name?'

'Yar, old Tom, um ... That's right, Tom the bank johnnie down at Nakuru.'

'Tom a father, eh? Well, well.' The man scratched his beard yet again.

'Mister?' he said to Grogan's back as he turned from the door. 'Arrh, won't you come in for a cuppa tea? Mister?'

Grogan mounted his horse and galloped away without replying. The shock of Dalton's death had been overcome by the relief that it wasn't Jessie. After that emotion subsided, he became angry, but he wasn't sure why. He thought it might be that Jessie had been deceitful in not letting him know, firstly, that she hadn't married Quentin, and, secondly, that she *had* married the banker, Tom. She seemed somehow ungrateful, although he had difficulty explaining the logic, even to himself.

He was usually able to dissect his thoughts if he persevered, and after some time he came to the conclusion he was angry with himself. He had lost his chance with Jessie because he wouldn't take the time to visit what he thought was the farm of an old friend. Had he done so, he would have found Jessie living alone. The reason he hadn't called in was because he had placed Dalton among the many other friends and associates he had discarded on his rise to the top.

As he neared the station he really became angry when he realised he had three days to wait for the next train to Kisumu.

Grogan's Somali headman, Ibrahim, and the three Swahili porters he had recruited on the coast were waiting for him at the small army camp in Kisumu.

Ibrahim had found six more candidates for porters into the Congo, and after a few questions given under Grogan's fierce gaze, he chose three, bringing the little band to ten counting the three armed *askaris*. It was a small caravan that would be able to move swiftly and silently through the bush.

Grogan then threw himself into the final preparations, including a 'sea' trial of the motorboat the military command had commandeered for the dash across Lake Victoria. The *Fifi* was a wide-beamed, steel-hulled craft that rode low in the water — a feature that made crossing the lake in bad weather a hazard, but one that would make it a more difficult quarry for the heavily armed steamer that the Germans used to terrorise the lake.

Two days later, as Grogan and his troop neared the western shore of Lake Victoria in the *Fifi*, they saw a plume of smoke rising above the southern horizon. A check through his binoculars confirmed to Grogan it was the German steamer, *Muansa*, on a course that would soon bring them into visual range.

Grogan ordered the French captain to put on full speed. The Frenchman, who had volunteered to captain his commandeered craft on the assumption he would be more likely to get it back in one piece if he did so, objected, saying his boat could go no faster in that weather. Grogan drew his revolver and convinced him otherwise, and as the heavily laden craft surged through the swell, sending water jets over the bows, Grogan's men bailed.

They were making good progress, and the *Muansa* continued on a course that would take it a few miles to the stern of them. Grogan began to think they would slip away undetected by the Germans.

Suddenly the smoke plume changed shape, and through the glasses Grogan could see the *Muansa* steaming directly towards them.

The captain told him they were still about thirty miles from Bukakata — the town on mainland Uganda where they would begin their trek. The *Muansa* was gaining ground. Grogan saw a puff of smoke from the steamer followed by a muffled boom and a whistling sound. A shell hit the water fifty yards behind them.

Grogan searched the water ahead. A scattering of small islands lay a couple of miles to the north.

'What's the water like among those islands?' Grogan yelled over the noise of the motor.

'I don't know,' shouted the Frenchman. 'Shallow, I think. Only small fishing boats can go in some of those channels.'

'Good,' Grogan said. Pushing the captain from the helm, he spun the wheel to the right.

'*Mon Dieu!*' the captain cried as the boat heeled over, bringing a wave pouring over the gunwales.

A moment later, a whistling shell flew overhead and sent an exploding geyser of water into the air immediately ahead on their original course.

Grogan began to throw the boat into a number of lumbering zigzags, while still on a heading towards the islands, now agonisingly close. A narrow channel lay immediately ahead, but until they got through it there was little chance of taking evasive action.

Grogan tried to get more speed out of the boat, but it was already at full throttle. They would soon be in range of the *Muansa*'s two machine guns.

Another exploding shell sent green water spilling into the boat. The captain moaned and put his face in his hands.

The boat shot towards a channel guarded by a bar on one side and rocks on the other. Grogan had prayed for a narrow channel, but was now worried that not only the *Muansa* but the *Fifi* would not clear the bottom.

'*Non, non!*' the captain moaned as the hull clipped a submerged rock, but in another moment they were through.

A roar went up from the porters. Behind them the *Muansa* had run aground, flinging her forward gunner into the sea.

The *Fifi* had escaped the net, leaving the *Muansa* high and dry in the soft mud of the lake.

No doubt the French captain was pleased to see Grogan and his team leave him at the small fishing village of Bukakata and head west into the tall grass of the swamplands surrounding the town. Their first assignment was to investigate rumours that the town of Mbarara, and perhaps ultimately British Uganda itself, were in imminent danger of invasion.

Grogan felt immensely satisfied to be at last doing something constructive, and having at one time said he didn't care if he never saw Central Africa again, he was pleased to be back. The feel of the grass against bare legs; the earthy, wet smell of the swamp; the adrenaline rush at the crash or splash of fleeing animals. Memories flooded back, some pleasant, many disturbingly reminiscent of days when hunger and thirst cast a veil of suffering over the otherwise beautiful landscape.

They made fair going on the first two days, then Grogan felt the crippling joint pains and building fever of the onset of malaria. He cursed the old reminder of his early trek, but knew better than to ignore it. He decided to rest and restricted their marches to the early morning and late afternoon. It gave him the chance to make an assessment of his men. They were good, but he knew it wasn't until they faced more stressful situations that he would know if they could remain cohesive as a group.

By the sixth day, the malaria had responded to the heavy doses of quinine, and Grogan was pleased to make a respectable twenty miles per day through difficult terrain.

Soon the country opened out into a rolling savanna studded with large round boulders where troops of baboons congregated to hurl abuse at the trespassers, and where, at evening meals, his men rejoiced in the bounty of fresh meat from the abundant plains.

Villagers stared at them as they passed. Sometimes the chief sent a cautious spokesman to enquire if it were true the Watusi were amassing to the south in preparation for an all-out attack.

Mbarara, which Grogan expected to be a substantial town, was in fact little more than a large native village incorporating a number of European and Indian traders.

A young Englishman wearing short khaki trousers and long white socks, and who immediately annoyed Grogan, due to his habit of frequently wiping the sweat from his thick spectacles and his overwhelmingly bossy manner, identified himself as the local administrative officer. He escorted Grogan and his men through a throng of townsfolk who had gathered in numbers to witness their arrival. When they came to his office, the administrator demanded to know details about the imminent German invasion, as well as the Watusi from the south, who were now swarming through the hills towards them.

'Mr Smith,' Grogan began.

'Smythe,' the administrative officer corrected.

Grogan ignored the interruption. 'The Watusi are at least two hundred miles to the south. The reason they are there, and not here, is that between the two is an extensive tsetse fly area.'

Smythe's myopic eyes blinked.

Grogan could see he needed to elaborate. 'They are not in Mbarara today,' he added, 'for the same reason they have never been in Mbarara. As you are probably aware, a fly area means death to livestock, and since the Watusi will not travel a day without their beloved cattle, I can assure you that you have nothing to fear so far as the Watusi invasion is concerned.'

Smythe removed his glasses and gave them a hurried wipe. 'Well . . .' he began.

'As for the Germans,' Grogan continued, 'I can't be so sure. That's one of the reasons I am here. I intend to survey the area to the south. If there is anything to report, you'll hear about it.' He stood to indicate the end of the conversation. 'Now, if you'll excuse me, I have to see to my men.'

'Captain Grogan,' Smythe called, stopping him at the door.

'Yes?'

'You may not be aware of it, but there's some very rough country down south. There's even talk of cannibals.'

Grogan nodded. 'Thank you, Mr Smith. I'll keep that in mind.'

The young soldier lying on the bed reminded Gertrude of Ewart at about the same age. He had those youthful good looks that belied his twenty or more years. His hair was fair and parted just off-centre, as was Ewart's. When he opened his eyes, the resemblance disappeared. They were brown and full of fear.

The young man was a member of the Fusiliers. The Boozaliers as Ewart liked to call them. He said they had a reputation for heroism and alcoholism, and were surely the most extraordinary military unit in British history because of the unique individuals who formed their ranks. They included the American millionaire Northrup MacMillan, with a sixty-inch sword belt and a personality to match, who'd made his money in Rumanian oil and Malayan rubber; and the old frontiersman Frederick Selous, more than sixty years old, whom Grogan had met fighting the Ndebele in South Africa. There were Texas Rangers, Arctic seal-poachers, veterans of the

French Foreign Legion, a former footman at Buckingham Palace. There were even an acrobat and a clown — escapees from a travelling circus.

In comparison, this young man looked quite ordinary, except that he was dying.

His ward was Chiromo's old drawing room. The paintings, brocaded curtains and other finery had been removed. Only the deep terracotta-coloured walls remained to remind Gertrude of what it had been.

She sat at the young man's bedside as she had done every waking moment for days, and swabbed the sweat from his face and chest with a towel. His features were now heavily jaundiced. Chills racked his body, and he continued to vomit although there was nothing left in his stomach. His eyelids fluttered, but the effort to open them was beyond him. The doctors said they could do no more. They said that when the blackwater fever affected the kidneys, as it had in this young man's case, there was nothing that could be done.

Gertrude couldn't accept it. She felt that by her sheer willpower she could save him. So she sat at his side and willed him to live.

The young soldier had survived the storming of Bukoba, only to succumb to malaria and the later complications. The press said Bukoba, on the western shore of Lake Victoria, was a great victory and a sign that the campaign was turning in the Allied colonists' favour. Without Bukoba, they said, the Germans would be unable to hold the Belgians at bay; that was, when the Belgians finally entered the war.

Unlike many other women with husbands, brothers and fathers in the war, Gertrude had no idea where Ewart was. He was not allowed to send messages when he was on one of his secret missions, and the vacuum meant that every bloody altercation, in any theatre of the war, could possibly involve him. She sighed and tried to put those thoughts from her head.

She took up the towel, and was about to pat the young man's brow, when she noticed he was staring at her. She smiled at him before realising his eyes were fixed, unblinking.

She knew she shouldn't, but she allowed herself one small tear before raising the sheet to cover him.

CHAPTER 59

Grogan and his men boarded three sturdy canoes and took the sometimes turbulent waters of a tributary down to the Kagera River. When he crossed the river into German East Africa, he crossed the line between combatant and spy. He would be shot if he were caught.

He led his men through enemy territory, travelling mainly at night, and making surveillance sorties by day. They were starved of fresh meat, but avoided shooting game and lighting cooking fires to conceal their position.

They found only one small German detachment on patrol along the border, but they were headed east and, Grogan thought, back to their base camp. He decided to complete his survey of the northern area, then travel east to establish the Germans' position, if possible.

After a week, they were deep in German East African territory. It appeared that the scrubby country through which they were passing was in the midst of a drought. Game was scarce, and the small streams they used to replenish their water canisters were dry. Grogan had avoided waterholes as they were more likely to be watched by German patrols, but after a few days without finding an alternative source, he decided they had to take the risk.

They found a useful waterhole, and watched it through the day from the safety of a hill with a little tree cover. By late afternoon, having seen nothing suspicious, Grogan left Ibrahim in charge and walked to the waterhole with two porters carrying water canisters.

Once on the flat ground approaching the waterhole, he felt the old sensation that told him of imminent danger — the hair on the back of his neck bristled. He signalled the porters to halt, then crept ahead, his every sense tuned to detect the presence of soldiers.

Near the waterhole, where the dried mud made a forty-yard clearing, he squatted in the grass and waited. Nobody appeared. He went back to bring the porters forward, wondering if his years of absence from the bush had dulled his skills.

The men quickly filled their canisters while Grogan stood over them, scanning the perimeter grassland for any sign of movement. When the containers were nearly filled, he said, 'Sowa, sowa,' meaning it was enough and they should leave. The two porters screwed the caps tight and hoisted the water canisters to their shoulders.

Grogan turned to lead them back to their hillside hideaway. In the grass fringing the waterhole was a crouching golden-maned lion, ears twitching and its yellow-green eyes — illuminated by the setting sun — fixed intently on the three men.

Grogan signalled to the men to put down their containers, unshouldered his rifle, and levered a cartridge into the breech.

The lion was tense, alert to his every movement. From his hunting days, Grogan knew the animal was ready to pounce, merely awaiting the inner trigger that instinct told it was the perfect moment to charge.

Although he had less than forty yards within which to aim and fire after the lion made its dash, Grogan had no doubt he could bring it down with his service weapon. The problem was that his shot would alert every German within a half-day's march. He had to avoid firing unless it was absolutely necessary.

Grogan guessed that the lion was a young adult because its hide and ears — the first parts damaged in scuffles with prey or rivals — were unmarked. If he gambled correctly, the animal may not have quite reached the confidence that it would inherit with its size.

He slowly reached for his felt hat and placed it over the barrel of his rifle. Inch by inch he lifted it above his head to arm's length. As he had hoped, the lion's piercing gaze shifted to the hat above Grogan's head.

Now he began to wave the rifle and hat from side to side, and at the same time he made an attempt at impersonating a lion's growl.

The beast at the edge of the grass blinked and licked its chops. It was the signal that Grogan had prayed for.

He pressed his advantage. His guttural growl said he was an angry animal, and the hat and rifle above his head demonstrated he was big enough to beat the young golden-mane.

The lion's iron muscles relaxed, and with hardly a sidewise glance it skulked off into the tall grass.

Whispered voices came from behind him, and when Grogan turned to give the order to move on, he found the porters' eyes were wide with wonder.

Grogan and his troop headed east for another week to search for signs of a German presence, but found nothing.

By now, their *posho* supplies were almost exhausted. To supplement the dry maize meal, they added what protein they could catch with their bare hands. Grasshoppers, snake and rodent meat were cut up, dried and added to their meagre ration of cold *posho*.

The insidious malaria returned to exacerbate Grogan's weakened state, reminding him how difficult the climate and terrain could become when the fever struck. It reminded him too that it had been fifteen years since he had last attempted such a physically demanding task. He was forced to rest for three days to recoup.

With their supplies at a perilous level, and no sign of the feared German invasion, Grogan decided it was time to head west for his rendezvous with the Belgians.

He had managed to find his way around German East Africa by using maps he had been given years before by a German timber baron whom he'd visited to exchange views on forestry methods. But he had no maps of the German territory of Ruanda through which they would travel to reach Uganda and the Rutchuru Valley. Once he was on the Rutchuru, which was familiar to him from his trek, he knew he could find the Belgians' headquarters on Lake Kivu.

He needed local knowledge, but knew it was unlikely he would find someone willing to act as a guide in any of the villages in German territory — the people were too fearful of the wrath of the German administration to agree to that. He would have to kidnap someone.

They had bypassed a number of small villages in their journey through GEA. One or two flew a German flag, indicating it was a volunteer, or colloquially, a *ruga-ruga* watching post. They were now camped near one of those villages, and at their breakfast of half a cup of *posho*, Grogan explained what he intended to do.

'They may have many weapons,' Ibrahim said. 'We will go into village with you, *Kapteni Simba*.'

Grogan had overheard the men using the term *Kapteni Simba* a number of times and decided to get to the bottom of it. 'What's this *Kapteni Simba* nonsense, Ibrahim?' he asked.

'Sorry, sorry, Captain Grogan. I forgot,' the old Somali scout said, revealing a number of gaps in his toothy grin.

'But what does it mean?'

'It mean Captain Lion, *bwana*.'

'I know that dammit, man, but what's it refer to?'

'Oh, it mean you, Captain. These *Swahilis*,' he said, nodding deprecatingly towards the men, 'already think Captain's eyes are all same lion's eyes. Then they hear you make sound, *grrrrrr*, like lion also. Now they say you *simba* too much.'

'Oh, for God's sake ... Well, never mind that. I'll decide how we get into the village and snatch our man when we get there.'

It was an hour after dawn when they crept through thin scrub to the outskirts of the village. Grogan sent Ibrahim forward to reconnoitre, and he came back to say there was no way into the village without being seen. It could only be done in darkness. However, there would be no problem in finding the *ruga-ruga*'s hut because it had a little German national flag fluttering on a stick above the entrance.

Grogan could not afford to waste another day, and decided to try something a little unconventional to avoid bloodshed. He unbuckled his trousers and slipped them off.

Ibrahim looked from Grogan to the other *askaris* and porters.

'Don't worry, Ibrahim,' he said, removing the belt and fastening it around his bare midriff. 'I'm not mad ... yet. Just using a bit of psychology.' He covered the belt with his shirt tails.

'Yes, *bwana*,' Ibrahim answered cautiously.

He removed his blue- and red-striped underpants and arranged them on his head. Ibrahim now had a rather worried expression on his face.

'I told you not to worry, Ibrahim,' Grogan said. 'There's method in my madness.'

His headman looked anything but convinced.

Grogan took his revolver and, reaching around, slipped it into the back of the belt under his shirt. Then he patted Ibrahim reassuringly on the shoulder and headed towards the village.

At the edge of the clearing surrounding the village, he paused for a moment to take a deep breath, then he marched with a quick step, arms swinging, towards the first of the huts. As soon as the warning call went up, he started to whistle *Yankee Doodle Dandy*. He had no idea how it came to mind, but thought it appropriate under the circumstances. As he had hoped, the villagers poured from their huts to stare and laugh at the strange apparition.

A man wearing the dull green shorts of a German *askari* came out of the hut that flew the German flag and, like all of his fellow villagers, stared in bemused surprise at the naked white man.

Grogan marched up to the volunteer *askari* and slipped the concealed revolver from his belt. 'Come,' he said with the barrel at the man's head, and pushed him ahead of him, while managing to slip his underpants on as he walked.

They passed through the village unhindered. When he reached his men's concealed position in the scrub, he ordered their retreat on the double.

Old Ibrahim had great difficulty concealing his smirk.

Immediately they crossed the border into Uganda, Ibrahim and another *askari* were despatched to find game. They brought back a kongoni, and for the first time in a month the troop feasted on fresh meat.

In Uganda, the patrol could find their way to the government post at Kigezi by making enquiries of the locals, and Grogan sent the *ruga-ruga* on his way with the advice that he should consider keeping his services to the British Intelligence Unit to himself.

When Grogan arrived in Kigezi six days later, he sent off a runner to Nairobi with his report. Then he spent three days replenishing his supplies and allowing his men to recuperate.

Good news arrived before they set off for the Congo. The terror of Lake Victoria — the German steamer *Muansa* — had been sunk in an island group off Bukakata. The report said that it appeared the *Muansa* had taken refuge to repair damage to its steering gear, and had been unable to manoeuvre in the tight confines of the channel when discovered by an under-equipped British boat.

Grogan allowed himself a modest smile of satisfaction as he handed the report file back to the clerk.

Tom had told her, 'All in good time, girl.' It was Tom's way. He had the unshakeable belief that anything could be done, given enough time. It was because he was methodical. Fastidious even. Things couldn't be done methodically or well unless there was enough time.

He'd said this after Jessie collapsed, sobbing, in his arms and told him she didn't think she would ever get over such a senseless loss. She thought it was the banker in him that spoke, but she didn't think unkindly of him for it. In some ways he was right. Time was her friend. Each day she felt a little better, a little stronger. After two weeks she was able to venture into the Kisumu stores.

When Tom had to go back to the front, she had a relapse, crying at odd times of the day and night. But time had again eased it, and now she hardly cried at all. Time had replaced the pain of baby Tom's death with a kind of numbness.

She looked at the tiny knitted pale blue jacket that lay in her hand, barely covering it. She brought it to her face, sniffed it. He had worn it just once — to his christening. It had the faintest hint of the baby smell, but time would soon take that away too.

It was good that she was packing all these clothes away. They only served to remind her of the baby. She could never re-use them, even if they did eventually have another. The jacket was the next to last item and the biscuit tin was nowhere near filled. Packing the tin was the last task she had given herself before offering her services to the Red Cross. It would bring to an end her time of grief and allow her to rebuild her spirit.

She patted the pale blue bonnet flat on the table, then lifted it again and slipped it over her fist. With her other hand she drew the little straps over it and turned it from side to side. She smiled, remembering little Tom's wrinkled face and his milky blue eyes, scrunched up as he tried to find his mouth with his fist.

Time. In good time she would feel complete again.

She took the bonnet off her hand and placed on top of the clothes in the biscuit tin. After one last look, she closed it, letting her tears wet the label on its lid.

CHAPTER 60

The journey south along the Rutchuru Valley was immediately familiar. Across the shimmering salt pans to the south rose the thickly forested slopes below the volcanic mountains of Götzen, Battersby and Eyres. Grogan knew that on those tortured slopes had once lived the Baleka cannibals, who might even yet terrorise the surrounding tribes, and beyond them were the handsome, dancing Watusi and the elusive pygmies. There too was beautiful Lake Kivu, whose cold, deep blue waters and thousand islands would be a balm for his salt-burned eyes.

The climb into the thin air of the mountains slowed progress, and the cutting edges of the lava flows tore at their boots. All of these trials were forgotten when, rounding a thickly wooded ridge, Lake Kivu revealed itself in all its splendour. Ibrahim, the porters and *askaris* — men inured by a tough life, where any appreciation of the beauty of the land through which they passed might understandably be ignored — were enraptured.

Grogan let them savour the sight, somehow feeling a proprietary right to the vista, and a barely concealed pride in having led them to it. The scenery and the men's enjoyment of it revived memories of the man he was when, at the age of twenty-five, he had first passed this way to prove himself worthy of the woman he loved. With a pang of guilt he recalled the unforgivable pain he must have caused Gertrude by his hateful comment that he had walked Africa for every reason except to win her hand in marriage. He felt wretched at the thought of it. He wondered what demon had possessed him to utter such a despicable lie.

Perhaps it was the beauty of Kivu that promoted a reflective insight on his past misdeeds, for they came back to him with stark clarity.

He realised that in recent years he had spent little time with his children. Where once he had found joy in joining them in their games and entertaining them with his tricks, he now barely gave them a glance. There were always more pressing matters afoot, like his business empire and his obsession with the world of politics. There was never time to sit and watch his children play.

And what had happened to him and Gertrude? When he last feasted his eyes on Kivu, he'd experienced the poignancy of finding such beauty without the chance to share it with the one he loved. Across Africa, there hadn't been a step taken without Gertrude being foremost in his mind.

Being so far away, in a jungle that evoked such sweet memories of her, it distressed him to find he couldn't recall the last time they had made love. His own needs had not gone wanting in that regard — a fact that must have been painfully, cruelly obvious to her. There always seemed to be women available to him, and although he had vague recollections of past resolutions to change, he now swore an oath on the surrounding volcanoes that, hereafter, he would remain faithful to Gertrude, and recapture the happiness they had enjoyed on their arrival in Africa.

Grogan had no trouble finding Archie Battersby's old camp site, and a few miles further on was the Belgian Headquarters under the command of Colonel Henri, one of the Belgian officers he had met on the Nile.

Henri hugged Grogan then kissed him fervently on each cheek. After a lot of backslapping and affable teasing about the good old days, they sat and talked.

Henri told him the Belgians had fifteen thousand men including two hundred and fifty officers throughout the Congo awaiting permission from the Minister of Colonies to enter the war.

Grogan whistled in appreciation. It was more than all the troops presently available to British East Africa, including the recent influx of men from South Africa and Northern Rhodesia.

'But getting them out here to where we can use them against the Germans is difficult. Very difficult. My last detachment took six months to get here from Stanleyville. We lost half of them before they reached here. Dysentery, malaria, blackwater fever. Others, the newcomers to Africa, were totally unprepared and lion, hippo, even hyena, took them. The tsetse fly finished their horses within a few weeks, and the men had to become their own beasts of burden.' Henri ran a hand down his stubbled chin. 'And when they get here, we can't even properly feed them. I'm sure the sick die quicker because of our miserable rations.'

Grogan had noticed how dishevelled Henri and his officers were. The camp had a look of poverty about it, and Henri confirmed that they were severely under-provisioned.

An African *askari* passed the tent where Grogan and Henri sat talking.

'Is that fellow a Manyema?' Grogan asked.

'*Oui*,' Henri answered. 'The Manyema are fine fighters, but recruiting cannibals has its problems.' He nodded towards a machine-gun emplacement. One gun pointed outwards from the camp, the second was pointed at a group of rondavels a hundred yards inside the camp. 'That group of huts is the Manyemas' barracks,' he said.

'I had similar problems on my trek through these parts.'

'*Oui*, I remember you told me about them when we met on the Nile. I must admit, I am not sure I was believing you then. But now ... well, when I made my first sortie into Ruanda, I took a few small posts along the border there. In one I captured their log books, you know? To see what was what. I know a little German, but for a while I couldn't believe what I was reading: Private so-and-so missing, believed eaten.' Henri laughed nervously. 'There were so many of them. I couldn't believe it, but now ...'

'Hmm,' Grogan said, 'The answer to your problems seems to be food.'

'*Absolument*,' Henri answered. 'But our supply lines are, how is it you say ...? Incredible.'

'What about game meat?' Grogan asked, but realised he had seen very little game as they approached Lake Kivu. It had been a similar situation in '99.

'Pah! A few very little monkeys, and not much else. My men are not hunters, and I can't afford to send the Manyema in case they find some game more to their liking among the villages.'

'Then why not go to a Ugandan town or village and buy some while you're waiting for your supplies to arrive? There are trade stores in Mbarara, for example.'

'Ah, but good-hearted though you Englishmen may be, I'm sure the store owners will demand payment.'

Grogan nodded. 'I see ... you have no pounds.'

'*Sacrebleu, mon ami.* We have no *francs*!'

Grogan knew he would have no luck convincing Henri to commit troops to the war until they were fed. Solving their hunger was an urgent priority, but if they were to be an effective frontline force, they had to have a shorter supply line than across the trackless miles of the Belgian Congo.

'I have a proposition for you, Colonel Henri,' he said, sitting straighter in his chair to pull a waxed folder from his back pocket. 'I will give the Belgian High Command the sum of one hundred pounds for the purchase of foodstuffs from the British Protectorate of Uganda.' He slapped the hundred pound note onto the table.

Henri raised his eyebrows and moved to the edge of his chair.

'It probably won't improve your situation for a month or so, but in the meantime I will take a few of my *askaris*, and fifty of your porters, and bring you back a couple of ton of meat to tide you over.'

'Go on Captain, I am interested.'

'In return for the meat and improved supply lines, you will come with me to Kampala to discuss the terms of Belgium's engagement in the war against the Germans with the Governor, Frederick Jackson.'

Grogan had forgotten how difficult it was to bag elephant in the heavily wooded hills around Kivu. After a week spent trying

463

to find, then follow, fresh spoor all over the mountainside, the creatures remained elusive, or their spoor disappeared on the rocky volcanic outcrops.

His best chance came as he and his gun-bearer were crossing a tortuous expanse of rock, using it as a short-cut to the jungle beyond. The desolate expanse of petrified lava was about half a mile wide and cut a swathe through what would have been dense forest before the molten lava fled to the valley floor. Grogan postulated it had been formed perhaps as recently as a decade ago, as the charred remains of enormous trees stood in rubble where the lava had been diverted for some reason, forming islands in the rock. Grogan had not expected to find any game on the lava flow, so when the bull elephant appeared above them, he couldn't believe his luck.

The wind was from the right quarter, but he felt sure the elephant, which was only a couple of hundred yards away, should have seen them when they came stumbling around the outcrop that had concealed them.

Grogan slowly took the .404 from his man and, taking what cover he could from the scattering of boulders, crept up the slope to make sure of the shot.

The elephant stood rocking backwards and forwards, as if testing the ground at its feet. Grogan had never seen such extraordinary behaviour, but appreciated whatever it was that was distracting his target.

At a hundred yards he felt he had pressed his luck far enough. The elephant had already raised its trunk in his direction once, making Grogan's breath catch in his throat, before returning to again prod at the ground.

He held the vee of his sights on the space between eye and ear, and slowly squeezed the trigger. The .404 exploded against his shoulder, and the elephant staggered one step, then fell backwards, out of sight.

Grogan signalled to his gun-bearer and hurried forward.

When he arrived near the place where the elephant had stood not more than a minute before, he could see nothing but the flat expanse of lava that seemed to be unbroken from the crater's lip to the valley floor.

When he reached the exact place, he found a patch of bare earth, and a narrow chasm behind it where the lava had been diverted. He threw in a stone and heard it bounce into endless depths. The mountain had swallowed his elephant.

An examination of what Grogan had taken to be bare earth revealed a number of ribs and a section of an elephant's skull. His elephant had been rubbing at the dirt and lava shale to expose the bones.

He looked into the pit, which was now the final resting place of Colonel Henri's meat supplies for two weeks. It was gone forever — another elephant's grave, but this one to remain unattended by any of its kind.

Colonel Henri slapped Grogan on the back and gave him a Gallic embrace when he returned to camp. '*Mon ami*,' he said, with tears of joy in his eyes, 'you have saved the honour of the regiment.'

'You are most welcome, Colonel. The Belgians and British are in this war together.' Grogan had not forgotten the primary purpose of his mission. 'I found hippo easier to get than elephant. I hope you don't mind.'

'Ah, yes, your beautiful hippo meat has been coming these last three weeks. Lucky for us. It would have been a great embarrassment for Belgian soldiers to starve to death in their own territory, no?'

'Indeed, Colonel.'

I am in your debt, Captain,' he said. 'What do you want me to do?'

'We can go into details later, but briefly, we need your men to act as a pincer movement on von Lettow-Vorbeck's troops as we chase them out of the east.'

'So long as we can use your supply lines in Mbarara, this is possible, but as you are aware, I cannot make the final decision. That is a matter for the High Command.'

'That's understood, Colonel, but if you and Governor Jackson can agree on a draft of the protocols, it will be a good start.'

'I can promise you that I will do my best.'

'That's all I can ask.'

'*Excellent*. Now, let us celebrate our mutual success. I have a little something that I have been saving for, how do you English put it? A rainy day? *Oui*, a rainy day.'

Henri beckoned Grogan to follow him to his tent where he fished a quarter of a bottle of cognac from his kit and poured a good measure of it into two glasses.

They toasted the success of their joint operations.

'Ah,' Henri said, taking a sip of the cognac, '*c'est bon*. Now, please, my friend, sit.' He offered Grogan his only canvas chair. 'Do you mind if I sit on your parcel?' He pointed to the canvas-covered bundle that Grogan had asked him to keep safe while he was hunting for meat.

'Not at all,' Grogan replied.

Henri tried to drag it across the ground. 'Oof, it is very heavy, no? What is in this parcel of yours, ah?'

'Before you sit, let me show you. I have to start breaking it into smaller packets anyhow.' Grogan pulled out his pocket knife, cut the binding and unwrapped the canvas. Inside was another wrapping of thick brown paper, which Grogan unfolded.

Henri gasped. '*Sacrebleu*!' he muttered. 'What is all that for?'

Grogan tossed a bundle of crisp German East Africa rupees at him. 'Two hundred thousand rupees. For you to spread around GEA.'

Henri's eyes widened. 'What are you up to, Grogan? Is this ...? Is it —?'

'Legal? No. Of course not. But we *are* at war, and very fortunately the Germans' African rupee is a very simple currency to copy. Even the government printer in Nairobi can knock them up in no time.'

'Counterfeit.'

'Quite so. And it's my job to spread as much of this rubbish around German territory as I can. In the process I'll also try to find a few sympathetic, or at least avaricious, souls, who prefer the real thing, to keep me informed of the enemy's movements.'

Henri smiled, tossing the bundle of notes from one hand to the other.

'That bundle's yours, old friend,' Grogan said. 'Make a good fellow of yourself next time you visit one of the GEA villages.'

466

CHAPTER 61

It seemed to Jeevanjee that everything that could go wrong did go wrong just when he really needed a little better luck. The commissioning of his SS *Cananore* was delayed in Bombay awaiting completion of sea trials, and the SS *Calicut* had been held up for five weeks because of some minor error in the paperwork.

Again, it was the Mombasa port captain who made things difficult. Even sending a telegraph to Bombay took days because he said the frequency was needed for military traffic.

When the matters were finally settled in Bombay, Jeevanjee spent a nervous week as the *Calicut* sailed across the Indian Ocean without, for some unexplained reason, a naval escort.

To placate his bankers, Pandit and Pavitt, Jeevanjee invited them to attend the maiden voyage that would finally launch the *Calicut* into revenue-making service. He nervously paced the Kilindini wharf as the *Calicut* was loaded and prepared to sail. Again, it was not a substantial inventory, but he had the hold covered before Pandit and Pavitt arrived for the promised tour of inspection. At the end of the tour, they stood with Jeevanjee and actually smiled. He took it as a good omen for their continuing relationship. It was seldom that they smiled in his company these days.

The *Calicut* broke ground and steamed serenely out past Fort Jesus on a normal course. It was a small step to retrieve his lost fortune, but it was a step in the right direction.

Jeevanjee allowed himself to breathe a sigh of relief. He smiled at Pandit and Pavitt. They smiled back.

Suddenly the ship veered off course towards English Point.

Jeevanjee felt as though he was watching a sleepwalker putting one careful foot after another towards the edge of a precipice. A cry caught in his throat — a strange strangled sound, as if he had been stabbed in the heart. But it was worse than that. The *Calicut* was headed for the Levin Reef, and he was headed towards certain financial death.

Grogan's return trip across Lake Victoria was in contrast to his first, months earlier. The Germans had lost control of the lake with the sinking of the *Muansa*, and the benign weather made for a smooth crossing.

The army camp at Kisumu had been upgraded in his absence, and he had orders awaiting him from Colonel Meinertzhagen: he and his men were to remain in Kisumu until the colonel returned from a mission of his own.

The officer in charge of the camp told Grogan that the Red Cross were handling all mail for out-postings such as Kisumu, and gave him instructions on how to find them.

The Red Cross had set up their makeshift hospital near the wharf in a long low building that had once been a warehouse. A handful of men in bandages or on crutches were sitting in an amenities area when Grogan arrived. One of them directed him to the end of the area where a small office sat beside a door marked 'No Admittance — Red Cross Staff Only'.

Grogan introduced himself to a bespectacled, grey-headed woman, and asked if the Red Cross were holding any postal items for him. She told him to make himself a cup of tea while she went to check. Grogan flicked through the newspapers on a nearby table. A story caught his eye and he began to read it.

'Captain Grogan,' a soft voice called from the office counter.

Grogan could not draw himself away from the newspaper.

'Captain Ewart Grogan,' she persisted.

He turned to ask for a moment more, and saw Jessie in the doorway, a tentative smile on her lips, and a bundle of letters in her hand.

The newspaper dropped to the floor. He quickly stooped to collect the scatter of pages. 'Jessie ...' he said, dumping the pile of paper on the table. 'You're ... It's you.'

She nodded, continuing to smile self-consciously. 'Yes, it's me.'

He went to her and took her hand in his, but sensing her unease at his familiarity, he released it. Pointing to the letters in her other hand, he asked, 'Are they all mine?'

'They are,' she said, handing them to him. 'From 17th September last year to the one that arrived just three days ago — 19th November.'

Her face was just as bright and youthful as the last time he had seen her, but behind the smiling hazel eyes was a quality he couldn't immediately recognise. Perhaps it was the maturity that some young people reached with the passing of years, or after life had revealed some of its realities.

'How are you, Jessie?' he asked, realising he had been staring at her for some time.

'I'm very well, Ewart. And you?'

'Not bad for an old soldier,' he said.

She nodded, smiled. The silence grew to become awkward.

They both began to speak at once, then stopped together.

'You first,' she said.

'I've heard you're married?'

She dropped her gaze to her left hand, then slipped it into her apron pocket. 'Yes,' she said.

'Congratulations. Who's the fortunate fellow?'

'Tom ... Thomas Burridge. Captain Thomas Burridge. He's down somewhere near Taveta, but you're never sure, are you? I mean, he could be anywhere in East Africa, and ... well, anyway ... How are you? How's Gertrude? And the children?'

'Gertrude's helping out at the hospital. We converted Chiromo into a hospital. Did you know? No, of course not.'

'And the children?'

'Oh, we sent them all to England. Just in case.'

Jessie was still slim-waisted, but fuller in figure than he recalled. Her breasts pressed against her starched white apron.

'The people I met at your farm — I mean, your father's old place — told me you have a baby.'

Jessie's smile flickered and was lost. 'I *had* a baby,' she said. 'We lost him in July.'

'Oh, I'm sorry.'

'It was a few months after we moved here from Londiani. Before Tom got his posting. I suppose there is some truth in the story that the highlands have a healthier climate. Here on the lake it's a lot hotter, don't you think? I certainly do. Anyway, he became ill, the poor little mite. He was just six weeks old, and well, a child like that hasn't much of a chance and ...' Tears rolled down her cheeks.

Grogan took her hand then drew her to him, holding her to his chest. It had been months since he'd held a woman in his arms.

She didn't resist his embrace, but her arms remained at her sides. After a moment he dropped his arms from around her.

She lifted her chin to meet his eyes. Her face was tear-streaked, but she had stopped weeping. Her expression told him nothing.

'I thought I had done with all that,' she said, dabbing at her nose with her handkerchief.

'Can we sit here and talk?' He pointed to the table of newspapers.

She shook her head. 'I really shouldn't. I'm on duty in the hospital.'

'You're a nurse?'

'A volunteer nurse's assistant. I only came out here because ... Well, I asked Lil to tell me if someone came to collect mail for Captain Grogan.' She smiled defensively. 'I just wanted to see you one more time.'

'Jessie —'

'No ... Please, no.'

She disappeared through the door to the hospital.

Jessie watched him go from the hospital ward's window. So straight, so tall. He had lost none of his swagger and confidence. Meanwhile, she felt like a bumbling adolescent girl again, overawed in his presence.

It surprised her that he could still have that effect on her after four years — four years in which she had done her best to put him into her past, but still couldn't resist scribbling, *Lil — Call Jessie if he comes*, on a note attached to his bundle of mail. It was just so she could renew acquaintances with an old friend, as she told the curious Lil, but to herself she had to admit it was more than that.

She had been married to Tom — her dependable, safe harbour — for over a year. Tom rescued her when her life had delivered two terrible blows to her spirit: her father had died, and she had run away from the man she loved with another that she clearly didn't.

Leaving the note for Lil to alert her to Ewart's arrival was a means of testing herself. Now she knew she had failed the test in every regard. She wanted him as much, if not more than ever.

Grogan untied the ribbon and arranged the envelopes into groups. There was a large bundle addressed in Gertrude's handwriting, a few from Philip that he expected would be about mundane business matters — the result of his brother's punctilious personality; and a few brown OHMS ones from the military.

Next, he arranged them into chronological order. He wasn't usually so regimented, but he expected to have many days, if not weeks, while waiting for his next orders, and he wanted to string out the enjoyment of reading the letters as long as possible.

Gertrude's first letter, written a week after they'd separated on Nairobi station, was a little matter of fact, describing the situation in Nairobi with the general call to arms affecting all aspects of daily life. She wrote that, in spite of censorship, the information doing the rounds of the women at home was that the men were having a hard time of it. Many had yet to confront the enemy, but casualties were high. Apart from the usual scourges of *siafu* ants, snakes, jigger fleas and scorpions, it was the weather — either sweltering hot or constant rain and mud. Mosquitoes followed the rain and laid many low with malaria. Others were sent home suffering from tick or blackwater fever, dysentery or ugly jungle sores. Having dashed off with barely a thought for supplies, many were near starvation.

She said that she had received letters from the children and Ewart's sister, whom they were staying with, and that all was well although the girls were a bit teary from time to time.

Her second letter was dated 9 October, and the tone was as if the first letter had never been written. She described the preparations for race week in December, the work at the hospital, the new curtains she had made for the guest quarters where they had moved to vacate Chiromo and how she had such a dreadful job finding plain cotton material. She told him how Bowker's Horse, bivouacked near Longido, had been surprised by the Germans who rustled all their mounts, and that Bowker's Horse were now surreptitiously referred to as Bowker's Foot.

She said she tried not to worry about him, but it was especially difficult in her case because, unlike the wives of regular troops, she had no idea where he was and worried about every incident she heard of. *Be safe, my love*, she said at the end.

Gertrude's letters developed a familiar routine: brief summaries of life in Nairobi, reports from Ewart's sister regarding the children, and admonishments to be careful.

In one of her envelopes she included a letter from Edmund, addressed to him. Gertrude had opened it, no doubt unable to resist the urge to partake of the rare communication between them — made more significant as their son had instigated it. Grogan was not surprised to find Edmund had very neat, carefully crafted handwriting.

Dear Papa, he wrote.

I am hoping this finds you safe. How is the war?

It is the last days of summer holidays. Emma and Sarah say that Aunt Dorothy says it won't last. She told them that the horns of winter will be soon upon us. They don't know what she means. I tell them I don't know what she means either.

Mama sent us some pocket money although there isn't much to buy.

Tomorrow I go to the river with Nicky to try to catch a fish. He is very good. I am not so good as him but I try.

Papa, I remember what you said on the wharf at Mombasa about doing some things together when we come back after the war. You said that we could do things that I would like to do. Well I think I would like to go fishing with you, if that is what you would like also.

Your loving son, Edmund Grogan.

Grogan rubbed his nose and sniffed. He read the last paragraph a second time. He was pleased that Edmund had written. It showed maturity. It was just the type of thing he had been trying to teach him all along. Then it occurred to him that he had put no pressure on his son to act in this manner. It had come unprompted. Perhaps it had arisen in that very brief, intimate moment they had shared on Mombasa wharf.

It made him wonder about his tactics with Edmund. He couldn't remember a time when he and his older son had shared more than a few minutes of enjoyment together, before Grogan found cause to try to exert his iron will on Edmund so he would behave in what he, Grogan, thought to be an appropriate manner. Yet here was that same, tentative boy reaching a hand to him.

Now that he was so far away, he regretted those missed opportunities to better know Edmund. He missed all of his children, but strangely, it was Edmund who now tugged at his heart.

He sighed, and turned to Gertrude's last letter. She started with the usual list of problems they were having at the hospital. At the end she wrote:

I didn't rush to pen this, as I knew it would arrive after you had departed on whatever secret mission Colonel Meinertzhagen has chosen for you, but also because I felt the need to reflect upon a number of matters affecting you and me.

I shouldn't include you in that sentence, because I am not at all sure you are affected by anything, or share my concerns, which are of course to do with our marriage. You have said you love me often enough, and there are times when I truly want to believe it. But there are others when you appear to be so much enraptured by your own life, you have no space in it for me or anyone else.

Yes, I am again harking back to your various love affairs, and yes, I know you have denied they continue, but the hurt that remains is not diminished by your denials. That you choose to give some of your precious attention to another when I starve for it is painful beyond belief.

I regret to find the days of our passion seem to have passed us by. Once we were lovers. There was a time when I believed you walked Africa for me. How could these things have changed without my notice?

She ended with, *Your loving wife, Gertrude.*

Grogan stood and paced the space between his bed and the table, dodging the knotted roll of mosquito netting at the end of his army cot, and bumping his head on the kerosene lantern that hung from the ridgepole.

He ducked under the flap into the warm evening, cursing and rubbing his forehead. The crickets had begun chirruping, and from the direction of the lake the frogs were well into their nightly chorus. He circumnavigated his tent with deliberate steps, trying to compose himself.

Inside again, he stared at the letter. He'd put it with the others on the small table that served as a writing desk. It looked as innocent as the earlier ones, but had a hidden barb that had caught him by surprise.

He unhooked the lantern and set it beside the pile of letters. The pale blue ribbon that had bound them lay beside them. Had Jessie tied that ribbon in her little post office? He immediately put her from his mind, returning to thoughts of Gertrude and wondering if now, months later, she still held such bitter thoughts of him. He hoped it was perhaps one of those temporary things that women sometimes developed, and quite soon forgot. But no, there had been no following letters. It hurt to know that the last recorded thought of him had been such a clinical demolishment of his feelings for her.

She was wrong! How could she make such a cruel assessment? How dare she imply he didn't love her!

He snatched a notepad and began to scribble a reply. After three attempts to address her criticisms, he couldn't get his message straight. Instead he decided to write about more mundane matters to settle him. He told her that, without fear of the censor's scissors, he was pleased to report that he was alive

474

and well and living in Kisumu in what was relatively salubrious accommodation when compared with his recent digs.

Had she heard any further news from the children? He said he thought the letter from Edmund was interesting, then crossed it out and wrote wonderful. He told her that from all he had read, there was no likelihood of English soil being invaded, and that she should have no fears in that regard.

He started to say that he hoped to get to Nairobi as soon as Meinertzhagen returned, but was certain the censor would have a problem with that, so he simply said he couldn't get leave at the moment but hoped to see her soon.

He took a deep breath and wrote:

I was sad, very sad, to read how wretched I have made you feel. This is of course quite the opposite to my intentions, which are to make you happy. You say I don't love you, but that is not true. Over these past months I have come to realise how much you and the children mean to me. There is nothing quite like the prospect of meeting your maker to cause a man to reflect upon life. I have done that, and I know I love you. Pity it has taken me a war to remember it.

When I get back we will make a new start, you and I. I want to make a fresh start with the children too, if that is at all possible.

He paused to consider what else he could say that would undo her poor impressions of him. He read her last letter again, and wondered if any amount of words could mend their damaged relationship, and decided to draw to a close.

He signed it, *Love always, ESG.*

He folded it and slipped it into an envelope, before turning down the lamp and sliding into bed.

In the morning he would take his letter to the Red Cross post office. He fell asleep with the distant bellow of hippos and the songs of frogs in his ears, and thoughts of Jessie on his mind.

CHAPTER 62

Delamere took the *East African Standard* into the lounge of the Muthaiga Club. He nodded to an acquaintance before sinking into a heavily padded chair and straightening the newspaper with a brisk flick of his wrists.

Under the headline of *Strange Happenings on the Coast — Ship's Terrible All-night Ordeal*, he read: *About 4.45 pm on Wednesday afternoon, Mombasa Island was startled by the insistent shrill scream of sirens and the deep blast of the horn of the SS* Calicut.

Observers reported nothing untoward as the ship steamed out on the normal sea lane past Levin Reef, just off English Point.

Suddenly the ship veered to starboard, to the consternation of witnesses, and ploughed head-on into the harsh coral rocks of the reef. There she lay, repeatedly dashed by the waves — a picture of abject misery, helplessness and despair.

There were no immediate fears for the safety of the thirty-eight Indian crewmen and the English captain, although the running seas made it difficult to immediately mount a rescue effort.

Around 3.30 on Thursday morning the captain and crew took to the boats and landed safely on Nyali beach.

Authorities advised your reporter that no efforts will be made to drag the Calicut *from the rocks because it was obvious that the ship could not remain afloat. There were fears that if a salvage were attempted and the* Calicut *was sunk, she would create a navigational hazard in the harbour.*

The ship's owner, Mr Jeevanjee, a strong advocate of the Indian cause, was not available for comment.

Grogan had been waiting impatiently from dawn until a time that he expected Jessie would be at the Red Cross office.

He had watched the sun rise from a cool, pale blue sky. By the time he started out, the sky was the endless vivid blue that had dominated since his arrival in Kisumu, and the sun fell scorching hot upon him, beating down on his shoulders and head with a relentless fury. By the time he reached the Red Cross offices his khaki shirt was saturated with sweat.

He handed in his letter for posting to Nairobi. He had one letter waiting for him. By the look of the handwriting, it was another from Philip.

'Thank you,' he said to the grey-headed woman, a little disappointed not to find Jessie there. 'Um ... I wonder if I might have a word with my friend, Jessie.'

'Oh, Jessie's not here this morning, Captain. It's her day off.'

He wrestled with the urge to ask where he might find her, but resisted it.

Outside, again in the sun, his pace was much slower as he returned to camp. Passing through the small group of *dukas* and shops, his eye was caught by a small red parasol, which concealed its owner, but the body shape, the curve of the hips, the tanned ankles, could be none other.

'Jessie,' he said, drawing alongside her.

She covered her mouth in surprise, 'Oh, Ewart,' she said, smiling. He thought her surprise seemed a little false.

'Good morning,' he added. 'It's wonderful to see you. I've just been down to the Red Cross, to check on my mail, and ... well ... what a surprise to find you here.'

'I was just doing a little shopping before it gets too hot, but I'm afraid it's caught me out after all.'

'Yes, it's hell. It must be the lake. I'm sure it's not so hot further inland.'

'No. I'm sure you're right.'

After a moment's silence he said, 'I'm sorry if I said something to upset you yesterday.'

'Upset me? No. I was just ... embarrassed.'

'Embarrassed? Why ever for?'

'About my behaviour, you know ... back in Nairobi.'

'No need to be embarrassed about it. In my own bumbling way, I was trying to protect you. I know what my brother is like. I was just concerned that you were taking a great risk — I mean ... running off like that.'

She smiled. 'It was a little rash of me, wasn't it? Never mind.'

Her red umbrella cast a pink shade over her features. She might have been blushing, but he wouldn't have known.

'How *is* your brother?' she asked as they resumed their stroll.

'Quentin? I haven't had any news, really. He joined the East African Supply Corps — hates horses, you know — and last heard was with the 29th Punjabis. He was lucky to escape with his life in that debacle at Longido.'

'Oh, this war! They said it would be finished by last Christmas. Now it's been going for over a year, and no sign of an ending to it.' She put her hand on his arm and appealed to him with her eyes. 'You will be careful, Ewart?'

He placed his hand over hers. 'I will.'

When Gertrude received Ewart's letter she was overwhelmed with relief. She had written her note in a moment of deep despair, desperate to rescue their marriage before it totally unravelled. She had spent the following months dreading that she had pushed him further away from her. Now that his reply was so full of contrition and hope for a new start between them, she was ecstatic.

She rushed to her writing desk and pulled out the last piece of her precious embossed stationery.

My Darling, being so near Nairobi is wonderful news. When will you be able to come down on leave? Or can I come up? No — that would never do — we continue to receive too many wounded from the various campaigns.

I do hope you can get down here soon. It would be simply wonderful to have you home for even a few days.

I will write again soon, and I promise it will have more news. I simply wanted to send you this quick message of love while I have the moment to spare.

One last thing. Maggie Braithwaite will be visiting Kisumu. Do you recall her? Probably not. She's about sixty, and a member of our auxiliary. She leaves today to visit the Red Cross unit in Kisumu, and you might well see her if you go there, although I know you're not one for engaging in the silly games that tend to be organised for the enlisted men. She is on an official visit, but is hoping to catch up with an old schoolmate who works in the Red Cross post office. I've asked her to enquire about your health if she has a chance.

Hearing from you made me so happy, but hearing your reassuring words of love was the magic I needed to survive until I see you again.

As always, I love you.

Grogan and Jessie had developed a routine. On the days when military matters did not intrude, he would meet her for tea in the Red Cross canteen. They would chat and laugh about nothing in particular, and then Lil would hover around their table, and Jessie would have to excuse herself and return to the hospital laundry, or whatever else was her shift for the week.

'Before you go,' he said, touching her hand. 'May I walk you home this evening after your shift ends?'

She hesitated a moment, and then nodded.

He watched her go before opening his military envelope. It was from the Intelligence Unit's headquarters. Meinertzhagen was on his way to Kisumu. Grogan's war was about to resume.

Lake flies came from the darkness and buzzed around them in clouds. If it were in Londiani, Jessie would say that the heavy moist air was a warning of imminent rain, but in Kisumu it seemed to be forever like that. Not that she cared much about the climate or conditions as she strolled along Kisumu's main street with Ewart Grogan at her side.

'You work long hours,' he said.

'I don't mind. With Tom away there's nothing at home for me.'

'Which reminds me, where is home?'

'Not far. Why? Are you afraid of me, Captain Grogan?'

'Terrified.'

She chuckled. 'Tom is, was, the bank manager here. We have a house out of town, but it's easier while he's away to live in the flat above the bank.'

'How did you two meet?' he asked.

'After my father died, I decided to sell out. Tom handled the transactions for me. It went on from there. He was transferred to Kisumu shortly after we were married.'

'Do you love him?'

The question took her by surprise. She glanced at him, and caught a glimpse of his green-blue eyes in the moonlight. He was far too serious, and she didn't want to be serious that night. 'You once told me I wouldn't know what love is.'

'Did I? Well, do you?'

'Do you remember? It was just after I accused you of sending Quentin away because you were in love with me.'

'Maybe you were right. Who knows?'

'Here we are,' she said, nodding to the stairs beside the bank building.

He turned to her. 'You haven't answered me.'

'Haven't I?'

'No ... I said, do you know what love is?' He put his arm around her and moved his body close to hers.

'Yes,' she said.

Gentle lips caressed hers, making her almost fall into his arms, but she held back.

'I need you, Jessie,' he whispered, his hoarse voice barely audible in the moist night air.

'I know,' she said, sounding as she always did in his presence — gormless and immature.

'Let me —'

'No,' she said, stepping back to regain her control. 'You asked if I know what love is. Can a fifteen-year-old know love? Because

I've loved you for as long as I've known you. With the benefit of all this time, I think I should know it well enough by now.'

She covered her mouth with her hand, surprised that she had admitted to thoughts she had tried to keep out of her head these last few years. 'I can't ... No,' she said, and made a move towards the stairs, but turned back and impulsively kissed him on the lips, lingering a moment more, teasing herself at the prospect of making love to him. Then she ran up the stairs and closed the door on him, and on the terrible temptation.

Gertrude thought she saw Maggie Braithwaite disappear into Dobie's Jewellery on Government Road, and remembered that Maggie had promised to let her know if she'd seen Ewart during her visit to Kisumu. It had been three weeks and she therefore assumed she'd had no luck, but thought she'd enquire to be sure.

'Maggie,' she said as the older woman came out the door.

'Oh, my God!' Maggie gasped, holding her hand to her heart. She looked as if she might faint with fright.

'I'm sorry, Maggie, I didn't mean to startle you.'

'You didn't! No. Well, perhaps a little. I wasn't expecting you.'

'I thought it was you going into Dobie's. Buying a present for someone special?'

'Me? No. Just looking.'

'I've been hoping to see you around after your visit to Kisumu.'

'Kisumu. Yes, a rush. Busy. I hardly had a moment's peace.'

'You must be glad to be back. Did you see your friend, what's her name?'

'Lil.'

'Yes, Lil. Did you see her?'

'I did. She's well. Very well. Everything's well.'

'That's good to hear. I don't suppose you saw my Ewart, did you?'

'No, I'm afraid I didn't, Gertrude. But I'm sure he's all right. The Red Cross do such a wonderful job for the men up there.'

'Does Lil know of him?'

'Lil? No. Why would she? I mean, no, she said the name wasn't familiar.'

'Oh,' Gertrude said. 'Well ... thanks for trying.'

'You're welcome, Gertrude. Well, must dash. I'll see you next week, at the meeting? Good. Cheerio then.'

Maggie bustled away without a backward glance.

Gertrude felt uneasy about the conversation. It usually took wild horses to drag Maggie away from a good natter. She felt a touch of alarm. It seemed as though Maggie was trying to hide something. Something to do with Ewart. Her heart skipped a beat. What if he was hurt and she couldn't bring herself to divulge it?

'Maggie!' she called after her. 'Maggie, wait up a bit!'

Maggie turned and waited for her to come up. She looked like a bird caught in a trap.

'Maggie, there's something wrong, isn't there? Something's happened to Ewart.'

'No! I swear, Gertrude. He's quite well.'

'But you said you hadn't seen him. How do you know he's well?'

'Well ... I saw him, or at least Lil saw him, and he's perfectly all right.'

'Maggie.' Gertrude took her hand, and looked directly into her eyes. 'Tell me.'

Maggie sighed and looked miserable. 'I didn't want to be the one to tell you this, Gertrude.'

'Please tell me, Maggie.'

Maggie looked down at Gertrude's hand holding hers. She brought her other hand up and placed it on top. 'Ewart is ... Ewart is seeing one of the women in the town.'

Gertrude opened her mouth to speak, but couldn't.

'Lil knows it for a fact, because it's one of the Red Cross volunteers. A young woman by the name of Jessie.'

Gertrude's heart thumped in her chest and pounded in her ears. It sent a blinding jolt of pain into her head. She gasped, and put a hand over the side of her face, hunkering down in an effort to make it stop. It felt like a red-hot poker had been rammed into her ear.

'Oh, Gertrude, Gertrude!' Maggie said. 'Here, come inside and sit down.' She helped her into the haberdashery. 'There, there,' she said, sitting beside her on a bench seat. 'It must be such a shock. I'm so sorry. I didn't want to do this. Oh, how I tried to avoid it.'

As the pain in Gertrude's head subsided, the pain in her heart grew to take its place.

CHAPTER 63

An old letter from Philip that he hadn't read. His earlier letters had nothing but bad news about business. Grogan quickly scanned the contents.

The Colonial Office had scrapped any discussion of the spur line although Philip continued to argue that it was a matter of strategic defence. Grogan had expected the railway initiative would falter at least for the time being, and wasn't too concerned as he wouldn't be able to work the concession until after the war was won.

Philip mentioned the collapse of A M Jeevanjee and Company. Receivers had been called in. Philip said he fully expected Jeevanjee to fail in his bid to extricate himself from a messy legal wrangle. Grogan felt a twinge of sadness at this. He had been a bitter opponent of the Indians winning an even greater share of the country's economy, but he didn't have any personal ill-feeling against his old partner.

There were a few names of business associates who had been killed or injured in the war.

He was about to toss the letter into the rubbish when he chanced upon Gertrude's name near the end.

Gertrude has probably mentioned it, but we were all a little worried for a while.

Doctor Ribeiro says it's fortunate that it seems to have settled down as mastoiditis can be a very worrying condition, although how you can put any faith in the words of a man who rides upon a zebra's back I do not know.

For goodness' sake, Ewart, I wish you would take my advice and use one of the other, very respectable English doctors we now have in abundance here in Nairobi.

Grogan had never heard of mastoiditis, but thought it had something to do with the inner ear. He was surprised that Gertrude hadn't mentioned it. She was not a person to dramatise her ailments, but Philip hinted at something more important. He dashed off a letter to her, asking about it, and went immediately to the post office to send it.

There were no letters awaiting him from Gertrude, which was odd, and more than a little worrying given that she had seemed so positive in her last note.

Either Gertrude had taken ill again, or Maggie Braithwaite, who had arrived and departed before he'd received the letter from Gertrude to say she was coming, had returned to Nairobi with bad news of her own.

When he reached his tent there was a soldier waiting to say that Colonel Richard Meinertzhagen wanted to see him urgently. Grogan hurried through the night to the old offices of the Lake Steamship Company, which the military had taken over.

Meinertzhagen sat behind his desk looking tanned, tired and a stone lighter than when Grogan had last seen him nearly twelve months previously. When Grogan handed the colonel his report on his activities in the Congo and German East Africa, Meinertzhagen asked for a brief summary.

At the end of it, the colonel nodded. 'Well done, Captain Grogan. I'll read the detail tonight, but from all accounts, a very successful mission. Now ...' He straightened and stretched, then took a step to the window where he stood for a moment, rocking slightly on his heels and watching the lights moving around the wharf as men loaded cargo for a dawn voyage. 'There is a more difficult, but equally important task that Command has asked us to carry out.' He returned to his desk and dropped into his chair. 'It requires subtlety, considerable diplomacy — even charm.'

'Charm?' Grogan said, wrinkling his brow and smiling.

'Quite.' Meinertzhagen passed over a cigar humidor. 'Try one of these, Ewart. Do you know that Cuba's best tobacco is grown in a climate very much like that of British East? Favourable rainfall, relative humidity of seventy-nine per cent, and an average annual temperature of 77° Fahrenheit. You watch, someone will plant tobacco out here one day and make an absolute fortune.' He watched Grogan light his cigar. 'Who knows, it may even be you. Anyway, as I was saying, Command wants us to win some hearts and minds.'

'Richard, are you quite all right? You're not making any sense.'

'Our inspirational Governor seems content to sit out the bloody war sea-fishing off the Mombasa and Malindi coasts. If we could find German ships as easily as he hooks marlin we'd have no worries. As it is, we're getting our arses kicked by von Lettow-Vorbeck in charge of a couple of hundred German officers and a bunch of illiterate black savages. Disaster after disaster. First we lose a cruiser, then we have the enemy surrounded and outnumbered eight to one — can you believe it? — eight to bloody one.' He paused to take a puff on his cigar. 'And he not only wins the battle, he gets away with most of our guns and ammunition. Then we have his supply lines blocked, and damn it if two German ships don't slip through our blockade.'

'They did? I hadn't heard.'

'Just a week or so ago. It's still hush-hush. Those supplies will keep von Lettow-Vorbeck going for months, maybe a year or more. I tell you, Ewart ... Oh, let's not go on with all that. What I'm saying is, the country's lost its spirit. Command are not happy with our war efforts. They want more from British East Africa. We need to rally them all — soldiers, officials, settlers. Everyone.'

'I hear that General Tighe is making a difference.'

'Yes, Mickey Tighe is a different sort to Aitken and Old Wappy, but he needs the entire country to get behind him.' He leaned forward. 'We need someone to inspire our people — man and woman, official and coolie. We need a man who is known as a leader — someone to inspire with his oratory.'

Meinertzhagen put down his cigar. 'I don't know anyone better to do it than Cape-to-Cairo Grogan.'

Jessie came down the steps shortly after dawn to find Ewart standing at the bottom of them. She quickly checked the street, and was relieved to find it was too early for the neighbours to be about.

'Ewart! What are you doing here?' she whispered, again searching the street for prying eyes.

'I'm leaving,' he said.

Her smile faded. 'When?'

'On tomorrow's train.'

'Oh, no. What can we do?' Again, she had let fall words she shouldn't have used. 'Where are they sending you?' she added. The previous night now seemed a vital lost opportunity.

'It's only to Nairobi. For some damn speaking engagement of all things. Jessie . . .' He also seemed nervous about the risk they were taking, and drew her into the seclusion of the staircase. He took her into his arms and kissed her.

She clung to him, feeling the strength of his body, the urgency of his lips.

'Jessie, I must know what it's like to have you in my arms before I go.'

'Oh, my darling. I'm afraid. Afraid of what we might be starting.'

'I don't care. I've wanted you since seeing you that night at your party.'

'And I've wanted you since the day I set eyes on you.'

He kissed her again. His delicious tongue teased hers.

'Tonight,' he said. 'After your shift at the hospital.'

'Yes, oh yes.'

'Around six then.' He kissed her quickly and was gone.

Grogan spent the remainder of the day in almost unbearable anticipation. Jessie was a jewel — an unimaginable temptation. Every part of him desired her. He wanted her like a starving man craved food. His body ached for her.

He tried to fill his mind with other things, and spent the day stowing his gear and packing the few items he needed in Nairobi.

He went to pick up his mail, but didn't try to see Jessie. Seeing her would simply make the wait worse. There was only one letter for him. By the handwriting he knew it was from Philip. He shoved it in his pocket and went for a brisk walk to the lake.

Lake Victoria was a nervous piece of water, always shifting. It gave Grogan the impression it was uncomfortable being there, waiting. Ahead lay its magnificent journey down the Nile to the sea. And the lake waters trembled at the prospect.

But that day the lake was calm, calmer than he'd ever seen it. He sat on a rock and absorbed its peace.

Gertrude came to mind, and her letter in which she revealed how much he had hurt her by his selfish behaviour. It had never occurred to him that she could be so affected by it. His dalliances meant nothing to him, but her reaction made him wonder about his perception of others. How could he be so blind to her feelings?

Was the affair he was planning with Jessie just another of those meaningless flings? How would he manage the outcome if it wasn't?

He was again evaluating the situation from his own perspective. What would be the consequences of the affair for Jessie? He began to feel uneasy about what they were planning. He sensed that she was ready to give up everything for him. What was he prepared to offer in return?

Having an affair in a small town like Kisumu almost guaranteed the end of her marriage. The frightening question was: Was he prepared to give up his marriage for her?

He sat at the lakeside until the sun started to dip behind the headlands guarding the Kavarondo Gulf. He had made his decision. As much as he wanted her, he could not treat Jessie as he had all the others. She was too young, too vulnerable. And maybe he was too close to love this time to risk it. Knowing that she had held strong feelings for him for so long made matters worse. She would expect more from him than he could give.

But apart from Jessie, there was Gertrude, whom he had hurt many times by his failures, and now, in the ultimate irony, he was contemplating failing himself. Back at Lake Kivu, under his own volition, he had made a promise to himself that he would change his ways, and now, at the first real test of it, was ready to fail again.

His whole life had been one of confronting challenges, one after another. That he succeeded was what made him the person he was. He despised failure in all its forms. He would not fail himself.

He climbed stiffly to his feet and dusted himself down. He would go to Jessie and tell her he couldn't, and shouldn't, go through with it.

He found Philip's letter in his pocket and idly opened it to read it before darkness fell.

Dear Brother,

I would not normally convey such alarming news by post, but as matters here are so dire, and worsening rapidly, I must resort to this in the hope that you can arrange an immediate return.

I am distressed to report that the mastoiditis that recently so cruelly attacked Gertrude has returned with vengeance. Her headaches are almost unbearable for her.

Dr Ribeiro advises immediate surgery to remove the part of the mastoid bone that is infected, but we are awaiting a second opinion. As you can imagine, such delicate brain surgery as this implies cannot be taken lightly, certainly not here in the colonies. However, here's the rub — we may not have the luxury of time for her repatriation to England and its civilised medical facilities.

I had planned to advise you of the developing situation long before this, but was forbidden to do so by Gertrude. At first I thought it was to avoid concerning you needlessly, in the hope that the situation would improve, but a later conversation with her revealed that she did not want you near her regardless of the state of her health. In her words, she never wanted to see you again.

I can only hope this is but a temporary symptom of the poor lady's distress, for I can't imagine what would have put her in such a state of mind.

In the meantime, I will do all I can to encourage the medicos to relieve poor Gertrude's suffering.

If at all possible, I beg you to return 'post haste'.

Philip.

Jessie stood in front of her mirror and gave another touch to her hair, which she had let loose. It hung in bouncy gold waves to touch her shoulders.

The clock said seven ten; five minutes had passed since she last looked. Ewart had said six; after sunset. Maybe she had got confused about the time.

Confusion had filled her days since Ewart had come charging back into her life. She was swept along with him, as usual, but could not regret it, even if it meant her marriage, as she suspected it would. Lil was sweet, but a notorious gossip. She couldn't keep a secret to save her soul. Tom would hear about it. She would tell him first.

Why did she always have the feeling she was on a runaway train whenever she was with Ewart? He had such power, he consumed her. She never could resist him. She wouldn't start now. This may be her last opportunity to seize the chance to know what it was like to be with this indomitable man.

Seven fifteen. She went to the window and drew the curtains gently aside. The military's night train was drawing out of the station.

It gave a breathy whistle, as if it didn't have the heart to leave.

Grogan looked through the dusty window of the guard's van at the twinkling lanterns on Kisumu station. He was still trying to catch his breath, having made a mad dash to catch the military train as it prepared to do the night run to Nairobi and Mombasa.

He was leaving Jessie without a chance to explain.

The Uganda Railway was again involved in an important event in his life. Women and the Uganda Railway — were they forever linked? The determinants of his life: the destination and the journey.

The stationmaster blew his whistle, the train screeched a reply and gave a jolt. It moved off.

From the corner of his eye he saw a woman standing under the platform light. It made him turn his head. But the platform was empty. It only looked like a faint reflection of Jessie — some trick of the window glass perhaps.

CHAPTER 64

Philip spotted Ewart's carriage approaching as he was about to leave Chiromo.

'Ewart! Thank God you're here,' he said when their carriages drew together at Chiromo's gate. 'I need to —'

'Where is she, Philip?'

'In her bed. But we need to talk about —'

'Driver! Carry on,' Grogan said. His carriage driver gave a flick of the reins, and they left Philip spluttering in their wake.

Grogan vaulted from the carriage and ran to Chiromo's door. A uniformed nurse asked who he was looking for, and he realised his house was now a military hospital and that Philip had meant the guest house.

Taking the steps two at a time, he sprinted down the path, passing Philip on his way. At the guest house door, he paused to draw breath before letting himself in.

The bedroom was well lit by the morning sun. Gertrude was lying in bed — pale, eyes closed. He edged forward and took her hand.

Her eyes slowly opened and she stared at him for a long moment. There was nothing in her eyes; no pain, no joy, no recognition.

She withdrew her hand from his. 'Go,' she said in a whisper, and again closed her eyes.

'Darling, it's me, Ewart.'

'I don't want you near me, Ewart. What are you doing here?'

'I came as soon as I heard.'

'Then go back to her. I don't want you here.'

Her words stung like a lash. 'I love you, Gertie.'

She opened her eyes and this time he could see the suffering, far beyond the physical. 'Get out of this place. Get out of my life.' Her voice was gaining in strength. 'I don't recognise you any more. You don't exist. I don't love you any more. Understand me, Ewart?'

She tried to sit up, and shut her eyes as a pain spasm passed over her, but she would not concede. 'I have nothing more to give you,' she said. 'You have taken all I have and now I'm empty.' She winced. 'Oh! For the love of God, leave me!'

Philip was at his side, tugging at his sleave. 'Ewart,' he said in a soft voice, 'this is not good ...'

Ewart glared at him, wanting to lash out to relieve his anger and feeling of injustice.

'Come, Ewart,' he repeated. 'Come.'

Grogan shrugged him off and left the room.

Grogan circled the gardens of the European Hospital, preferring their anonymous surrounds to the accusatory company of Gertrude's closest friends waiting inside for the results of the operation. He even imagined the silent admonishment of his own family members, Philip and Quentin, although at least, publicly, they remained supportive of him.

He hated the barracks-like appearance of the European Hospital. He should have insisted she have the operation at Chiromo. At least it was inviting and more familiar to Gertrude.

He had taken a room at the Muthaiga Club, and had spent the last three days trying to arrange a meeting with his wife before she went under the knife. Even Quentin could not sway her.

He picked up a stone and hurled it towards the road.

'Ho, ho,' a voice came from behind him. 'Tossing stones at clouds, are you?'

It was Jeevanjee, waddling towards him down the gravel path.

'Jeevanjee,' he said, reluctantly extending his hand. 'How are you?'

'I thought I might find you here. I have come to pay my respects to you in your time of trouble.' His solemn smile showed sincerity. 'I hope dear Mrs Grogan will be all right.'

'Well, thank you, Jeevanjee. It's very good of you. I imagine it will be some time yet until we learn if ... I mean, until we hear something.'

'Such things cannot be hurried.'

'No, they can't.'

'Shall we sit?' Jeevanjee indicated a garden bench seat.

Grogan obliged, although he didn't particularly want the company, but Jeevanjee had made a kind gesture, which was more than he expected as they had been bitter business rivals over recent years.

'Tossing stones at clouds,' Jeevanjee said, repeating his odd comment. 'Is that an expression you have in English?'

'No, I don't believe so.'

'It is a very good one, I think. In my family we use it when someone is being silly.'

'Really?' Grogan was not particularly interested, but was trying to be polite.

'When you think about it, it can be two different things. Most people think it means you are trying to achieve the impossible. But there is another interpretation. It can also mean that the task you have set yourself, the objective, is actually quite trivial — a piece of fluff. A vapour. Something not worthy of your efforts.'

'Ah-huh.'

They sat in silence, watching a sunbird hover among the hibiscus.

'You know, Mr Grogan, I have never been on safari. Not even once. But if I ever did, I think I would seek birds, not animals. They are so beautiful and plentiful here in Africa. Not so in Karachi. No.'

The sunbird moved on to another shrub.

'The other reason I came is to say goodbye,' Jeevanjee went on. 'I am leaving Nairobi; leaving Africa.'

'Why?' Grogan was curious in spite of his earlier disinterest.

'Because I realise I have done all that I wanted to do; all I *can* do.' He turned to Grogan. 'Do you realise that we are very much alike, you and I, Mr Grogan?'

Grogan smiled. 'It hadn't occurred to me, no.'

'We are both attracted by the new and different — the unattainable, maybe even dangerous, things. I am talking about our business interests, of course. The truly innovative solution is more fun, more challenging, and ultimately more profitable. It was what attracted us both to a useless piece of land in what is now the centre of Nairobi. Most people saw the swamp as one of those clouds I was telling you about — unachievable fluff. But not you and I.

'These days it is difficult to find that something that thrills the heart with its opportunities. Maybe I have lost the urge to seek them out. Instead I spend my time defending what I already have. Family — of all people — my family, would steal what I have from me. Can you believe that, Mr Grogan?' He shook his head and patted his enormous girth. 'Yes, family.'

He roused himself into a brighter attitude. 'Ah, so they can have it. I go back to Karachi. I again sleep with my dear wife. I play with the grandchildren. What more can an old man ask?'

Grogan nodded, unsure of how to respond to Jeevanjee's obvious sadness.

'So ... I have bothered you enough for this day, Mr Grogan ... Ewart.' He smiled as he rose to his feet and offered his hand. 'One more little piece of advice from an old friend. Maybe at times an old opponent too, no?' His smile broadened. 'I have heard you are sleeping at the club since you came home.' Jeevanjee held up a hand to halt his retort. 'You are right — it is none of my business, but this town is full of gossip. As if there isn't more to do in these times of war, but the gossip-gossip goes on. You are looking at another victim of such nasty gossip.' He raised a finger skywards. 'Don't throw stones at clouds. Find what is important. Seize it.'

With that, Jeevanjee turned and waddled down the path, through darting bulbuls and hovering sunbirds. Grogan watched him follow the path towards the gate and an enormous bougainvillea that guarded the entrance. As he disappeared behind the riotous tower of purple, Philip and Quentin approached from the hospital building.

He knew his brothers had come with news of Gertrude and it terrified him. It was far too soon to have a good result. The doctors had warned them that it would be a protracted and difficult procedure. Grogan sat rooted to the garden bench, trying to interpret something from their expressions. He could read nothing in their eyes.

When they stood before him, Quentin looked at Philip who nodded that he should speak for them. 'Dr Milne said the pressure has been eased.'

Grogan tried to decipher the calamity concealed in his words. Surely releasing the pressure was the desired outcome, but he couldn't allow himself to believe the news was good until he was certain.

When he made no response, Quentin added, 'It was a complete success, Ewart. Gertrude's going to be all right.'

Grogan dropped his face into his hands and wept.

Gertrude's bed was empty when Grogan went to visit. He searched, and found her alone in the garden, sitting on the bench where he and Jeevanjee had spoken on the day of the operation. She wore a pale pink frockcoat, buttoned to her throat, and a pair of blue slippers. Her ear was lightly bandaged, but a clump of her lustrous brown hair spilled from the furl of white cotton. It reminded him of one of the more outrageous hats that she often wore when they were younger — in the days when they still enjoyed tilting at convention.

'Why are you here, Ewart?' she asked without having even glanced in his direction.

'How did you know it was me?'

'I don't want you here.'

'Gertie, I need to speak with you.'

He sat on the far end of the bench, resisting the urge to take her hand.

'There's nothing to talk about,' she insisted, still not turning to face him.

'Gertie, I never meant to hurt you. There was no need for you to know about ... about anything. None of those other women meant a thing to me. I know this doesn't excuse my conduct, but I want you to know you are the only woman in my life.'

She sat in silence, her hands clasped calmly in her lap, staring at the mass of purple bougainvillea that had climbed one of Ainsworth's resolute young gums and was in danger of devouring it.

'I've always had difficulty expressing my love. It's something I have been conscious of all my life. I loved my mother dearly, yet I can't remember ever having told her so. When she was gone, it haunted me. I tried hard to remember, to convince myself that there had been times when we were together and I told her, or at least showed her how much I cared, but I was never sure.

'Gertie, I miss not having your love around me. I realise now it is the important part of my life that has been missing these last few years. Did you stop loving me, or did I stop noticing?'

Gertrude retained her rigid pose. She was half turned away from him and he couldn't read her expression.

'When I say I have trouble revealing my love, I mean love in both the physical and platonic sense. To me it is a form of surrender. It makes me feel vulnerable — a feeling I've fought since childhood. I even have trouble expressing brotherly love.'

He waited, hoping for a response of some kind, but she remained resolute.

'Gertrude?' he said.

She showed no sign of having heard a word he had said.

'What I am asking is for you to open your heart to me like you once did. I promise you, I've changed.'

'I'm sorry, Ewart; I would dearly love to say I want you back, but I can't. My love is dying. Or maybe, like this old head of mine, it needs time to heal. It's best that you just leave me be.'

He wasn't prepared for such a firm rebuff. He had never known Gertrude to be so unyielding. 'Well ... if you wish, I'll go. I just wanted to tell you that I've changed, and that I've proved to myself that I can be trusted with your love.'

He stood, about to leave, but turned back to her. 'Gertrude, I'm still curious — how *did* you know it was me?'

She turned to face him for the first time. Her eyes were grey and distant. 'I'm not surprised you don't understand it. You see, when a person is totally attached to another, when all you need is to be with that person to make you feel enfolded ... Is that the right description? Perhaps *part of him* is better. You learn to sense his presence. It's the aura, or the electricity. You get used to it surrounding you. It's like a blanket of love. In spite of my changed feelings about you, it appears I still sense that aura. Maybe it's an instinct that I can't turn off. I suppose in that regard I'm like one of those animals in the bush you know so much about. We have an instinct to stay close when lions roar.'

'When you put it like that, I envy you. I wish I could experience that feeling, but I can't.'

'Then I am truly sorry for you, Ewart.'

He nodded. 'Me too,' and walked down the path to the road.

CHAPTER 65

'How's the speech going, big brother?' Quentin said, breezing into Grogan's office.

'Oh ... Quentin,' Grogan answered. 'I didn't notice you come in.' He looked back at his page of notes. 'It's going all right, I suppose.'

'Having trouble finding the words?'

'I never actually write a speech. I just prepare a few points to work from.'

'You seem worried.'

'Just a little distracted. Finding it difficult to get into it.'

'I've just been to see Gertrude. She's coming along nicely.'

Grogan nodded. 'Good,' he said. Friends had kept him informed of her convalescence. 'Did she have anything to say ... I mean, any message for me?'

Quentin shook his head. 'For God's sake, Ewart, why don't you let me tell her the truth? Or at least convince her to let you have a chance to explain?'

'It's not as simple as that. Even if she knew the truth, I'm not sure it would make much difference. It seems that she has finally had enough of me. I can't say she hasn't been patient.' He pushed his notes aside and looked up at his brother. 'It's ironic, isn't it? For the first time in my life I was put severely to the test and resisted, only to find that Gertrude had already made up her mind that I had failed her again.' He fiddled with his pencil. 'She's probably condemned me on the strength of past experiences.'

'Women will always condemn us as sinners, Ewart,' Quentin said, taking a seat opposite his brother. 'It's their nature. Even repentant sinners are seldom forgiven in the long run. It must stay buried somewhere deep in their brain. I can't say I understand the creatures all that well, but surely if you go to Gertrude with the truth, she will give you another chance?'

'Another chance? It sounds simple enough, but I don't think it is.'

He wasn't prepared to share his private thoughts with his brother, but he felt that Gertrude had already been hurt beyond the point of forgiveness. It would be a severe test for her to restore the love she had once given him so lavishly.

'Before I left for the Congo, she told me she had to think about things. She seemed to have hardened her position when I went to see her before her operation. She needs to reach a decision about our future without inducements from me, or anyone else for that matter.' He turned his gaze on his brother. 'Do you understand me, Quentin?'

'Of course I do, Ewart. Have I ever defied you? But seriously, I think it's stupid letting yourself be blamed for a sin you didn't commit. Surely she's not about to give up after all this time? Not after tolerating your disgraceful carryings-on for all these years.'

Grogan nodded glumly. 'I can't take issue with that.'

'Oh, no. There you go again — taking me at my word. Bloody hell, Ewart, I'm only joking!'

Grogan nodded and forced a smile. 'I'm sorry, but I'm afraid my sense of humour is a bit shaky at the moment.'

'Well, buck up.' Quentin arose from his chair and took his hat from the rack. 'You're supposed to be delivering an inspirational speech to the whole population in a few days. At the moment, you couldn't raise a three-cheers for His Majesty.'

When Quentin had gone, Grogan leaned forward to rest his head in his hands. He felt exhausted. His nights had been lost to sleep since his conversation with Gertrude. He recalled it well. She had said her love was dying. The word had haunted him since. *Dying*. She made it sound as if it was something that had once been healthy, but now had no chance of survival. Something to be mourned in its passing, but equally, something that could not be resurrected.

After all the lies, he wanted to tell her the truth, but what would the truth mean to her? He believed what he'd told Quentin, that Gertrude had to find a level upon which to rebuild the love they'd once had. The truth that he had been tempted by Jessie, but managed to resist her, was of lesser importance.

He was proud that he had set himself the promise to change his ways and been up to the challenge in what would surely be its toughest test. If he won another chance with Gertrude, he would not disappoint her again.

It had to be Momposhe, but she couldn't believe it. Tall, straight. Elegant. Too preoccupied by the clothing items in the Kisumu Drapery and Tailoring shop to notice Jessie staring at him from across the main street.

It could only be Momposhe. The way he held his head when thinking — just slightly askew. His stance — weight to one side, his free foot resting against the ankle of the other, but not quite making that final, defining gesture of pressing it against the knee as his fellow Maasai typically did. His long hair tightly braided.

The only missing element was the Drury Lane suit. In its place was a short piece of red fabric slung nonchalantly across a shoulder. His hardwood club, the *orinka*, rested in the crook of his arm, and his long-bladed spear lay balanced in his curled fingers.

Jessie crossed the street, stepped onto the wooden kerb and headed directly towards him. When she entered his field of vision, he inclined his head in her direction, but kept his gaze on the shop window. She stood a mere pace from him, restraining herself and enjoying the moment.

Finally he turned to face her, wearing an annoyed expression.

A moment passed. 'Jessie!' he said, stunned disbelief on his face.

She flung her arms around his neck without a thought. 'Momposhe! What are you doing here?'

He spluttered, mildly resisting her embrace. 'For goodness' sake, Jessie. What will people think?' He glanced around them. 'You don't know who's watching.' Despite his protest, there was no mistaking his joy at seeing her.

'Who cares who sees us?' she said, resigned to the fact that her reputation was probably terminally wounded after her time with Ewart. 'I'm just so thrilled to see you. Where have you been? What are you doing these days?'

They babbled incoherently. Questions and answers intermingled, until they paused for breath. Jessie used the break to draw Momposhe onto the bench seat outside the drapery, where the chatter continued unabated for some time.

'So you found your people in the Uasin Gishu?'

'Yes. And I led them south, as ordered by the Administration.'

She saw the sadness in his eyes. 'And was it bad?'

He stared at her for a moment, as if deciding how much he could tell her. Finally, he said, 'It was very bad, Jessie. Many died. Nearly all our herd and flock. It took us two years and ...' He shook his head. 'Even now, we are still suffering.' He shrugged. It was obviously a demon he had often wrestled, and knew it could not be beaten.

'But you were accepted back into the section?'

His expression brightened. 'Yes. I am now a *morani*. Fully initiated.' There was more than a touch of pride in his smile. 'I have cattle, and already one wife.'

'One already? My, my.' She was tempted to tease him further, but sensed that he was not the same young man who had once stoically tolerated her interminable childish chiding. He was different. She might have said he had aged, but the boyish good looks remained. Whatever had happened to him in his two-year trek across the Mau Escarpment into the Serengeti Plains, Momposhe had changed.

'Why are you here?' she asked.

'I have come to get some children's books.'

'You have a child?'

'Not yet. But I am teaching English to the children of my *enkang*. The school here arranged to buy some books for me.'

502

'So you live nearby? Wonderful. We'll be able to meet.'

He shook his head with a smile. 'No. It is far. But the teacher here is the only one who agreed to help me. It has taken me five days to come from the Serengeti.'

'Wouldn't you like to live in a town again?' she asked, hopefully.

'No.' He searched the façades along the dusty Kisumu street as if looking for a welcoming sign. 'I have no need for life in a town. In the towns people see a Maasai and believe he is an ignorant savage. Here in Kisumu, people talk about me as if I'm not here.'

Jessie patted his hand, which lay on his bare leg. 'Are you happy, Momposhe?'

He was taken aback by her question. 'Yes,' he answered after a moment. 'I am. And you?'

'Tom is at the war, and ... well, I'm just waiting.'

She realised she hadn't answered the question. Momposhe didn't seem to notice. He told her he had to be at the local school to meet the teacher. They stood to make their farewells. This time they were more reserved.

Jessie kissed him on the cheek. 'Will I see you again?'

He nodded and smiled. 'Maybe.'

'Go well, Momposhe.'

'Go well, *Enkiti*,' he replied, and picked up his spear. At the kerb he turned back to her. 'It is strange how a life so well planned can change in ways we can never imagine. Isn't that so, *Enkiti*?'

She studied his eyes, unable to know whether he was harking back to his question about happiness or not. She decided to be equally ambiguous. 'Yes, my brother, it is very strange.'

The news item was hidden on page five in a small box headed *Merchant Prince Departs*. The reporter said that one of the founders of A M Jeevanjee and Company had divested himself of all responsibilities in the company and was leaving on the afternoon train for Mombasa, and Karachi.

The article went on:

Mr Jeevanjee is presently a partner in the firm which numbers among its interests substantial property in Nairobi, stevedoring, port facilities and property in Mombasa, and a labyrinthine array of similar interests in India.

Recently Mr Jeevanjee has been beset with legal and financial problems. A court case between Jeevanjee and three of his brothers is pending regarding the substantive ownership of the business, A M Jeevanjee and Company. It is unclear if Jeevanjee will contest the suit in view of his imminent departure for Karachi.

Jeevanjee's financial affairs are similarly clouded by his suit against his insurance company and the government over the loss of two of his ships in recent months. Messrs Pandit and Pavitt of Rajah Banking Corporation have instigated their own proceedings in regard to monies outstanding and underwritten against Mr Jeevanjee's shipping assets.

The whole matter seems to be quite a mess.

Mr Jeevanjee's departure on this afternoon's train will be met with mixed feelings. His detractors would say that he received very favourable concessions from the government and often under dubious circumstances. His political agitations within the Indian community drew the ire of many a Settler. Others might point to the charitable and community work he contributed to over the years.

All will agree that Nairobi will be a different place without the merchant prince.

Grogan closed the newspaper, and took it to the hanging rack in the Muthaiga Club's reading room, where shelves of leatherbound books lined the walls. He checked his timepiece.

Outside the club he stepped into the carriage that was reserved to ferry members to and from the town, and told the driver to take him to the station.

Grogan arrived in time to hear the final 'All Aboard' call from the stationmaster. The train was pulling out of the station as he stepped onto the platform, but he spotted Jeevanjee's white turban at a carriage window. There appeared to be no one in the crowd to see him off, for Jeevanjee peered out with vacant eyes. Then he saw Grogan. A smile replaced his momentary surprise, and a heavily-ringed hand rose to make a discreet acknowledgement of Grogan's presence.

Grogan nodded, and waved his farewell.

Lil handed Jessie the letter with a sniff of disapproval. Jessie stared at it for a long moment. It was from Ewart.

It burned inside her pocket until her shift ended, and she resisted it some more until she reached the flat, and her bedroom.

She sat on the bed, the letter lying on the flat of her hand. It was a brief note. She could tell by the weight and thickness. What could such a note say? It was too thin to be an explanation of the military matters that had forced him to leave without a word. Military matters were heavy, requiring pages. Nor could it be about pressing business issues. Complicated and weighty.

She slit the envelope open.

It was written on a single leaf of Norfolk Hotel stationery.

My dear Jessie,

There is no other way to tell you this. I have had a change of heart. My feelings for you are too strong to be able to spend just one night with you. I must possess you if I am to have you at all. And that is impossible. We both have important others in our lives.

Speaking for myself, I have had an awakening of sorts. I realise that I can't continue my selfish ways. Yes, I would dearly love to love you, but I can't do that to my wife and family. Nor can I do it to you.

Forgive me.

Jessie read the note again, and walked out of the bedroom with it.

She stood at the kitchen stove and tore the note into tiny pieces, and then dropped them, a piece at a time, into the fire box.

CHAPTER 66

'Ah, there you are, Grogan.' Meinertzhagen's voice boomed through the empty theatre. 'Come up here. Come, my boy — feel the ambience.'

Grogan strolled down the aisle of the Theatre Royal, his eyes climbing the Grecian columns to the curlicued cornices. Cherubs and dragons waged war across the plaster of Paris ceiling. Red, white and blue bunting hung in festoons down each side of the stage where Meinertzhagen stood, beaming.

'What do you say, eh? Isn't this just what the doctor ordered?'

Grogan joined him on the stage and nodded, not quite sure what the doctor had had in mind, but prepared to acknowledge that the theatre — the biggest in East Africa — was impressively decked out. 'Do you think we can do justice to all this?' he asked, noticing the workmen on ladders at the rear of the theatre, fastening bunting to the Grecian columns.

'Do it justice?' Meinertzhagen scoffed. 'We'd better. If we don't do something about our war response, we'll be kicked out of the bloody Empire! Did you read what the Sec of State said in the weekend paper? He said that British East is the only Protectorate in the Empire that needed to call on outside help.'

'I still blame Belfield,' Grogan replied. 'Telling the farmers they needn't bother with the war, to get on with their farming and leave the fighting to the military.'

'Exactly, so it's no wonder that people have drifted back to their quiet lives. We must give them a wake up; get them to rally to our support. Seriously, Ewart, this is not a little fundraiser. If we can't get the people behind us — that is, if *you* can't get the people behind us — we might as well give the show away.' He lowered his voice. 'I don't need to pander to your ego, but you are the only man I know who is capable of turning these people around.'

'I'll do what I can.'

Meinertzhagen nodded. 'Northrup MacMillan is behind us all the way. As you can see,' he swept an arm to indicate the theatre preparations, 'at least he's got the right spirit. And he's not even British!'

'The Americans will join us eventually.'

'I hope so. Anyway, we are letting the newspapers know a little about your speech in advance — to whet their appetites, and those of our audience. We've said you'll be calling the slackers to account, that you'll be naming names, and that you will be telling everyone exactly how we can win the war. If that doesn't stir their patriotic spirit, nothing will.'

'Hmm, I should think that if they were at all patriotic there wouldn't be a need for all this hullabaloo.' He ran his eyes around the auditorium yet again. 'Do you really think we can fill this place?'

A half-hour before the event was due to commence, the Theatre Royal was packed from the doors to the ceiling.

That morning, Tuesday 7 September, 1915, Nairobi's newspaper had run a full-page announcement, and stories to the effect that the event at the Theatre Royal that evening would mark the most important day in the history of the Protectorate.

People arrived at the theatre in late afternoon, greeting one another as they did in the festive season. The bunting strung along Government Road and Sixth Avenue added to the celebratory air.

Grogan had always been known as an outspoken champion against the mindless bureaucracy of government. The fifteen hundred people who filled the hall fully expected Captain Ewart Grogan to again pull no punches in his opinions on what was wrong in British East Africa, and what must be done to defeat the Germans.

Outside the night was crisp, but the hall held the remnant heat of the day, which had been a typical one for September — intensely bright, with the sun unrelenting in a vivid blue sky. By eight o'clock, the cumulative body heat had raised the temperature inside the theatre to become uncomfortably warm.

Grogan joined General Tighe and all the other military brass in the front row. Town councillors and senior administrators formed up in strict pecking order in the reserved seats behind them. The seat beside Grogan was vacant, reserved by him for Gertrude. She had been present for every important address he had made to the Legislative Council, and he now felt alone in that vast auditorium without her. Until that moment he hadn't realised how much he enjoyed her presence on those occasions. It was not that he needed moral support — he was a very confident speaker — but he took pleasure in the look of pride she wore whenever he spoke in public.

When the musical introduction began, he had to concede the obvious: Gertrude would not be present.

The orchestra — an ensemble consisting of the military band and a few local enthusiasts — launched into a string of military marches and stirring patriotic songs. As the conductor flailed his baton, the fervour lifted a further notch, inspiring those gathered to raise their voices in song.

The orchestra marched off and a buzz of excitement skirted the theatre, but the crowd became restive when nothing appeared to be happening after several minutes. When the gargantuan Northrup MacMillan clambered to the stage — all twenty-four stone of him — it brought rousing applause from the assembly.

MacMillan held up his arms for quiet, and, like a circus ringmaster about to announce his climactic act, waited for a complete hush to fall before he spoke.

'General Tighe and staff,' he bellowed in his slight Yankee accent. 'Senior government administrators, Nairobi councillors, ladies and gentlemen. Tonight we are honoured to have a great local identity and member of our armed forces share with us his thoughts on the war and how it affects us all here in Nairobi and the Protectorate at large.' His beaming smile encompassed everyone in the theatre. 'You all know this gentleman very well, I'm sure. Down in Mombasa his port delivers goods that eventually arrive on your tables; he probably supplied the timber that was used to construct your house. Who knows? He might even *own* your bloody house!'

A howl of laughter filled the theatre.

'I have in my hand a large number of congratulatory telegrams.' He held the bundle aloft. 'I will read but a few.' He shuffled through the pile. 'Ah, from the Right Honourable Mr Bonar Law, the Secretary of State for Colonies: *I commend your efforts on 15th. There is no more important duty than that every man, woman and child in this Empire of ours puts heart and soul into war efforts. Good luck with your mission.*

'From Winston Churchill. Some of you will recall his visit to Nairobi when he was Under Secretary of State. He writes: *Dearest Ewart, I vividly recall our meeting years ago, and I have followed the continuing success of your many endeavours ever since. So too have I watched the growth of British East Africa, our fledgling colony. These troubled times demand men of conviction. More power to your arm in your address of the 15th. I can think of no better man to sound the rallying call than you. Sincerest regards. Winston.*

'There are more, many more. Here's one from Teddy Roosevelt who was here on a hunting trip a few years ago: *Good luck, Ewart. Knock 'em dead.* And Lord Elgin, Lord Alfred Milner, and, of course, our own Lords Delamere, Hindlip, Cranworth, and Cardross.

'But that is perhaps enough by way of introduction. Let me now get to the stuff of the matter, the reason we are all here tonight — our special speaker. Ladies and gentlemen, here is a man who, at the tender age of twenty-two, went off to fight the fierce Matabele for Cecil Rhodes. He acquitted himself admirably in that conflict, nearly giving his life for the cause. But a little later he came to our attention as Cape-to-Cairo

Grogan — a man who braved countless miles of savage country for no other purpose than to serve his Empire, his sovereign and his country. A man who at twenty-four years of age conquered the continent of Africa for these ideals; ideals that he still holds most dearly.' He paused to draw breath, and to let the suspense build, before flinging a hand towards the front row and crying, 'Please welcome, Captain Ewart Scott Grogan!'

A tumultuous roar erupted from fifteen hundred throats when Grogan mounted the steps, resplendent in the braids and medals of his captain's uniform. He crossed the stage as the fire-proof curtain went up, sending the bunting billowing from its fixtures above the stage and revealing a huge Union Jack that hung suspended high above his head.

The crowd were on their feet, cheering and applauding. The ladies wore fashionable gowns and fancy hats; the men were in their best starched collars. Many were in uniform. Some wore the reminders of earlier wars, with feathers in sun helmets and ribbons on their chests.

Major Ringer of the Norfolk Hotel was in the crowd, and the Indian stationmaster from Londiani. There was a scattering of familiar faces from upcountry — farmers and their wives. There were people he hadn't seen for years; people who had helped him on his way up the ladder, but of whom he had lost sight as he neared the top. Ronald Preston was in an aisle, waving his hat.

He was in no hurry to silence them, but let the tumult run its course. When the theatre was in total silence he waited another moment, sensing the tension in the air. There were a few muffled coughs, and the sound of people getting settled in their seats.

He began. 'Ladies and gentlemen. Fellow countrymen. My friends. I am here today to speak of honour. And duty, and ... Empire.

'First, let me tell you we are in a period of our history when the very fabric of our way of life teeters on a knife edge. Across the border,' he pointed to the south, 'no more than one hundred and fifty miles away, lies the enemy. He is powerful. He is cunning. He is hell-bent on destroying your life and mine. Why?

Because he knows that if he can destroy the Protectorate — one small element of this great Empire of ours — it will send a tremor through all of His Majesty's realm. If one pole or beam of our mighty British Empire falls, it imperils the stability of the whole structure.

'We stand with our fellow colonists. The South Africans ...' This brought a chorus of cheers, which was repeated on his mention of New Zealanders, Canadians, and Australians. 'All are doing a magnificent job. And it is well that they are. The enemy is audacious. He is also inventive. I have taken a walk through his territory of late, and have seen it first-hand. Every German farmer is training his native workers. They are ready. They wait for von Lettow-Vorbeck's call to arms. And they will fight. Make no mistake, the native can be a most capable soldier. Give him a firm leader, train him well, and he will perform quite admirably. You have no further to look than to our own King's African Rifles, among whose ranks are many trustworthy natives. Many more support our fighting troops in the Carrier Corp.

'But I am not here to praise the natives or anyone else. I come here tonight to speak to you, my friends. I am talking to you, Mr Administrator, Mr Trader, and you, Mr Settler.' He held their attention on the pointed finger of his outstretched arm. His blazing eyes might have kept the audience transfixed for an age, but he continued. 'Many have done what is expected of them. In that I include our men in uniform, both black and white, who are prepared to make the ultimate sacrifice for the Empire. But there are others who do not do enough. I go so far as to say that every man and woman in this Protectorate of ours can do more.'

He paused, as if daring anyone to disagree.

'Let me reveal to you my vision of what can be achieved.' He expounded proposals to bring the Protectorate onto a proper war footing and to coordinate the many resources of the war effort. 'I propose we form a War Council within which to direct our efforts. We cannot afford to squander our resources on duplication and waste.' He went on to explain in detail what the War Council would do.

Grogan sensed the crowd was with him, and decided to take a leap of faith on the strength of his intuition. Nobody within the military command or civil administration had dared to risk it. Even the British government had not raised it.

'The measures we propose cannot deliver victory of their own accord. Nothing has been achieved in the long history of our Empire without the sweat and muscle of people such as yourselves.' He swept his arm around the theatre. 'And again it is to you — the sturdy stock of Empire — to whom we must turn if we are to seize victory. We must mobilise every able-bodied man to the cause.'

The applause began to build.

'We must liberate the power within our numbers. There can be no exceptions. Everyone has a part to play. The answer is universal conscription.'

When the crowd howled their support, he knew he had every single person in the auditorium under his spell. As the din subsided, he continued. 'I say we should all play our part in this war. By that I mean our full part. Any one of you can walk into a club or pub in this town, and I dare say in any other part of the Protectorate, and see a half-dozen young blades sitting with a beer at their elbow and an illustrated newspaper in their lap. Oh, for the life of the gentry, what?'

The crowd laughed.

'Or you can take a stroll up the hill,' he pointed in the direction of Nairobi Hill, 'amongst the elite and well-to-do and find a host of pretty gardens and tennis courts. You will ask yourself, no doubt, what is all this nonsense about a war? For you will see no sign of it up there. Oh no.'

He praised and damned. He stalked the stage like a caged leopard, at times pounding his fist into his palm and threatening, at others pleading and cajoling. He used words like a rapier, sharp and cutting. Or he caressed and soothed with them. He added a sprinkling of humour to entertain and lighten the moment, or often turned it into an allegory to illustrate a point. He extolled the simple virtues like plain hard work.

'Government offices are populated by men on fine salaries, but doing nothing to help the war effort. I feel, and I think you will agree, that this is no time for slacking, for penny-ha'penny bits of business and pottering about in gardens. This is no time for tea parties and silly games. *We are at war!*'

The crowd surged to their feet, whistling, stamping and cheering.

He nodded, and raised his hands to encourage the crowd to give vent to their emotions. His eyes glistened in the stage lights.

'I met a young man on the street who said he had a farm to run. He said that it was the government's job to run the war. I told him his outlook was that of a rabbit. But not even a wild rabbit who takes its chances in the bush with the daily battle to survive, but a white rabbit who sits in its cage waiting for someone to bring it a lettuce.'

'Who's to blame for all this nonsense then, Captain Grogan?' cried a voice beyond the footlights.

'Whose fault is it, you ask? Why, it is our fault, my friend. Many men do their best, but we must remember this is a war like no other. There is no warrior class. There is no settlers class. We are all British subjects. We stand or fall together. '

More loud applause.

'We cannot afford the distinction between settler and soldier, farmer and official. We must all shoulder the burden of this war.'

Cries of 'Here, here!' rang out.

He had been speaking for the best part of an hour. The theatre was thick with smoke, and windows had been opened in an attempt to clear and cool the air. People who had been unable to enter clung to the window frames and hung through the openings to hear Grogan's words.

The air on stage was trapped behind a fetid, smoky barricade. Seeing beyond the footlights to the first rows was like trying to peer through a blazing campfire. Faces melted, distorted in the heat. Perspiration trickled down Grogan's face to his collar.

'We will win this war by the efforts of all people in the Protectorate. We cannot allow the situation to arise where one man stays home to make money, while the men at the front do battle for a shilling a day.'

Another deafening roar.

'The War Council will keep us to the task. Our first duty is to our self-respect. We are members of a proud fighting race — the British race. We will brook no interference in our way of life. We will cleanse this country of the invader.'

His last words were barely audible over the building applause. He pressed on.

'When it's time for history to make its decision ... When the gentle folk of this generation and the next ask for an account of our stewardship ... Or when you stand before your God long after the dust has settled on the battlefield ... And when your children ask, Papa, what did you do in the war? Let no man dare answer in any other way than to say: *I fought for the British Empire. And we won*!'

While Grogan took a deep draught from his water glass, MacMillan swept onto the stage like a wheeling battleship, leading a sustained round of applause.

Through the clouds of tobacco smoke Grogan caught a glimpse of a tall woman in a long, fitted empire line dress. An opened overlay skirt draped from the bodice and was trimmed with satin ribbon. His breath caught in his chest. The woman was standing in the aisle, a few rows back from the stage, as if she had entered late. The hat, which had first captured his eye, was flouncy and typical of the modern style. It was something Gertrude would wear to shock more than to impress. For a moment he was able to convince himself it was she.

When he realised it wasn't, he felt as if he had been struck in the midriff with a bag of wheat. At that moment he knew how much he would miss her if she was irretrievably gone.

Having thought he had seen her in the crowd, Grogan became convinced she was there — somewhere. If she was, it would prove he still had a chance with her. He moved to the edge of the footlights, where he was able to avoid the brightest light, and through the fog of smoke and the glare of lights he peered into the faces of the crowd.

He would find her by her eyes — she had such expressive eyes — and when he did, he would somehow convey a promise across the space between them. He would tell her of the stupidity that nearly lost her, and the regret he felt for hurting her. He would ask her forgiveness. And if she could love him again as she always had, he would never fail her again.

Grogan heard none of the Master of Ceremonies' words as he summarised the evening's address. He felt an almost unendurable ache for Gertrude. He needed her; needed to feel the reassuring warmth of her body against his. Realising he was now without her, he felt utterly alone. He was trapped on stage under the harsh scrutiny of the footlights awaiting his chance to escape. But the Master of Ceremonies droned on.

He found Quentin standing along the back wall, arms folded in characteristic style. If she were to come with anyone, it would be with his brother, but Gertrude was not there either.

MacMillan's mention of his name brought him back to his presence on the stage. '... who, as I said earlier, accomplished amazing deeds for his country. Before he leaves us, I wonder if he has a few last words for us.' He turned to Grogan. 'Captain Grogan ... if you please.'

Grogan reluctantly returned to centre stage. He faced his audience like a condemned man facing his executioners. After a minute, he opened his mouth to speak, but there was nothing to say. It was as if his life had evaporated — every thought and feeling erased. He stared at the fifteen hundred people who were expecting a final rousing climax to send them home feeling empowered and determined, but his mind was a vacuum, devoid of words and feelings.

Whispered voices and shuffling feet disturbed the otherwise utter silence in the room.

'Captain Grogan?' MacMillan said with an anxious note in his voice.

'Yes ... yes. To tell the truth, Mr MacMillan, I ... I am not at all sure ...'

'Tell us about your march for the Empire, Captain Grogan,' a voice cried.

A general murmur of accord worked its way through the theatre.

'My march for the Empire ...' Grogan responded uncertainly. 'You are perhaps referring to my walk from the Cape to Cairo?'

Murmurs of assent came from the audience.

He tried to shake off the depressing emptiness in his heart and find something meaningful to say, but Gertrude's loss dominated his thoughts.

'Well ... what more can be said about that?' he asked, stalling. 'In the context of this evening's speech, I suppose I could say that I had in mind the ... the triumph, yes, the triumph that such a walk would engender in the hearts of every Englishman. Yes, every Englishman. Man, woman and child ...'

In desperation he tried to find something more illuminating from his trek to use. An obscure memory popped into his mind. 'Do you know,' he said, with a return of some enthusiasm, 'that I shot an elephant on the Nile. A beautiful creature with tusks of eighty pound apiece. It was to feed starving Dinka people.' He could see the immensely tall, dignified, naked black men as if they were standing before him. 'I told them of my regret at having to leave such wonderful ivory behind because I had no porters to carry it. The Dinka promised to send the tusks to me at an address in London. What a great laugh we had at that.' He smiled, alone with the memory. 'Well, those tusks miraculously arrived in London, COD, eight months later ...'

Other faces came to him. Smiling Makanjira. The supremely confident Zowanji. The cook boy from Ujiji. The Manyema porters. The Waruanda. He wanted the assembly to understand what a wonderful experience it had been to forge such a strong bond of brotherhood between those black men and himself. For some reason it was suddenly the most important message of the night, but he couldn't find a way to express it.

The silence became awkward.

Grogan patted his pockets for his notes. They were not there. It had always been his proud boast that he needed no notes, no matter how long his speech. Now his fragmented thoughts would not coalesce to form a single intelligent comment.

Some instinct of self-preservation forced his vocal chords to react. In a voice he hardly recognised, he said, 'You know, as a boy I dreamed of glorious exploits in Africa. Of doing things that would make my loved ones proud of me. I read everything I could about Africa. I studied its geology and geography. Its flora and fauna. I loved Africa long before I witnessed its beauty.'

He coughed and tried to lift his voice now that he had the scrap of an idea to focus upon, although its relevance was not immediately apparent.

'I was not a robust child, but my heroes were Livingstone, Stanley, Burton and Speke. And there was Grant and Baker. Men who dominated their day.

'I began by climbing mountains in Europe. Large, terrifying mountains, to test myself. Then there was a war to try. I developed a fierce nationalism. I would fight my country's enemies to the death if necessary. I very nearly died. There were near misses at the hands of the enemy, certainly, but also from illnesses I carried from childhood, and from new ones I collected while fighting the Matabele with Rhodes.

'I was, and still am, a great admirer of Mr Cecil Rhodes, and in particular of his vision of Empire — a string of British colonies running through the spine of Africa. Colonies linked like a string of pearls by the silver thread of a railway.' His voice trailed off and again he lapsed into silence.

'I could say that I was a compulsive boy, who had four driving ambitions — to shoot a lion, a rhino and an elephant. Nowadays, I wonder what drove me to such a pointless pursuit, but I was young then, and, I suppose, was attracted by the danger. I also wanted to set eyes on that most exotic of waters — Lake Tanganyika. That, and many other unforgettable vistas, still lives in my memory.

'But now that you have taken me back to those days, I think I should state for the sake of the record, that in all honesty, there was something even more important than my country that drove me to achieve all I did.

'A wise man — who also happens to be an old friend — recently gave me some advice. He told me not to throw stones at clouds. I had no idea what he meant, but he explained that to throw stones at clouds meant to attempt the impossible, and that even if I attained it, the prize could never justify the effort. As a result, I would appear foolish.'

He stopped, realising he had allowed the strong images of recent days to invade.

'Ladies and gentlemen, I must apologise for this rambling diversion ... It occurs to me now that there is, after all, a link between what my friend told me and what has occurred in my life. I believe it is also pertinent to what I have been talking about tonight.

'I must have had this sentiment of stones and clouds in mind before I started out across Africa, because I kept my objective to myself in case I failed. Nobody likes to be thought a fool, for even as cocky a young blood as I was, I had to admit that traversing Africa with little more than a high ideal and a few porters was quite possibly a little silly. As it turned out I succeeded. But because I had so successfully kept my objectives a secret, nobody knew about it until it was done.'

A few people in the crowd chuckled politely.

'And when it was done, nobody knew why I'd done it.'

More laughter.

'I realise now that I didn't want to appear to have been tossing stones at clouds, so I invented some important reasons for making the attempt. As is often quoted, these were for the honour and glory of Queen and country, and to survey a possible route for Mr Rhodes' railway.

'In my talk this evening, I believe I have made it known that our glorious sovereign needs no more glory on my account. Ditto the Empire. As for Cecil Rhodes' railway, well, I'll leave that to his engineers.

'The truth is that I was in love with a beautiful young lady, but her stepfather was not at all sure he should give her away to what he no doubt perceived to be a feckless youth. I needed a plan so improbable that even that irascible old gentleman would take note. I believed then, as I do today, that nothing is impossible if it is tackled by a healthy body and a determined mind. So I boldly stated that I would march the length of Africa to prove I had the stuff to make her a worthy husband.

'Why would I say such a thing? Why are we compelled at times to attempt the very difficult? The answer, my friends, is that there comes a time when even the impossible must be attempted if we are to be who we can be.

'Well, history has recorded that I succeeded in my little walk. And I proved to my father-in-law that I had the necessary grit. However, I imagine there have been times when my dear wife might have wondered if indeed I had the character to make a good husband after all.

'I said this evening that we can always find excuses to avoid our responsibilities. There are always seemingly more important matters to attend to; more demands on our time. Ladies and gentlemen, I feel that tonight we have all promised to do more for our country. I have another promise to add. I am promising to renew my energies, to be worthy of the respect of a woman who has given me her love unreservedly, and unselfishly, since the day we met.

'When you toss a stone at a cloud the commitment is absolute. I have no option but to make another long journey to recover the love I had, and perhaps lost.'

As he stepped from the spot-lit stage amid the final applause and commenced his descent of the stairs, he paused to give a farewell salute in acknowledgement to the crowd.

He ran his eye around the sea of faces, again finding friends and acquaintances.

Quentin was still standing at the rear wall.

Beside him, wearing a hat with an outrageous ostrich feather stuck on a wide brim with a raffish sweep, was Gertrude.

AUTHOR'S NOTE

Roar of the Lion is a work of fiction based on the life of Ewart Scott Grogan. Many other people — some who shared his experiences and some who influenced them from afar — also appear in the narrative.

In reconstructing Grogan's life in the period roughly from 1898 to 1920, I have drawn on two important sources. They are: *Lost Lion of Empire: The Life of Cape-to-Cairo Grogan* by Edward Paice (HarperCollins Publishers, London, 2001) and *From the Cape to Cairo: The First Traverse of Africa from South to North* by Ewart Scott Grogan and Arthur H Sharp (Thomas Nelson & Sons Ltd, London, 1908).

In addition, I acknowledge Zarina Patel's *Challenge to Colonialism: The Struggle of Alibhai Mulla Jeevanjee for Equal Rights in Kenya* (published by Zarina Patel, PO Box 80430, Mombasa, 1997).

I have taken many liberties in depicting Grogan and other characters for the purpose of adding dramatic effect, therefore the novel should not be taken as an accurate historical representation of the people in it, or of the true directions their lives took.